SHOSHAMAN

Voices from Asia

Shoshaman

A Tale of Corporate Japan

ARAI SHINYA
Translated by Chieko Mulhern

UNIVERSITY OF CALIFORNIA PRESS
Berkeley   Los Angeles   Oxford

University of California Press
Berkeley and Los Angeles, California

University of California Press, Ltd.
Oxford, England

Shoshaman: A Tale of Corporate Japan by Arai Shinya
Translation by Chieko I. Mulhern
Copyright © 1991 by Sumitomo Corporation
All Rights Reserved

Library of Congress Cataloging-in-Publication Data
Arai, Shinya.
    [Kigyōka sararīman. English]
    Shoshaman : a tale of corporate Japan / Arai Shinya ; translated
    by Chieko Mulhern.
        p. cm. – (Voices from Asia ; 3)
    Translation of : Kigyōka sararīman.
    ISBN 0-520-07141-7. — ISBN 0-520-07142-5 (pbk.)
    I. Title. II. Series.
PL845.R246K5413 1991
895.6′35—dc20   90-24137
                                                                CIP

The paper used in this publication meets the minimum
requiremeŋts of American National Standard for
Information Sciences—Permanence of Paper for Printed
Library Materials, ANSI Z39.48-1984. ∞

Printed in the United States of America
9 8 7 6 5 4 3 2 1

CONTENTS

INTRODUCTION

The Japanese Business Novel

By Chieko Mulhern

In Japan, the business novel constitutes a distinct literary genre that boasts an impressive history harking back to feudal times. From the beginning, such novels have not only been marked by critical acclaim but have proved tremendously popular.

Japan's first writer of best-sellers, Ihara Saikaku (1642–1693), was born into an Osaka merchant family and became a superb chronicler of the business world, producing numerous fact-based stories as well as financial advice in fiction form. His 1688 work entitled *The Japanese Storehouse; or, the Millionaire's Gospel Modernized,* which was translated into English in 1959, offers thirty tales of business successes and failures. One traces the rise of Mitsui, a powerful merchant who was building his fortune with an innovative cash and carry discount in kimono retail along with a money exchange service. Saikaku proved prophetic: three years later, in 1691, Mitsui secured exclusive rights as the shogunate's official broker in bills of exchange, laying the foundation for the powerful Mitsui Group of today.

Two centuries later, when Japan opened its doors to the West, the 1870 Japanese translation of *Self Help* (1859) by Samuel Smiles (1812–1904) became one of the best-sellers of the Meiji period (1868–1912). This Victorian collection of success stories inspired a Horatio Alger–type of popular fiction as well as serious literature dealing with social ambition and business ethics. A classic example is "The Five-storied Pagoda" (1892), available in translation in *Pagoda, Skull, and Samurai* (Tuttle, 1985). Written by a major novelist and scholar, Kōda Rohan (1867–1947), the story delves into decision making and psychological warfare among carpenter-architects over construction bids.

Today, the full-fledged business novel *(keizai* or *kigyō, shōsetsu)* encompasses various subgenres and enjoys high visibility thanks to many top-rated novelists and a dedicated "business novel critic"— Sataka Makoto (b. 1945), former chief editor of a business magazine. Sataka provides the most (and probably the only) comprehensive survey of this ever-growing field to date in two of his books. *How to Read Business Novels* (1980; revised paperback edition, 1986) discusses seventy authors and two hundred works. In the appendix, Sataka gives his selection of the best one hundred titles, grouping them by industry: *shōsha,* trading company, leads the list with nineteen, followed by banks (sixteen counting *Money Changers*) and the auto industry (ten with *Wheels*), Arthur Hailey being the only foreign author cited. *Guide to Corporate Anthropology* (originally serialized in the *Evening Fuji* newspaper in 1982 and 1983; revised paperback edition, 1986) elucidates the social significance of issues dramatized in major business novels and the lessons to be derived from them. The jacket of *Guide to Corporate Anthropology* whets the Japanese appetite for practical knowledge, undiminished since Saikaku's days: "This book analyzes the world view and behavior patterns of the Business Tribe inhabiting the Japonesia archipelago, as substantiated by the data in the form of business novels; in short, it shines light deep into the collective unconscious of your superiors and colleagues."

The Businessman as Literary Subject

The modern Japanese business novel established itself in the literary mainstream in 1957, when Shiroyama Saburō (b. 1927) won the coveted Bungakkai New Writer Award for his story "Export." Ever since, the shoshamen have been eulogized by Shiroyama as courageous corporate warriors turned pathetic scapegoats, abandoned abroad or sacrificed for the sake of global economic expansion. Two of his works in this vein are introduced in *Made in Japan and*

Other Japanese Business Novels (M. E. Sharpe, 1989). The title story, "Made in Japan" (1963), describes the moral dilemma of Japanese exporters in the 1950s, caused by the U.S. government's requirement of the Made in Japan imprint. "In Los Angeles" (1972) traces the fate of shoshamen caught between impossible orders from their Tokyo office and the contractual demands of California fruit growers. During World War II Shiroyama had been a teenage Navy pilot trainee. This brief military experience predisposed him to turn into a "foot soldier of literature," skeptical of any system with the power to dehumanize and driven by a sense of mission to carry on his battle of resistance with the pen.

The war metaphor is closely associated with trade and industry, and Japanese business novels are often equated with *senki* (war chronicles). Fukada Yūsuke (b. 1931), a best-selling novelist since the late 1950s, traveled around the globe on business until 1983, when he left his job as a public relations manager with Japan Air Lines. He is a self-styled combat-zone correspondent of the trade wars. Among his many novels, *The Revolution Merchant* (1979) exposes the in-fighting among shōsha supporting the former or current administrations in Chile, at a time when Fukada's own cousin headed Mitsui's trading company there. *The Merchant of Scorching Heat* (1982), which deals with the Japanese rush to import Filipino lumber that triggered the 1971 murder of a shōsha executive in Manila, earned Fukada the Naoki Prize, the most prestigious award in popular literature.

Insider knowledge also enhances the fiction of Sakimura Kan (1930–1988), who gave up his twenty-three-year career with Sumitomo Warehouse Company in 1976, when he had risen to deputy chief of their Tokyo office. Following *Demotion* (1977), describing internal promotion wars, his 1983 novel *The Shōsha Tribe: The Grain War* seemed as if to take up where Frank Norris's *The Octopus* left off in 1901. Set at a time when extreme weather conditions threaten Japan with nationwide famine, Sakimura's apocalyptic novel describes shoshamen outbidding one another in a desperate logistical race to secure portside silos in the United States to circumvent the tight control of American giants known as the Grain Majors.

Preceding Sakimura by three decades was another Sumitomo manager, Genji Keita (1912–1985), twenty-six years in service. Before

Cameron Hawley's *Executive Suite* (1952) reached Japan in its 1954 movie version, Genji's first big success, *The Third-rate Executive* (1951), had already contributed the term "salaryman executive" to the popular vocabulary and created a subgenre of tragicomedy depicting the modest joys and sometimes biting sorrows of salarymen at work and at home. Typical of this subgenre are *The Ogre and Other Stories of Japanese Salaryman* and *The Guardian God of Golf* (both available in translation from Japan Times, Inc., 1972). Another middle-management writer, Nakamura Takeshi (b. 1909), who was with Japan National Railway for thirty years, began a series of salaryman novels in 1953 that delineated the mundane lives of underachievers. Nakamura's work paved the way for the 1956 movie based on Sloan Wilson's *The Man in the Grey Flannel Suit* (1955) to become a hit in Japan.

The salaryman novel took on social significance and emotional firepower with the emergence of a blockbuster novelist who would join Shiroyama in dominating the market. A desk clerk at Hotel New Otani, Morimura Seiichi (b. 1933) made a spectacular debut in 1968 with *The False Castle of Silver,* which would sell over 700,000 copies. No cousin of Hailey's *Hotel* (1964), Morimura's business thriller is an incisive indictment of hotel management tactics such as, according to this fictional scenario, sending employees on undercover missions to sabotage rival establishments. Since winning the Edogawa Rampo Mystery Award in 1969 for *The Blind Spot in High-risers,* Morimura has been producing one best-seller after another, each spotlighting a business crime or a controversial social issue and focusing on victimized customers and salarymen—themes evident in titles such as *Corporate Slaves* and *Company Funeral* (a movie version of which was released in 1989).

The Law as Business

The first to write successful mysteries featuring industrial espionage was Kajiyama Toshiyuki (1930–1975), whose first novel, *The Trial Car in Black* (1962), not only ran up sales figures of 250,000 but also set off a business mystery novel boom ten years prior to *Wheels* and Harold Robbins's *The Betsy.* Formerly an investigative reporter, Kajiyama proved a prolific writer of great range. He was sued by Devi Sukarno for *The Human Offering* (1967), an exposé of the scandal over war damage reparations to Indonesia that implicated the prime minister Kishi Shinsuke. It had sold 100,000 copies before it went out of print under the terms of an out-of-court settlement.

Representing Kajiyama in this defamation case was a prosecutor turned lawyer, Saga Sen (1909–1970), himself an established writer with a Rampo Award for *A Cheerful Corpse* (1962). Several of his murder mysteries also fall into the category of the business novel, including *A Diet Member under Arrest* and *The Prime Minister's Aide,* the latter about the death of Prime Minister Ikeda Hayato's aide during the investigation of a 1964 fund-raising scandal. The courtroom drama is popular: E. S. Gardner and his Perry Mason have their fans in Japan. Currently dominating this subgenre is lawyer-novelist Waku Shunzō (b. 1930), who gave up his job as a newspaper reporter, passed the bar in 1967, and has since been successful both in his private law practice and in creative writing. His innovative novels synthesize courtroom drama and the business thriller. Among them are the award-winning *Masqued Trial* (1972), about real estate fraud; *Billion-yen Invaders,* which pits computer hackers against a bank's on-line security specialist; *Murder in a Multinational Corporation;* and an economic mystery, *The Deflation Conspiracy.* Waku concentrates on the whodunit without corpses. Making use of civil and commercial laws still unfamiliar to the public in solving his hypothetical litigations and mundane crimes, Waku turns civil cases into the stuff of suspense stories.

To expand the possibilities of the mystery genre in this way is no small contribution to the field, since Japan's judicial system—with no jury trials or plea bargaining—leaves little room for courtroom grandstanding. The titles of American lawyer-novelist Scott Turow's best-sellers *Presumed Innocent* (1987) and *The Burden of Proof* (1990) are pure fantasy in a country where a 1989 TV-movie about an elderly attorney fighting for a not-guilty verdict is entitled *The One-percent Wall.* The figure is rounded out: Japanese legal statistics show a conviction rate of 99.9 percent over the years. To stand trial, at least in a Japanese criminal court, is to be presumed guilty. Only civil courts provide a fair ground for the legal battle of wits and offer the chance to win a reversal in higher courts.

Turow happened to spark great interest ten years ago, when his first published work, *One L* (1977), chronicling his days as a first-year law student at Harvard, sold 25,000 copies in Japan (see *Time* magazine, June 11, 1990). There, if one hopes for an elite career in government or business, a Todai (Tokyo University) degree, particularly in law or economics, is seen as the greatest single asset, if not an absolute prerequisite. Hence, Turow's insider view of the American equivalent of Todai Law was avidly consumed by businessmen who hoped to gain a valuable perspective on their own superiors and rivals as well as the government officials in charge of various business fields.

Small wonder, then, that a Japanese publisher paid $300,000 for the translation rights to Pat Choate's *Agents of Influence* (1990), which the Japanese can read as a how-to book on lobbying for Japanese interests in the United States, one which offers case studies replete with exact dollar figures and relevant names. Likewise, Americans have turned to Japanese literature for insights into business. *A Book of Five Rings* (1625; tr. Kodansha International, 1974), in which legendary swordsman Miyamoto Musashi (1584?–1645) reveals the cosmic significance of swordplay, was not only adapted by Eric van Lustbader and Trevanian in their ninja action adventures but also studied by American executives as a text in business strategy. A fictionalized life of this undefeated samurai duelist written by the historical novelist Yoshikawa Eiji (1892–1962) became a top earner among translated Japanese novels in its English edition, *Musashi* (1935–1939; tr. Kodansha International, 1981).

The Bureaucrats

As can be deduced from the fact that John Ehrlichman's *The Company* (1976) is often counted as a business novel in Japan because it depicts the White House's interaction with the CIA, government agencies and key officials are a conspicuous component in Japanese business fiction. Ever since Matsumoto Seichō (b. 1909) followed his Freeman Crofts–style alibi-cracking trail in *Points and Lines* (1957–1958; tr. 1970) to the evil inherent in a system that allows corrupt bureaucrats to enjoy the spoils of office with impunity, Japanese mystery of the "post-Seichō" era has strived for realism, immediacy, and social concern. Convincing glimpses of the central bureaucracy shrouded in a tantalizing mist of prestige, sometimes tinged with the black of political intrigue, make for suspenseful and enlightening reading. A notable example is *Bank of Japan* (1963) by Shiroyama Saburō, who previously taught economic theory at university. It remains a long-standing best-seller because of, rather than in spite of, lengthy quotations from official documents and German treatises on monetary policies, woven into a plot that centers on the struggle of Japan's state bank through postwar fiscal crises, culminating in the arrival of Joseph Dodge to put his anti-inflation measures to effect.

Shiroyama won the Mainichi Cultural Publication Award as well as a popular fiction award for *War Criminal: The Life and Death of Hirota Kōki* (1974; tr. 1977). In portraying this career diplomat and wartime prime minister, who was the only civilian Class-A defendant of the Tokyo Trials to be executed (along with six Army generals), this documentary novel sheds light on the decision-making mechanisms within the Ministry of Foreign Affairs and the dynamics of its relation to the Cabinet and party leaders. In *The Summer of Bureaucrats* (1974), Shiroyama steps inside the Ministry of International Trade and Industry, modeling his protagonist on a former vice minister whose real-life byname was Mr. MITI. Neither laudatory nor censorious, this well-researched novel highlights MITI's precarious position within the government hierarchy and the desperate power game its senior managers must play with and against their own short-term ministers and the tight-fisted Ministry of Finance. In so doing, it belies the common image prevalent in the West of MITI as an all-powerful dictator of trade policies.

Japan's central government can count several prominent novelists in its upper echelons. In 1956 an economic research official, Kojima Naoki (b. 1919), was nominated for the top award in serious fiction, the Akutagawa Prize, for his story "Human Chair" dealing with enforcement of the black market law. Subsequently serving for ten years as a manager of the Bridgestone Tire Company, Kojima has continued to produce business novels of high caliber. The 1956 winner of the prize over Kojima was Ishihara Shintarō (b. 1932), who would succeed in simultaneous careers as a leading novelist of serious literature, a Diet member since 1968, and most recently a self-appointed advocate of national rights, coauthoring *Japan That Can Say No* with Sony's Morita Akio, which provoked heated debates both in Tokyo and on Capitol Hill. One MITI manager shocked the

Japanese public in 1975 with his first novel entitled *Yudan!*—which means "caught off guard" as well as "out of oil." Three years after this "panic" novel built on an imaginative use of statistics conjured up the dire consequences of an oil shortage, its author, Sakaiya Taichi (b. 1935), launched on his second and even more influential career to emerge as a versatile writer of television drama and fiction, a sample of which, "Baby Boom Generation," can be found in *Made in Japan and Other Japanese Business Novels.*

The Stock Market

The same collection also introduces a peculiar Japanese profession that borders on economic crime: "Kinjō the Corporate Bouncer" (1958) brought the Naoki Prize to its author Shiroyama and threw light on the darker side of the business world. Such feats as Michael Douglas's scathing oration in *Wall Street* (1989) and Judy Holliday's innocently lethal questioning in *Solid Gold Cadillac* (1956) could never take place at all, let alone wreak havoc, at a general meeting of stockholders (*sōkai*) in Japan. Until a recent law took effect, corporate managements had been forced to hire or pay off *sōkai-ya*, gangsterlike professional filibusterers cum heckler guards, if they wanted to conclude their annual meetings expeditiously and without disturbance. The dread duty of handling *sōkai-ya*, black journalists, and patent thieves fell to the head of the department of general affairs, commonly called the CIA of corporations. The harrowing experiences that can result are the subject of an autobiographical business novel with the straightforward title *The Chief of General Affairs Dies in Rage* (1978), by Odakane Jirō (b. 1911), who held that position in Nihon Rayon Company until 1970, while building his literary reputation as poet and biographer (for example, of artist Munakata Shikō).

The stock market itself provides the arena for a former reporter on its turf, Shimizu Ikkō (b. 1931). In 1966, the same year Louis Auchincloss published *The Embezzler,* its main character modeled on an acting head of the New York Stock Exchange who was sent to Sing Sing in 1938, Shimizu's first novel became a runaway hit. It sold 18,000 copies in one day to go into twenty-five printings in the first month, its total sales mounting to 200,000. Named for Japan's equivalent to Wall Street, his *Kabutochō* ("the Island" in jargon) features a stockbroker of the lone wolf–type. The character is cast in the mold of a sales executive of Nikkō Securities who played an unbroken series of winning bets on then little-favored stocks like Honda and Ricoh to become a legend on Kabutochō as the last of the great speculators, before the modern methods of the big brokerage houses took over the market. Shimizu is a relentless vivisector of the big business that he scrutinized from the back door in his youth as a radical trade union organizer traveling around the country. With his fifteen titles he tops the chronological list of the 107 notable business novels published between 1956 and 1985 in the appendix of *Guide to Corporate Anthropology. Made in Japan and Other Japanese Business Novels* contains one of his stories, "Silver Sanctuary."

Kabutochō has produced another writer with more orthodox credentials. A second-generation stock analyst running an investment consultant firm founded with his celebrated father, Yasuda Jirō (b. 1949) is considered the bane of brokerage houses for his novels such as *The Black Wolf of Kabutochō*. This work lays bare an underground economy in which strategic buy and sell maneuvers are used to launder great quantities of funds for wealthy clients wishing to evade taxes, while *The Collapse of Kabutochō* (1982) warns against the exploitation of the stock market by political fund-raisers. Yasuda has had little to lose ever since his first novel, which would later appear as *Money Hunter* (1980), was abruptly returned by a major publisher under pressure from securities companies alarmed by its uncomfortably realistic plot. The novel revolves around a scheme of Ministry of Finance officials to turn Kabutochō into what amounts to a state-operated casino through the methodical manipulation of stock prices.

Women Writers with Clout

Shaking up a specific industry or even the central government with a work of fiction is by no means a male monopoly in Japan. Men are actually latecomers to the field, centuries behind the court ladies who produced the sophisticated prose literature epitomized by *The Tale of Genji* of Lady Murasaki Shikibu (fl. ca. 1000), which rivals Proust in its volume and Joyce in its narrative technique.

Contemporary American authors such as Judith Krantz, Barbara Taylor Bradford, Danielle Steel, and the late executive novelist Helen van Slyke have loyal followers in Japan, who derive vicarious pleasure from epics in which Western women build glorious careers and fabulous fortunes. But the modern Japanese women who appear consistently on the best-seller lists are quite different from these authors, and from the romance queens Janet Dailey and Joanna Lindsey, who also command a steady Japanese readership. Women are conspicuous in the mainstream of serious literature and have in recent decades been earning more than half the major literary prizes and new writer awards as their ranks continue to swell with ever younger and more innovative members. Suffice it here to cite a few business-related novels of several major writers whose works are already accessible in the West.

An acknowledged leader in business fiction is Yamazaki Toyoko (b. 1924), who makes frontal attacks on the corruption of bureaucrats and the abuse of power by big businesses. Daughter of a venerable Osaka merchant family, she worked as a fashion reporter for the *Mainichi* newspaper before winning the Naoki Prize for *Flower Curtains* (1958), about a widowed owner-manager determined to keep her *yose* theater for traditional storytellers open. After earning the Osaka Culture Award for *Bonchi* ("the spoiled heir," 1959; tr. University of Hawaii Press, 1982), an insider account of the lifestyle of Osaka's commercial elite, Yamazaki weighed in with heavy, hard-line novels often featuring powerfully realistic villains.

Predating Hailey's *Money Changers* by two years, Yamazaki's *The Magnificent Clan* (1973) delves into the great evil that a strong-armed banker can breed in collusion with corrupt bureaucrats. One of her million-sellers is *The Barren Zone* (1973–1978; tr. University of Hawaii Press, 1985), a shōsha story of epic proportions based solidly on intensive research including interviews with 377 people. Her hero is modeled on a vice president of C. Itoh & Company who brought about the affiliation of General Motors and Isuzu Motors; the model for his nemesis, a character involved in procuring planes for the Defense Agency, is the vice president of Nissho-Iwai Trading Company. He was convicted in the Douglas-Grumman scandal that came to light in 1979, a year after the conclusion of Yamazaki's serialized work that dealt with the same subject, depicting the fierce competition among trading companies.

More traditional roles provide a domestic focus for heroism in the socially significant works of Ariyoshi Sawako (1931–1984). Her celebrated *River* tetralogy features married women who single-handedly carry on their family trades: silk weaving in *The River Kinu* (1950) and tangerine growing in *The River Arida*. Ariyoshi's personal observations during a ten-month research stay at Sarah Lawrence College on a Rockefeller grant from 1959 to 1960 yielded *Not Because of Color* (1963; translated in *Heroic with Grace: Legendary Women of Japan*, M. E. Sharpe, 1991). In this novel Ariyoshi tackles the issue of race and class discrimination in America as manifested in the problems facing four Japanese GI brides employed at a Japanese restaurant in New York City. Her best-seller *The Doctor's Wife* (1967; tr. Kodansha International, 1978), which features a cast of historical figures, focuses on the wife's contributions as assistant and human guinea pig in the development of a herbal anesthetic by samurai surgeon Hanaoka Seishū (1760–1835), who made medical history in 1805 by performing the world's first successful operation using general anesthesia.

Ariyoshi was also instrumental in prompting the tax bureau to liberalize restrictions on charitable donations. Her 1972 novel, *The Twilight Years* (tr. Kodansha International, 1984), about a legal secretary's courageous endeavor to take independent care of her senile father-in-law for lack of adequate nursing homes, stirred up criticism of the government's inaction on this issue and earned more than 100 million yen in royalties in the first half year. When tax agents stopped Ariyoshi from donating the entire sum to facilities for the aged, the ensuing public furor led to a change in the tax law. *The Twilight Years* rendered an immeasurable social service in raising public consciousness about the imminent problem of an aging population, at a time when the average life span in Japan was becoming the world's longest. It not only spurred scholarly researchers to take up gerontology but prompted legislatures and government agencies to study the conditions in proprietary nursing homes and take measures to remedy the woeful shortage of public facilities for the aged.

The next time Ariyoshi entered the ring, the impact of her punches reached the Diet floors and corporate executive suites. Her meticulous investigative novel *Compound Pollution* (1974–1975) warns against the untold effects of industrial pollutants that may not be immediately harmful but may very well prove lethal when they accumulate and combine in the environment and in human bodies. Her annotated data and persuasive caveats were quoted by opposition party politicians firing questions at the Cabinet members during the Diet session. They have also been often introduced as evidence in court by attorneys representing industrial pollution victims such as those afflicted by mercury poisoning in the Minamata case in Kyushu, which is so vividly presented by Ishimure Michiko (b. 1927) in her *Paradise in the Sea of Sorrow* (1969; tr. Yamaguchi-shoten, Kyoto, 1990).

Natsuki Shizuko (b. 1938) made her name with sensitive domestic mysteries such as "Cry from the Cliff," published in *Japanese Golden Dozen* edited by Ellery Queen (Tuttle, 1978), and *The Third Lady* (tr. Ballantine Books, 1987). In honor of *The XYZ Murders* (1961) by Ellery Queen, with whom (or, more precisely, with one of whom, Frederick Danney) she was personally acquainted, Natsuki wrote *The W Murder* in 1982. The initial is for Women and the female psychology at work in the death of a business patriarch. In the novel's English translation, the title is rendered *Murder at Mt. Fuji* (St. Martin's, 1984).

Before the usury law capped the interest rate that *sarakin,* or the "salaryman financing service," could charge on loans to individuals, Natsuki called attention to the human toll claimed by these institutionalized loan sharks, who were free to set the rate as high as 200 percent and collect on schedule with the help of gangsters. Her *End of the Way Home* (1981) portrays a couple of modest income driven to family suicide by mushrooming mortgage obligations and relentless collectors.

In her acclaimed business novel, *Distant Promise* (1977), she takes up the field of life insurance. The backdrop for her plot, which centers on the stock acquisition race in an internal power struggle, is fictional: only four of the twenty-three life insurance companies then operating in Japan were joint stock corporations, the rest being mutual companies (aside from the foreign-funded Sony Prudential and Seibu Allstate). But her well-researched delineation of the plight and moral dilemma of employees who must rely on sweet promises to sell life insurance policies filled with loopholes received a grateful accolade from the outside sales force working on commission, comprised mostly of mature, unskilled women. What interested Natsuki most, however, was the executive (or enterprise) insurance that medium to small businesses took out, as if using their officers as human collateral against default.

Executive Novels

Japanese business fiction can thus be categorized by subject matter. One type features a particular industry as its virtual protagonist, as in many of Hailey's works and, for example, Kojima Naoki's popular *Mitsui Corporation* (1969), which sold 200,000 copies. The second dramatizes a specific incident in the public domain, such as succession disputes involving corporate leaders, mergers, bankruptcy, financial feats, and criminal indictment. But the particular Japanese favorite is a type that can be called the executive novel. Aside from Theodore Dreiser's *The Financier* (1912) and its sequel *The Titan* (1914), stories about historical figures of the managerial class have not exactly been a mainstay of modern American fiction, even counting F. Scott Fitzgerald's unfinished work, *The Last Tycoon* (1941). But modern Japanese fiction abounds in novels about contemporary business leaders.

Just to cite a few that may be of interest to Western readers, *Operation Colors* (1963) by Kunimitsu Shirō (b. 1922) recounts the meteoric career of an executive dubbed the "Rainbow Vendor" who set fashion trends through his marketing coups at Toray Textile Corporation, crowned by the success of the miniskirt campaign (with Twiggy as their image girl) and the "peacock revolution" that put businessmen into colored shirts. This novel recaptured attention in 1982, when the undisguised model for its protagonist moved to Kanebo, Toray's rival, in the biggest executive trade in textile merchandising, albeit within the Mitsui Group. Many Japanese novels of this type dramatize the heroic endeavors and professional craft of high-ranking executives who appear under their real names, as in Shimizu Ikkō's *Burn to the Limit* (1972). This novel is a requiem for President Makita Yōichirō of Mitsubishi Heavy Industries, who had died in office the year before, leaving the legend of "Fighting Maki" as testimony to the aggressive progressivism he demonstrated in pulling off ventures such as Mitsubishi's affiliation with Caterpillar and Chrysler.

An executive perspective from a different vantage point informs the fiction of Takasugi Ryō (b. 1939). His debut work, *The False Castle* (1976), clearly modeled on Idemitsu Oil Company, led the press to surmise that an inside whistle-blower had written it under a pen name, and rumor attributed its sale of 30,000 copies within the first three months to the effort of Idemitsu employees to take it out of circulation. Takasugi indeed was an insider of the oil industry but as chief editor of a trade paper. His 1981 novel, *The Tower of Bandal*, follows the president of Mitsui Corporation through the ill-fated Iran-Japan Petrochemical Project. But Takasugi is also concerned with the tribulations and pitfalls of middle management: his story "From Paris," included in *Made in Japan and Other Japanese Business Novels*, evokes Joseph Conrad's study of moral degeneration in *Heart of Darkness*. As befits its Japanese title, which literally means "The Breakdown of a Civilian Bureaucrat," its shoshaman protagonist falls victim to the taste of managerial power on his ten-year tour of duty in France and eventually finds himself banished to a dead-end post in Africa.

Good and evil are not readily distinguishable in business fiction any more than they are in real life, and characters of dubious reputation tangle with prominent public figures in many fact-based novels. One example is *The Tiger and the Wolf* (1960) by Kumaō Tokuhei (b. 1906), which covers the dramatic exchange of transportation stocks between two takeover kings. The tiger is the nationalist-connected money man behind Tanaka Kakuei, who was to become postwar Japan's youngest prime minister in 1972 only to be ousted and convicted in the Lockheed graft case. The wolf is Tsutsumi "Pistol" Yasujirō (1889–1964), a Diet member since 1924 (he served thirteen terms), president of the House of Representatives in 1953, and the railroad baron who established the Seibu financial kingdom to bequeath to his two sons.

Today, the younger son is head of Seibu Railroad, president of Prince Hotels, and owner of a major league baseball team, the Seibu Lions. But his elder brother, Tsutsumi Seiji (b. 1927), who commands the Seibu Saison Group (consisting of ninety-eight companies), the Seibu Department Stores, and the Seiyū market chain, is also an award-winning author of serious literature under the pen name Tsujii Takashi. His long autobiographical novel, *In the Season of Wandering* (1969), maps out the ideological trail that took him from active student communist (he left the Party in 1951) to crack capitalist leader.

Among executive novelists of contemporary Japan, Tsutsumi Seiji is probably the highest in social rank, but he has an illustrious predecessor who may outrank him in many regards—Kikuchi Kan (1888–1948). Kikuchi was a prolific novelist who wrote many best-sellers including *Lady Pearl* (1920) about a beautiful woman's revenge on her nouveau riche husband that established an archetype of popular fiction in Japan in the style of Sidney Sheldon and Shirley Conran. In 1923 Kikuchi founded the publishing house Bungei-shunjū and inaugurated the magazine by that name; in 1935 he established parallel literary awards, the Akutagawa Prize for serious literature and the Naoki Prize for popular literature; and in 1943 he became president of Daiei Motion Picture Company. In his 1918 story, "On the Conduct of Lord Tadanao" (published in *Modern Japanese Stories*, Tuttle, 1987), Kikuchi depicted the loneliness of command that drove a young feudal lord to inflict all manner of cruelties on his loyal retainers. This historical tale can be read as an allegory of modern salarymen, who must endure the unendurable at work in a social milieu where the lifetime employment system leaves individuals little choice but to die in their company's service.

Foreign novelists who are also experienced business leaders command respect and popularity in Japan for their professional knowledge, regardless of the ultimate fate of their careers. The author of *Kane and Abel* (1979), Jeffrey Archer (b. 1940), who became the youngest member of the House of Commons and then Deputy Chairman of the Conservative Party, was the promoter of a business venture that soon collapsed. And Paul Erdman (b. 1932), vice chairman of the failed United California Bank in Basel, Switzerland, is often cited as an executive novelist of business fiction for *The Billion Dollar Sure Thing* (1973), which he completed in Swiss prison to win a new mystery writer award, and *The Crash of 1979* (1976), his very popular business suspense novel on oil politics.

Perhaps next only to Tsutsumi Seiji in the Japanese business hierarchy of today stands executive novelist Arai Shinya (b. 1937; pen name, Azuchi Satoshi), director of Sumitomo Corporation, a major integrated trading company, executive vice president of Summit Inc., a supermarket chain founded by Sumitomo with technical assistance from Safeway Stores, and author of the novel whose translation follows. *Shoshaman: A Tale of Corporate Japan* (1986) focuses on the course of careers in senior management and in particular on the agonizing choices that management executives face—such as Nakasato's, between an assignment as the CEO of a subsidiary abroad and the coveted role of member of the president's trusted executive staff in the Tokyo headquarters of the parent company.

Arai's earlier novel, *Supermarket* (1980), not only takes the readers down to the shop floors but up into the boardroom to witness the power struggles at the top, the managerial strategies, the brainstorming behind innovative merchandising, and the human drama born of the business environment. Other stores and many food retail study groups have used this novel as a textbook in employee training programs. Similar use has been made of Shiroyama's *Price Down* (1969), a portrait of that revolutionary of consumer economy, Nakauchi Isao (b. 1922), whose great realm includes the Daiei chain of discount department stores that he built up from Japan's first "discount shop for housewives," the Daiei Hawks major league baseball team, and Retail Business College that he recently founded.

Although most Japanese readers are probably unaware of Arthur Hailey's brief stints as an RAF flier and a sales and ad executive in Canada, Japan's relatively young and modest advertising field has produced some novelists of repute. Among his other duties, Kaikō Takeshi (1930–1989) worked in Suntory's publicity department editing *Suntory Kingdom* until 1957, when he launched his successful career as a mainstream novelist on the force of the Akutagawa Prize that he had just earned for *The King's New Clothes.* Kaikō was to collect many more awards including the Kikuchi Kan Prize for *Into a Black Sun* (1979; tr. Kodansha, 1989), an account of his combat-zone observations as a volunteer correspondent in Vietnam. All the while, he remained a familiar face in Suntory whiskey commercials; "Giants and Toys," published in *Made in Japan and Other Japanese Business Novels,* is set in Suntory's publicity office. Hailing from the major advertising firm of Hakuhōdō is Ausaka Gō (b. 1943), deputy chief of its ad division. His award-winning *The Red Star of Cadiz*

(1987) is an adventure suspense featuring a Japanese ad executive caught in a deadly game of cat and mouse between the secret police and radical terrorists in Spain.

Japan's medical field, which has been made a subject of business fiction, can boast a number of major novelists who are also practicing psychiatrists or surgeons. Even the pharmaceutical industry incubated a writer—Kadota Yasuaki (b. 1940). This author, known for his medical stories such as the televised *Scalpel in the Cancer Ward* and *White Crevice* (1985), used to be head of general affairs at a large company that manufactures vaccines. His 1981 novel, *White Ambition*, portrays hospitals as profit-making enterprises and exposes a three-way conspiracy of physicians, pharmaceutical companies, and Welfare Ministry officials in which cash payoffs are used to influence the testing of new drugs on human subjects.

In Japanese fiction, medicine is color-coded white. *The Great White Tower*, Yamazaki Toyoko's 1965 best-seller, depicts a no-holds-barred power play in the election campaign for a lucrative medical school deanship involving the faculty, alumni, medical supply firms, and the local physicians' association. Takasugi Ryō set his *The White Revolt* (1977) in the pharmaceutical industry, but unlike Hailey's *Strong Medicine*, which traces the rise of a woman sales executive, Takasugi's novel indicts the widespread exploitation of commissioned salesmen by arrogant doctors and slave-driving sales executives.

When Takasugi takes critical aim at the upper circles of the business world, however, labor leaders are not spared either. His fact-based *Race to Destruction* (1984) exposes the duplicity and tyranny of the former chairman of Nissan Motors and the president of the National Federation of Automobile Workers Unions, who together nearly wrecked Nissan. Power does corrupt, and being a union leader can prove a dangerous business in Japan, though not as lethal as in Steinbeck's *In Dubious Battle* (1936) and other American novels that show management and unionists in violent confrontation.

A case in point is Watanabe Kazuo (b. 1928), who served as chairman of a company union in the course of his steady climb to become general manager of Daimaru Department Store in 1971. Then he won the Japan Writers Club Award for his first novel, *The Chair of Wild Ambition* (1976), only to receive hate mail from his colleagues accusing him of dragging out the company's dirty linen. For his next novel, *Need Not Report to Work* (1978), Watanabe was demoted to manager, and he had his year-end bonus reduced for an essay "Why Discriminate Against Middle-aged Employees?" carried in the Japanese *Economist.* Undaunted, Watanabe published *Feeding on the Company* in 1979. Its cast of characters includes a greedy self-seeking pair consisting of managing director and general manager, a left-wing union openly critical of their devious activities, and the chairman of their own right-wing union who is ordered to squeeze the left-wing union out of existence. Watanabe was again demoted, this time to section manager, for the story was based on his own painful memories: he was the right-wing union chairman. It was to expiate his guilt for having played the company's puppet in union bashing on his way to senior management that he began to write exposé novels in the first place. His 1980 novel, *A Letter of Resignation,* became a minor best-seller, and he was accordingly relegated to a no-man's-land at the office where he had nothing to do and practically quarantined as a member of the *madogiwa-zoku,* the Windowside Tribe. Before long Watanabe developed an ulcer and gave up his thirty-year career with Daimaru, a notable casualty among executive novelists.

Another union leader turned writer is Saki Ryūzō (b. 1937), who had a four-year stint as a rolling machine operator in the plant of Yawata Steel before moving on to office work in general affairs. His experience as a member of the central executive committee of their labor union yielded *General Strike* (1961), which brought him the New Japanese Literature Prize and enabled him to leave his job in 1964. A successful blue-collar executive novelist ten years later, he won the Naoki Prize for *Revenge is Mine* (1975), a documentary novel about a serial killer on death row reminiscent of Truman Capote's *In Cold Blood,* which shook Japan in its day. Meanwhile, Saki's former employer, Yawata Steel, merged with Fuji Steel to form the world's largest steel producer, Shin Nittetsu (New Nippon Steel). Saki visited their state-of-the-art plants, and iron refineries in China and Brazil, to conduct on-site research for his serialized novel, *Cold Lump of Steel* (1979–1980). It features a blue-collar novelist very much like himself as protagonist and delineates the effects on the labor force of hierarchical differentials in fringe benefits and working conditions.

The view from the top during the greatest merger in the history of the steel industry is presented by Akimoto Hideo (b. 1926) in *Shin*

Nittetsu, a novel which reveals the foresight, global vision, and negotiation skill of the patriarchs of the industry that went into the merger. Akimoto seems a reliable source as well as a convincing reporter of such behind-the-scene events, for he was managing editor of economic news at the *Yomiuri* newspaper until his resignation in 1971. Thereafter Akimoto published business novels such as *Keidanren* (1977), about a colorful executive vice chairman of the Federation of Economic Organizations and the Federation's power politics. Since 1983 he has been known as Mr. Today for his late-night television news program, "Information Desk Today."

The order of executive novelists is growing in both number and visibility. In 1979, the Nikkei (Nihon Keizai) Newspaper Company ran a contest for *keizai shōsetsu* ("economic fiction") between 350 and 500 pages in length. This elicited manuscripts from 138 amateur writers, most of them businessmen in their forties and fifties. The first prize of three million yen went to *Post-bankruptcy Procedures* by Tsuru Rokuhei (b. 1924), a director of Mitsui Bank. In their second contest two years later, the winner, this time out of 103 submissions, was *Young Executive* by Yagi Daisuke (b. 1926), who was deputy general manager of the machinery division at Mitsubishi Corporation at the time, having served as vice president of their trading company in Columbia in the 1960s. Under his real name he was elected to the Diet in 1983 as a representative of the newly formed Salaryman Party, serving a six-year term in Japan's equivalent of the Senate.

With major publishing houses coming out with one high-earning paperback series after another, such as Shueisha's Corporate Fiction Fair and Kodansha's Occupational Information Novel Series and Business Novel Fair, the Japanese appetite for writing as well as reading business fiction is clearly growing.

Chieko Mulhern
University of Illinois
Urbana: October 1990

SHOSHAMAN

The Intruder

April

Suddenly a high-pitched voice cut across the calm of the promotion ceremony about to begin. Ebisawa Shiro, president of Nissei Corporation, was on his feet and the general manager of personnel was ready to make his opening announcement to the assembled employees.

In the front row of the hundred men in dark suits stood Nakasato Michio, general manager of project development, who was to be appointed to Management Grade One today. He glanced toward the entrance and instantly recognized the intruder as Ojima. He and Ojima had entered the company the same year.

Planting himself in the doorway, Ojima called to the president in a voice wild with agitation: "Hold everything, please! Before you hand out those appointments, I want you to answer my questions."

Tension froze the room. Even the personnel staff were rooted to the spot staring at the intruder, unable to understand what was taking place before their eyes.

"*I* should have been invited here today. For twenty-five years I have served Nissei with devotion and loyalty, carrying out all my assignments perfectly. No one else could have done them better." His voice faltered momentarily. "My performance record is unblemished. Therefore I deserve to be promoted to Management Grade One today. But I have been passed over. Why? Please tell me why. Can Nissei betray its most loyal, devoted employee?"

Personnel Manager Yamabe Seiji rushed up and whispered something to Ojima, taking him by the shoulders. Shrugging off Yamabe's hands, Ojima raised his voice again.

"True, Section Two of Iron and Steel Import and Export, my department, suffered massive cutbacks. And ten months ago I was assigned out to our subsidiary, Nissei Steel Sales. But I am not to blame for the decline in steel export. Why should I be punished for it? Keeping my full faith in Nissei Corporation, I have lived only . . . "

As Ojima's cry rose in pitch, Yamabe shouted to cut him off. Harsh voices joined in, yelling "Shut up!" and "Get out!" The murmur of voices rippled through the once quiet room. As if anticipating physical violence, some of the promotion nominees moved to stand vigilantly around the president.

Nakasato noted the expression on Ebisawa's deeply lined patrician face framed in silver-white hair. No trace of fear there. Absolutely unperturbed, cool and dignified, invulnerable in a crisis—exactly according to his reputation, thought Nakasato admiringly.

Ojima's screams were no longer making sense. Two staff members and several other men surrounded Ojima, helping the personnel manager push him through the doorway.

"I . . . I trust . . . trust in Nissei. I do trust . . . "

Trailing a cry behind him, Ojima disappeared with his unwanted escorts behind the heavy wooden door.

"We shall wait," President Ebisawa said softly. He sat down in a front seat as if nothing untoward had occurred.

"Gentlemen, please stand by," announced an alert personnel staffer who caught the president's remark. The commotion quickly subsided, and a solemn atmosphere pervaded the room.

Nakasato straightened his back and assumed a calm expression, but his mind was still reeling from the impact of the incident he had witnessed.

·   ·   ·

Nakasato and Ojima began their life at Nissei in the same year, even assigned to the same room in the orientation camp for new employees. Ojima seemed rather serious, of good family, with a business degree from a prestigious national university. Nakasato rejoiced in his good fortune at finding a suitable friend among colleagues at the start of what would be a lifetime career together.

At the same time, he was aware of a certain psychological distance separating him from Ojima. For one thing, Nissei Corporation was the whole world for Ojima.

"I was a high school student when I first heard of Nissei," Ojima confided in Nakasato. "A *sōgō shōsha*, an integrated trading company—it has the entire globe as one huge market! It's the core of the internationally renowned Nissei Group. Working for Nissei Corporation's been my only goal in life ever since. At last, today I can call myself an employee of this same company. I'm not dreaming, am I? A Nissei man now. Can you believe that!"

As if to convince himself, Ojima slapped his body all over and lightly pinched his cheek.

"I feel pain all right. This must be real. Hard to believe it but still real," cried Ojima jumping to his feet. He began to pace the narrow tatami-matted room of the bachelor quarters. It had been the last night of the new-hire training camp.

"To tell the truth, I've got another dream. Can you guess what it is?"

"Let me see . . . ," Nakasato pondered as he poured cheap whiskey into their glasses. "An assignment overseas?"

"Sure, that's a dream, but it goes with the territory. Now that I'm a Nissei man, that dream's as good as granted."

"The presidency, then."

"Too big for me."

"Oh. The board room?"

"No, no. I'm not talking about the company. Another kind of dream altogether."

"You mean a hobby? Going around the world, visiting foreign museums, or something like that?"

"You've got a one-track mind. Can't you think beyond 'overseas'?"

"Then what is it?" asked Nakasato halfheartedly, tiring of the subject.

"It's a woman. I'm in love and want to marry her. If I can manage that, my life's dream will be fulfilled."

"Completely?"

"Yes, 100 percent."

"Are you sure there isn't more to life?"

"Aside from the usual, like good health and so on, I need nothing more. To work for Nissei, marry the woman I love—that's all. A magnificent dream, I'd say."

Nakasato drained his glass in silence. He could find nothing appropriate to say, completely out of touch with Ojima's perception.

Nakasato was certainly happy to have been accepted into Nissei Corporation, but not without apprehension. What sort of assignments would he be required to carry out? Did he really have a natural aptitude to succeed as a shoshaman? He knew nothing of the human relationships at the office. Suppose he found himself caught in a feudal hierarchy that operated on a collective mentality as some of the college sports teams did? Landing this job meant no guarantee of happiness for him.

Love was not much different. During college, Nakasato had involved himself with his share of women, but only one at a time. He thought he was honorable enough but never believed that marriage with any particular woman would fulfill his life's dream. On the contrary, he'd even thought that he might be better off staying single to pursue his dream. He found it hard to picture himself as satisfied as Ojima claimed to be by a job with Nissei and marriage to a woman he loved.

Three years after their talk in the training camp, he got an invitation to Ojima's wedding. While Nakasato served in the sober Accounting Department, Ojima had been exultant in Iron and Steel Import and Export, the glamorous mainstay of Nissei's primary operations. Then he married the woman of his heart's desire. The bride was beautiful, radiating a sensuous charm that overwhelmed the young Nakasato. On his way home from Ojima's reception, Nakasato made up his mind to get married as soon as he could.

The two men continued to have little association with each other. Not that they fell out of friendship—they simply went through the usual stages in life and career where each was much too occupied with socializing among business associates and newer acquaintances to find time or inclination to discuss world views with friends from youthful days. Over the years, their personal contact involved only occasional greetings in the office corridor.

Then, on this day, Ojima forced his way into the promotion ceremony, made an unprecedented speech, and was hustled out. It was impossible to fathom his thoughts, but his words were straightforward and clear enough. Ojima felt he had been unfairly passed over for promotion to the managerial top rank and crashed the ceremony to state his complaint.

What could he possibly get out of such a drastic action?

.   .   .

"Mr. Nakasato Michio."

A voice broke into Nakasato's train of thought. The presentation had begun. He stepped forward to stand before Ebisawa.

"I appoint you to Management Grade One," pronounced the president softly, holding out a piece of paper. Nakasato received it, bowed, and returned to his place.

Relief washed over him. Making Management Grade One in the first round of competition for his class virtually guaranteed him a reserved seat on the express to senior management. Basking in the glow of his peers' envy, Nakasato had entered the last stretch of a career track, its glorious finish line in sight.

What a close call! Nakasato shuddered, recalling his recent trip to the United States. Was I lucky to escape the fate of being sidetracked into a post away from Nissei's mainstream! If I expect to be the first in my class to make it into senior management, I must position myself in the head office as near as possible to Ebisawa Shiro, who is handing out appointments now. I must avoid a sideline assignment, no matter how significant, to say nothing of hanging my fate on an American restaurant chain! The important thing is to stay put in the nerve center of this high-rise building, where I can be noticed by the important men running the headquarters. That's where Ojima failed. Hapless enough to be caught in the scale-down of the steel department, he was assigned out to a subsidiary, and his career course began to go awry.

No sooner did Nakasato's thought return full circle to settle on Ojima than he was seized by a frightful notion—Ojima may kill himself! How else can he make amends for today's fiasco? No. There is another possibility: was it a last act of defiant protest before quitting the company? Not likely. Past observation had taught Nakasato that a man about to resign is not inclined to remonstrate with his company at great cost to himself, for he needs a favorable reference from his former employer to show at his next place of employment.

Yes. Ojima does intend to kill himself!

The sudden conviction nearly jolted Nakasato into action. He wanted to rush out that instant and do something. And yet he might be reading too much into the situation. Nakasato debated with himself. After all, a man who'd claimed complete career and personal fulfillment in work for Nissei Corporation and marriage to his beloved could not possibly choose death to end it all. Nakasato felt somewhat comforted by this thought, but the relief was short-lived. By a reverse logic, the same philosophy could just as well drive Ojima to suicide.

Thus Nakasato pondered for the duration of the ceremony. When at last he bounded out of the executive conference room, he found Yamabe, probably in a similar state of mind, hurrying down the hallway.

"I roomed with Ojima in the new-hire training camp," Nakasato said.

"That fool!" the personnel manager spat out, ignoring the younger man's comment, apparently still enraged by the incident. A majority of Nissei's personnel managers had been dignified and discreet; Yamabe was one of the few with a sharp tongue.

At the personnel office, Nakasato learned that Ojima had shaken loose the men restraining him and run off.

"I'm worried about him," Nakasato blurted out, but Yamabe brushed off his concern.

"No need to be. A man who gets hysterical over a delay in his promotion hasn't got the guts to commit suicide."

Yamabe's brusque words nonetheless betrayed that the possibility of Ojima's suicide had also crossed his mind. At that moment, the tall form of the General Affairs section chief dashed into the room, his face drained of color.

"A man dived under the subway train at Otemachi Station. Looks like it was our Ojima."

Yamabe clicked his tongue and signaled for Nakasato to leave.

Within an hour, the news of Ojima's suicide had spread throughout the Nissei building. During lunch Nakasato heard here and there such spontaneous exclamations as "Whatever happened?" and "How dreadful!" but they did not last long. No measure of any kind had been taken to make it a forbidden subject, but the employees seemed reluctant to speak of the incident. Since the company was not to blame in any way, it never became an issue to require official handling.

The death of Ojima faded into oblivion, a flash of lightning, leaving no trace whatever.

New York

March

1

One day in mid-March, a few weeks before the promotion ceremony, Nakasato Michio had returned from a staff meeting to his
general manager's desk in Project Development. The digital clock
face set in his paperweight showed 3:30. One hour before his next
meeting to negotiate on a project for tourism in Okinawa. As he was
expected at an early dinner meeting hosted by a major construction
firm, he could not idle away this precious hour. He set to work on a
pile of papers awaiting his decision.

Acknowledging a welcome cup of tea that a young woman clerk
brought him, Nakasato swiveled his chair round to take in the view
outside the window. A small cry of surprise escaped him. It was
snowing. He had no idea that the morning rain had turned into a
heavy snow. It must have been coming down for some time and already covered the pine trees fringing the hotel across the street in a
few inches of white. Even on adults, snow kept an undiminished exhilarating effect. Now with this white makeup, everything familiar—building, street, car, and human—put on a fresh face.

Nakasato was enjoying his tea and the refreshing view, when a
voice behind him spoke. "Snow-watching?"

"Oh, hi, Yoshida! Taking a break from the endless chore of reading documents."

Yoshida Shizuo was chief of the Marine Products section. They had been on friendly terms for some time, ever since they worked together on the launching of a herring roe processing company. Well up on office gossip, he passed pieces of useful information to Nakasato from time to time.

"You can't tell from here, but it's pretty cold outside. Blowing hard, too."

"Looks like quite a wind." Following the dance of snowflakes with his eyes, Nakasato asked, "Been outside?"

"Yes. I just came in."

"I ought to get out more often. Here in this building I tend to lose touch with what's going on outside."

"Exactly my point. I've got some information that may interest you." Yoshida leaned over and lowered his voice. "Do you know about the plan to buy an American restaurant chain and get into the food service business on the East Coast?"

"What! Which shosha are you talking about?"

"Our own, of course."

"Well, no. I haven't heard anything about it."

"You haven't?" Yoshida eagerly explained that the acquisition plan involved American Gourmet Company, a medium-scale restaurant chain with 180 locations.

"Can't work," Nakasato laughed. "Just the sort of fatuous scheme you'd dream up in an office with central heating. How can you handle restaurants way over on the American East Coast, when you can't even feel the cold on the other side of a window?"

"True," Yoshida allowed but added, "Still, Nissei America seems serious."

Nissei America Ltd. consisted of a network of Nissei Corporation's former regional offices that had been incorporated in the United States, its headquarters occupying the premises of the old New York branch.

"What does President Tobita of Nissei America say? He must know better than to take up such a plan even to look at."

Tobita Tokihiko had been the youngest senior managing director of Nissei Corporation two years ago, when he was installed as president of Nissei America in New York City. Nakasato had encountered his overcaution during Tobita's tenure as general manager of Internal Audit, when he subjected every proposal to his wary scrutiny.

"But Mr. Nakasato, I've been told that President Tobita is most enthusiastic about the acquisition."

"Who told you that?"

"Mr. Kano. He emphasized this particular point in his letter to me. In the first place, Mr. Kano is the one who proposed the plan."

"Oh, he did?"

Kano Taichiro joined the company the same year Nakasato did, but Kano had been no more than a casual acquaintance in college. A quick-thinking extrovert, Kano had thrived in sales specializing in soft goods such as textiles and general merchandise. Apparently appreciated by his superiors, he was one of the front-runners in the promotion race, as was Nakasato.

"Mr. Kano heads the General Products Department at Nissei America. Last year's structural streamlining also put him in charge of Foodstuff."

"I remember. But how do you know him so well, Yoshida?"

"I worked for him in Sydney years ago. A typical shoshaman and an ambitious manager. He didn't spare the rod in—well, he took good care of us, all right."

"I see. But I'm surprised he's proposing to buy a restaurant chain. When I was on our supermarket job, he used to criticize the very idea of a trading company running grocery stores. What changed, circumstances or Kano?"

"Both, I imagine. Trading companies nowadays are in trouble— what the media call 'shosha's winter.' Soft goods have been particularly hard hit. The time's gone when the shosha could make money just moving merchandise from right to left."

"At any rate, tell him not to promote any other high-flying ideas. Lately everybody's coming up with a new venture and a diversification plan and what not. But trading companies can't possibly succeed in retail or food service. Twenty years ago, getting into the supermarket business was their favorite sport, but most attempts failed."

"Shosha types are probably too soft for the task."

"Not a matter of strength, but the task is certainly beyond us. It's absolutely impossible for us to run a restaurant chain, and in Amer-

ica to boot! I've no idea what Kano's saying, but the plan will just
fizzle out."

"Most likely. But I thought I'd keep you informed."

"I appreciate your telling me. Shoshamen *are* a breed apart—
more interested in figuring out what to do than how to do it. Nothing can be accomplished that way."

"That's why our herring roe processing company failed," said
Yoshida, getting to his feet. "I'd better take off before I incriminate
myself."

Excusing himself with a joke, Yoshida left the room. The absurd
story about a food service project in America vanished from Nakasato's mind. But not for long. On the following day, even before the
spring snow had melted, he heard the same story from President
Ebisawa.

2

Nakasato was summoned to the president's office along with his superior, Enomoto Shinsaku, a managing director in charge of project development.

"An interesting proposal has come from Tobita in New York. At
first sight, it seems totally out of our line, but a bit of flexible thinking may make it worth considering."

An aura of dignity emanated from Ebisawa's slender frame
graced with silver-white hair. His eyes were always smiling yet conveyed his strong will and vitality.

Nakasato remembered the previous day's story. His intuition was
soon proved right. The project Ebisawa proceeded to outline did
concern the acquisition of American Gourmet.

"Sogo shosha, the integrated trading company, has long enjoyed
steady growth, earning commissions as an agent mediating in trade
deals. But we can't expect that growth to continue, even on the
strength of our ample revolving funds. It's time we ventured into
unexplored territories to carve out a future for ourselves. Stepping
over the bounds of the shosha *function* would be a first step in the
right direction. A major merit of the idea to buy and operate American Gourmet Company lies in its tandem purpose—to reconfirm
our primary function as a *world business* and branch out into a

downstream industry to expand our capabilities. Transcend the sho-sha function and enhance the shosha image all at the same time. A stroke of genius, wouldn't you say?"

Ebisawa looked Nakasato in the eye with confidence. The president displayed an enthusiasm uncharacteristic of his usual prudent self. The insight impressed Nakasato, but the younger man would not act as a yes-man.

"I will get a *feasibility study* under way. Competition in the food service field in America is *tough*. We must be well prepared before we make the plunge." In responding to Ebisawa, Nakasato found himself peppering his sentences with English terms, as the president routinely did.

"Of course. It won't do to go in blind. Conduct a full-scale study by all means. I want you to go to New York and personally check out the situation. Haven't you been cooped up here lately, with no over-seas trip?"

"Not exactly. Last summer I was in Hong Kong and Singapore and off to the Middle East in the fall. No time to keep my chair warm."

"Ah, well, if you say so. But I wonder, was it all business?" Ebisawa teased Nakasato, laughing. They had established a rapport a dozen years ago in their work together in the Los Angeles office.

"I'm fairly working myself into the ground for you," Nakasato responded in kind. "Off to New York directly, to attend to the American Gourmet business, then."

"Good."

"By the way, where does this American Gourmet Company rank in American restaurant chains?" asked Managing Director Eno-moto, at last seizing a pause in the easy exchange between the oth-ers. A punctilious man who had worked his way up strictly within the administrative sphere, Enomoto was well known for his deliber-ate pace of action. Certainly a personal virtue, it did not suit him to direct project development. Well aware of his limitations, he con-ceded de facto leadership to Nakasato, announcing, "I'm in charge of development in name but leave day-to-day operations to you." But instead of keeping out of Nakasato's way, at odd moments he would interpose his opinions.

"About lower middle, I'd say," Ebisawa informed him. "Tobita's report indicates 310 million dollars in annual revenue from 180 loca-tions combined."

"So many stores? What's their sales volume, I wonder? Let me see: 310 million dollars—how much is it in yen?"

"Approximately 75 billion yen," said Nakasato, making a quick mental calculation with the latest exchange rate.

"Is that all? Seventy-five billion isn't much. A number of business units within our own company reach a similar figure."

"Director Enomoto, you can't apply the shosha criteria to the food service business in comparing trade volume," Nakasato interjected. "Our profit margin is 1.5 percent, but theirs probably exceeds 50 percent."

"Fifty? Sir, does that mean their purchase cost is less than a half of their sales?"

"Tobita suggests here," said Ebisawa, scanning the data sheets, "that we need to secure an aggregate profit margin of over 65 percent. If you adjust the figure at that margin, American Gourmet Company is equivalent in scale to a trading company with 3 trillion yen in annual revenues."

"Three trillion!" exclaimed Enomoto, astonished. "That's almost 20 percent of Nissei Corporation's gross trading volume. A giant enterprise indeed."

"Quite an undertaking to buy up such a big company. If anything goes wrong, Nissei itself may not come out unscathed." Nakasato cast a worried glance toward Ebisawa.

"Quite true. We don't come across a project this big more than once in ten years. Proceed *quickly and carefully.*"

Quickly and carefully was Ebisawa's favorite phrase, which he had frequently used even when he headed the Los Angeles office.

"President Ebisawa. You may not be pleased to hear a negative opinion at this early stage. But as a simple matter of general policy, I find it unwise to undertake this project. Some years ago I managed our supermarket operation, and it certainly proved beyond the range of shosha expertise," Nakasato boldly offered his honest opinion but chose his words with care.

"I know. You told me about it often enough in L.A.—I remember it distinctly. You blamed our failure to break into the food-supply field on our inability to shed the shosha mentality. I agree with you there," said Ebisawa, his eyes gleaming. "But listen, that's just the point of this project. Go beyond the shosha *function*, I said earlier—but we must rid ourselves of the mentality that defined the shosha function in the first place. We need to make it the first order of the day, if we want to succeed in this project. My job at the top is to create conditions for a successful changeover. To be more specific, I personally guarantee three conditions for this project: assignment of the best man for the job, *direct supervision* by a ranking executive officer, and nonintervention by Nissei's management."

"What do you mean, sir, by nonintervention?" asked Enomoto. A stickler for clarity, even with the president or important clients Enomoto never failed to check the meaning of words. This habit often made his subordinates cringe in embarrassment, but Nakasato guessed it might have helped him on his way to the managing directorship. Ebisawa flashed him an amused look, obviously familiar with Enomoto's predilection, and set out patiently to explain.

"If the acquisition goes through, American Gourmet Company becomes our subsidiary—well, Nissei America's—but there's not much difference, since it comes under the supervision of one of Nissei's departments, Development, Sales, or some other related unit. Now, here's where the trouble begins."

Ebisawa paused and gazed at the two men. One of his idiosyncrasies, unusual for a man in the position of highest authority, was to take great pains to make his meaning clear. Some deplored this trait, saying it diminished the mysterious aura a shosha president was expected to possess.

"You see, it's through the supervisory channel that the shosha mentality passes to a subsidiary. All to the good if the subsidiary's in a similar business such as commercial finance, middleman transactions, and export-import. But when it comes to other types of companies—say, manufacturing (except for our subcontractors), retail, and food service—good intentions could backfire. Theoretically, everything's fine if the supervisory unit doesn't impose the shosha mentality on such businesses, but that's easier said than done. For one thing, the departmental chiefs are *middle management*, caught between the officers above, subordinates below, and the conflicting interests of their own peers. They have no choice but conform to the shosha spirit. Asking a middle manager to rise above it is like telling him to go against the flow of rush-hour commuters on the station platform."

Obviously pleased with his metaphor, Ebisawa went on to illustrate that an organization operated on the same rush-hour dynamics.

"The top management is free to move whatever the rush-hour human current, but some of the older officers lose their mental agility. Everything hinges on the individual heading a project—a competent and imaginative leader can work wonders. My intention is to appoint such a man to head American Gourmet Company. If necessary, I'm determined to take on the responsibility myself. Building up a business totally new to us is an ambitious task. It certainly calls for that much commitment on our part."

The president must have put a lot of thought into this, Nakasato surmised. Thoroughly accustomed to Ebisawa's method and approach ever since their five years together in Los Angeles, Nakasato could tell when Ebisawa was taking genuine interest in a project. If he stopped at introducing a proposal for general discussion, it meant that his mind was not made up one way or another. This time, though, he started right off by spelling out the responsibilities he himself would shoulder.

Yes, he's ready to give the go sign at the first opportunity, Nakasato thought. Contingent only on the feasibility study.

Once outside the president's office, Enomoto looked searchingly at Nakasato and asked, "Do you think he's serious?"

"I think he is."

"I have the same feeling."

"I'm worried."

"Why should you be?"

"This company may show possibilities as an enterprise, but whether a shosha can manage it properly is entirely another matter."

"We can't dismiss the project outright. The president all but said he wants to supervise it personally. He also promised to assign the best man."

"That's just the point. No problem if we've got such a talent at hand, but no shoshaman around can possibly handle the retail food business."

"What's the difference? It's nothing more than a glorified cafeteria after all, isn't it? You're probably overrating the project."

Nakasato said nothing. Simplistic explanation would be useless. He himself had had to learn it the hard way fifteen years ago. Why

bother to explain? There was no pressing need to enlighten Enomoto. After all was said and done, the whole thing would be dumped
on Nakasato anyway. His mind was already absorbed in working out
how to dispose of this unexpected, weighty project.

3

Nakasato Michio scheduled a one-week trip to the United States toward the end of March. That left him little time for preparation, but
his choice was either that or postpone the trip till mid-April. He had
three important appointments lined up in early April, and he told
his secretary that he must be in Tokyo to keep them. But he had an
ulterior motive for getting the U.S. trip out of the way during
March—he anticipated promotion to Management Grade One effective April 1.

His promotion was unconfirmed as yet. He would receive the customary preliminary notification from Managing Director Enomoto
only several days before the ceremony. But Nakasato felt certain
he'd make MG-1.

Out of the nearly two hundred men who entered Nissei Corporation twenty-five years ago, only a handful would be appointed this
year to management's top grade—the cream of the crop, winners of
the first round. Reaching MG-1 ahead of his peers would greatly improve his odds for making officer status within the next several
years. As a consequence, the screening of candidates for promotion
from MG-2 to MG-1 was exacting.

Around this time every year, Nissei employees talked of nothing
else but the promotion issue, even over drinks after work. Speculation about the MG-1 list was a matter of critical concern to all,
next in importance only to each individual's own chances for
promotion.

Nakasato was confident of passing through the narrow gate, but
he wasn't there yet. There was always a negative possibility, even a
small one. Whether or not he stayed put in his own office between
the preliminary notification in late March and the appointment
ceremony on April 1 had no effect whatever on the selection committee's decision. So being away in the United States would not alter
his fate.

Then why was he so reluctant to schedule a business trip that week? A schoolboy eagerness to beat others in checking the scoreboard posted at school to confirm the results of an exam on which he knew he'd done well? Or a superstitious fear that something would go wrong if he absented himself from the promotion ceremony—a ritual as solemn as a ground-breaking or roof-raising rite.

Was Ebisawa deliberately sending him away at this particular time? Nakasato felt uneasy. By now the president must have made up his mind whether to promote Nakasato this year. It was entirely possible that he'd been passed over, and in all kindness Ebisawa was arranging for him to be out of the country on his day of disappointment. Ebisawa was exceptionally considerate, protective enough of his men to take such a measure. In that case, Nakasato should accept his kindness and go with grace.

Then again, he might be assuming too much. Who could expect the president to realize that Nakasato's class had accrued the seniority for MG-1 this year, even before Personnel submitted the finalized nominations for his approval? The chief executive officer commanding more than ten thousand employees could hardly keep track of personnel matters below the executive ranks. All he could be expected to do was to congratulate each man who came to him in grateful acknowledgment of promotion. All the more reason, Nakasato felt, he ought to stay in Tokyo on April 1. That day's obligatory round of thanksgiving visits to the officers of the company would get him off to a good start in his race to the final corporate destination.

After more vacillation, he set an itinerary that would get him back in time for the preliminary notification. Paperwork for overseas business trips was processed by the foreign travel section of the Overseas Personnel Department. Nakasato was absorbed in figuring out the amount of foreign currencies to take with him and filling out requisition forms, when his telephone rang.

"Hello, is this Nissei Corporation?" a male voice said. Evidently unfamiliar with the direct dial system, the caller must have anticipated a female operator to come on. The man repeated his question to confirm the company and asked for a Mr. Nakasato.

"Speaking."

"Nakasato-san? It's been a long time."

"Oh?" Nakasato could not place the voice, which sounded vaguely familiar, as if he'd heard it before but not recently. Yet the man spoke as if he knew Nakasato rather well.

"May I ask . . . "

"I didn't expect you to recognize me. This is Inuzuka."

The name meant little to Nakasato. He once knew a man named Inuzuka, but there was no reason why that man should be calling him now.

"I worked with you in the Food Department."

"Oh, Inuzuka-san! It *has* been a long time."

A warning sounded in Nakasato's head. It was Inuzuka Keigoro after all. That name conjured up unpleasant memories.

"You sound charged up. I've been hearing how well you are doing. General manager of project development now, right?"

"Yes."

"Wonderful. Holding the key to Nissei's strategic future planning. You can do a great job of it. Nissei's management is a good judge of men."

"You're too kind."

What's this all about? What does he want from me? Nakasato's mind worked fast as he carried on the conversation. Must be something he wants—a job for a relative or a friend? Or some donation? Why should he call me up, if not to ask a favor?

Some fifteen years ago, he was Nakasato's immediate superior for six months. Not long in the span of a business career, but their brief contact had destroyed one of Nakasato's cherished dreams. Why was the man who had done the damage talking to him now as if they'd been close friends? Besides, several years ago Inuzuka had resigned from his post as general manager to leave Nissei well before the mandatory retirement age, while some of his peers became corporate officers. No tie of any kind was left to link Inuzuka to Nakasato.

"What can I do for you?" urged Nakasato, sensing the other man's hesitation.

"Sorry to trouble you when you're so busy. I have something I'd like to discuss with you in person. Can you make time for me?"

"I'd be glad to—but if it's something that can be discussed on the phone, please tell me now."

"Well, not on the phone."

"What's it about?"

"Something to do with a project from the days you and I worked together."

"Worked together? You mean on the supermarket job? What on earth . . . "

"Please meet me, and you will find out."

"Well, I would but . . . "

Nakasato curbed an impulse to say no. Even if he was justified in turning Inuzuka down, he might be criticized for lacking even the common courtesy to agree to a meeting. He had reached a position where complaints of this sort could hurt him.

"Can you come to the office the day after tomorrow?"

"No, not the office. I'm sorry to insist, but I'd like to call at your home."

"My home! That would never do, whatever business you have with me. I make it a rule not to take my work home."

"Yes, I understand how you feel. I do see, but I beg you to bend the rule just this once. Otherwise, I can't even die in peace. To keep it short, I just want to apologize to you."

"Apologize? Whatever for? I wouldn't know what to do if you apologized for something that happened fifteen years ago. In the first place, I can't think of anything you owe me an apology for."

"But I can. I'll explain to you in person."

"I don't know what to say."

Even to himself, Nakasato sounded plaintive. He was annoyed by Inuzuka's high-handed manner, but it would be childish to respond in kind. He had no intention, though, of letting Inuzuka call at his house on such a dubious pretext.

"Please come to the office anyhow. I'll hear you out then."

"Nakasato-san, this doesn't seem to be a good time for you. I'll contact you another time. Until then." Inuzuka abruptly concluded the conversation and hung up.

Nakasato sat stunned for some time, the receiver still in his hand. What's all this about? He wants to apologize. For what? And at this late date? Does he intend to say, "Sorry I transferred you against your will"? How ridiculous! All that happened a long, long time ago.

Nakasato replaced the receiver in its cradle and picked up a pen to concentrate on the requisition forms. He shrugged aside the strange call from Inuzuka.

4

"Mr. Inuzuka dropped in," Rieko informed Nakasato when he returned home from a business dinner that night. His wife was in a sullen mood. "He said he'd given you a call. Why didn't you warn me?"

"It never occurred to me he would drop in tonight. I certainly didn't invite him."

"He took me by surprise, and I didn't know how to treat him. After all, he's not a stranger but your boss."

"Not my boss any more. So, you invited him in?"

"What else could I do?"

Rieko's voice rose in pitch, words taking on sharp edges as they always did whenever her feelings were hurt. In her this common sign of ill humor was particularly pronounced. In some ways she was like a child incapable of self-restraint.

Twenty years earlier when Nakasato first noticed her immature side, the couple had been married several weeks, long enough for the initial reserve to wear off. It was too late. Her childishness gave rise to quarrels, but this was not a difference that quarrels could cure. In time Nakasato learned simply to ignore her outbursts.

Attributing her personal flaw to inadequate discipline in childhood, Nakasato had prayed that their children would grow up free of the trait. Lately, however, their eldest son in high school was already exhibiting an attitude and even a facial expression identical to his mother's. It seemed to prove that this trait, far from being instilled in childhood, had been programmed indelibly into the genes. According to Mendel's law of heredity, a certain percentage of Nakasato's descendants would be born with it in perpetuity, to strain their spouses' patience and pose trouble for their colleagues.

Seemingly trivial, such an idiosyncracy would be inadmissible as a cause for divorce. But it had led Nakasato to think seriously of getting a divorce at one time. More specifically, when he fell in love with another woman and dreamed of a new life with an ideal companion, this particular shortcoming of his wife's added fuel to his desire to dissolve their marriage.

Inuzuka had been his immediate superior during that phase of his life.

"He left something," said Rieko from behind his back, as he took off his shoes in silence and stepped into the dining room.

"What is it?"

"A painting. See for yourself."

It was on the living room table, nestled in the open wrapper. An oil depicting an elderly man and a youth in a setting suggestive of the mid 1920s, around the end of the Taisho era or the beginning of the Showa. Perhaps a father seeing his son off, the older man's desolate expression in contrast to the younger one's bright face.

"This is a scene, he said, where a father who'd never been able to do anything for his son wishes him good luck as he sets out on a journey."

"A lovely picture," Nakasato commented honestly. "Well done, too. Mr. Inuzuka couldn't have painted this himself, could he?"

"This tells about the painter."

Enclosed in the box was a printed history of the artist's career. A man born in 1927 with an impressive list of honors won at various exhibits.

"The painting looks terribly expensive. Considering the size, I figure it cost no less than half a million yen. Why such an expensive . . . "

"How should I know?"

"I wasn't asking your opinion. I just want you to tell me what Mr. Inuzuka said about it. Did he say this was a gift for us?"

"Sounded that way."

"What a nuisance! I can't accept this."

Nakasato ran through a number of likely explanations in his mind. None of them seemed plausible enough.—This may be his first move in some elaborate revenge plan. It isn't beyond the realm of possibility that for some reason Inuzuka blames me for his own failure to achieve success and devised a petty scheme to avenge an imagined wrong. But I can't see him resorting to such a measure. As far as I know, Inuzuka is straightforward, far from a neurotic type capable of staging a sinister revenge play. In the first place, what evil purpose could he possibly serve by visiting someone's house with a costly art object?

Is there any significance in the picture itself, then? Nakasato scrutinized the composition in oil. The expression clouding the kimono-clad father's face fit a scene of leave-taking. Viewed as a whole, in fact, a composition of serene lyricism, not gloom.

"Didn't Mr. Inuzuka say anything else?"

"He was rambling on about a lot of things, but they made no sense to me. He was wrong to have abandoned Century Stores, it was too late for regrets now, you were right all along, and things like that he kept repeating over and over. Toward the end, he actually had tears in his eyes. Made me terribly nervous."

"Abandoned Century Stores? Now I'm beginning to get it."

Century Stores was a supermarket chain that Nissei Corporation had founded in equal partnership with a Tokyo department store around 1960, some ten years before Nakasato and Inuzuka were assigned to the Food Department. It was an ambitious project that the sogo shosha—specializing in distribution of resources and raw materials—had launched in an attempt to branch out into the consumer goods market. But within ten years Nissei withdrew from this new field and sold off the Century stocks to its department store partner. The man who overruled Nakasato's objections and maneuvered the company toward this decision was Inuzuka.

"Quite odd, isn't he? He says that after he quit the company, he looked back on his business life and realized how many serious mistakes he made on the job. One of the two worst was the Century Stores case, he thinks."

"He's right. Even in hindsight, or perhaps especially in hindsight, it has to be called a grave misjudgment. It permanently destroyed a bridgehead Nissei had begun to build in the consumer goods market. It's only right that Inuzuka feels guilty about it."

"But what's the use of his coming to you in apology bearing a gift at this late date?"

"Well, did he say what his other mistake was?"

"Er . . . Kimura Company or something, I think."

"He means Kijima."

"Some name like that. He squashed a plan to build warehouses, and it proved fatal to the company, he explained."

"I know what he's talking about. It happened while we were away in Los Angeles."

Kijima Company was a foodstuff wholesale house controlled by Nissei, its majority stockholder. It had been in serious trouble at the time of the takeover, and Nissei's attempt to turn it around faced tough going. Around 1970, just about the time of Nakasato's transfer overseas, some younger members of the Food Department proposed a plan to build modern distribution centers to facilitate the flow of merchandise and expedite Kijima's recovery. Its most ardent advocate was Nukaya Kiichiro, Nakasato's junior by two years. The expansion plan was scuttled by Inuzuka on the grounds that sinking a capital investment of such a scale into an ailing wholesale house would be throwing good money after bad. Thereafter Kijima Company was forced to scrape along precariously on inadequate facilities and a retrenchment budget.

It was under a new general manager who succeeded Inuzuka that Nukaya's insistence paid off at last and the plan was approved to build warehouses on a 12,000-square-yard site. No sooner had construction begun than the oil crisis of 1973 shocked the world economy. Consumption dropped off in the aftermath, Kijima's deficits climbed sky high, and the extraordinary increase in the construction costs mired Kijima in red ink. Nukaya, who had proposed the distribution center construction, tried his desperate best to bail the company out but the violent changes in economic conditions proved beyond his power. He ended up with a nervous breakdown and took a leave of absence to recuperate. The news of his misfortune reached Nakasato in Los Angeles. When Nukaya returned to work, he was a changed man with no trace of the burning passion characteristic of his earlier self. At present he sat passively in a corner of the Foodstuff Division holding a sinecure post of manager without subordinates. Still young but already consigned to the no-man's-land of the business world. Kijima Company, which floundered on with no chance to recover, was absorbed into a large wholesale house several years ago.

Inasmuch as the warehouse construction had hurt the company instead of helping it, Kijima's later tribulations seemed to validate the soundness of Inuzuka's decision. But a collective judgment of the Foodstuff Division staff was that Kijima's fate had been sealed by Inuzuka's opposition. It caused them to pass up the optimum timing for adding warehouses.

"As far as Kijima Company is concerned, Inuzuka certainly has a personal reason to apologize to Nukaya. But my own career improved, if anything, thanks to the sale of Century Stores. He owes me no apologies."

"That's right. If you hadn't been transferred to L.A. because of it, you wouldn't have come into contact with President Ebisawa."

"So runs the businessman's luck. By the way, I'm wondering if Inuzuka also paid Nukaya a visit."

"No idea. I didn't bother to ask him questions."

Rieko didn't even try to hide her lack of interest in such matters. But Nakasato wanted to clear up a few more points.

"What's come over him? Maybe Inuzuka is a case of senile dementia. It isn't normal to worry so much over what he did fifteen years ago. Didn't you notice anything strange about him?"

"I suppose you can call it strange—he got tearful as he talked, but his face looked ruddy and younger than his age. He hasn't changed much."

"Ruddiness in the elderly isn't always a sign of robust health. High blood pressure tends to flush the skin."

"His voice sounded more powerful than I remembered."

"He must have been bluffing."

"I did have that impression, too."

"Did you, now? Just to relieve the loneliness of old age, he reaches out into the past and makes the rounds looking up former acquaintances, or something like that. How sad! I wonder how his wife is doing."

The only time Nakasato was invited to Inuzuka's house, on some occasion he could no longer remember, he and Rieko were entertained by Mrs. Inuzuka. A very favorable impression was etched in Nakasato's memory: she was a gracious hostess, attentive and considerate in every way. A quiet beauty with a slender elegant face, she had a distinctive tenderness in her voice and speech that warmed the hearts of her guests. Afterward Nakasato commented that he liked Mrs. Inuzuka far better than her husband.

"That reminds me. They're divorced. Isn't it awful?"

"Divorced? Since when?"

"Just recently, it seems."

"Awful indeed! Inuzuka lost the only good thing he ever had," said Nakasato with feeling. "He's been abandoned. Deserted by his own wife."

"That's what I thought."

"What a terrible thing to happen to anybody!"

Nakasato slumped down on the living room couch to contemplate the prospect of the deserted husband. "Pitiful beyond words. He didn't do well in his career, either. He had to watch his peers pass him right by as they stepped into senior management. It proved too much for him, and he left the company before the retirement age. He must have gone through any number of lesser jobs after that. Then in his midsixties, he was deserted by his wife. Now that he's alone, all he has to cherish are memories of his best days as general manager at Nissei. But even those memories are far from sweet. He's haunted by mistakes he made in the past, costing the company dearly and hurting some people. No wonder he's depressed."

"That's right. You'd better take care you don't end up like him after retirement. It'd be trouble enough having you hang around the house all day, garrulous in your old age. I'd be so ashamed if you went around apologizing to your former subordinates, carrying a painting or something."

"What a mean thing to say! To be honest, I do feel despondent whenever I think of my life after Nissei. Senile dementia or not, I'd go crazy if I had nothing to do in my old age. Mr. Inuzuka today, me tomorrow?"

"But he does have something to do."

"Oh? What does he do?"

"He teaches Japanese dance."

"Japanese dance, eh?"

Nakasato suddenly remembered. He had played golf with Inuzuka just once. He himself was a beginner plagued with a wild slice, a long way from making decent scores. By contrast, Inuzuka was a masterful player, probably one of the best in Nissei's upper echelon teeming with accomplished golfers. What impressed Nakasato most, though, was not Inuzuka's score but his swing. Most amateurs could make passable practice swings, but when it came to hitting the ball they tended to go stiff and awkward. Not Inuzuka. Nakasato was surprised time and again by the sound of a shot while watching Inuzuka make what seemed like a practice swing. He kept the same timing in his practice and actual strokes so that his tee shots had both distance and accuracy.

"Form is the first thing taught in Japanese dance lessons. I swing the club as if making a dance movement. That's all," Inuzuka explained in response to Nakasato's compliments. For the first time then Nakasato learned that Inuzuka was head of a school of Japanese classical dance.

"Well, well. Occupying his twilight years with Japanese dance, is he?" Nakasato said to Rieko. "He's fortunate to have a hobby. But it couldn't possibly amount to much, when an old man suddenly begins to give lessons in classical theatrical dance."

"Probably not."

"In any case, we can't keep his gift," said Nakasato, gazing at the picture on the table. "What a nuisance! He may be trying to reestablish contact with us. I'll meet him to find out. Better get in touch with Nukaya. He must have had a visit too. But I'll tend to this matter after I come back from America."

"America? Are you being sent overseas again?"

"Yes, on short notice."

Nakasato hardly ever discussed business with Rieko, making it a rule to tell her no more than the destination and the date, even in the case of travel abroad. She never seemed interested enough to ask for details. Yet she had a lot to say about the nonbusiness ramifications of his trips.

"I wish you didn't go so often. Overseas travel costs us a lot extra for miscellaneous expenses. I have to buy you new toiletries and socks and underwear every time. Is this a long trip?"

"No, just one week. I want to get back by April 1. I'm expecting a promotion to MG-1."

"Promotion? How nice! It'll mean some increase in your salary, I hope. But don't bring home much beef jerky from this trip, as you did the last time. Unless, of course, you pay for it out of your own monthly allowance."

He had thought of telling Rieko about Nissei's plan to affiliate with American Gourmet Company but lost heart as he listened to her. He stood up to change from his suit.

"Trading companies are going through a tough time, but I'm doing better than most businessmen. Don't tell me we're short of cash."

Rieko looked eager to retort, but Nakasato strode out of the living room. He knew what she'd say—with the household budget so strained by the children's school expenses, she was struggling to make ends meet, or some such story. No use for him to listen, for there was nothing more he could do: as always, he turned his entire pay over to her. For all that, Rieko would no doubt start fuming if Nakasato as much as questioned her management of family finance.

"Put this picture away yourself. I don't want to be accused of damaging such a valuable article." Her voice pursued Nakasato out into the hallway.

5

Headquarters of Nissei America Ltd. was in a midtown skyscraper one block off Fifth Avenue. Walking to the office from his hotel, Nakasato found himself overwhelmed once again by the energy that New York City exuded. This, after all, was the center of the world.

Bits of news funneled through the Japanese mass media tended to create an impression that America had turned into a sick country. The media reports focused mostly on murder, sex crimes, unemployment, and the gay issue. During and immediately after the Vietnam War, the country had been in a state of desolation that Nakasato observed on his earlier short visits.

No longer. New York City had regained its radiance, and a radiant New York was more like Tokyo than any other city in the world. Differences in ethnic composition notwithstanding, the people of these two cities wore similar facial expressions and walked at the same speed. But in sheer energy New York outdid Tokyo.

If anything, this impression grew as Nakasato listened to the exposition on the American Gourmet acquisition plan in the spacious meeting room of Nissei America. The expositor was Hoshino Daisuke, assistant to the general manager of the Food Department. Only one other man was present, Food Section Chief Emura Hiroshi. Kano Taichiro, the assumed initiator of this project, was inexplicably absent. As if he sensed a question in Nakasato's mind, Hoshino opened the meeting by explaining why Kano was not with them.

"Mr. Kano, our general manager, has been called to Taiwan on urgent business, but he'll be back the day after tomorrow. In the meantime, I have orders to fill in as your guide and informant. I'm at your service."

Hoshino rose slightly from the couch to bow. This man with a youthfully expressive face was not familiar to Nakasato.

"How long have you been stationed here?"

"A year and a half now."

"Where did you belong in Tokyo?"

"To Planning and Coordination of the Foodstuff Division. Here, I'm in project development related to foodstuff."

"Ah," Nakasato murmured, wondering why Hoshino had failed to notify him of his new assignment before reporting to New York.

"I went to your office just before I left Japan, but you happened to be in Europe at the time."

"Oh, was it you who left me that business card?"

"Yes," Hoshino grinned, exposing his prominent teeth. He looked like a mischievous little boy: his narrow eyes all but disappeared in laughter lines that turned his face into the generic Japanese image of Western cartoons. He wore the inevitable pair of glasses. On Nakasato's return from Europe, he had found the business card waiting on his desk. The printed name circled in red pencil made it stand out; it resembled nothing so much as a menu from some shabby Chinese restaurant. A message written in ungainly but accurate block script read: "I am transferred to Nissei America, assigned to project development in Foodstuff. Hope to generate projects truly worthy of the term 'development.' Please favor me with help and guidance!"

What a peculiar individual to find in a corporation like Nissei, Nakasato had thought at the time, as he wondered at the message and dropped the card into his desk drawer. Now he found himself face to face with its author.

"Assuming you read our report on American Gourmet Company, I'll make this briefing short. The firm isn't listed on the stock exchange, but it's a sizable chain of restaurants owned by Zadick Corporation, a well-known meat-processing company. The food-service industry is a complex field and enterprises vary greatly in type and scale. Aside from restaurant chains, they range from school-lunch programs, suppliers to military mess halls and hospitals, and airline caterers, down to eating facilities in other businesses—hotels, drugstores, and retail outlets. These enterprises may seem unrelated, but because they make it their business to provide food and drink, they actually have close relationships—sometimes cooperating for collective procurement of foodstuff and at other times competing. So we have to study the industry as a whole, uncommon types of business and all, if we buy American Gourmet Company and get into the field. But for now, I'll cover the orthodox type, that is, the one with a chain-store structure, which is where American Gourmet belongs."

Hoshino leaned over to peer into Nakasato's eyes, to read his reaction. Hoshino's spontaneous gesture had an appealing charm that made Nakasato smile.

"The prototype of the chain store is the *fast-food* shop serving hamburgers on short order. This type can be subdivided by specialties such as doughnuts, pizza, fried chicken, and so on. In substance it's a snack bar performing the same social function as the noodle shop in Japan. At this kind of establishment, the typical customer spends an average of three dollars on the main item—say, a hamburger—plus one drink such as a cola, and a side order of french fries. The fast-food chain is considered the king of the food-service industry in the United States. American Gourmet Company, now, is a chain of family restaurants. Please look at this chart."

Hoshino spread out on the table a sheet showing graphs and lists.

"This study of menu variety and price range compares main dishes, side orders, and drinks available at different types of shops. As you can see in these parallel columns, the family restaurant matches the fast-food shop in price range but clearly outstrips it in the number of menu items. Similar to or slightly better than the fast-food shop, the family restaurant is an informal dining facility where customers can get a light but full meal for the price of fast food."

"It appears to be different fast-food shops rolled into one, just like the supermarket made up of butcher and grocer under one roof," Nakasato observed.

"I thought so, too, at first, but that's not the case. The chains of restaurants offering substantial menus—like Big Boy, Denny's, and Sambo—established themselves first in the field, where the limited-menu fast-food shops barged in later and eventually dominated the market. Sambo was squeezed out of business several years ago as a result."

"American Gourmet belongs to a type of enterprise on the wane, doesn't it?"

"Not as simple as that," countered Hoshino, leaning forward in excitement. He stared up at Nakasato and gripped the edge of the coffee table for support as if ready to lunge at him. "True, the family restaurant lost some ground to fast food. American Gourmet itself showed little growth for the past several years. Its owners, Zadick Corporation, put it up for sale in an obvious attempt to get it off their hands while they could still expect a decent bid. That's why we can buy it for a bargain price of 60 million dollars. But some of us believe the family restaurant is not the waning business it appears to be. For two reasons."

Hoshino's narrow eyes gleamed behind the glasses.

"First, there's the aging of the American population to consider. It's certainly growing older at an accelerated pace. Fast food burgeoned because of the postwar baby-boomers, but that generation is just entering middle age. It's hard to imagine that baby-boomers in their fifties will still mob fast-food shops. Ten years from now, they're more likely to head for the family restaurant—I'd call it a mid-life counterpart of fast-food shops. The family restaurant has a better than fair chance to entice the customers back from fast food. Second, there's a steady rise in Americans' health consciousness and taste for Japanese food. Family restaurants lost out in the first round of competition, because they failed to keep up with new trends. This time around, the Japanese food boom can play a key role. If we buy American Gourmet Company, we ought to expand its menu with Japanese items. I believe we can't go wrong with this strategy. Any questions so far?"

Snapping momentarily out of the spell of his own heated speech, Hoshino peered at Nakasato apprehensively.

"No. Your presentation is clear enough. I'll hold my questions until you finish. Now, I want to know more about major types other than fast food and the family restaurant."

"I understand," Hoshino said, with a touch of relief in his voice. He resumed his exposition, going into the chains of dinner restaurants and steak houses that catered to more sophisticated tastes.

"As you can probably tell by now, the food-service industry encompasses all types of enterprises that provide meals outside the home. In this sense, it supplements the function of the supermarket, which supplies the foodstuff that is to be prepared and served at home. From another perspective, though, we can say these two industries are fighting over their share of the same market. As a matter of fact, food service grew fat by eating into the supermarket's trade, but in recent years the supermarket has gone all out on the offensive to drive back the encroaching food service. In my opinion, both are essential industries, firmly entrenched in the American social structure, and it will be well worth the sogo shosha's effort to build a solid foothold in their field."

Hoshino ended on a conclusive note. He waited, as if bracing himself for tough questions. Nakasato started to express his opinion.

"Now I see where the family restaurant stands in the food-service industry. But I'm still unclear why we should go in for direct management. Building a foothold is an abstract idea. To be more precise, what can Nissei expect to gain by entering the field? I can think of two things. One is the profit to be earned from competent management of American Gourmet Company. It can come in stock dividends or in proceeds from the total or partial sale of capital assets after building up their net worth—capital gains either way. The other possibility is new revenues to be generated by marketing Nissei's products through American Gourmet. Which of the two objectives is Nissei America aiming at, Hoshino?"

"If you pin me down to one or the other, then I'd have to say it's capital gains. We're not even thinking of the other possibility."

"I see," said Nakasato simply. The answer took the wind out of his sail. He had expected the other answer, eager to point out its fallacy. "Is that your own opinion? Or is Kano of the same mind?"

"Both Mr. Kano and President Tobita share this view. Or rather, I should say the president is even more progressive in his thinking."

"What do you mean by progressive?"

"He's thinking beyond capital gains. He seems to believe some sectors of our operation ought to move out of traditional shosha territory and relocate into a downstream field like food service."

"Relocate?"

"Yes. Keep intact the units that can still carry on the shosha function as effectively as ever, but let the least shosha-like sector in, say, consumer goods distribution, find a new world to develop."

"A grand vision worthy of President Tobita! By the way, Nissei Corporation has changed so much, hasn't it?" sighed Nakasato with feeling. "Fifteen years ago, we no sooner stepped into the supermarket business than we beat a hasty retreat. Know why? Direct management of the supermarket doesn't bring enough sales volume by the shosha standard, and nothing better can be expected from Nissei's indirect participation, either. The project has no profit potential. So went the verdict."

"I know. I heard the story just the other day. You had a hard time, didn't you?"

"Who on earth was rehashing an old story like that?"

"A Mr. Inuzuka was here."

"What! You can't mean Inuzuka Keigoro?"

"I think that was his name. He said he used to be your boss."

"Then that's him. I wonder what brought him to New York City." The unexpected mention of Inuzuka's name intrigued Nakasato. His image of a depressed old man defied mental association with a trip to New York.

"I ran into President Tobita at a sushi bar here during lunch hour. He was with Mr. Inuzuka. A college classmate, he said."

"That's it! They did attend the same university. That explains why they met here," Nakasato reasoned. "By the way, is Mr. Tobita in today?"

"The president is in South America, on business about ores, I think. He'll return to the U.S. by the weekend, but he's scheduled to go directly to Seattle. The president of Nissei Heavy Industries is to arrive there from Japan."

"Hmm. Well, I'm going to miss him this time."

"Yes. President Tobita was very disappointed you had only March free for this trip, but there was nothing he could do. He ordered me to bring you up to date on the American Gourmet project."

Nakasato somewhat regretted having moved up his trip in anticipation of his promotion. He had telexed New York that he would be tied down by three priority appointments from late March to early April, and Nissei America had been obliged to leave him out of their plans.

Had he delayed his trip, he would have been able to meet President Tobita and learn much about Inuzuka. Preposterous as it seemed, the possibility of Inuzuka's involvement in the American Gourmet acquisition plan could not be ruled out altogether. The timing of his sudden call was too uncanny to be mere coincidence. But there was no way to ascertain it, short of checking with Tobita in person.

"Relocating some business units into a downstream field is certainly a good idea, Hoshino, but not easy to carry out," Nakasato said, reverting to the primary subject. "The downstream of the consumer-service industry is not an area where a shoshaman can orient himself immediately to start operating effectively. Whether in food service or retail, most small shops are too rudimentary to be called 'enterprise,' and you can't even imagine the difficulties involved in trying to expand or scale up their operation. Basically, food service and retail stores are commercial businesses, but they're also like manufacturing plants in that they process fresh foodstuff. The set-up in chain stores is inevitable if you want to consolidate food service and retail. You may find it hard to believe, but the chain store is a highly sophisticated concept in structuring commercial organizations. But the shosha never had the manufacturing industry's instinct or the know-how to structure a chain of stores. Without them it can't survive in the downstream field. Hard enough to carry it off in Japan, but you're trying to do it in America! I wouldn't go so far as to say it's impossible, but your chances are about nil."

Nakasato explained his views with care as Hoshino listened in rapt attention, his eyes wide.

"In America, you face difficulties ten times more serious than in Japan. Take the management of American personnel, for instance. The overseas shosha offices hire local staff, but restaurant employees are another story. And the American labor market has craft unions and union shops very different from the company unions common in Japan. You can't overlook the kinetic energy of this country: imagine what it takes to topple a giant chain like Sambo. As you illustrated so vividly, competition in the American service industry often forces a fight to the death. Can Nissei men find their footing and survive there? *That* is the question."

Nakasato paused for a moment to see if Hoshino was following him so far. Then he softened his tone to continue: "I'm sorry to be a wet blanket here. But I can't endorse a plan to buy and manage American Gourmet unless you give me some exceptional reasons to recommend it."

"I see," Hoshino mumbled, looking like a primitive clay figurine for the moment, all expression wiped from his face, which had registered lively changes during the course of their conversation. Instantly recovering, he asked with a glimmer in his eyes, "All you need is exceptional reasons, right?"

"Ah, you believe in positive thinking, don't you?" Nakasato burst out laughing in spite of himself. "Got to be super exceptional to convince me, you know."

"First, I'd like you to see the restaurants for yourself. Let's make the rounds this afternoon and tomorrow, checking the American Gourmet shops and the competition in this neighborhood. The day after tomorrow, when Mr. Kano is back, we'll take you to see the M & A manager at Griffin Securities—they're the intermediaries in this negotiation."

In recent years, Nakasato knew, Japanese securities companies had begun to set up separate sections specifically to handle M & A transactions, modeled on the merger and acquisition unit in American stock brokerage houses. But their activities were held in check by a strong psychological resistance, innate in the Japanese corporate mind, against treating companies as objects for sale or purchase. American companies, though, considered M & A an important line of brokerage business and pegged an agent's fees to the net worth of the enterprises they traded, as they did in buying and selling merchandise or real estate properties.

"We still need confirmation, but we may be able to get you an appointment with McGavan, chairman of Zadick Corporation. They own American Gourmet Company. It'll be for the day after tomorrow, or three days from now at the most."

"I see. In the meantime, we should run a thorough check and come to a decision we won't regret later. By the way, Hoshino, I almost forgot to ask an important question about the acquisition plan. Did Griffin Securities make the initial contact with us, or did we send out feelers for a good buy on the market?"

"We made the first move."

"Then Nissei America had no previous dealings with American Gourmet Company, I take it."

"None at all."

"Good," Nakasato breathed, relaxing his brows. He had seen many cases where meticulous investigation uncovered bad debts concealed behind some plausible pretext for selling a company or capital stocks. And he was wary of a shosha type who manipulated his colleagues more than he did outsiders. "Well, what's the use of my coming out here, if we stay holed up in a room talking? Let's get going and look over American Gourmet restaurants."

At Nakasato's suggestion, Hoshino fairly catapulted himself out of the chair. Emura, the food section chief, also rose to his feet and left the room, uttering no more than a curt good-bye in a disgruntled voice. Nakasato wondered whether Emura was naturally morose, a rare type among shoshamen, or happened to be displeased about something in particular. His casual concern soon dissipated as he talked with Hoshino.

6

For four days Nakasato followed a grueling schedule packed full by Hoshino. He visited innumerable restaurants in the American Gourmet chain spread across the New York suburbs and met with both the M & A manager of Griffin Securities and the chairman of Zadick Corporation. Kano returned from Taiwan on the third day to join Nakasato and Hoshino in their breathless excursions.

As a young man twenty years earlier, Kano had epitomized the urbane shoshaman, but now in his middle years he cut an even more stylish figure. Nakasato had had little contact with Kano since they entered Nissei in the same year, but within five minutes of their reunion at Nissei America's office, the prerogative of peers led them to dispense with protocol and revert to the familiar tone of their trainee days.

"Quite a problem you dropped in our lap," Nakasato charged.

"No problem," Kano dodged deftly. "Just take a cool but *severe* look at the tight spot the sogo shosha is in these days, and you'll come to the same conclusion."

"Do you really believe this project will succeed?"

"It can't fail. Other restaurant chains are making it in the U.S. Why not American Gourmet? Look, it's doing well right now," Kano reasoned with confidence.

American Gourmet Company certainly seemed to enjoy sound financial health. Nakasato had this assessment confirmed on his visits to Griffin Securities and Zadick Corporation. If Nissei's management could keep profits at the current level, its capital spending for the purchase would run little risk of loss. At worst no greater than usual for an investment in low-yield stocks and bonds.

But can a Nissei-appointed management hold the rate of return at the current level? Nakasato wondered.

He tossed the question at Kano and received a ready answer: "Our company is a treasure house of human resources. There must be any number of men who can easily handle a restaurant chain or even two."

"But Kano, this field is clearly out of shosha territory. Even if you found a man with the highest potential, he'd need many years just to acclimatize himself to an unfamiliar field."

"That kind of thinking keeps us forever from launching into other fields. At most, all he'd need is a year to learn his way around."

"I don't think it's so easy. Even assuming he can manage somehow, he'll be stuck there for a long time. If worst comes to worst before he gets back to Nissei, he may go down with a bunch of foreign restaurants."

"It won't come to that, but the tour of duty will have to be a long one. After all, relocation to a new continent requires at least that much commitment."

This conversation took place in snatches during the drive between American Gourmet shops and business appointments. In the relaxed atmosphere in the back seat of the Ford Hoshino was driving, Nakasato found himself voicing frank opinions that might sound caustic face-to-face.

"Well, you might be right there," said Nakasato, crossing his arms over his chest to brace himself for serious thinking. "Relocation to a new continent indeed. Who's going to be put in charge? Shoshamen talk about leaving their bones in overseas posts—but they know they'll be called back sooner or later. Their ultimate goal is to earn a deserved place in the hierarchy of Nissei's home offices.

Settling down on a new continent . . . now that's a different story. Once a man's assigned to a restaurant chain, he may never make it back to the home office—maybe not even to Japan, for that matter. Do you think Nissei has a merit system to evaluate and reward a man for this kind of service? Anyway, Kano, the food retailing industry is like moss that clings to the ground to survive, it's a business that needs roots. But the shosha is like a bird, it must ride the skies. Buying the restaurant chain is a momentous decision, no matter how you look at it." Nakasato shuddered, for a moment feeling as if he himself had drawn the assignment to manage American Gourmet.

"Don't worry. Lay the foundation in five to seven years, and the man can come home in glory. Why brood over it, Nakasato? You don't have to handle this job." Kano cast a teasing glance at Nakasato. "Still much too serious, aren't you?"

"Five to seven years won't be nearly enough," Nakasato went on, ignoring Kano's banter. "Since I worked on the supermarket project some time ago, I think I have a pretty good understanding of how a chain store operates. It's a centralized system, the exact opposite of the shosha in structure. In a way, the chain store's an organic body—a highly evolved animal in which all elements are neatly coordinated. The chief executive officer is its brain, and the chain store grows or dies based on his ability. Some experts even say the chain store can't ever prosper under any CEO but an autocratic owner-manager. I don't think the top officer should be changed in five to seven years. But the issue is purely academic, because Nissei men aren't up to the job anyway. I bet there'll be no volunteers."

"I, for one—I'd like to try my hand at it," threw in Hoshino from the wheel. "I don't mind hard work. I don't care even if I never return to Nissei or have to live in the U.S. permanently. I'm willing to stake my life on a promising project as long as there's a chance I can turn it into a success with my own effort."

"Really?" Nakasato was amazed.

"Listen to the famous Hoshino tune," Kano commented with no sign of astonishment. "This man tells me, Nakasato, he's bored to death with a businessman's life. He even wonders why he's still leading so absurd a life and if this isn't a bad dream. He's looking awfully fit and full of smiles for all that, don't you think?"

"He certainly doesn't look bored. Seems he's enjoying his business life to the full," Nakasato went along with Kano's jibe at Hoshino.

"Not a chance! Enjoying it to the full, no, I'm not. But I'm not as despondent as Mr. Kano made me out, either. Only . . . "

"Only what?"

"Only I keep wondering if this is the way I should live. To be honest, I don't have all that much work to do. But come payday, I get paid just the same—better than the going rate at that. It really bothers me."

"Too much spare time on your hands?"

"No, I don't mean that. I'm as busy as can be, same as back in Japan. I've been working after hours every day and coming to the office some weekends."

"In that case, anyone else would think the salary is too low. What makes you feel yours is excessive?"

"If I quit Nissei, I'll never earn the same salary for the same amount of work anywhere else."

"True enough. We salarymen all have security and protection in our company. We'd never earn as much on the outside."

"That's what disgusts me, this feeling of being on alms. Worse yet, overpaid as I am for the work I put in, I find my life hard to take."

"What? You mean you aren't paid enough?"

"Yes, I do."

"You make no sense at all."

"It's like going through incomplete combustion. I'm not using all the energy I've got. I'm capable of giving more service to the world. My salary's much smaller than the reward I'd earn from accomplishing a more worthy task. But I'm afraid I can never take on a useful job as long as I stay with Nissei Corporation."

"Can you, if you move on to a restaurant chain?"

"Yes. I believe managing a restaurant chain is such a job."

"Hey, watch out!" Kano cried out in alarm. "No need to look at us while you're talking. We hear you."

In his mounting excitement, Hoshino frequently turned his head sideways or peered into the rearview mirror as he drove. Nakasato watched with apprehension. They were traveling on a three-lane highway in New Jersey. Few other cars were in sight at the moment, and no danger imminent, but a little carelessness could lead to a big accident. Hoshino seemed an excitable type, whose imagination was liable to get overheated unless someone cooled it for him from time to time.

"I'm all right," Hoshino assured them, perfectly calm. "A restaurant cooks food, serves it, and brings in revenue depending on its customers' satisfaction level. If you serve unsatisfactory meals, you'll go right out of business. On the other hand, if you manage it well, you steadily increase your profits. I want to bet on that chance."

Nakasato felt a long-forgotten memory stirring to life. He once used to say the same things Hoshino did: I want to arm myself with some skill that would allow me to wean myself from the company and go my own way.—Yes, that's how I put it. Fifteen years ago.

Fifteen years ago, he had been genuinely motivated to make a success of the supermarket job. That dream of his, Inuzuka Keigoro had killed it. His aspiration to make his own way in life had been buried, forgotten ever since.

"How about that, Nakasato? Here's one man eager to take on a tough job. Hoshino's no exception. When the word gets around about our affiliation with American Gourmet, you'll see no end of volunteers from Nissei's ranks."

"That may be, but not one will be up to the job. No way a shosha-man can manage a chain store."

Even as he voiced this negative opinion, Nakasato was eagerly searching his thoughts for the exact circumstances of his experience that lay at the root of his reaction. Old memories returned to him in bits and pieces.

At the same time, his heart was undergoing a change that belied his words. The American Gourmet acquisition plan, which had seemed no more substantial than a daydream back in Tokyo, was beginning to look like a choice project offering realistic possibilities. Now that he had felt the American soil under his feet, looked over the restaurants, and canvassed their management performance records, his new insights were rapidly altering his thinking. Another factor that made an impact was Hoshino's blazing passion.

This young man with a gleam in his eyes, spouting hope and ambition, reminded Nakasato of himself in days long ago. He could almost believe Hoshino capable of accomplishing any task, no matter how difficult. I'd like to let him try, Nakasato thought, filled with nostalgia for his own distant youthful self.

Even if he wanted to, Nakasato knew, he could never put Hoshino in charge of this project. Nissei Corporation considered a thirty-year-old no more than a beginner. Hoshino would need a ranking supervisor to report to—a youngish senior executive or a crack veteran manager. In his mind, Nakasato counted off possible candidates—but none of them measured up to his standard. Well, consult with the general manager of personnel and see, he told himself. His mind was already leaning toward an affirmative decision.

7

The day before his scheduled departure, Nakasato invited Hoshino to dinner. The younger man suggested Japanese cuisine, but Nakasato insisted on steak. Whenever he was entertained by the Nissei men stationed overseas, they never failed to steer him toward a Japanese restaurant. You must miss familiar foods while traveling, they'd say, but in truth they were the ones who craved Japanese dishes. Eager for every opportunity to try out indigenous Western specialties, Nakasato made it a rule to assert his preference. Since he was treating Hoshino this time, perhaps he should have been gracious enough to accommodate Hoshino's preference, but Nakasato was intent on ordering steak—that quintessential piece of Americana—before he left the country.

"In that case, there's a place we ought to try, now that we contemplate going into the same business," Hoshino said and named an exclusive restaurant in downtown Manhattan. "It's doing so well that waiting over one hour for a table is nothing unusual. But, Mr. Nakasato, can you guess what the popular menu item is, at this most American of restaurants? Teriyaki steak! The American taste for Japanese cuisine has gone well past a temporary fad. Now it's a case of cultural assimilation."

"Thank you but no," Nakasato said, flinching inwardly from the younger man's occupational fixation. "Maybe next time. I'm beat after the forced marches we took. I have some packing to do tonight for an early start in the morning. Let's grab a steak at the restaurant in my hotel."

"I see what you mean. Fine with me," said Hoshino understand-ingly. His understanding went only as far as the choice of restau-rant. Entirely unaware that he was a major cause of Nakasato's ex-haustion, he launched into an interminable discourse as soon as they were seated at the hotel restaurant.

"I think American Gourmet has three problems. First, it hasn't kept pace with the times, witness the absence of Japanese cuisine on their menu Second, their service policies are far from cost-effi-cient. Haven't you noticed, Mr. Nakasato, that in productivity the American Gourmet employees fall behind their counterparts in ri-val establishments? They make contact with each set of customers one or two times more than employees do at other restaurants."

Hoshino's scenario went something like this. When customers come into the family restaurant, the waitress seats each party and passes out the menus. Rarely does she get orders on this first con-tact. More likely she walks away and waits for what seems an opti-mum time. If she returns too soon, the customers may be still unde-cided or ready to give only a partial order, say, for the children. Too long and they get restless. The timing for taking drink orders is deli-cate. Dessert can cost her another two trips.

"All this may sound trivial, but in my opinion here's the most crucial weakness in personnel cost-efficiency. If American Gourmet wait-resses make two extra customer contacts per table, that alone lowers their productivity 15 percent below their competitors' average."

"Look, an attractive lady's here to make contact." Nakasato called Hoshino's attention to an exceedingly tall brunette who had just ar-rived at their table.

"Steak for you, too, Hoshino?"

"Yes."

"What'll you drink? A beer?"

"How about a California wine?"

"Not a bad idea."

Nakasato ordered their food and Hoshino their wine. This order was taken by another tall woman. Showing himself a connoisseur, Hoshino traded comments with her on varieties of wine incompre-hensible to Nakasato. Evidently he applied his exceptional enthusi-asm to this area as well.

"Rather expensive. Would you mind?"

"How expensive?"

"She recommends this, a red wine, from Cabernet Sauvignon grapes. Fairly dry and full, she says."

Hoshino pointed to the line on the wine list, (bottle) $32. On the expensive side as he says, but if that's what he wants, Nakasato thought and gave him a nod.

"The third problem with American Gourmet is," Hoshino began, picking up his original topic as soon as the wine talk was over, "they've got no distinct corporate identity." He studied Nakasato's expression through his slitted eyes. "Pointing this out to you, a general manager, is like preaching to a buddha, I know. But corporate identity holds the personality of an enterprise. The store's physical layout and decor, menu items, employees' appearance and attitude, background music—all these and other elements that make up a company express its creed and philosophy. In a sensibly organized enterprise, all the key elements interrelate and mesh into a distinctive corporate personality. But American Gourmet lacks focus, because these elements aren't coordinated. To start with, their white stuccoed Spanish architecture clashes with their name."

"But you talk about introducing Japanese cuisine there. Wouldn't it dilute their identity even more?"

"No, it wouldn't," Hoshino countered, reacting in earnest to Nakasato's bantering question.

Corporate identity reflects the basic stance of the company, while the decision on Japanese food is just short-term marketing strategy; since the Spanish-style facade is part of the long-lasting physical structure, it has much to do with the company's stance itself—so went Hoshino's argument. He seemed intent on clearing up a misunderstanding on Nakasato's part.

Unhurriedly Nakasato consumed his soup. Its flavor saturated his taste buds.

"Stop talking and start eating. Your soup's getting cold."

"Yes, I'd better."

Hoshino fell to immediately. The spoon had made no more than a few trips to his mouth when he asked, grim-faced, "Mr. Nakasato, do you anticipate a *go sign* on this project?" The soup was already forgotten. "I've learned much just following you around the past few days. I always wanted to get to know you, and this opportunity showed me my expectations had been well founded. All the more now, I'm impatient to get the council of managing directors to approve this project so I can work with you.''

Hoshino's words caught Nakasato by surprise.

What does he mean by working with me? Most likely, he expects we'll meet many more times before the approved project can be launched. But why do I have this feeling Hoshino meant something else? Giving Nakasato no chance to pursue this thought, Hoshino posed a question of his own: "Have you seen the cathedral of Cologne, on the Rhine?"

"Yes, I have. Majestic and sublime. I wanted to take a picture of it but never could. I didn't have a wide-angle lens."

"The construction of the cathedral began in 1248 and ended in 1880. It took over six hundred years."

"So I've heard. The work was interrupted many times by war but eventually carried through. I understand paintings of the city of Cologne can be dated by the number of stories the cathedral has in the picture."

"That's right. They didn't just finish the project after so many centuries. The amazing thing is, they adhered faithfully to the exact original specifications. Architectural technology and machinery had made tremendous progress over the centuries, but they used nothing but thirteenth-century techniques and implements to incarnate the ideal as it had been initially envisioned. When I first heard this story, I was spellbound, awed. It dawned on me—we don't come into the world merely to die; there does exist some idea or principle transcending the individual body that can be transmitted down through the ages. As a college student I'd strained and scrimped to finance the trip to Europe. This one precious insight I gained at Cologne made it well worth all the trouble."

"I see." Nakasato responded automatically, preoccupied, but without understanding why Hoshino brought up the story of the Cologne cathedral.

"I think it embodies the dream of the human race. Man discovered a certain idea that'd never existed on earth before and aspired to express it in a tangible form. Draw up a blueprint of it, for example. But this concept was so grand that it proved beyond the effort of one individual or even one generation. So people sharing the same aspiration worked in concert over the centuries to complete it. Mr. Nakasato, I want to create something equally meaningful."

"I see." Nakasato temporized by echoing himself but still failed to get Hoshino's point.

"Can't we turn American Gourmet Company into a Cologne cathedral of our own? As a means to dream our dream and embody it? It'll give us the pleasure of creative endeavor—something that's missing in the shosha's normal activities. We won't be dealing in some other company's products or acting as intermediary in a transaction between companies A and B. Of course I'm not denying that shosha business has its own creative aspects. I just don't see the same quality of creativity we'd need to build up a restaurant chain."

That's the very reason the downstream operation is too difficult for the shosha to handle, Nakasato wanted to remind Hoshino, but he could not get a word in edgewise as the young man kept up his nonstop discourse, leaning forward in his ardor.

"Maybe you want to criticize me for presumption, but I mean no harm. I suppose it'll cause problems at home and elsewhere for you, but our top management rarely shows this much interest in a project like this. The famous winter freeze is forcing integrated trading companies to change their ways, but without your consent this project will fall through. For the future of Nissei Corporation and for the sake of the new generation of shoshamen, please lend us your support."

"Hey, Hoshino, wait a second! Problems at home? Lend you *my* support? What in the world are you talking about?"

"What! Didn't you know?" Hoshino widened his eyes and blew a silent whistle. "Well. Now that I think back, Mr. Kano did say something to the effect that you don't have to handle this job."

"Handle this job? Am I slated to be assigned out to American Gourmet, when the acquisition goes through? Is that part of the plan?"

Just then the waitress brought their food. Nakasato picked up knife and fork, cut into the steak, and put a piece of meat into his mouth. He could taste nothing. His dinner was ruined by the shock of the startling revelation.

"Yes, President Tobita considers your appointment the most crucial factor. He insists you're the only man in our company who's capable of accomplishing this task. I hear President Ebisawa has no objections, provided you are willing. I simply assumed you came on this trip fully informed of all this."

"No. I know nothing about it. I was ordered here to conduct a feasibility study on the proposed plan to go into the family restaurant business in America."

"In that case, did I say something I shouldn't have?"

"It's okay. In fact, I appreciate your telling me. Now I understand the situation better."

"That may be so but . . . "

Hoshino sounded thoroughly demoralized, no vestige of his earlier fervor in evidence. But he was not the type to sustain a negative mood for long. Soon his face brightened.

"What's done is done. Maybe I was wrong to speak out, but everything I told you is true. So please lend us a helping hand. I beg of you."

Nakasato merely grunted in response, his thoughts whirling in complex reaction to the facts so unexpectedly brought to light.

Annoying enough to learn that close associates had been plotting behind his back to use him. Managing Director Enomoto, his immediate superior, must have been in on it. Not only his peer, Kano, but even his junior, Hoshino, knew all about it. He himself was the last to find out, and by sheer accident at that. The injustice of it all! The more he thought about it, the more annoyed he became.

The biggest jolt was the news that President Ebisawa was in favor of the idea. He had flattered himself into thinking he was Ebisawa's right-hand man. But now he faced the very real danger of being assigned out of the headquarters by the president himself to a post that threatened to mean his banishment to America.

What's more, Hoshino was correct in predicting trouble at home.

How would Rieko react, if Nakasato told her they'd live in the United States until his retirement? Once she was happy living in Los Angeles. So she wouldn't be averse to life in America as such. But now the children were older, the family's circumstances were totally different. Unthinkable to uproot the two children at this critical juncture, as they prepared frantically for examination hell, to get into higher schools.—Please, leave us behind and go by yourself— he could all but hear his wife's voice urging him. The move would break up his home. As it was, his marriage coasted along, nothing more than a habit.

What a mess! Who concocted such an absurd plan? By chance, was it Inuzuka himself?

"Mr. Nakasato, let's build our own Cologne cathedral together," Nakasato heard Hoshino saying.

Shut up! cried Nakasato inwardly. I hate maudlin romanticism like that. You talk too much anyway.

Nakasato fell into silence, his face grim. His displeasure at last reached Hoshino. They finished their meal in a constrained mood.

"I'm sorry. I shouldn't have talked so much." Hoshino apologized in obvious distress, bowing to Nakasato many times in the hotel lobby.

"No, it's not your fault. You've done a lot for me. Thank you. Please give my regards to President Tobita."

Taking pity on Hoshino after all, Nakasato extended his right hand to give him a friendly handshake.

8

"Please give me a call. Doesn't matter how late the hour." The message was waiting for Nakasato, when he saw Hoshino off and went to the front desk for his room key. Judging by the Japanese written in an accomplished hand, it was not a message left by phone but one delivered by the writer in person.

The signature read Emura Hiroshi.

It took Nakasato a few seconds to connect the name with the food section chief at Nissei America. The man had made so slight an impression on Nakasato that he had trouble remembering him. They'd met on the day of his arrival in New York City, but Emura kept silent while Hoshino talked himself into a fever. A taciturn type unusual for a shoshaman, Nakasato had thought at the time.

Did an urgent message come in from Tokyo? Entering his room, Nakasato dropped his attaché case on the bed and immediately dialed the number noted on the message slip. Emura must have been waiting by the phone, for he answered on the first ring.

"Something up?" Nakasato asked.

"No, nothing's up," Emura assured him but faltered momentarily. "It's just that there's something I'd like you to know." His voice sounded as gloomy as Nakasato's first impression of him.

"What would that be?"

"It concerns the American Gourmet acquisition plan. I think Hoshino's presentation wasn't quite the whole truth."

"Not the whole truth?"

"He told you this deal came not from Griffin Securities but through our search for a good buy."

"Yes, he did."

"That much is accurate."

"So?"

Emura's grudging phrases were getting on Nakasato's nerves, and he struggled to keep irritation out of his voice.

"Then you asked if we'd ever had any dealings with American Gourmet Company, and Hoshino said no."

"Oh. We actually had some?"

"No, we never did."

"Then what's your problem?"

"The problem concerns what your question was getting at. What you really wanted was confirmation that the American Gourmet acquisition plan was no last-ditch effort on Nissei's part to write off delinquent debts by buying out the debtor, wasn't it?"

"That's right. Disreputable deals of that sort aren't uncommon. Under certain circumstances, of course, the takeover of a company to recover bad debts isn't necessarily discreditable, but it's dishonest to cover up the fact with pretentious justification. Now, are you saying this project has a smell of dishonesty?"

"Yes. To tell you the truth, the General Products Department of Nissei America is currently encumbered by a huge stockpile of unmarketable merchandise. I think this bad overstock has something to do with the acquisition plan."

"Give me the full details."

As Nakasato began to get the gist of Emura's story, he realized the seriousness of it. He sat down on the bed to listen with more attention.

"General Products handles third-party trade, importing general merchandise and textiles made in Taiwan to the United States—

wooden tables, small furniture, uniforms, fabric, and so forth. It's a sector that Mr. Ishida, the general manager before Mr. Kano, developed with painstaking care."

"Ishida Ichiro, right? A steadfast hard worker. I know him well."

"The outlets for these items are American supermarkets and food service shops. Our biggest customer is Ferguson Burgers, the well-known fast-food chain on the East Coast. We've been their exclusive supplier of wood and textile products, ranging from store fixtures, furnishings, curtains, tablecloths, down to employees' uniforms."

"Now I remember. I heard about it as a success story in downstream marketing."

"But this account began to go sour several months ago."

"Go sour?"

"Yes. A new man took over as vice-president of purchasing at Ferguson and changed their policies. As our current contracts on various items come up for renewal, they're being rejected one after another."

"That's a shame. But it means merely a loss of new business. That entails no further risk."

"You're right there. But Nissei America never anticipated such a turn of events and had large standing orders placed with manufacturers in Taiwan based on sales forecasts."

"How dreadful! I assume our contracts guaranteed them outright purchase."

"I don't know the details, but even if we made no legally binding commitment to purchase the products in their entirety, the fact remains that they were manufactured in good faith on our standing order. So the responsibility lies with Nissei America. If we failed to accept the shipments, there'd be the devil to pay. The damage would go much further than this particular deal, making it almost impossible for Nissei to trade with Taiwan in any other field."

"Oh, that explains why Kano went to Taiwan, doesn't it?"

"I think so."

Nakasato recalled his momentary misgiving when he arrived in New York to find Kano absent. No wonder. An emergency was brewing in Taiwan at the time. But on his return Kano never mentioned it to Nakasato.

If Emura's allegation was valid, Kano's very silence on this matter constituted circumstantial evidence testifying that a cause-and-effect relationship did indeed exist between the questionable stock and the acquisition plan.

"What's the amount involved?"

"The amount?"

"I mean, the amount of money needed to honor the purchase contracts."

"I think I heard the figure of one million dollars mentioned."

"That's roughly 250 million yen at the current exchange rate. By no means negligible if it turns out to be a total loss."

"A total loss isn't likely but neither is a decrease in the ultimate damage."

"So you believe this matter is related in some way to the American Gourmet acquisition plan."

"Yes, I do," Emura said, a sudden tensing in his voice palpable over the line.

Why is Emura telling me all this? Nakasato could not begin to fathom the mind of a man he hardly knew as yet. Aside from his apparent loyalty to Nissei, Emura might be motivated by some grudge against Kano.

"When Ferguson Burgers began to demur on contract renewals, Mr. Kano didn't take the situation seriously enough. He dismissed it lightly, saying the new vice-president was merely trying to prove his mettle by arguing the price down and we'd have to play along by conceding him some points. Apparently Mr. Kano never expected an across-the-board termination, and he did nothing more than occasionally mention the issue in casual conversations. But the state of affairs turned out to be more serious than his estimate. As the contract renewal negotiations went on the rocks, Mr. Kano fell silent on the subject. It happened to be around the same time that the American Gourmet plan suddenly surfaced."

"But it's out of all proportion to buy a whole enterprise for the sole purpose of moving a stockpile worth no more than one million dollars."

"True, if you see it from Nissei's vantage point—incongruous enough to elude suspicion, I'd say. Still, on the individual level, a million-dollar loss would seem lethal to any sales manager. When it comes to weighing his own career survival against the corporate interest, a manager in trouble may go so far as to buy a food-service chain at any cost to the company. He may not even hesitate to sell his own company out, for that matter."

"You don't mince words, do you? Kano and I have been friends ever since college, and I can tell you he's not an unscrupulous man."

"I apologize. I didn't mean Mr. Kano would sell his company out. I was talking about the common nature of businessmen in general."

Unpleasant as Emura's view was, it had a convincing ring to it. Nakasato had to admit that an individual might preach the virtue of giving priority to the corporate interest over personal gains but shade his actions toward the other direction. No wonder the business world was infested with toadyism and play-safe attitudes that undermined the system from within.

"Mr. Nakasato, at first I had no intention of telling you about this. I saw no reason to, because I didn't believe such a wild scheme as buying American Gourmet would get anywhere. After you'd been here a few days, I couldn't help noticing a change in your thinking. I was afraid that, astute as you are, you might have fallen under the spell of Hoshino's eccentric presentation. If you sanction the plan, Nissei Corporation will implement it. So I decided to report all this to you, hoping you'd make judicious use of the knowledge. Too many opportunists nowadays just use the downturn in the shosha's fortunes as an excuse to jump at any novel venture. These would-be reconstructionists endanger the company. We must protect Nissei Corporation. I hope you understand how I feel."

"I understand," Nakasato said and managed to thank Emura before hanging up. He felt heartsick.

Emura must have sincerely wanted to protect the interest of their company by making the disclosure. But his action smacked of tattling and Nakasato found it repulsive. Couldn't Emura find some other use for the sensitive information? Perhaps in his position, Emura saw no alternative. He could explain the situation to President Tobita and leave it to him to monitor Kano's moves? But that line of action would work only if Emura enjoyed Tobita's implicit trust to begin with, and besides it ran the risk of doing Kano more drastic harm, more than confiding in Nakasato.

Does President Tobita know all about the stock of Taiwanese merchandise? In any event, can American Gourmet restaurants actually use the furnishings and tablecloths made to order for another restaurant chain? In reviewing the conversation in a calmer mind, Nakasato found many points that needed clarification.

Call Emura again and ask him—Nakasato picked up the receiver but returned it to its cradle at once. No need. He'd lost all desire to endorse the American Gourmet acquisition plan.

Why give up my elite management post that took me over twenty years of hard work to reach? And why accept an indefinite tour of duty in America and throw in my lot with a new enterprise of questionable prospects? Who cares whether Emura's information is true or false!

Nakasato got up slowly and dragged his suitcase out to the middle of the room to start packing. Fatigue plastered every inch of his body.

9

"How's American Gourmet coming along?" Ebisawa asked, his expression warm, as soon as he saw Nakasato come into his suite and before the younger man had a chance to make his salutations.

"President Ebisawa, I have been honored with the preliminary notice of promotion upon my return. I shall strive to be worthy of it."

"Congratulations!" Ebisawa acknowledged. He rose with the agility of a much younger man, walked from his desk toward the armchairs, and invited Nakasato to sit down.

"How does it feel?"

"Well, I still have to draw a conclusion." Nakasato began his report as he had outlined it in his mind. "American Gourmet Company seems to exceed all my expectations. Currently it even shows profits. In Japan, no owner would dream of selling a company that's doing so well. The only question concerns future prospects."

"Is there any cause for worry?"

"Not American Gourmet Company itself. But this type of operation faces a rather uncertain future."

"How do you mean?"

"American Gourmet stores belong to the family restaurant category. Other types of food service include fast food and the dinner restaurant," Nakasato introduced the knowledge supplied by Ho-shino. "In substance, a food-service chain can be one of many types, some with great growth potential and others already on the decline. The family restaurant seems closer to the latter case. I think Zadick Corporation's decision to sell American Gourmet Company was based on such a prognosis."

"So family restaurants are on the way out."

"Not exactly on the way out, but their future is far from bright. There's an imminent danger for us: we may flee from the shosha's winter only to get stuck in late autumn."

"Which type of food service has the best prospects?"

"The hub of the field will remain fast-food chains. They're prey-ing on the family restaurant. But the dinner restaurant has a growth potential, though it won't expand too much."

"I see."

Ebisawa gazed up at the ceiling, arms crossed over his chest and lips tight. His face, long known even outside Nissei's organization through his climb to the summit of this colossus, looked wistful for a moment.

"Now that Japanese cuisine has passed the fad stage to take its place in Americans' eating habits, moving into the food service in-dustry in the United States makes good sense. Looking over the country with that idea in mind on this trip, I've become even more confirmed in my view. Americans don't generally get attentive care and considerate service."

"It isn't a country known for softness anyway."

"Indifference is more and more perceptible and widespread. At stores and restaurants, the waiting time's too long and the available merchandise and service are poor in quality. I've heard many tales of woe. A top department store packs two right shoes in the box and gives the customer a hard time when he comes back to exchange one duplicate for a matching left shoe. Or a mix-up in hotel reservations leaves a guest in the lurch." Nakasato recounted a number of exper-iences he'd gleaned from Nissei men in the New York office.

"All too true. The last time I was in California, a manager in our San Francisco office told me he'd had great trouble getting accom-modations for me."

"Naturally Americans aren't happy with this situation. They aren't as finicky as Japanese customers, but these days poor merchandise and service are wearing their patience so thin that they welcome Japanese-made products and cars over there. The food-service industry is no exception. Under the circumstances, I recommend that we give serious thought to entering the food service business, aside from the issue of whether the acquisition of American Gourmet is feasible."

"All right. Where will you start?"

"I'll run another thorough investigation on American Gourmet. In the meantime, I'll canvass other types of food-service operations with better growth potentials to find a suitable property for sale."

"Good. Thank you for a job well done," Ebisawa said, relaxing his brows. He stood up, his back ramrod straight.

"Nakasato, Tanabe Motors informed us of their decision to switch to direct export."

"Oh, no! When did it happen?"

"Just last week."

"Is that so? At last. Europe, too."

Tanabe Motors was a leading motorcycle maker whose fortunes shot up after World War II but included many financial crises. Each time, Nissei Corporation bailed the company out. After its management performance stabilized, Nissei also helped expand its exports during the high-growth phase of Japan's economy. Just about the time when French President de Gaulle derided Japan's Prime Minister Ikeda Hayato as a transistor salesman, Nissei men were going around the world selling motorcycles, if not transistor radios. Tanabe Motors lacked foreign language competence and business acumen in international trading and had no employees with overseas sales experience. It achieved footholds in foreign countries entirely through Nissei's efforts and expertise. Without them Tanabe would have had no chance at all against competitors like Honda and Yamaha.

Over the past ten years, however, the situation had been reversing itself. Tanabe now had its own employees stationed at key areas around the globe. Their qualifications had steadily improved to the point that these days Tanabe's overseas staff boasted multilingual proficiency and trade expertise fortified with knowledge about motorcycles easily surpassing that of Nissei men.

Already Tanabe had put its direct trade policy into effect in America, Southeast Asia, and Australia. It was closing out its agent, Nissei, from one lucrative region after another down the list in descending order by sales volume.

"Fits their pattern, doesn't it?"

"Yes. Tanabe is *clever*." Ebisawa used the English word for emphasis. "They don't cut us off at a stroke. First, they take over the actual business transactions but keep paying sinecure commissions to Nissei. When our men get complacent and neglectful of their primary function as trade agent, Tanabe declares a direct trade arrangement to match the actual practice. This unique tactic of Tanabe's causes an initial increase to show in our profits. Naive men on our staff welcome more return for less work, but it's nothing to celebrate."

"No function performed, no long-term gains earned, as you say." Nakasato quoted Ebisawa's favorite aphorism.

"Right you are. If anything, this winter freeze will only deepen for the shosha. But none of the other shoshas seem to be scoring success in new ventures they try as countermeasures. Operation downstream, new media, information service, biotechnology—all you see is a flood of trendy terms from new fields. The actual state of our business doesn't get any better. Now the question is, which shosha can make a forward leap ahead of the others?" Ebisawa looked straight at Nakasato. "It's a job for the general manager of project development. Give it your best shot."

"Yes," Nakasato said but averted his eyes. He wondered if Ebisawa had seen through his secret intent to squash the American Gourmet acquisition plan. But Ebisawa said nothing more.

"I'll take my leave now." Nakasato bowed deeply and left the president's office.

What and how to report back to President Ebisawa? That decision had been a matter of critical importance to Nakasato. Even subtle nuances of the wording in his first report fresh off the trip might leave an indelible mark in Ebisawa's memory. So Nakasato had carefully worked out a presentation strategy before he went to see the president.

Revealing his true thoughts to Ebisawa was out of the question, he had decided first off. If he came right out and said, "I'm against this project because I seem to be the one singled out to head it," he'd be tagged, instantly, as unenterprising and unmotivated. He could emphasize that running a food-service company in America was impractical. But that would mean outright refutation of the president's personal judgment in favor of the plan. He might try to change Ebisawa's mind by stressing the anticipated difficulties in direct management of American restaurants. But Ebisawa could simply toss everything back to him by saying, "It's your job to overcome them." Nakasato would find himself cornered. By all means, he must kill the plan without denigrating it. Should he say, my study uncovered many problems that make American Gourmet unsuitable for our takeover? An explanation of this sort would be easily accepted but was distinctly untrue. American Gourmet turned out to be an excellent company. Any other assessment would be a lie. If exposed, a false report would cause irreparable damage to Nakasato's credibility.

Having considered a whole range of alternatives, he had put into effect what seemed the best plan—to dissuade Ebisawa while ostensibly briefing him on the prospects of various modes of food-service operations. Hardly knowledgeable in this area, the president could be sidetracked smoothly with a comparative appraisal of growth potentials. Nakasato's tactic was designed to jumble the issue to death while discussing it from a positive perspective.

There's some uncertainty in their growth potential, so we'll wait for the finding of a further study.—That's all I have to say, Nakasato told himself on his way out of the presidential suite. While I'm stalling, the plan will simply evaporate. American Gourmet makes a tempting enough target for some other buyer to snap up. After our survey of the field finds other types of food-service operations to be more promising, a new search will begin. The American market should have any number of companies up for sale. When a likely candidate is located, its standing will be evaluated against American Gourmet's, since the computation of profit margins and projected returns on investments is basically the same whatever the differences in corporate form and mode of operation. I doubt we'll come across a property that can outshine American Gourmet. While the search and reject process is going on, the market situation will change. If an abrupt upswing in the economy sparks substantial increases in import of raw materials and export of steel and machinery, the shosha winter will recede and no one will wonder whether the sudden warming signals an unseasonable thaw or burgeoning spring. Real gains on the balance sheet never fail to help everything along. Under such circumstances, the idea of getting into the food service business, to say nothing of buying American Gourmet Company, will melt away, completely forgotten.

Thus Nakasato plotted a silent death for the acquisition plan without a single word in explicit opposition. Unnerved as he was by President Ebisawa's piercing eyes, he had already played out his first hand—no choice but move ahead as planned.

His peace of mind, however, was soon disturbed by a younger staff member of Project Development, Sumoto Kazuhiko.

"Mr. Nakasato, you've just explained various reasons why you don't actively endorse the acquisition plan. But what's your primary reason?" Sumoto asked in a brash manner, bending his lanky body forward.

They were at the dinner party that departmental staff had arranged to celebrate Nakasato's promotion. The occasion was an informal gathering of in-house associates, all of whom Nakasato outranked. Lulled into a false sense of security, Nakasato had just stated his views on the American Gourmet issue: The family restaurant has doubtful growth potential; Hoshino in New York is most enthusiastic about the plan but not astute enough in his judgment; there's reason to suspect the proposal was impelled by a need to dispose of the unmarketable stock that New York's General Products Department is saddled with.

Nakasato's seven subordinates listened to his narration with keen interest. No sooner had he finished than Sumoto, the youngest among them, shot the question at him.

"My primary reason? Hard to pick one. If I must, then I'd say the poor prospects of the family restaurant."

"But Mr. Nakasato, even if it has no prospects, the family restaurant isn't about to disappear altogether, is it? I assume you mean that no growth above the current level can be expected. If so, I'd think that American Gourmet, one of the best firms in that particular category, has the making of an ideal base for Nissei, because there's little danger of new competitors crowding into the field one after another."

"Oh, well, that's one way to look at it, I suppose. Then again, the orthodox approach in making capital investment is to choose an operation with the highest growth potential."

"Doesn't seem to fit somehow. I have a feeling you left out your real reason."

Sumoto's eyes seemed to bore into Nakasato's mind. I see the real reason, his glance implied. Nettled as he was, Nakasato summoned a smile to his face to mask his emotion.

"There's no real reason or false reason. I've just laid out everything."

"Did you really?" Sumoto would not back down. "You used to be in charge of our supermarket project. That makes you one of the few Nissei managers with actual experience in downstream operations. Isn't that true?"

Here it comes, Nakasato said inwardly, bracing himself.

"I believe," Sumoto continued, "your reservations concerning the current issue have a lot to do with your particular experience in the past. If that's the case, I'm afraid you'll never approve any other project of this kind, no matter what business is involved."

"Not necessarily." Nakasato barely managed to breathe that much, but his tongue felt too heavy to produce intelligible sounds. How shameful, letting a green subordinate inquisition him. But he couldn't simply dismiss his questions. All the men of his department were present, listening to their exchange with rapt attention. Mishandle this situation, and the consequences could undermine his effectiveness as manager.

"My guess is, you believe the shosha cannot function in the downstream field."

"What?"

"Well, don't you?"

"No, I'm not so dogmatic about it, but . . . ," Nakasato faltered, his mind preoccupied—did I misunderstand the intent of Sumoto's question? Did my own guilty conscience turn his youthful probe into sharp interrogation?

"Mr. Nakasato, what in the world happened years ago when Nissei failed in the direct management of a supermarket chain? Didn't you live through some events that convinced you the shosha mentality was good at the role of trade intermediary but absolutely unfit to dive into the downstream and set up a new enterprise? That's why you objected once before to the proposal to establish a produce distribution network, isn't it?"

Relief flooded Nakasato's heart. His real motive hadn't been penetrated after all.

A nationwide network of produce distribution centers was originally conceived to expedite the flow of vegetables and fruits and cut costs. First touted as a revolutionary concept to streamline merchandise distribution, on closer examination the project revealed its inadequate understanding of the existing marketing system and even posed legal snags that made it unfeasible. Nakasato had turned it down for that and no other reason.

Still, Nakasato found Sumoto's superficial interpretation opportune. It served his immediate purpose. If everybody believed it, all the better for him. He could easily dress it up and pass it off as his real reason.

"You're right, Sumoto. To be honest, none of the reasons I listed are lies, but they aren't decisive factors either. To narrow down to a single most important reason, I'd have to cite the shoshaman's inability to function in the downstream of consumer goods distribution field—for the present, at any rate."

"So I was right all along. In your judgment, then, any kind of downstream operation will fail under the shosha's direct management. Isn't that so?"

"No. It isn't. I refrained from mentioning the particular reason precisely to prevent this sort of misunderstanding, but . . . "

"Please tell us whatever is on your mind," Sumoto urged, looking serious. "It's a matter of grave concern for all of us. This severe business environment everyone compares to the winter climate is forcing integrated trading companies to probe new fields. Downstream commercial operations—like retail shops, restaurants, and service industry—seem more important and easier for the shosha to take up than upstream fields like manufacturing, since the shosha is primarily commercial capital in itself." Sumoto paused for a moment and addressed Nakasato. "But you maintain the downstream is beyond the shosha's capabilities. You made the same point once before. Ever since the American Gourmet plan came up, I've been watching you with great interest. I believe you're ready to pass a negative judgment again. If the shosha can never hope to break into the downstream, as you say, are we left with no choice but to sit in our winter until we freeze to death?"

Intoxicated by his own words, Sumoto was sliding into an oratorical tone. "It may be impertinent of me to say this in your presence. But as general manager of project development, you hold the key to Nissei's advance into untouched territories. Your negative stand all but closes off Nissei's exploration into the downstream of the commercial world. Do you really think it's the right attitude to take?"

"No need for drama," Nakasato mollified him. "The shosha may be going through winter now, but it doesn't mean there's no future. You needn't be afraid we'll freeze to death unless we make it to the downstream. Let a fear like that panic you into jumping in the water without proper preparations or convictions and you're sure to drown. Exactly the point I've been trying to make."

"You mean to say you're not necessarily against all downstream operations?"

"If the men in charge are well prepared and firmly resolved, and if the enterprise in question shows sufficient growth potential, there's no reason why I should rule against the plan." Nakasato glanced around at his men. "You are so kind as to honor me with this party. Let's drop business talk for now and enjoy the dinner. After we finish here, I'll buy you all drinks somewhere else," Nakasato said to cut off the discussion. Sumoto still looked unsatisfied.

Nakasato's real motive was safe from exposure for the moment, but talking about the downstream operation had made him nervous. Somehow Sumoto's questions had stirred fifteen-year-old memories and perturbed his heart. At the bar to which he led the party for afterdinner drinks, Nakasato's mind wandered among those memories even as he carried on trivial conversation with his companions.

Fifteen years ago. Struggling desperately to escape from the salaryman's lot but with no exit in sight, he tried to dedicate his life to the supermarket project he'd been assigned to, but his way was blocked. Indifferent managers and employees. Filth and stench of the fish-packing room. Cherry blossoms in full bloom. And a woman.

Hozumi Masako. Where is Masako now? Nakasato wondered. To drive away her image that had come back to him after a long respite, Nakasato raised his whiskey glass and drained it in one breath.

The Turning Point

Fifteen Years Ago

1

Nissei Corporation went into the supermarket business in 1960. It founded Century Stores Inc. in equal partnership with Metropolitan Department Store, an affiliate that Nissei Bank financed. Initially Century's sales personnel were on loan from Metropolitan, but Nissei Corporation controlled its management and administration.

An alarmist prognosis of the day held that integrated trading companies were heading into the corporate sunset. Shosha groups stampeded into the supermarket business to gain an American-type chain store, the necessary first stage to leadership in the retail future. Some invested in existing supermarkets; others tied up with foreign companies. Each shosha tried its own course. The fevered pace slowed within half a decade, its momentum checked by the dismal performance of all shosha-affiliated supermarkets.

As the other integrated trading companies dropped out of the race one after another, Nissei surged ahead and expanded. By 1967, Century Stores had spread a chain of thirteen markets across the southwestern sector of Tokyo. In financial terms, however, it did no better than other shosha-affiliated supermarkets. In the red from the outset, the company was running up deficits that kept pace with its corporate expansion.

The supervisory unit at Nissei's headquarters, the Foodstuff Division, held many emergency meetings but failed to pinpoint causes for Century's troubles.

The president of Century Stores was Hatakeyama Shinsaku, an assignee from Nissei. Smallish, ordinary, and nondescript—and therefore unusual among the shosha's stylish types—he looked like his nickname, Woodchuck. His dedication to the job was beyond question, though, for he was more often on the shop floor than in his office. He was not unpopular with the employees. There was no obvious problem in labor relations.

The geographical locations and dimensions of Century's stores were reviewed, but no conclusive findings emerged. Since similar chain stores all around the country were doing quite well, this corporate structure could not be blamed for Century's problems. True, the sales counters in Century's stores were poorly tended: their perishables were far from fresh, and some items were out of stock. But Nissei's supervisory staff dismissed the sorry condition by saying, What more can you expect from a supermarket, nothing more than a low-priced self-service store?

As losses mounted month after month with no apparent reason, the director of the Foodstuff Division at Nissei ordered a temporary halt to new capital spending in Century Stores and made reducing its deficit a top priority. At this point the supermarket changed its status from a progressive project to a backsliding one on Nissei's chart. Before long the veteran staffer in charge was transferred out of Foodstuff. Nakasato was his replacement, assigned from Accounting and quite unaware of the circumstances behind Century's case history.

Nakasato's initial enthusiasm soon gave way to disillusionment in the new job. Handling the Century Stores project was like nursing a terminally ill patient. All he was required to do was check requisition forms submitted to Nissei and pare the requested amounts down to the minimum. It was not a job to inspire a sense of mission. Nakasato had been languishing through dark days of disappointment, when his heart caught fire and burst into blazing flame.

It happened on a warm day in early April.

What made this particular day so memorable for Nakasato were the cherry trees in full bloom. Along both banks of a dirty river clandestinely running through the exclusive residential area of Setagaya Ward in Tokyo, aged trees spread their boughs heavy with clusters of delicate petals. Beyond the canopy of red-tinged white flowers stood the Setagaya Century Store.

On that day Nakasato went to inspect Century's meat and fish packing room, which the store's management proposed to renovate at an estimated cost of 10 million yen.

Personally serving as his escort, President Hatakeyama commented, "Appalling, isn't it? The public health office served us an ultimatum: it threatens to revoke our license unless we correct the condition promptly."

"Appalling indeed!" Nakasato grimaced at the stench saturating the air.

The concrete floor was uneven and badly cracked. Waste water full of meat and fish slops stagnated everywhere underfoot in the yawning gaps, its odor suffusing the 180 square feet of work space.

"How could they have bungled things so badly? Plants and stores all over Japan process raw foodstuff. If this room had been designed with the same floor plan and drainage system they use, its dreadful mess could have been prevented."

"Well, reality defies logic, you know. A supermarket is a cheap food shop after all. It can't afford the facilities of modern food-processing plants."

"Modern food-processing plants . . . ," Nakasato murmured as, triggered by Hatakeyama's words, a vision took shape in his mind— a room designated for handling perishable food and constructed to keep out germs and slow the growth of bacteria. Its temperature much lower than that of outside. Disinfectants in abundant supply, and clean work clothes for employees, who are required to wash their hands often. A floor designed to remain dry to hold bacterial growth to a minimum, no matter how much water is used.——This vision was no fantasy. Nakasato had seen it six months earlier in a plant producing ready-to-serve packaged food.

"President Hatakeyama, a modern food-processing plant *is* the answer. Why not?" Nakasato felt something surge in his heart. Then it ignited, and the flame engulfed his being.

"A modern plant is not only immaculate but efficient too. You raise productivity when you use an assembly-line operation." Nakasato seized Hatakeyama's arm in his excitement, stirred up by a force that was literally shaking him from deep within. "Please, look at the way they're working here," Nakasato signaled with his eyes to direct Hatakeyama's attention toward the two young men nearby.

The older one with long hair was slicing tuna fillets and arranging them in neat rows on small trays. A little distance away, the younger man in a crew cut was putting wrappers on mackerel-packed trays.

"That's not an assembly-line operation. The man who slices the raw tuna will pack the fillets, weigh the trays, stick on price labels, and take them to the sales counter. Just watch him go through the whole process by himself. In terms of industrial standards, this is strictly a sixteenth-century method," Nakasato rattled on heatedly. Hatakeyama remained silent, visibly ill at ease.

"If you modernize this process, you'll never run out of fresh meat and fish on your shelves, because the processing time is dramatically shortened. Just divide the labor and assign a man exclusively to each stage as cutter, packer, wrapper, pricer, and stacker, and you improve your productivity more than tenfold. If the floor supervisor does his job well—keeping track of the stock on shelves and coordinating the line's operation—fresh stock is supplied as fast as it sells."

Don't you remember, Nakasato wanted to say, what Adam Smith said at the beginning of *The Wealth of Nations?* In his excitement he nearly blurted it out—"The greatest improvement in the productive powers of labour, and the greatest part of the skill, dexterity, and judgment . . . have been the effect of the division of labour." But the undisguised displeasure on Hatakeyama's face made him swallow his words.

"Nakasato-kun, I respect the enthusiasm you showed, taking the trouble to leave the comfortable shosha office for a spot inspection of our store. But a store doesn't run on logic, especially its meat and fish department. Maybe it's not clear to someone like you who writes reports sitting in an office, but what matters most to the on-site management is the here and now. Today's reality is more important to us than tomorrow's ideal. What I want you to do is push our renovation proposal through the channels and get us a decision as soon as possible."

"I understand but . . . ," Nakasato hesitated for a moment but then failed to hold back the words that gushed from his heart. "When you turn this filthy place into a modern food-processing plant, your employees stand to reap the most benefit, because it makes their work much easier. This is one improvement that on-site workers will welcome, I think."

"Nakasato-kun," Hatakeyama began in a serious tone. "You don't know the on-site situation. See the fish chief over there? He flew into a rage—waving his knife around—when the store manager said something the other day about how fish was sliced into fillets. Don't you see? These are artisans. They have professional pride. Success or failure of the supermarket operation depends on a manager's ability to handle these artisans. If you so much as mention an assembly-line system that will turn them into cutters and packers, you're liable to get yourself knifed to death."

But if *you* go on giving in to their pride, you can never hope to attain the corporate objectives, Nakasato wanted to say but stifled the urge. Winning this argument with Hatakeyama would settle nothing. Evidently he was stuck with his belief that the best on-site management was a laissez-faire policy, to allow the artisan mentality free rein.

Holding his own emotion in check, Nakasato thanked Hatakeyama properly for the personally guided tour. He managed to stay behind in the meat and fish room, pleading his need to make a closer study.

Two hours later, when he emerged into the afternoon air along the river lined with cherry trees, Nakasato experienced an excitement unlike anything he'd felt in all his years with Nissei. His head was still in turmoil, but he was now firmly convinced: updating the meat and fish department was the only way to save Century Stores.

· · ·

"Are you telling me other supermarkets are equipped with modern facilities?" asked Nakasato's immediate superior, Natsukawa Tetsuji. The general manager of the food department stared at Nakasato, his eyes large in his golf-tanned face.

"No, they aren't. Not yet," Nakasato answered truthfully. To say yes might have helped his argument, but since he'd personally checked some large chains and found their conditions to be no better, to lie would go against the grain.

"Oh?" Natsukawa's face registered disappointment. "Does that mean it's only your own idea?"

"Yes, it is."

"Well, now. That's something." His expression contradicted his words. Leaning back in the general manager's chair and stretching his impressively long legs alongside the desk, Natsukawa looked straight at Nakasato.

"It'll cost us extra, won't it?"

"Yes, somewhat."

"Can you keep it at 'somewhat'?"

"I can't make accurate estimates until the blueprint is drawn with all the concrete details worked out. But the final figure may be considerable."

More like 30 or 40 million yen, Nakasato reckoned, instead of the 10 million originally requested for stop-gap repairs, but refrained from mentioning it.

"Century Stores is deep in the red, as you know."

"I'm aware of that. But if the renovation works, it can boast the best meat and fish department in Japan. All the better for us, if no other supermarket can make a similar claim."

"Well, keep up your research. But fixing up the meat-packing room at the Setagaya store can't wait. Get the wheels rolling. Send their requisition through the proper channels."

"Yes, I will," Nakasato agreed, encouraged by the fact that his suggestion had not met outright rejection. The young man did not suspect that veteran managers were skilled at snuffing out a subordinate's troublesome idea without appearing to oppose it.

Nakasato threw himself into the research. The more he studied the subject, the more convinced he became of the soundness of his idea. His most surprising discovery was that fresh meat departments, a problem he'd thought peculiar to Century Stores, were in fact the Achilles' heel of all supermarkets. Some prospering chains beat Century in employee discipline and morale but their meat-packing rooms belonged to a period before Adam Smith, or, more precisely, to the stage of manual labor guilds. It was hard to believe that any store could get by with such an archaic system. Larger chains with high sales volume compensated by turning themselves into versions of a department store to increase their earnings—with expanded floor space and a wider range of merchandise, including apparel and appliances.

No supermarket with an efficiently run fresh meat department existed in Japan—this startling revelation propelled Nakasato into action. He used all his personal connections to get permission to visit food-processing plants and talk with their architects and with managers of the construction companies that built them. He made his way to Century's various stores to observe and record the entire procedure that turned each raw food into packed merchandise.

When it came to working out a modernization plan, the greatest technical problem was that a conveyor belt could not be used. Not only did it take up too much space, it was unfit to handle a large variety of items in small quantities. After much concentration, Nakasato came up with the idea of placing the partly prepared food on large trays to pass along to the next processing stage.

What excitement, to discover a worthy objective. The dream of technological reform. Patient labor over research and evaluation of collected data. Anxious hours of racking the brain. And the boundless joy of hitting on a solution.

Nakasato was caught in a riptide. But there was not a soul with whom he could share his feelings and thoughts. General manager Natsukawa and the staff showed some interest at first, only to revert to the view that such technical matters should be left to on-site management: the job for Nissei's supervisory unit was to work out marketing strategies from a broader perspective worthy of the shosha.

"On-site technical reform goes hand in hand with strategic planning—the one is useless without the other." Over and over Nakasato explained his reasoning. But before long he noticed a sneer would spread on his colleagues' faces at the mention of modern food-processing plants.

His wife, Rieko, was preoccupied with the care of their young children. To begin with, Nakasato knew, she was the type who expected nothing more from her husband than his paycheck. She was not a companion able and willing to comfort him in his lonely creative battle.

Every month Century Stores continued to run up enormous losses. Natsukawa was quick to dismiss Nakasato's suggestion but offered no plan to implement in its place.

Nakasato was drowning in a sea of anguish when Hozumi Masako, a young woman working in a nearby office of the Foodstuff Division, came in contact with him.

2

Masako stepped up to Nakasato's desk one afternoon. The other desks in his work station were deserted. It was likely that she had been waiting for just such a moment.

"Excuse me, but may I talk to you?" Nakasato looked up to find a young woman standing before him with a tense expression on her face.

"Oh? What is it?"

"I have a favor to ask of you."

"What kind of favor?"

Nakasato knew her by sight. What distinguished her from the other women was her straight black hair bobbed unpretentiously like a little girl's. She was a high-school graduate who entered Nissei a few years behind Nakasato—so she had to be five or six years younger. Belonging to the same division and working on the same floor, they often passed each other and exchanged greetings. She looked a sensitive type. But this was the first time he actually talked with the woman he knew next to nothing about.

"It's something personal."

"Personal?"

When a young woman talked this way, a man's imagination spread its wings. Nakasato must have looked disconcerted, for she hastened to explain: "But it has to do with your work."

"Whatever it is, please sit down," Nakasato pulled a neighbor's chair over for her.

"Please . . . well, I'd like you to teach me about chain stores."

"Chain stores? How do you mean?"

"Century *is* a chain store, isn't it?"

"Well, you can call it that. Mired in red ink, but still a chain store."

"That's what I thought."

"Anyway, please do sit down." To overcome her reserve, Nakasato offered the chair once more but she remained on her feet.

"I have questions. In fact, I have too many to ask here and now. If you don't mind, I'd like to do it over dinner. Will you teach me?"

"Yes. I'd be happy to—but my knowledge doesn't go beyond a floundering supermarket. You're sure you want to hear my story?"

"Yes, very much."

"In that case, this evening's fine with me."

"I'll be grateful."

That night at a restaurant in Shinjuku, and later at a whiskey bar very much in vogue at the time, Masako shot questions at him in quick succession and in all seriousness.

What is a chain store? Does any enterprise that opens more than one shop become a chain store? Or must all its shops be of the same type? What criteria, then, do you use to determine the same type? What advantages can you derive from the chain structure? Does it take special management skill to run a chain with many stores?

To her barrage of rapid-fire questions Nakasato did his best to respond sincerely. Having read several books in the field to arm himself with practical knowledge as Nissei's supervisory staffer in charge of Century Stores, he managed to provide passable answers. But all the while her probes made him acutely aware of the inadequacy of his knowledge.

Evidently Masako had done a considerable amount of homework.

"Why are you interested in chain stores, of all things?" Nakasato asked her for the second time that night over a drink at the bar. Earlier, when he posed the same question, she had somehow deflected it without giving him a straight answer.

"Please don't laugh," she said this time.

"I won't. You *are* serious, aren't you?"

"Very serious. That's why I'm afraid you'll laugh."

"Well?"

"I . . . want to open a chain store."

"What!"

"See, you're laughing!"

"No, not laughing. But I don't understand what you said. Do you intend to operate a supermarket for yourself?"

"A supermarket probably takes a great deal of capital investment I can't afford to make. I've set my heart on a dress boutique. Not a run-of-the-mill apparel shop but one based on a new concept to fit the new age. To tell you the truth, my family runs an apparel shop at Ogikubo."

"Oh, that's how it is."

"Please don't jump to conclusions. I have no intention of getting into the family business. It's doomed anyway. Bigger stores moved into the neighborhood one after another to take the trade away from us. My older brother gave up hope and opted to work for others. My father has been ill, and it's just a matter of time before he must close up shop."

"Then why do you want to run a chain store?"

"I had no such ambition until several years ago. At first I was happy simply to have a job with Nissei. As I worked here my thinking underwent gradual changes. I didn't meet anyone suitable to marry. But I couldn't see any sense in spending the rest of my working life at Nissei. Unlike our male colleagues, we women have no hope of getting meaningful and challenging assignments."

"But you're much too young to give up marriage."

"I can't seem to find the right man. This might sound arrogant— but I no longer wish to be the wife of a businessman, even if my family finds a suitable candidate."

"Why?"

"Well, because that's just the way I feel," Masako said in a small voice and watched anxiously for Nakasato's reaction as if she were afraid she had hurt his feelings. "At any rate, I've already made up my mind to have a chain of dress boutiques."

Nakasato hardly knew what to make of Masako's declaration. In all his time on the supermarket project, running a chain store for himself had never occurred to him. By now the employee mentality might be second nature, but Nakasato told himself he hadn't thought of turning entrepreneur because he knew too well the difficulties involved in such a venture.

"Thank you. You've taught me a great deal."

"Was this what you wanted?"

"Yes." Masako placed a white envelope on the table. "Please take this."

"What is it?"

"I'm sorry it's so little."

"Money?" Nakasato gazed at Masako searchingly. Was it a joke? Or was she testing him? But he could detect nothing but seriousness in her face.

"You are unconventional, aren't you?" Nakasato found his voice to say. "This kind of thing might make some people angry, you know."

"Do you think so? I don't really know the protocol about such matters. Once I read a book that said the Japanese didn't know you must pay for information according to its value, and such ignorance marks us as culturally underdeveloped. I thought it was so true. That's why I've come today, determined to pay my tuition even if you consider it unconventional."

"Never mind. The pleasure of talking with an attractive woman like you was reward enough for me. Anyway, I'll take you to see a Century store next Sunday. You can get a better understanding of the chain system from observation."

"Do you mean it? Oh, I beg you to show me!" Masako exclaimed and abruptly bowed, bracing her hands on her knees in a formal manner. As the crisp movement sent her short black hair falling over her face, she raised her left hand to brush it back. Mature femininity flashed in her spontaneous gesture.

That might have been the very instant Nakasato began to feel strongly attracted to Masako, unassuming as she was in speech and appearance.

3

"Why is this store doing poorly?" asked Masasko, sharp-eyed with serious interest.

"Mmm, well. Bad location. They used poor judgment in choosing the site for this store," Nakasato informed her. Both were dressed casually on this Sunday outing. They were in a coffeehouse opposite the shopping district that faced a station on the independent railroad line between Shinjuku and the western suburbs.

"What's wrong with the location? This Century store is on the shopping street. I can't see anything that makes it a bad choice."

"But of their thirteen stores, this one is running up the biggest deficit."

"Well, the aisles were certainly far from crowded. But why? There must be competition nearby."

"Yes, you've got it. There's a large Toto store across from the station."

"Now I see. The Century store is losing out, isn't it?"

"Quite true, but that's not the whole story."

"Why not?"

"You see, this store opened last May. Century's management hung its hopes on this new addition. But within half a year it proved nothing but a dream."

"Because Toto built one of its own right here?"

"That's right. Three times larger than ours and in the best location opposite the station."

"Then there's no help for it."

"Is that so? No help for it? I happen to think otherwise." Nakasato's tone sharpened, and Masako stared in surprise.

"A store that plunges into the red just because a larger competitor settles in front of the station shouldn't have been opened in the first place. Of course, it would be perfect if no competition crops up. But as long as we operate in the free enterprise system we can't just wish our competitors away. As a matter of fact, only a store that can hold its own against any rival stands a fair chance of thriving in the retail field for any length of time."

"I can understand that but . . . "

"In this store's case, its location is the problem. I'll show you."

Nakasato spread a map on the table, and Masako leaned over for a closer look, eyes wide to scrutinize it.

"Now. The station's here, the big Toto store is there. And here's Century. What do you see?"

"Oh, no! This is no good," Masako sighed after a careful study. Her tone was as somber as if she were mourning her own store's defeat.

"How's that?"

"There's the university. The station road ends within two hundred yards right at its main gate onto the big campus. That drastically cuts down Century's commercial territory. Probably it made no critical difference before the Toto store came in, but now Century's shut up tight as in a blind alley."

"Exactly."

"An unfortunate choice of location after all. Can't something be done about it?"

"It might be possible to make up for the geographical disadvantage, if Century could beat Toto in store size and offer a big parking lot besides. More than anything else, a strong meat department could help overcome a powerful rival. But I'm sorry to say that Century can't even bring its meat-packing room anywhere close to Toto's standard."

"Why is that?"

"To be blunt, it's because bad-tempered artisan types are lording over it. Top management just spoils them—and that includes the Nissei assignees, who leave the operation of the meat department to them."

"Do you mean that the managers have no grip on the floor-level operation?"

"It comes down to that. Century's management advocates the priority of on-site needs but avoids getting involved on the floor. You can't run a store that way. The manager must get down to the floor."

"Quite difficult to do, isn't it?"

"No matter how difficult, it has to be done because there's no other way to ensure results. In getting down there, however, it won't do to join the artisans in their old ways. There has to be a different approach. There *is* one."

Nakasato began to explain the idea of turning the meat-packing room into a modern food-processing plant. Soon he reproached himself for starting on a topic that must bore her—but he couldn't very well stop midway. He talked on, resolved to cut it short the moment he detected a sign of boredom on her face. Far from becoming bored, however, Masako listened in rapt attention, her eyes gleaming with interest.

"How exciting!" she exclaimed as soon as Nakasato finished his exposition. "That's *technological innovation,* isn't it?"

"What?" Nakasato was astonished. "You know big words!"

"Am I wrong?"

"No, you aren't. My idea can contribute technological innovation to retail business management."

"*Innovation*—one of my favorite English words. I feel it's packed full with the greatness that human beings are capable of reaching."

"Amazing," Nakasato murmured, but Masako looked unaffected.

"Your explanation of geographical location was enlightening. If you don't mind, I'd like to walk around some more. We can look over the Toto store, study the lay of the shopping district, and pay another visit to Century's premises. I can learn much more about store location this way."

"All right. We'll do it. Retail is often called a locating business because the store site plays a decisive role. I imagine it'd be the same with a dress boutique."

For two hours after leaving the coffeehouse, they covered the oblong area half a mile in diameter that lay between the station and the Century store. The commercial zone led into a residential district and then to another shopping zone on the far side. Masako kept up with Nakasato's rapid strides, her eyes observing everything. A feel of summer still lingered in the air, and their faces were flushed from walking.

"Surveying the neighborhood on foot like this, I can see the negative aspects of Century's location. How did the planners make such a mistake?"

"Misinterpretation, it seems."

"Misinterpretation?"

"Yes. This is a fairly busy commercial district."

"Yes, it is. That's why I failed to notice its disadvantages at first."

"On weekdays, quite a crowd passes this street in the evening."

"Really? Oh, but they're students, aren't they?"

"Right. See those two over there?" With his eyes, Nakasato indicated a young couple walking ahead of them. "No doubt these are students who must have come to attend a Sunday meeting of their college club or something. Now, do they look like students?"

"Now that you mention it, they do. Yet at first sight they appear to be working people."

"That's one reason why our planners made the mistake of labeling this area a good enough location. There are some other reasons. Look carefully at the shops around here."

"A tofu shop."

"And?"

"Apparel shop, bookstore, grocer, then the gas company office, stationery store, and public bathhouse."

"This is a commercial district all right, but not a simple ordinary one."

"I've got it! This district caters to the needs of students. There *are* shops serving housewives but only few in number and meager in scale—like the tofu shop and the grocer. They're not exactly thriving, by the looks of them."

"That's right, but Century's management failed to perceive it."

"How?" Masako asked, and Nakasato burst out laughing.

"What's so funny?"

He was still laughing.

"Did I say something funny?"

"No, it's not that you said anything funny."

"Then, why . . . "

"That's what made me laugh. You want to know everything. Why? How? You ask a question at every turn."

"Oh." Masako blushed. She covered her mouth with a hand and stared at Nakasato uncertainly, looking for all the world like a schoolgirl. "My mother keeps telling me, 'Until you stop your whys and hows, you'll never find anyone to marry you.' "

"I don't agree," Nakasato said, turning serious. "It's just the opposite. I for one find your habit most charming. But . . . " He began to laugh again. "Anyway, you are a very unusual person to have so much curiosity and enthusiasm. And you are exceptionally logical, for a Japanese."

"I'm sorry," Masako said, pursing her full, sensuous lips.

"No need to apologize. I'm complimenting you, in fact. Now, let's take in another Century store. We have all day to play the question-and-answer game."

"Yes, let's." Her eyes flashed her pleasure. "I've been chided for talking too logically, but this is the first time anyone complimented me for it." She laughed in apparent relief, tilting her head slightly to one side.

When they finished their self-imposed march, Nakasato invited Masako to dinner. "I want to talk about things other than business," he said, and she nodded with a vivacious smile. They took the subway to Akasaka Mitsuke. After dinner in a German restaurant, they settled down at a hotel bar.

As Nakasato talked with Masako at close quarters in the soft haze of the indirect lighting, the real world seemed to fade into a distance. Vanished also from his mind were the job that never improved no matter how much he agonized over it and the stagnant marriage that offered no peace or empathy. Only a chimerically exquisite zone spanned the space between him and Masako, who silently lifted a cocktail glass. Nakasato felt his heart being drawn inexorably toward her.

He had a feeling that she was attracted to him as much as he was to her. Is this really happening? Isn't it a fantasy induced by the pleasant physical exhaustion and the drink in semidarkness? Nakasato was submerged in a glorious apprehension.

"You are a very mysterious person," Masako said, as if confirming each word.

"Me? No! You're the one who's mysterious. How strange, to be called mysterious by a mysterious woman."

"I don't exactly know how to explain . . . Well, you have an intensity, an awesome intensity. Other Nissei men of your age don't display such force or energy. I've been aware of the difference for some time. You haven't buried yourself in the company. Or should I say, you slipped away?"

"I do make an effort not to get buried in the company."

"Perhaps that's why. I'm even more convinced now, after spending a whole day with you. When you're looking over the Century stores or explaining about them, you have a marvelous expression on your face."

"I was impressed by your eagerness." Nakasato gestured with the whiskey glass in his hand. "Miss Hozumi, let's make another round of Century stores next week. Some we skipped today," he said with more fervor than the simple invitation to a survey trip warranted.

"I'll be most grateful," Masako said, gazing at Nakasato with eyes as unwavering as her straight hair. The fiery glimmer in her ardent dark eyes bound his whole being in an exquisite magic web.

"What a beautiful woman you are!" His thought materialized as whispered words and melted into the soft music.

"Next Sunday, same time, same place." Masako's lips fluttered like butterfly wings, just as airy and vibrant. Nakasato gave himself up to a rush of emotion.

4

In the Shinjuku district, the lively entertainment zone ended abruptly at a large street beyond which lay an area of nearly deserted alleys. As colorful yet silent as sea anemones and starfish in the rock-bound darkness of the ocean beneath shoals of flitting fish, small rendezvous hotels hugged the narrow side streets, their signs glowing in red and purple.

It was Sunday, and they were returning from their second visit to Century supermarkets.

"All right with you?" Nakasato asked, looking back at Masako as they crossed the street. She had acceded to his suggestion and come with him this far, but still he felt compelled to reconfirm her assent.

"Yes," she whispered and nodded, her expression strained.

Nakasato turned quickly into a dimly lit alley, Masako following a few steps behind. Several breathless paces later, he practically flung himself through a small side door behind its screen of shrubbery and swung round to wait for Masako. Their eyes locked for a few seconds. Then, holding her by the shoulder, he led her into the lobby.

A maid showed them to their room and left. Alone at last in the spacious Japanese-style room secured by an inside lock, they stood gazing at each other in silence for some time. Nakasato still had the strap of a tote bag on his shoulder and Masako held on to her handbag.

Slowly Nakasato extended both arms and placed his hands lightly on the shoulders of Masako's short-sleeved yellow blouse.

"You must be tired from all that walking," he said in a questioning tone. She smiled, closed her eyes, and shook her head. Drawing her closer with care, Nakasato covered the trace of a smile still lingering about her mouth with his lips. As his body caught fire, urging him on, Masako pulled away and said, "I'll make tea." Her handbag fell to the tatami-matted floor with a loud thud, startling them.

Masako sat down at the table, arranged Japanese teacups on wooden saucers, and lifted the lid of a teapot. Momentarily at a loss, Nakasato headed for the bathroom to draw a bath. He felt strange, as if caught in a dimension where time stood still. When the tub was full of steaming water, he returned to the room. Masako was sitting on the tatami floor by the table, her back straight and her knees tucked under her in ceremonial posture.

"I'm going to open my chain of stores after all," she said, looking extremely serious.

"Making a solemn announcement at this juncture? What a girl!"

"Today I made up my mind, after you showed me more stores."

"Do you mean to say your mind wasn't made up until today?" Nakasato cast her a teasing look across the table.

"Your tea's already cold. I'll make a fresh pot."

"No. This is fine with me," Nakasato reassured her, picking up his cup.

"To tell you the truth, the first tour of the stores scared me. I'd no idea there were so many things to consider. Competition, geographical factors, and such."

"If you let such things daunt you, you can't start any project at all."

"You're right. I reached the same conclusion after thinking hard for a whole week. This time around I studied the stores with one objective in mind—figure out how to beat the competition."

"That's why you wanted to see so many rival stores today!"

"Yes. I have a great deal more to learn," she said with a nod followed by a smile. "Knowledge of merchandise is a must, and professional skill in dressmaking. Display techniques take special training to master, too."

"Competence in bookkeeping and accounting as well, if you are to run your own company."

"Yes. I already have the Grade Three certificate in commercial bookkeeping."

"Good for you!"

Getting to his feet, Nakasato said, "Bathwater gets cold rather quickly. Let's save your story for later. Now, will you join me in the bath?"

"Well, would it be all right if I waited until you finish?"

As soon as the subject changed from chain stores, Masako's voice became faint and uncertain. She was masking her nervousness with all that business talk, Nakasato noted.

"I'll go first," he said, picking up a bar of soap and a fresh night kimono provided by the hotel.

.　　.　　.

The sound of water ceased. In a breath or two, the bathroom door slid open and shut. Nakasato stretched out in the bedding, the lamp by his pillow turned down to a dim glow. Masako was long in reaching the anteroom, perhaps taking time to tidy up. He could sense a nearly imperceptible human presence in the stillness. Draping the towel over the hanger now? Slipping into her night kimono next? He waited with bated breath.

At last his ear caught the sound of footsteps as of a small animal stealing into the next room. Unobtrusive but rhythmic, it found an echo in his wild heartbeats.

The paper sliding door sighed open.

"Come here," Nakasato whispered.

Masako seemed to hesitate but only for a moment. With her slender fingers she lifted an edge of the quilt Nakasato had turned up for her and slid silently into the bedding to lie alongside him. Buried to the neck under the coverlet, she straightened the kimono to wrap it around her body. Nakasato turned toward her, pressed his lips on hers, and slipped his hand between the folds of her kimono. Her skin felt soft and slightly chilled after the bath beneath the underwear she had modestly put on.

"Love you." Nakasato voiced his thought as he unloosed her sash.

· · ·

"That takes courage, doesn't it?" Nakasato said at length, staring up at the ceiling in the half-light. They lay in separate realms, a single quilt covering the two bodies that had shared a blazing passion moments earlier.

"Mmm. What?" Masako's small detached voice sounded like a child awakened from a dream.

"Opening your own chain of dress shops, I mean. You can't afford to fail."

"True enough," she began languidly but snapped from repose to continue in a firmer tone. "You're right, but I don't think I will fail. Can't possibly—though I won't go so far as to predict success."

"How do you mean?"

For a second Nakasato wondered if she was confused in choosing her words but soon realized that was not the case.

"I intend to pick out a location easily accessible to women who like the line of dresses I plan to carry and create a kind of shop they find attractive. It will draw customers, don't you think? Or am I being too optimistic?"

"No, not too optimistic. Carry out your plan, Masako, and customers will certainly come in, if only to look around in the beginning."

It was the first time that Nakasato called her Masako, but the name rolled off his tongue with no resistance at all. Masako did not seem to catch her own name.

"They *will* come in, won't they?" Nevertheless, her speech had by subtle changes taken on a shade of informality natural between lovers. "They'll drop in at least once. My shop will have nothing but dresses chosen exclusively for them. In other words, by making the rounds of wholesale houses and placing select orders, I serve as a delegate or proxy buyer for the type of women I envision as my primary clientele."

In the still night Masako's mellow alto flowed on as if reciting a poem.

"My display will be more than just visually beautiful, because the garments will be arranged with customers' convenience in mind. For instance, picture a woman going through a rack of dresses suitable for her age and taste. If she suddenly comes on an item totally alien to her needs or preferences, she'll get an unpleasant jolt. Won't she lose interest in looking at dresses after that?"

"Just like that?" Nakasato responded vaguely, never having wasted serious thought on buying clothes for himself.

"Yes, just like that," Masako affirmed with conviction. "That's why in my shop I'll group dresses by style and customers' age range. Some items can also be classified by the intended use, say, for everyday wear at home or for a semiformal outing. If I pay attention to such small but important details, I create a sensible shop where my customers quickly spot the counters or racks carrying the particular article they have in mind and head directly for them. One thing follows another, doesn't it?"

"Yes, if you get to implement the plan."

"The customer examines the merchandise. Picks out a dress, reads the price tag, fingers the material, turns out the lining, checks the color against her skin tone in front of the mirror, and . . ."

As if she could see the still intangible sales rack, Masako raised her hands and twisted an imaginary dress back and forth in midair. The slight pull on the quilt conveyed her every movement to Nakasato.

"The instant some dress catches a customer's fancy, I speak to her."

"Reeling in the line on cue!"

"Oh, no. Nothing like that!" Masako shook her head and shoulders in denial, laughing happily. Nakasato savored the feel of her soft naked body brushing against his side, like a playful animal in an affectionate mood.

"I'll be fashion consultant to my customers. Give advice but never resort to high-pressure tactics or push items with larger markups. Put myself in my customers' place in searching for dresses to suit their tastes and their figures."

"Can you make enough sales that way?"

"When an item proves to be just right for my clientele and it sells well, I'll immediately stock up on similar items. Unless, of course, it's too late in the season."

"What if you have nothing to fit a particular customer?"

"I'll try to pinpoint the cause of her dissatisfaction or the poor fit. I may ask her specific questions—down to what shape of collar usually looks best on her—or I may go through other apparel shops to study their merchandise. But the most effective method of fashion research is to canvass the clothes women out on the street actually wear, I believe."

A vision flashed into Nakasato's imagination. Gold-tinted ginko trees lining a promenade carpeted with fallen leaves along which walk women in impeccable autumn outfits. Masako is seated at a white table on the terrace of a fashionable café. Beneath the bangs her alert eyes follow the passing women. And Nakasato himself watches her, never tiring of the sight. In time the ginkoes shed their leaves, snow flurries fill the sky, cherries blossom, and thunderclaps roll on. All the while Masako continues her vigil, watching the women on the street as Nakasato keeps up his, watching her.

"I won't stop till I learn what pleases my customers. Once I find out, I'll hunt for particular articles even if I have to comb the entire country, tracking down a wholesaler who can supply them. When some item I want isn't available wholesale, I'll buy it retail from another shop or department store and sell at cost. If I keep up my efforts, my shop will be filled with selections most appealing to my clients. Then first-time shoppers will come back again and again. So I think I can't fail."

"Not only that, you'll succeed without fail."

"Ah, but success is never a sure thing. There must be some people in this world who hit on the same idea. Some of them will become my rivals. Until I beat them, I can't call myself a success. I need luck to win."

Nakasato was astounded. Masako had apparently given this matter serious thought, meticulously taking all contingencies into account. Determined was the word for her. Masako would likely keep up her sidewalk fashion research any number of years, as she did in the fanciful scene that unfolded before his mind's eye moments ago. Her plan to open a chain of dress shops had sounded preposterous to him at first, but now she seemed perfectly capable of carrying it off.

"Rest assured, Lady Luck will smile on you."

Nakasato closed his eyes. A full tide of peace and contentment washed over him. His heart was serene, like an inlet glittering in the warm sunshine, no anxiety to cast dark shadows on it. Time seemed to stand still. He felt he was back where he really belonged. Not that he'd ever been on such intimate terms with any other woman before. Not even with his wife, Rieko, had he shared a time like this.

Much later he was to reason that he had felt so at home with Masako because he was at last back in the long-forgotten world of his own principles and beliefs where he was free to dream to his heart's content, without fear. Perhaps the single door separating their room and the hallway in this love hotel not only shielded their private act of love from the eyes of the world but also shut out the almighty influence of Nissei Corporation. It left no opening for the insatiable monster called the company that wanted to intrude and gobble up everything.

"Once you set your plan into motion," Nakasato heard himself say back in this real time, "you may very well run into unpredictable difficulties. But you have enough mettle to conquer them all."

"I'll do my best," Masako said, turning on her side to face him. "I hope you try likewise to make Century the best supermarket in Japan."

"Not that easy in my case," Nakasato said, feeling an ache in his chest. He rolled over toward Masako. "Supposing I work out what I believe to be a good plan?" Nakasato began, his legs entwined with hers, his face touching hers. "It'll get stalled if there's so much as a single voice raised in opposition at any stage of the deliberation process. As you say, a commonsense measure well executed will naturally yield good results. In the case of supermarkets, common sense tells you that meat and fish should be offered as fresh as possible and that this objective can't be achieved without sanitary and efficient packing facilities. Yet many people in our company have neither basic common sense nor an inclination to learn. It takes no more than one of them to scuttle any proposal. Come to think of it, sho-shamen can't be expected to understand anything about supermarket meat rooms. Too much to ask of them."

"But I was able to follow your reasoning on the meat-room issue. If you persist, you can surely convince your colleagues." Masako slowly ran her left index finger along Nakasato's chin with the tender artlessness of a small girl playing with flowers in a meadow. "Feels stubby," she giggled. The lips framing her white teeth were butterflies fluttering, and her face with the glittering eyes was a consummate cosmos that welcomed Nakasato.

"When you first told me about your plan to remodel the supermarket meat-packing room into a modern food-processing plant, I thought it was a truly wonderful idea. I'm not exaggerating the excitement I felt. Actually nobody has much confidence in the fresh foods on supermarket shelves. My mother buys all her meats, fish, and vegetables from the butcher and the fish vendor and the grocer in the neighborhood. Now that I've seen Century's meat room, I can really appreciate my mother's judgment. I'm convinced you can make a great contribution with your plan. If the company shows no understanding, I'd like to see you quit your job—accomplish it on your own. Yes, that's it! This may be the very chance for you: go independent and free yourself from the company and your superiors who are too slow to see the light."

"Whoa! Not so fast!" Nakasato gasped in astonishment. Perfectly logical to her, yes. But the matter was not so simple for a man: a man didn't have the woman's option of marriage as a way to escape if he failed. On the contrary. Marriage only added to his responsibilities.

Even as Nakasato rationalized to himself, a contradictory thought surfaced in a corner of his mind. If he had confidence in his own idea, he *should* be able to make it work without Nissei Corporation's auspices. With the real estate property he inherited from his parents, he could raise at least part of the capital he needed to start a modest business venture of his own. No pressing need for him to be an owner-president: maybe he could sell his ideas and services to some progressive supermarket management? All over Japan, many entrepreneurs were running retail outlets that went under the name of supermarket. Was he unrealistic to assume none of them would show interest in his idea?

No need to cling to Nissei Corporation after all!

Such a thought had never entered Nakasato's head before. In the past, all his thinking had hinged on the unquestioned premise: being a Nissei man. When Masako startled him with her suggestion, Nakasato had temporized by crying out, Not so fast! But at the same time, inwardly, he couldn't help admitting it was a viable idea. Or . . . did it seem so now just because here he was in the love hotel, insulated—if by a scant door—from the world dictated by Nissei's values?

"It may very well take that much commitment on my part to get Nissei men moving." Nakasato spoke to Masako in a tone of delivering the last word on the matter. He quietly took Masako's supple body into his arms.

The desire that had been becalmed in two separate bodies began to swell in hot billows, stirring up their fierce need to melt into each other in this world of their own. Fresh energy flooded into Nakasato's body.

With tenderness he laid Masako onto the bed and deliberately kissed her. As he slowly lowered himself upon her, she moved gently to welcome him.

Then they were one, and a great joy surged up and coursed through their bodies to soar into infinity. Their breathing suffused the quiet night until a faint sound resembling a sigh escaped Masako's lips. The involuntary tone held a profound sadness, like the whisper of sculls on a boat stealing from some distant fog-filled port, its destination unknown. This sensory impression that Nakasato experienced at the culmination of their physical pleasure seemed to foreshadow the boundless uncharted sea he and Masako were setting out together to cross.

5

Nakasato and Masako continued to see each other, twice each week, for the next three years. They would meet at the public telephone booth by the ticket gate of a National Railway station and proceed immediately to a hotel. In the beginning they had gone to dinner first, but Masako objected: that way, they wasted money. Thereafter she stopped at a department store or the shopping mall in the station building for sandwiches and packaged meals that they ate in their hotel room.

Masako was intent on scraping together the capital for her planned business venture, while Nakasato was as short of spending money as any other Japanese businessman on the customary monthly allowance doled out by his wife, as was the custom in middle-class families where managing the household finances was considered a wifely duty.

"Rather shabby-looking, but do you mind?" Nakasato asked when he picked out the inexpensive and inconspicuous hotel hidden in the residential district away from the gaudy entertainment zone.

"I don't mind anything, as long as you're with me," Masako answered in a tone half-playful, half-serious.

They usually spent four to five hours at the hotel. Initially the front manager seemed nervous about a couple staying long past the two-hour basic charge period; the clerk on duty would telephone their room to inquire whether they wished to extend their "short rest" by paying a surcharge for extra hours, or switch to the "overnight" basis. Before long, however, an elderly woman clerk took kindly notice of them and put a stop to such calls.

Their hours together came to follow a set pattern—first they made love, and afterward they talked. They talked on serious subjects, quite out of keeping with the love-hotel setting. From chain store and retail operations, their interest extended to commerce, business administration, economics, and psychology. That part of their twice-weekly trysts had all the appearance of a private tutoring session that allowed Masako serious lessons in a vast range of academic disciplines.

In the beginning Nakasato relied on his own stock of knowledge but soon took to preparing a sort of lecture in advance. For one thing, Masako's questions came to require more and more complex answers; for another, Nakasato found that advance research helped him not only in teaching Masako but also in reeducating himself. Being a Bachelor of Law meant a respected social standing, but Nakasato had felt the disadvantage of lacking structured knowledge in commerce and business administration long before he met Masako.

"When you advised me to quit my company and get into the supermarket business for myself, I was stunned. I never thought seriously about it before. But you made me realize what my biggest problem was—I had no confidence in my own ability and professional expertise. So I decided to educate myself while teaching you. I'm going to learn some skills that will let me make a living on my own—away from Nissei Corporation. I want to qualify as a specialist in commerce and management. Come to think of it, an ability to be independent would be valuable to Nissei, too. Or rather, anyone who lacks it can't claim to give real service to his company. In the first place, if a man can't survive without Nissei, how can he possibly stand firm on his own beliefs? Such a man would have no choice but to compromise himself—to back down every time someone of higher authority disagrees with him. One insight I've gained from all this self-reflection is that the misery of salaried businessmen stems from their inability to survive without company affiliation."

While explaining his views to Masako in this manner, Nakasato steadily expanded the range of his own knowledge. It was exciting to find that all academic disciplines, even commerce and management, meshed with such humanistic concerns as philosophies of life and views on human nature. Nakasato pored over a book popular in Japan at the time, by Drucker, an American expert on business administration. He read it in its original English edition and produced a synopsis in Japanese for Masako, investing almost a year in the endeavor.

A French engineer turned entrepreneur captured his interest: Henri Fayol (1841–1925), who established a reputation in corporate management for *fayolisme*. Nakasato eagerly recounted to Masako how Fayol took over a failing mine company and turned it around. His feat was nothing short of miraculous, for he accomplished it without changing mines, executive officers, labor force, marketing methods, or what they produced. The only thing he changed was management style. His innovative contribution—an ensemble approach based on a simple principle he termed *administration*.

Fayol's success story touched a responsive chord in Nakasato's heart. It provided exactly what Century Stores needed, a revitalization plan entailing no radical changes in management, workers, store locations, or its identity as a supermarket. Nakasato found it imperative to study the management principle that Fayol called "administration." His new insight made him realize that few sho-shamen were knowledgeable in this area.

Nakasato probed and explored all these books. To explain each concept in a manner clear enough for Masako to understand, he had to digest it until he could illustrate it through application to concrete examples. With such need and motivation, he absorbed knowledge much more effectively than he'd ever done in college.

"I want to get assigned out to Century so I can make use of everything I've learned about business administration," he said to Masako one day as if stating a conclusion.

On the following day, Nakasato went to his department chief, Natsukawa, and made a request for transfer. "I see. Let me sleep on it," the general manager told Nakasato. That turned out to be all he ever heard on the matter. He remained stuck where he was.

His status was not the only thing left unchanged, either. Everything around Nakasato at the office was stagnating in weariness. Nissei's policy for Century Stores simply stopped any new capital spending. In Nakasato's view it was the worst possible measure to impose on Century. To pull itself out of the deficit Century Stores needed aggressive capital spending—whether to break the impasse or to consolidate for a scale-down. Nissei's simplistic denial of all capital expenditures kept Century from moving in either direction. In effect the chain of supermarkets stood abandoned, half dead. Under the circumstances, Nakasato's proposal to renovate the meat room and modernize the processing method hadn't the ghost of a chance.

Nakasato took every possible opportunity to remind Natsukawa of it. The general manager's response was always noncommittal. Growing impatient, Nakasato pressed for a definite answer, and Natsukawa claimed that his hands were tied as long as the Affiliates Control Division refused to allow any more funds to be invested in Century.

Nakasato went to the Affiliates Control Division and checked with the officer in charge only to be told, "We have no standing directive to curtail capital spending so drastically. Your general manager, Natsukawa, is the one who enforces the policy. Now, with tight money, Finance may not approve your project anyway."

For all his effort, Nakasato was unable to find who was ultimately responsible for making policy. Half alive, Century languished on. Consequently its deficits kept mounting, and despair assailed Nakasato every time he sat in, an observer at Century's monthly meeting of operating officers in the conference room of Nissei headquarters.

"Utterly hopeless," Nakasato lamented to Masako one night. He hated to unload his depression on her but, sensing himself on the verge of collapsing under its weight, he desperately needed to share his feelings.

The pent-up misery only inflamed his passion for Masako, as a lover and as a teacher. Every time they met Nakasato claimed her body with fierce need. She seemed to blossom, as if senses that had slept within her were awakened one after another by his touch. And she studied all the more assiduously.

It was Nakasato who expressed a wish to make a new life with her. "I'll get a divorce," he began, "and I'll quit the company. Let's get married and run a chain of dress shops or supermarkets together."

They were in bed, their hearts and bodies fused. Masako did not reply. Nakasato had expected his announcement to make her happy. Apparently her feelings were not as simple as he'd thought. Only after repeating his statement did he note the trembling of her shoulder, which she had turned unobtrusively away from him at his first announcement. A slight vibration passed from her back directly to his chest as she lay in his embrace.

"What's the matter?" Nakasato asked, when he became aware of her weeping. There was no answer. In an effort to turn her body, he gently tugged at her shoulder with his right hand that lay draped over it, but Masako's body went rigid and remained turned away from him.

"What is it? Is it anything I said?"

Over and over Nakasato repeated the question, holding her body tight against his. Still no answer. He pushed himself up on his elbow to see her expression but she buried her face in the sheet, silent tremors shaking her body.

"I'm sorry. Please forgive me if I hurt your feelings."

Nakasato could not understand. He'd always thought a woman couldn't wait to get married. Announcing his intention to get a divorce and marry Masako was supposed to sound like the joyful proclamation of Masako's victory.

But all she did was dissolve in tears and sorrow.

Unable to fathom her reaction, Nakasato used his strength to turn her body over to cover it with his own. He licked the tears on her cheeks. Masako wrapped both arms around his neck, her eyes shut tight as if she were desperately forming a wish.

Nakasato never again brought up the subject.

6

One hot summer evening Nakasato returned to the air-conditioned office and was catching his breath, when he learned that the general manager of the food department, Natsukawa, had been reassigned to the London office and that Inuzuka Keigoro, due back from his San Francisco post, was to succeed Natsukawa.

Personnel reshuffling being routine in Japanese business life, there was nothing mysterious about Natsukawa's sudden transfer. But it had come as a complete surprise to Nakasato, and for some moments he found this incredible piece of news hard to believe. When he confirmed it, joy surged through his body.

Free at last! Now I can break the stranglehold!

Scarcely able to contain his excitement, he walked toward Masako's desk, pretended to trip over the chair leg, and stumbled forward. Extremely careful to keep their relationship secret, Nakasato had never even addressed her directly at the office before.

"Pardon me!" he apologized, clutching at her chair back as if for support. As Masako started up in alarm, he whispered into her ear, "Natsukawa's been transferred. Banzai!" Loudly he repeated his apologies and returned to his seat.

Quick-witted, Masako instantly grasped the significance of Nakasato's impulsive behavior. When he risked a discreet glance in her direction, she sent him a covert signal with her eyes and fingers. From beneath the distinctive fringe of black bangs, a bright smile beamed her wordless congratulations across the distance.

"You really startled me but made me very happy, too," Masako said when they were alone in their hotel room. "Besides, the new general manager, Mr. Inuzuka, is a fine man."

"How do you know so much about him?"

"Don't you remember, I used to work in the Transportation Department?"

"Oh. That's all?" Indeed, Masako's first assignment at Nissei had been in transportation. Until ordered out to San Francisco, Inuzuka had served as a section chief in her department.

"Masculine and decisive. A man who knows his own mind."

"It makes me jealous—to hear you speak so highly of him."

"Nothing personal. He was popular with the men too. They considered him honest and steadfast."

"He sounds too good to be true, doesn't he?"

"Some did criticize him for being too straightforward."

"Did they?"

An image of Inuzuka was rapidly forming in Nakasato's mind: the type who can make quick decisions and stand by them without wavering. Nakasato began to formulate his plan of action. If I can get him over to my side, he'll make a powerful and reliable ally. But let him take an opposing stand and he'll prove a formidable adversary. So my initial briefing will make a critical difference. I'd better feed him all the facts of the supermarket operation at the outset—I need to make a friend of him. Nakasato had his strategy all mapped out.

Inuzuka turned out to have an engaging personality, just as predicted. His full face impressed Nakasato with its unaffected conviviality; his voice was strong.

When Nakasato asked him to inspect Century's stores in person, Inuzuka promptly had a tour worked into his busy schedule, with no sign of reluctance. It was well within his duty as a supervisor, but Nakasato was grateful for Inuzuka's ready consent. A senior manager who'd bestir himself to conduct on-site inspections was rare indeed. To Nakasato's knowledge, Natsukawa had never set foot in Century's markets while he headed their supervisory unit.

In the car taking them from store to store, Nakasato did his best to explain the dynamics of supermarket business to Inuzuka. Naturally, he put most fervor into describing his own idea to turn the meat-packing room into a modern food-processing plant.

"By the way, what volume of goods does Century purchase through Nissei Corporation?" Inuzuka asked at one point.

"Negligible, I'm sorry to say. Their sales volume is way below Nissei's scale. Century grosses 3 billion yen in annual revenues from selling ten thousand commodities and products. That means it averages no more than 300,000 yen per item. As you know, Nissei handles bulk commodities—like herring roe or shrimp—by millions and even billions of yen per transaction. Altogether in a different league."

"In that case, what is Nissei's objective in directly managing this supermarket chain?"

"That is . . . well . . . ," Nakasato mumbled, lost for a reply. From past experience, Nakasato well knew that a satisfactory answer to this question was not easy to find. Inuzuka's question was actually the first thing to cross any shoshaman's mind. Since integrated trading companies earned money from acting as intermediaries in wholesale and other distribution transactions, a shosha's usual relation to a supermarket would be to help it buy merchandise. With too little volume, the supermarket would not be worth the shosha's effort.

All Nakasato had to offer at the moment was a weak argument: the ultimate aim was for capital gains or for an increase in value of capital assets. But shoshamen in sales and marketing worked under relentless pressure to show short-term gains on their semiannual balance sheets. For them, future profit and profit from sale of stock meant nothing more than a castle in the air. With Century Stores showing very tangible red figures, they'd laugh him away, saying, "Invest on capital growth? Hey, spare us the tired joke, will you?" Lamely, Nakasato presented his only argument to Inuzuka.

"Capital gains? Well, now." Inuzuka fell deep into thought. Slumping against the back seat of the car, he fixed his wide-eyed gaze on the empty space above for what seemed an agonizingly long time.

"No matter how I look at it, your idea seems impossible," Inuzuka slowly reasoned a few minutes later. "If we accept your theory, Nissei must invest in—and operate—all kinds of enterprises, even those that are alien to a trading firm's primary functions, as long as it deems profitable to do so. Such a policy might fit a conglomerate but not the sogo shosha. My personal view is that the trading company ought to concentrate on increasing profits to be gained from its principal activity, acting as a trade intermediary."

Taken aback, all Nakasato said was, "Yes. It's certainly possible to see it that way, but . . . " He thought rapidly. If I press the point any further, I'll sound argumentative. Tactically unwise to rub the new general manager the wrong way. Best to ease off this issue for the time being, Nakasato concluded, and kept his mouth shut thereafter.

Nissei Corporation will withdraw from the supermarket business. The supervisory unit is to make every effort to minimize our damages and to sell off Century Stores.

This directive was issued soon after Inuzuka's personal inspection of Century's premises. Inuzuka's opinion, Nakasato conceded, had constituted Nissei's last word on Operation Supermarket. On its heels came the notice of Nakasato's assignment to the Los Angeles office.

This bolt out of the blue, the second in a few days, hit Nakasato harder. The transfer order came as a fait accompli, preceded by no attempt to sound him out. Nissei's rules stipulated the lead time of three days between preliminary notice and official announcement, and three weeks before arrival at a new post.

"I appreciate your ambition. I was most impressed when you told me you wouldn't mind working for Century Stores for good. But I'd rather see you apply your ardor to something more meaningful. No matter how hard you try, you can never save Century's stores singlehanded. Even if they manage to show some profit, it's only a drop in the bucket for the shosha. What you really need at this point in your career is experience in overseas service."—Thus Inuzuka counseled Nakasato when he betrayed displeasure in reaction to the transfer order. In his panic-stricken state, Nakasato could spare no thought for Inuzuka's motives. What might have been his genuine concern for a young subordinate's future was lost on Nakasato. His mind was overloaded with one thought—what to do about his relationship with Masako.

He had no intention of giving her up: she was his raison d'être, the source of his life. He felt truly alive only when he was with her. They had known each other for nearly three years now. All his energy and professional drive, he felt, were generated during their hours together.

What if the day came when he could see Masako no more? The thought had crossed his mind in the past. Since they were not married to each other, it only needed Masako's change of heart to stop their trysts. If their relationship became known to anyone in the company, that too would spell an end for them. Out of necessity Nakasato should have prepared for the contingency, but he had never been able to contemplate the if and when. To him, the mental task was as tortuous and frightening as trying to imagine life after death.

Nakasato was resigned to the situation at home. His wife, Rieko, had long ago lost all emotional hold on him. Rieko was ensconced in the security of her married status. She did nothing but complain that it was hard to make ends meet with his salary. She was utterly self-centered in their sex life as well. Nakasato sometimes wondered, might Masako end up no different from Rieko after she married? But that never seemed possible.

Suppose I married Masako, he tried to picture in his mind. Would Masako lose her temper at every turn and fling sharp words at me as if aiming at my heart? Can this woman with so much intellectual curiosity and passion for learning turn into another Rieko, who reads nothing but gossipy weekly magazines and the social pages of newspapers or watches soap operas and variety shows on television for hours on end?

I can never let Masako go. Without her, my life would be nothing. Such were Nakasato's thoughts as he set out to meet Masako at the usual time and place. But he had yet to devise a practical plan of action to save their precious relationship.—Once I accept the Los Angeles job, the company will expect me to stay there for five years at the minimum, maybe ten years under certain circumstances. Can I ask her to wait as long as it takes? And to wait for what? For a man who brings back a body ten years older? Or for study sessions that resume ten years later?

For the first time Nakasato realized: without the benefit of legal sanction, he and Masako had no other means to validate their relationship except their physical contact, to confirm mutual love by meeting on a continual basis. Once an ocean between Japan and the

United States separated them, they'd be powerless to prevent time from dissolving their relationship.

In that case, why not resign from the company as he had contemplated before, to start a fashion apparel business with Masako? But the stakes were too high. It was a gamble that might well ruin him—in diametrical contrast to his job with Nissei Corporation, which accorded him security.

"Give me more time to think. I won't be able to work out a plan in two or three weeks. For the time being, I have no choice but to report to Los Angeles as ordered. Once I decide to drop everything and come home, I can do so at any time. Please give me a few months. I can never forget you."

In the bed they were unlikely to share again for a long time, Nakasato expressed his thoughts. Masako said little in response. Turned away from Nakasato with her eyes squeezed shut, she was frozen in agony as if bearing down on a heavy pain deep inside. When Nakasato touched her shoulder, he felt her quivering like a small animal trying to protect itself against bitter cold.

Time slipped by mercilessly.

"I don't want to leave!" Just as Nakasato left the bed and started for the bathroom to get dressed, Masako cried out. Deep-throated and loud, the voice was a totally alien sound of raw emotion that burst from the depths of her body with irrepressible force. Recoiling in fright, Nakasato swung round to look at the bed. The female form lay, eyes shut tight and hands gripping the edges of the sheets.

"What's the matter?" Nakasato asked, returning to her side.

Masako's eyelids snapped apart. These eyes Nakasato had never seen before—pupils wide, dilated, bulging, practically spilling out.

"I don't want to leave!" she howled again. "I can't go on living!" Lying stretched at full length on her back, she speared Nakasato with her eyes and petrified him with her voice.

"What is it?" he tried to ask, but his voice stuck in his throat.

"Going to leave me all alone, are you? What am I to do with myself?" Masako muttered, as if delirious, fevered. Her eyes were open but vacant, apparently registering nothing and utterly oblivious of Nakasato right next to her.

When he reached over the bed to touch her, she cried out once more, "Ah, I'm dying! I'll be dead! How do you expect me to find my way home now? Oh, I'll be reduced to zero. We were one—there'll be nothing left!"

She's lost her senses, Nakasato thought.

"There must be some mistake. You're going out of my life? Impossible!" Masako said softly and fell silent for a while, only to let out a full cry, "I'm going to die!"

At a complete loss, Nakasato stood rooted to the spot. If he touched her body, surely he would feel a high-voltage current streak into his own.

The telephone bell unfroze him.

"What's going on there, sir?" the front clerk asked. Apparently Masako's cries had been overheard. Perhaps an alarmed guest in a nearby room had alerted the management.

"I'm sorry, but it's nothing."

"Are you all right?"

"Yes, we are fine."

"I beg your pardon, but—please let me speak to the lady."

Do they suspect a murder? Nakasato wondered. He had no choice but to call Masako to the phone.

"Yes . . . yes . . . I'm all right . . . I'm sorry . . . ," she whispered into the telephone. Her rumpled hair swayed unsteadily. "We'll be leaving shortly. I am sorry."

Nakasato was relieved by her announcement. Seeing the state she was in, he had braced himself for the long night it might take to calm her down.

"I am sorry." Masako tendered her apology to Nakasato next, as she cradled the receiver. "I forgot myself."

Nakasato hugged her without a word. In scrambling out of bed, she had put the night kimono over her bare skin without taking time to find the sash. A shapely breast was peeking through the loose front folds. Nakasato pressed his lips on it, sucked, and then pulled the kimono's folds together to cover it carefully. He clasped her tightly, this time encircling her body with both arms.

· · ·

In the several days that remained before his scheduled departure, Nakasato tried to arrange one more intimate meeting with Masako. But the obligatory series of farewell parties and preparations for the trip took up all his evening hours.

As a last resort, Nakasato called Masako from an outside telephone one afternoon on his way back from a business appointment. They met at a coffee shop near the Nissei building. Their colleagues would have been astonished if they had happened by to catch sight of them together—and engaged in serious talk over coffee at that— when no one ever saw them so much as speak to each other at the office. Now their time was running out. Neither wasted any concern over the risk of a scandal at this juncture.

Masako looked haunted as she sipped her tea.

Nakasato, too, was lost for words. From the company envelope he had with him, Nakasato pulled out a small package. "Just a little something, but I want you to have this as a keepsake."

"May I open this now?"

"Please do," he nodded, after he looked around to make certain no one was watching.

"Oh, how lovely!"

Belying the spirit of the words, her voice was sad. Nevertheless she picked up a silver pendant from its soft nest and wound the chain around her finger. The design consisted of two slender boats joined together. At first glance, they looked like an abstract representation of bamboo leaves, long and sleek enough for use in children's water games.

"We are the boats in this design. Our hearts will never part."

"Certainly," Masako said in a barely audible voice. The butterflies that were her lips seemed weak and stiff.

"I bet it becomes you," Nakasato suggested.

She gave a nod but said nothing. Bending forward, she fastened the pendant around her neck.

"Now, look up and let me see." Nakasato tried to coax her into raising her downcast face, but she responded only by awkwardly turning her face away from him. The movement caused glistening streams of tears to course down her cheeks in straight lines paralleling the black hair. They hit the little boats and spattered.

"Patience. Just a few months," Nakasato said weakly.

Her head lowered, she groped in the handbag beside her and fished out a package as small as his.

"I've brought a present too." Her voice was all but drowning in tears. "I was afraid I might not get a chance to hand it to you."

Nakasato opened the little box to find matching tie pin and cuff links winking their opal eyes.

"Thank you. I'll regard this gift as your being and cherish it." He clipped all three pieces on his tie and cuffs.

"Don't cry any more. Let's face our fate as best we can."

"Yes," she agreed valiantly but struggled for a while to fight back the flood of tears.

Somehow she managed to regain self-control. When at last her eyes were dry, Nakasato touched her shoulder and said, "You leave first. Take care of yourself. Be sure to write to me. I'll write you, every day."

Masako forced a smile to her face. Slowly she rose from her chair and walked from the coffee shop. Moments later her face floated across the translucent patterns of the front windowpane, but her tear-clouded smile faded even before her figure itself disappeared from his sight.

7

The transfer to Los Angeles was a crucial turning point in Nakasato's life. In the beautiful sprawling metropolis that he reached in confusion and despair he earned the trust of Ebisawa Shiro, head of the Nissei office there.

A crack senior manager, Ebisawa already ranked among the top three in Nissei's marketing and sales at the time. Thereafter he continued his ascent of the corporate ladder until he reached its highest eminence. Nakasato could see that Ebisawa was endowed with all the mental faculties and special skills indispensable in a shoshaman, from reasoning power, leadership, and the art of negotiation down to foreign language competence. Still more, Ebisawa possessed a potently magnetic personality. His lean body exuded unequivocal sincerity and all-embracing warmth. He would seem energetic and fairly unbeatable in his vitality most of the time, but at other times as serene as ancient ceramics.

Nakasato thus became an instant captive of Ebisawa's charisma, and Ebisawa took him under his wing. As Nakasato's sense of fair dealing, which others had considered a negative quality in him, was tempered and reinforced on the job by this enlightened supervisor, Nakasato matured into a competent and redoubtable shoshaman.

In those days, the Los Angeles office was the operational base of Nissei's U.S. trade. For a time before New York City became a new focus of the business world, the Pacific Coast served as the gateway in all United States–Japan commercial transactions handled by Japanese trading companies. That was why a top executive of Ebisawa's caliber had been assigned to head Nissei's West Coast office.

There for the first time in his career Nakasato found himself in the corporate mainstream, working under one of Nissei's most powerful leaders. Representatives of most client firms showed their respect for Ebisawa whenever he took part in transactions. One time, for example, when a Japan-bound shipment of raw meat was held up in the United States, Ebisawa made a single telephone call to a prominent Japanese sausage company, whose top executive flew across the Pacific to settle the dispute.

Ebisawa's influence was strongest in Nissei's internal hierarchy. Much to Nakasato's amazement, time and again a deal with slim chances for approval would get the go order, or a proposal for cash loans that exceeded usual limits under the particular market conditions would receive approval—all on the force of Ebisawa's endorsement. Work could not fail to go well under such circumstances. His job became a pleasure that totally absorbed Nakasato. It was also the best way he could find to keep Masako out of his thoughts.

Communication with her fell off more and more as time passed. Before leaving Tokyo, he had worked out a safe procedure in corresponding with Masako: using a female pseudonym, Nakasato was to write her in care of the office; Masako had addressed the envelopes in her own hand. By the time he ran out of them, she would mail a new batch to Los Angeles. To forestall suspicion and gossip, they agreed to hold the frequency of his correspondence to twice a week.

Masako's letters to him, by contrast, posed no problem at all. She sent them directly to his apartment, since his family stayed behind in Tokyo for the time being.

When he arrived in Los Angeles, Nakasato wrote Masako many letters every day. Although he kept extremely busy, taking over new duties and trying to find his way around in new surroundings, Masako was never out of his heart for a moment. Of the many letters he wrote, he would choose a few to stuff into an envelope prepared by Masako and send it off.

In turn Masako's letters arrived practically at the rate of one a day. Whenever he beheld her script—neat yet asexual and stiff—like a schoolteacher's writing on the blackboard, he clutched the letter to his heart. And every time the feel of her lips and the memory of her body came back to him, with the acute sensation of a real touch. When Nakasato's family joined him in Los Angeles some months later, Masako mailed her letters to his office. Perhaps the necessity for such precaution inhibited her, for their correspondence began to decrease in frequency and volume from then on, never to regain its initial level.

About a half-year after his transfer to the United States Nakasato lost contact with Masako. By that time he had grown used to the long intervals between her letters. But after a whole month passed without hearing from her, he was worried enough to put a call through to her home, using an assumed name.

Her mother answered the telephone. Her replies to his questions were evasive. "Masako no longer lives at home," she informed Nakasato but would not divulge her new address.

Next day, again under an assumed name, he called Nissei's main office in Tokyo and asked for Masako only to be told, "Miss Hozumi is no longer with the company." The shock took his breath away. Is she dead? he feared for a moment. But in that case there would have been no need to hide the fact from him. Since her mother refused to give out her address, Masako had to be alive somewhere.

Nakasato thought of asking one of his close friends in Nissei's headquarters to trace her for him but could not bring himself to do so. After all, no matter how close, a colleague at the office was not the same as a college friend. Why risk setting up a fatal scandal himself? At best, he'd put himself forever in somebody's power. That kind of indiscretion could well cost him dear in the final laps of the corporate race.

Nakasato had yet to realize it but already his mind was preoccupied with the race for promotion and career success. Evidently he'd learned a new greed as he entered the company's mainstream via the Los Angeles office.

Thus Masako vanished out of Nakasato's life.

· · ·

One year later, Nakasato flew back to Tokyo on business. He dropped in at the Foodstuff Division and made a discreet inquiry into what had become of Masako but netted not a shred of information. A business firm had nothing like the college roster of graduates to keep track of former employees, as Nakasato learned to his sharp disappointment. A man can't expect even a trace of his own existence to remain after he's gone. That's life, he told himself sadly as he watched Tokyo Bay recede beneath his jet from Haneda Airport bound for Los Angeles.

In retrospect it seemed providential that he had been torn from Masako by an overseas assignment and that on her own accord she had disappeared. Had he been carried away by his supermarket fever and moved out to a deficit-ridden subsidiary, he would have killed all hope for a bright future in his career. And his love affair with Masako could have ruined his entire life.

Well, luck still rides with me, Nakasato thought with a deep sense of relief as he drifted into peaceful sleep—a sleep to span the next fifteen years that would roll on with hectic swiftness.

THREE

Black Hair

April

1

Nakasato took carefully calculated steps to squash the American Gourmet Company acquisition plan by slow and safe degrees. To create an impression that he was actively involved in the feasibility study, he must send to America for a sizable amount of data and hold staff meetings from time to time. He put the zealous Sumoto in charge of the project and scrupulously followed all the usual procedures.

"I thought you were against this plan," Sumoto blurted out, surprised, when Nakasato told him to ask Nissei America to make a particularly thorough study of the food-service industry in the United States.

"Who says I was against it? I said, if Nissei men demonstrated sufficient commitment and preparation and if the industry in question indicated growth potential, there'd be no reason not to implement the plan."

"Is that your feeling?" Sumoto sounded skeptical but continued as if to convince himself, "That means we must run a thorough check." They invited experts on the U.S. food-service market to come and give lectures. These prominent industry leaders, business consultants, and academics offered helpful hints but no inside information or advice of critical importance.

Nakasato had a serious talk with the personnel manager about what kind of a man to assign to American Gourmet Company if and when the takeover came through.

"Well, there's nobody else but you for the top spot," Yamabe said with his characteristic bluntness, a trait he bragged about as distinguishing him from the previous personnel managers at Nissei. He was senior to Nakasato by three years. "I bet the president has you in mind, too."

"Surely not!" Nakasato exclaimed, with the right note of alarm in his voice. "The job's too big for me. But of course, if it's a company order, I'll be happy to go to the United States."

"You say so now—but this job's no picnic. First of all, you can't expect to be called back in a couple of years like any other man posted overseas. As a worst case, you might be over there for good, buried there. I don't want another neurotic suicide on my hands, jumping under the subway train, you know," Yamabe said, obliquely referring to Ojima's death.

Finding Yamabe's remark in poor taste, Nakasato nonetheless said, "Not me. I won't mind living in America at all."

"Well, good for you. But you're one of the president's favorites, so maybe you aren't slated for a job like this. Now, then, who'd make the next best candidate?"

Even as he seemed to speak his mind with guileless candor, Yamabe never missed a chance to tickle the listener's vanity, as he had just done by working in an extra comment to pat Nakasato on the back. Yamabe read off several names on the personnel roster on his desk, but Nakasato knew in his heart that none of them would do. There was still nobody else but him.

"When the time comes to get down to business, I'll be back," Nakasato promised and left the personnel office.

Aside from official inquiries, Nakasato began his own probe into two matters that weighed heavily on his mind. The first one was the problem stock that Nissei America's general products department allegedly had on its hands. If matters stood as Emura told Nakasato on the phone the night before he left New York, the man responsible for the useless merchandise was Kano, now head of General Products at Nissei America and Nakasato's exact contemporary in the company. Large shipments, furnishings of wood and fabric custom-made in Taiwan for Ferguson Burgers, had to be stowed away when the large East Coast fast-food chain refused to renew its purchase contracts with Nissei. There was a good possibility, then, that Nissei America's need to dispose of the items in secret was behind the recommendation to buy American Gourmet Company.

And yet Nakasato wasn't sure he bought the story. For one thing, it was hard to believe that furnishings designed specifically for Ferguson Burgers could be used in American Gourmet's restaurants. For another, Nakasato was in the dark as to Emura's real motive in informing him of it. But still he could not dismiss the story outright: he could picture the desperation of a shoshaman under terrific pressure to collect bad debts or get rid of unsalable stock.

Now that Nakasato had made up his mind to scuttle the acquisition plan, the issue was moot. But he remained intent on learning the truth behind it anyway. It had a direct bearing on his relationship with Kano. No more than classmates on nodding terms back in college, since entering Nissei in the same year they had kept pace with each other, clearing every stage of the career course at the top of their class. Kano was indeed a presence to be reckoned with. They never worked together at the office, somehow drawing departments and posts distant from each other over the years. Nakasato learned of Kano's competence and expertise only through the office grapevine. Now for the first time they had direct contact over the acquisition of American Gourmet Company.

If the plan had been proposed solely to move the questionable stock that would otherwise count against Kano's performance record, he was in fact trying to use his "year-mate" Nakasato to cover up his own tracks. Not only use him, but perhaps even exile him almost permanently to the United States or saddle him with an impossible task that would ruin his reputation. Either way, Kano might well plan to take this chance of removing a rival from the internal competition. Unpardonable, if true. Nakasato felt compelled to get to the bottom of the ominous story. Depending on what his probe turned up, he could use his findings to kill the acquisition plan or, better yet, deal Kano out.

Nakasato was wondering where to start his investigation when Tamura, a section chief in the Internal Control Division three years his junior, came to report. Tamura had received a transfer order to the New York office. Not to miss this golden opportunity, Nakasato asked Tamura to look closely at the New York inventory situation and send his report back. Tamura and Nakasato had lived in the same bachelors' dormitory in their early years at Nissei and had come to know each other rather well.

The second matter of personal concern to Nakasato was Inuzuka, his one-time boss. By making a gift of what seemed to be a valuable painting for no credible reason, Inuzuka was forcing Nakasato to meet him. But now Nakasato had a reason of his own to see Inuzuka. He could not shake the feeling that Inuzuka somehow had a hand in the American Gourmet acquisition plan. That telephone call out of the blue had come so soon after the plan was dropped in Nakasato's lap. His timing was impeccable—or downright uncanny, if it had not been deliberate.

Moreover, Inuzuka had gone all the way to New York City one step ahead of Nakasato and had met President Tobita of Nissei America. Just old pals getting together in New York? Maybe. But then again, it was entirely possible that they discussed the acquisition of American Gourmet Company and settled on Nakasato as their choice for the man in charge. President Tobita had shown too much enthusiasm from the start, uncharacteristic of his usual overcautious self, Nakasato thought with a mounting sense of disquiet. He would not put it past Inuzuka to have concocted the whole plot by himself and talked Tobita into adopting it. Tobita could easily have been influenced by his best friend since college days, practically guaranteeing that Nakasato was just the man to make a success of it.

But does Inuzuka have so much power? A manager who failed to make senior rank and quit the company well before the mandatory retirement age; a man whose wife ran out on him; someone who felt compelled to make the rounds of his former subordinates to apologize. No matter how you look at him, he cuts a sorry figure, an aging man feeling wretched in failure and defeat. A melancholic, by the looks of him: is this a person to talk the CEO of a giant enterprise like Nissei Corporation into doing anything at all? Retired, with nothing more to do with Nissei, can Inuzuka even stick his head into company business again?

Nakasato suddenly realized that the last conjecture was well within the realm of possibilities. Even more than most Japanese firms, integrated trading companies moved more on the force of informal human relationships than of organizational structure. Each individual's assignment was totally unrelated to his colleagues' work, and there was no common yardstick to measure or compare the requirements of various projects. Thus, judgments and decisions were often based on the personal reputations of the men involved in each case. Since Nakasato handled the supermarket project many years ago, he had been consulted on and off ever since, through formal and informal channels, every time some problem cropped up in relation to the supermarket or retail business. It would be no surprise, therefore, if President Tobita should call in Inuzuka for consultation on the downstream operations, a field of his former expertise—assuming Tobita had implicit trust in his close friend of long standing.

Nevertheless, what prompted Inuzuka, a career dropout no less, to travel all the way to America at this time? However anxious Tobita may have been to get his opinion, it's unthinkable for Nissei America to have sent for Inuzuka at company expense. In any case, how is he getting by these days? I must learn more about his current circumstances before I meet him, Nakasato told himself.

He decided to get in touch with Nukaya Kiichiro. He had suffered a nervous breakdown as a direct result of Inuzuka's misjudgment regarding their affiliate company, Kijima. Like Nakasato, Nukaya was one of Inuzuka's former subordinates, startled by his belated apology.

Nakasato flipped through the pages of the internal telephone directory to find Nukaya's number.

2

"Hi!" Nakasato waved in friendly greeting as he walked into the coffee shop in the basement of their building.

"It's been a long time." Nukaya rose from the chair and bowed slightly.

"True. We work in the same building but have little chance to run into each other these days. It goes to show you how much Nissei's grown, doesn't it?"

"You may be right there," Nukaya agreed and then switched to a more formal tone. "Nakasato-san, congratulations on your promotion to MG-1!"

"Oh? Thanks. I've been lucky."

"No, you made it on your own merit. I hear there was some commotion at the ceremony."

"You mean Ojima?"

"Yes. I didn't know him well, but I was shocked to hear about him. What made him do it?"

Nervous breakdown, Nakasato was about to say, but checked himself in time. Nukaya sitting across from him at this very moment had a history of mental breakdown. Perhaps not completely cured yet. It would do no good to tell a neurotic man about another who had committed suicide.

"Well, doesn't matter now. Anyway, you look really well. Put on a bit of weight, I see," Nakasato said, tactfully changing the subject. For some time after he returned from an extended leave of absence following his breakdown, Nukaya had gone around the office wearing a morbid expression on his face that showed no spirit or ambition. Now even his skin had a glow.

"Thank you. I'm feeling much better these days. I fell into a good thing recently."

"Oh, did you?"

What good thing? He hasn't had a promotion or an upgrade reassignment lately that I know of—must have something to do with his family, Nakasato thought vaguely.

"I'll tell you about it later. First things first. What in the world is Mr. Inuzuka up to, anyway?"

"The fact that he paid you a visit too makes me think it's a case of senile melancholia after all. If he picked me out, I might have suspected some kind of a revenge attempt, though."

"What grudge could Mr. Inuzuka hold against you? The other way around, that I could understand better."

"Well, maybe so. But to put it bluntly, Mr. Inuzuka's a career dropout. In his steady progress up the corporate ladder, at some point he somehow climbed off and opted out by resigning from Nissei. He must have mixed feelings about the past. So I didn't rule out the possibility of guilt turned into a grudge against me."

"Knowing Mr. Inuzuka's personality as I do, I can't see him doing anything so underhanded. I grant you, he does have a tendency to be dogmatic at times, but . . ."

"Uncommonly dogmatic, or he wouldn't be coming around after all this time to give us expensive artworks and apologize without rhyme or reason."

"True enough." Nukaya laughed cheerfully. That good thing had apparently worked a complete change in his personality to brighten up his disposition. "But Nakasato-san, we can't very well accept his gift with polite thanks."

"In any case, let's all three get together. Aside from the painting, I have a business matter to discuss with Mr. Inuzuka."

Nakasato brought Nukaya up to date on the American Gourmet acquisition project.

"Say, I wonder if Mr. Inuzuka instigated the whole thing."

"Well, this is just my speculation. That's why I'm anxious to verify it."

"Tell me, do you really believe his opinion can be taken seriously by our senior executives at this point?"

"I don't know. I certainly don't know how, but it could be possible. Besides . . ." Nakasato hesitated for a moment, wondering whether to mention that he might be the one most likely to end up in the position of responsibility on this project. After all, since Nukaya was his junior and former coworker, Nakasato could feel free to explain the situation to him.

"It does have his touch all right. Suppose Mr. Inuzuka repents of his past action, he might have recommended you to make up for the wrong he thinks he's done you."

"That's just it. If you're right, he's meddling with my life. Once he destroyed a supermarket single-handed. And now he plots to make me run a restaurant chain against my will—and in America at that! The whole thing is absurd."

'May be fun to take him up on it, don't you think? Sounds pretty exciting to run a business in America."

"Look, this is no joke. What's so exciting about it? Nothing but exile in effect."

"Is it? Exile, eh?" Nukaya looked surprised. "Well, I suppose you could see it that way, but to me it's a dream come true. If I were you, I'd drop everything and go flying over there."

"What are you talking about? Listen! Running a restaurant chain in America means putting your life on the line just to survive in the

American food-service industry. In order to win the battle of survival, you must hold your own—stay tuned to American tastes and way
of life and beat your American competitors in the art of management. To use a simple example, it's like a man with little grasp of the
technical skills, or the differences in language and game rules, trying to manage a major league baseball team in a foreign country.
Nukaya, have you given any thought to the amount of time and effort it would take him, to overcome all those odds?"

"A formidable task, I imagine. But for someone like me who's already flunked the businessman's course, it's a task that looks su-
premely attractive, though clear out of my reach. A job well worth
taking on, even when I know I have little chance of success. But, looking at it from your vantage point, I can understand there's absolutely
no reason why you should engage in such a senseless endeavor."

"Makes no difference if it's you or me. This is one job that can't be
accomplished unless you're prepared to stay in America indefinitely."

"No. It does make a difference," Nukaya countered in an unexpected display of stubbornness. "You should never accept such an
assignment. Since everyone expects you to succeed, your success
won't get much accolade anyway. But your failure will wipe out in
one stroke all the influence and reputation you've built up over the
years. So long as President Ebisawa remains in his position, not even
failure can do you too much damage. But what if you get assigned
out to American Gourmet on President Ebisawa's order and he ab-
dicates before your term is up? Then you'll end up having climbed
upstairs only to get the ladder stolen, as the saying goes."

"It could very well come to that," Nakasato conceded. Nukaya
merely pointed out the precise contingency that worried Nakasato
the most.

President Ebisawa himself picked me for the tough job. So long as
I'm making a serious effort, Ebisawa will stand behind me even
when the going gets rougher than anticipated. But if he resigns, the
situation changes overnight. Certainly, considerate and judicious as
he is, even after he steps down he won't hesitate to use his influence
whenever I need help carrying out the difficult duty he himself assigned me. But nothing will be the same when the supreme power is
no longer in his hands. If he falls ill or retires outright, he has no
influence left to wield. This is no routine overseas assignment: the

American Gourmet position goes with an indefinite term. Odds are nearly a hundred to one that Ebisawa steps down before I get back from the United States. And when he does—when the command changes hands—I need to maneuver, find a favored position in the new regime. Here's where the real meaning of the mainstream comes into play. Stay in the mainstream, and I keep direct contact with the top command, no matter who takes over. But in the United States, no matter how hard I work in the food-service industry, my great performance record will soon be forgotten back at the main office. Not only that: while I'm with American Gourmet Company, I'll have no chance to make officer of Nissei Corporation!

"Ironic, isn't it?" Nukaya's voice roused Nakasato from his musing. "A has-been like me—with nothing more to lose—may be itching to take on any risky project, but the company has no faith in him. And someone like you—charging full steam ahead—can't afford to leave the mainstream and the central administration. A classic standoff."

Nukaya spoke plainly but without rancor, and Nakasato did not find it offensive.

"Nukaya-kun, let's meet Mr. Inuzuka. Maybe over dinner. But where?"

"You mean, a place to eat?"

"Somewhere quiet so we can talk. Not too expensive. Let me see . . ."

Nakasato ruled out the restaurants and clubs that he frequented for business entertainment: much too expensive for private use, in fact way beyond the average businessman's means. Even the general manager of a department in a prestigious trading company did hardly better than a clerk in terms of spending money.

"Leave that to me," Nukaya volunteered with unusual animation. "Which is your pleasure, Western cuisine or Japanese?"

"Hmm, you sound like a gourmet."

"More or less, I am. Shall we pick a place where they serve the famous calvados?"

"Calvados? What's that?"

"Here—this is it. See, it says here . . ." He dragged a pile of papers out of the bag he had placed on the chair next to him and fluttered through the sheets.

"Here it is," he said at last, holding out a sheet toward Nakasato. It looked like galley proof for a book. Here and there editorial corrections were marked in red. Nakasato began to read the section Nukaya's finger pointed out.

> The waiter was wiping off the table. "Pernod," Ravic told him.
> "With water, sir?"
> "No. But hold it," Ravic said, trying to think some more. "Forget Pernod."
> He felt like washing something right out of him. A bitter taste. A sweet liqueur like anise would not be enough to kill it.
> "Bring me a calvados," he said to the waiter. "A large one."
> "Yes, sir."

"What is this?"

"A scene from *The Arch of Triumph* by Remarque. Calvados is a liquor the Hollywood version of this novel made famous. It takes the name of an area in Normandy that is believed to come from *El Calvador,* one of the vessels in the invincible Spanish armada, which ran aground there. Calvados is distilled from apple cider. A brandy, you might call it. As for anise, it's a liqueur flavored with the seeds of a plant used to season food and in medicine."

"But what on earth is this all about?"

"This? These are the proofs of a book. I wrote it."

"You wrote a book?" Nakasato turned to another page.

> They had given the dining-room girl their order for a bottle of Gruaud Larose, but Hans Castorp was not satisfied with the temperature of the wine and sent her back to have it warmed. The meal was superb: asparagus soup, stuffed tomato, roast meat with trimmings, excellently prepared pudding, cheese, and fruit. Hans Castorp ate heartily.

"This scene is in chapter one of Thomas Mann's *Magic Mountain,* where a young man named Hans Castorp pays a visit to his cousin Joachim at a sanatorium on the mountaintop and dines with him. Gruaud Larose is a wine produced by Cordier at Saint-Julien in the famous Bordeaux region. A top-grade wine with an attractive mellow bouquet. When it comes to making a tasty asparagus soup, you need a certain knack . . ."

"Hold a minute there." Nakasato stopped Nukaya, who seemed to be warming up to the subject. "What's all this? A book about wine?"

"Not only about wine. It's entitled *Meals in World Literature.* It'll be in the bookstores two months from now."

This, then, was the good thing Nukaya had mentioned a while ago. Fairly bursting with pleasure, he began to tell his story before Nakasato had a chance to prompt him.

.　　.　　.

After a traumatic setback on the job triggered his nervous breakdown, Nukaya eventually returned to work but found himself kept out of challenging assignments. At first he took it as a benevolent gesture on the part of the management in consideration for his recent illness. But he was consigned to pushing papers in a no-man's-land year after year. Discontent began to gnaw him, but he knew that too much worrying would yield nothing but another breakdown. After much thinking, he reached the conclusion that he could never get out of the rut unless he changed his perspective. His mental search for a way out had preoccupied him for several months when he experienced a revelation.

Suddenly one day it dawned on him: He was too company-oriented in his thinking. That had been his trouble. The world must be full of important things beyond any job, he realized. Objectively speaking, Nissei Corporation occupied a negligible space within society as a whole. It was nothing short of farcical, to brood and rage under the mistaken impression that the insignificant sphere called Nissei was the whole world. If the company would not make full use of him, he must find another way of making himself useful to the world by developing some talent that had nothing to do with his job.

Although new thoughts stirred in Nukaya, how was he to hit on a concrete idea? He was entertaining a notion to volunteer as a baseball coach in the neighborhood little league, when his wife, Kiyoko, made a suggestion.

"Why don't you write a book?"

"Write a book? I have no literary talent."

"You don't need special talent. Anybody can write a book. Recount some unusual experiences of your own, or do research on a subject no one else ever explored."

"My personal experiences are all too common to be interesting."

"Then why not try research? I'll help, too."

"But I'm afraid any worthwhile subjects must be all taken now—by scholars who specialize in each field."

At first, Nukaya took a dim view of her idea. But Kiyoko was enthusiastic. After considering and rejecting a number of possible topics, she settled on one that was unique—meals in world literature.

"Surely, you can make a fascinating book out of this research. And there's absolutely no scholar specializing in this area. Just think of it. Do people normally do such a fool thing as reread the famous novels of the world all over again just to search out dining scenes?"

"But you're trying to get *me* to do the fool thing!"

"You're already a bookworm anyway. It takes no extra effort. All you have to do is fill out a card whenever you come on a food scene in the story you happen to be reading. Then you do some research on the drinks and dishes described in it. If possible, you actually cook the same items and photograph the results to make your file. I'll be your collaborator. If we keep at it for as long as it takes, I'm sure we can produce something meaningful, something to show that you and I really lived."

The Nukayas were childless. Apparently Kiyoko too had been assailed by a sense of regret and uselessness, watching time and her own life passing by.

Once embarked on what they thought would be a ten-year plan, they divided the volumes of an anthology of world literature between them and set to reading. Soon they realized they could cover more than just food scenes and began to make excerpts of passages describing other items—clothes, furniture, and vehicles. These extra sets of cards were to serve as source materials for their next book, should *Meals in World Literature* prove a success.

As Kiyoko astutely remarked, her husband was an avid reader by nature. Fiction was his particular passion. In no time Nukaya became absorbed in the task, making great strides in accumulating his share of cards. With increasing frequency, he and his wife dined out together to try the foods and wines they were researching. Before long, they not only became knowledgeable about the restaurants that offered international cuisine but also made friends with their master chefs and sommeliers.

In less than two years, Nukaya was enjoying a new world that had opened up before him, thanks solely to their research. The chefs and sommeliers of exclusive restaurants had a professional pride all their own. One wine steward could not answer the Nukayas' question to his own satisfaction. Mortified, he made a thorough private study of the particular brand and thanked them for the inspiration with a gift of wine worth as much as Nukaya's monthly personal allowance. The attitude and behavior of these people exceeded the measure of common sense Nukaya could expect from his colleagues in Nissei Corporation. Their artless, uninhibited good cheer belonged to a world Nukaya had never imagined.

One of the master chefs with whom he struck up friendship through his research helped him get his book published. He referred Nukaya to a publisher experienced in handling books on culinary art, and the manuscript of *Meals in World Literature* was promptly accepted for publication. It was a feat all the greater for being accomplished in less than half the time they originally set.

·   ·   ·

"At the risk of sounding like a lovesick fool, Nakasato-san," Nukaya said honestly, "I confess I owe everything to Kiyoko. My wife saved me by showing the way to another world that existed outside of Nissei Corporation."

"I'm happy for you. Nice to combine your hobby with making a profit."

"But profit is practically nil. Costs probably exceed earnings by far. I couldn't care less. How wonderful it feels to share interests, feelings, and laughter over things totally unrelated to my work at Nissei, with people who have nothing to do with Nissei—you yourself have to taste the joy to know it. I feel as if I'm restored to my own true self. The real Nukaya Kiichiro is the one who lives like this now. I'm not deprecating Nissei, you know. I just believe life would be dull if you let Nissei be your whole world." Nukaya concluded on a conciliatory note, perhaps fearing he had hurt Nakasato's feelings.

"I understand. Since you are a pro in matters of food, I'll leave it to you to choose a place for the dinner we host in Mr. Inuzuka's honor. Not too expensive, I beg you."

Nakasato attempted a light, joking tone but felt awkward. Nukaya's comment stuck in his mind: life would be dull if Nissei were the whole world. The words reached something deep in Nakasato's memory. Once upon a time they'd been his words. That was why he requested a transfer to Century Stores and fell in love with Hozumi Masako. But eventually Nakasato returned to the domain where Nissei's values reigned supreme, to lodge securely in the good graces of its top leader. To the present Nakasato, a world that operated on values other than Nissei's had no meaning whatsoever. It might as well not exist. And yet . . .

Yet Nukaya had written a book on food and derived genuine pleasure from that fact. No practical gains, he said. He claimed to feel alive thanks to his new contact with a world alien to Nissei's values. But after all, Nukaya got squeezed out of Nissei's domain. Restored to his own true self? Failed in one world and latched onto another of a different nature is more like it. Pitiful last-ditch struggles of a career burnout, that's all.

In direct contrast to Nukaya's case, Nakasato told himself, he had his rightful place in the central hierarchy. He personified Nissei's values and was fully capable of being his true self in the company's sphere. If only he kept clear of a dangerous sidetrack such as assignment to American Gourmet, he could easily stay put in the power center until his retirement. No need to go out of his way to seek trouble. Just climb one step at a time right on schedule. And some day he might even hold the supreme power in his own hands.

Nukaya's outlook on life was no more than a career failure's view—Nakasato settled his mind at that. Or tried to. But where would it leave him? Was I headed for burnout fifteen years ago? Those days I was saying things not much different from what Nukaya just said. If I as my old self of that period met up with the Nukaya of today, I would probably have empathized with his views. Does it mean that I too was on the verge of dropping out? That I was simply young and immature? Or was there something else?

The sensation that Nukaya's comment brought on remained within Nakasato's body, like that of a fish bone lodged in the throat.

3

Nakasato and Nukaya met Inuzuka Keigoro at a traditional Japanese-style restaurant in the Shinbashi district of Tokyo. Nukaya had made reservations at another place, but Inuzuka would not hear of it. Not by force but with matter-of-fact casualness, he had the reservations switched to the exclusive Shinbashi establishment of his choice.

Five minutes before the appointed time Nakasato and Nukaya arrived at the traditional wooden building with an impressive facade that suggested its top status. Inuzuka came out to welcome them with his air of conviviality as in the old days. If there was any change in his round face or large frame, he looked even younger. His voice was vigorous and his complexion healthy. No sooner had Nakasato set eyes on Inuzuka than he knew by intuition that the man was as far as possible from senile melancholia.

"This does nicely even for entertaining Americans," Inuzuka said with a genial smile after he had seated his two guests in the honored place before the alcove. Set in the center of a room that seemed much too spacious for three was a table with a square sunken area beneath it for their legs. They sat around the table instead of kneeling in Japanese style.

"Americans are 70 percent of the students attending my school," Inuzuka informed them. "In fact, what Japanese students we have were referred to us by the Americans. That's one reason why I prefer a Japanese-style room with bench-seat arrangements like this one. I often use this restaurant for social functions."

"Do you teach Japanese theatrical dance?"

"Right. I have a fairly small dance school. Nothing much, but enough to make a living."

"That's really impressive." Nukaya expressed his sincere admiration.

"One Japanese student of mine happens to own a supermarket in Kanagawa prefecture. About half a year ago, he insisted on showing me around his store."

A kimono-clad waitress with an attractive oval face entered and asked Inuzuka, "May we begin now?"

"Let's get started." He ordered beer and sake after checking with Nakasato and Nukaya. "This owner-president is obsessed with his work. A workaholic or a fanatic on supermarkets you might call him, but he radiates enthusiasm that touches even an outsider like me. He loves his business so much, he just can't wait to explain the supermarket operation to everybody."

Inuzuka poured beer for Nakasato and Nukaya and gracefully acknowledged Nakasato's offer to fill his glass.

"Let's drink a *kampai*," Inuzuka said, raising his glass to eye level. "To our health and happiness!"

After the toast, he poured a glass of sake and sipped it slowly as he resumed his story.

. . .

Frankly, Inuzuka had no desire to visit the supermarket. A guided tour would be wasted on him; he was no judge of retail business. But in the end the owner escorted him around the store. According to the owner, it displayed the highest standards in the field. A constant stream of his peers and industry specialists came to observe the operation.

Even to Inuzuka's untutored eyes, this store's superior standard was evident. Its foodstuff section was incredibly spacious and cheerful. The produce counters alone stretched from the entrance clear to the back of the store, piled high with vegetables and fruits in a profusion of bright colors as far as he could see. The massed variety of greengrocery had a visual impact of tremendous force. All the sales counters looked immaculate, abundant, and inviting, every item stacked neatly in some ingenious order. The store was crowded with customers carrying heavily loaded baskets and yet the shelves and counters remained full and neat, as if the store had just opened.

Inuzuka was greatly impressed. As he walked through the aisles, what he felt was simple admiration. Then he stepped into the meat-packing room in the back. Listening to the owner's impassioned explanation, he felt a weird sensation come over him: I heard about this store before, some time ago, somewhere, Inuzuka thought. But it couldn't possibly be the same store! When I served briefly as general manager of a unit overseeing a supermarket company in my Nissei days, my duty was to jettison the deficit-ridden retail business that was Nissei's ill-conceived venture into the downstream field. I never bothered to study up on supermarket management strategies. So why should this store seem so familiar to me now?

As Inuzuka was puzzling it out, something flashed into his head— Nakasato! The mystery was solved on the instant. The meat- and fish-packing room where he stood this very moment was exactly the kind of facility Nakasato had proposed fifteen years ago.

Let's remodel Century's back rooms into a modern food-processing plant capable of supplying meat and fish as fresh as they come in and as fast as they sell—so Nakasato had urged. At the time, however, no one at Nissei Corporation or Century Stores understood him. When Inuzuka was appointed the new general manager of the Food Department, his predecessor, Natsukawa, went so far as to make a special mention in his oral briefing of Nakasato's case—here was an example of personnel trouble Inuzuka ought to beware of.

"He's a hard worker all right, but he carries it much too far. Obsessed, I think."

"Obsessed?"

"Yes. He talks of nothing but the supermarket meat-packing room. He's obsessed with it. If you listen to him long enough, you'll end up believing that the poor condition of the meat-packing facility is to blame for everything wrong with Century stores, from their small sales volume and low earnings to their failure to beat the competition. Ask him what to do about it, and he'll tell you to make exorbitant capital expenditures. You'd think all other supermarkets have already done it—but that's not the case, he says. The whole thing's nothing but a wild notion he's got into his head. So I tried to impress on him that it was *not* Nissei's intention to turn Century into the best-rated supermarket in Japan. All we expected him to do was see to it that Century came up to par with average supermarkets such as Toto Stores or Kanto Stores."

"I see."

"But Nakasato's done extensive research, personally inspecting the food-processing facilities all over the country. He even drew up some remodeling plans of his own design: he specified that some cutting counters be reserved exclusively for pork and that meat and fish be carried on large aluminum trays rather than a conveyor belt to speed up the flow between different stages of the process. It goes to show what a hopeless case he is."

"To be sure, he sounds obsessed."

"If he keeps this up, he'll make himself useless as a shoshaman. I think we ought to do something to open his eyes before it's too late for him. Get him an overseas assignment, maybe? The sooner the better."

"I understand."

Inuzuka was not simpleminded enough to believe everything Natsukawa told him. To make his own judgment, he took pains to listen to what Nakasato had to say and went to the Century supermarkets to see for himself. As could be expected, however, he understood little. He did not think Nakasato was unbalanced, but neither did he consider the young man's idea to be as progressive as Nakasato seemed to believe. In the first place, Inuzuka was far from convinced that such remodeling, even assuming it went by Nakasato's specifications, would bring about any increase in Century's earnings.

Inuzuka decided to settle the matter once and for all. A trading company was unlikely to do a good job of running supermarkets and acting the part of butcher or fish vendor. Even at best, markets would contribute little to the shosha's overall trade volume. With cries of "Revolutionize consumer marketing!" trading companies had rushed to try their hands at supermarket operations. Some had been wise enough to drop it after a while. Nissei Corporation should do the same, and immediately, Inuzuka concluded.

Etched into his memory even now, fifteen years later, was the stunned expression that froze Nakasato's face as Inuzuka formally announced the withdrawal. Soon afterward he gave Nakasato his transfer notice and saw a look of madness come over his subordinate. Unhinged, unbalanced—such words flashed through Inuzuka's mind then. After Nakasato's move to Los Angeles, the young man went on to earn himself a high repute in marketing and sales. Nissei's share of Century Stores was sold at a decent price to its equal partner, Metropolitan Department Store. From Inuzuka's point of view, therefore, Nakasato and the supermarket were business matters that had been settled satisfactorily. As such they faded out of his mind before long. Now, touring the facilities of an ultramodern supermarket, Inuzuka experienced a moment of truth. How wrong he'd been.

The pride of the store's owner, his dance student, was one room that nearly equaled the entire sales area in floor space. Immaculate and odorfree, it hardly seemed like a place for dressing meat and fish. The room temperature was kept low enough to prevent the fresh food from spoiling during processing, and the employees washed their hands frequently as stipulated by the work rules. Clad in clean white coats, they carried on an assembly-line operation as efficiently as automobile factory workers building cars from parts passing along the conveyor belt.

This room exactly replicated the "modern food-processing plant" that Nakasato had advocated fifteen years earlier. Inuzuka's traumatic discovery spurred him to examine the consequences of his own judgment and policy decision from fifteen years ago.

He began by looking up his former colleagues, some of whom had already made senior management ranks. In the course of talking with these old associates, Inuzuka realized that the integrated trading companies were indeed in a tight spot, virtually closed out of the new consumer marketing field because of their traditional orientation toward distribution of materials and natural resources. In the economic climate commonly known as shosha winter, trading companies were desperately searching for new directions.

One former colleague, whether or not he knew Inuzuka's past assignment, contended that Nissei Corporation had made its greatest mistake when it sold Century Stores Inc.—after showing the foresight to set it up. Another asserted that what the shosha needed now was entrepreneurship: the employee mentality stood in the way of progress toward a brighter future. Only the type of man who made it his life's ambition to create a new business could help the shosha break out of the current impasse. But rare indeed was such a type among shoshamen—as witness most employees of Nissei Corporation who were settled in their ways, much too sensible and worldly wise.

The more Inuzuka listened to his old friends, the more convinced he became of his own mistake in the past. The realization took a great toll, self-confident as Inuzuka was. Until then he had been secure in the belief that all his decisions in the line of duty at Nissei had on the whole been fair and correct and that the company had fallen short of rewarding him properly for his contributions on the job.

Inuzuka was not a man to sit still or dawdle. Now that he knew he had made a grave mistake over Century Stores, he suspected that others lay buried within his impeccable past. So Inuzuka set out to pay another round of visits to his former associates. He followed up on the various business projects handled by his unit at Nissei to learn the consequences of his own decisions. His meticulous self-review eventually uncovered another serious mistake that had led to the downfall of a foodstuff wholesaler, Kijima Company. The failure included a human casualty—Nukaya, whose nervous breakdown in the aftermath ruined his business career.

Inuzuka commissioned a prominent artist among his dance students to paint two pictures. Bearing these works of art as valued gifts, he called on Nakasato and Nukaya at their respective homes.

.   .   .

"None of us has more than one life to live," Inuzuka commented with feeling. "How much value each of us puts on this one and only life, to make the most of it—that I think is the crucial question. Living in a competitive world as we do, we're obliged to fight hard. Once we confront our adversaries, we must do our best to knock them down. I never doubted that I'd done right by people who were my allies and associates. Now it turns out that I did great wrong—restraining the talents of my subordinates and causing them distress and despair, all with the best of intentions." Now Inuzuka addressed Nakasato and Nukaya. "I don't expect you to understand the full extent of my self-disgust, but it's so intense I can hardly bear it. Forgive me for imposing on you like this. I need to express my profound remorse and make restitution, even in a small measure."

Inuzuka would not resort to the histrionic gesture of prostrating himself on the floor. Instead, bracing both hands on his knees as he sat upright, he inclined his head slightly in an informal bow that nonetheless communicated the intensity of his emotion.

Involuntarily, Nakasato and Nukaya exchanged a look of astonishment.

"Inuzuka-san, there's no need for you to reproach yourself so severely," Nukaya said. "Kijima Company was done in by the oil crisis. At the time, no one could have foreseen such a drastic turn of events. It's just one of those things."

"Not necessarily. If I'd approved your proposal the first time you submitted it, the distribution centers would have been completed a few years before the oil crisis. Then they could have served as a bulwark against its shock waves. You may recall, the value of merchandise sitting in warehouses shot up overnight."

"Well, that's one way of looking at it but . . ." Nukaya made a stumbling effort to abate Inuzuka's self-recrimination.

"You needn't blame yourself on my account either." Nakasato took his turn to ease Inuzuka's mind. "I was sorry our supermarket operation folded the way it did—but at the time nothing guaranteed better results if I threw in my lot with Century Stores. In fact, my odds were no more than one or two in ten. To tell you the truth, I resented the fact you didn't study my proposal more carefully before reaching your decision. But speaking personally, the job transfer prompted a radical change of direction that helped my career course. Thanks to you, I went through the rite of passage on my tour of duty overseas and came back a full-fledged shoshaman."

"No, you had a greater life in store. You could have achieved a glory in the wider world far beyond a career success in Nissei Corporation, I believe."

"I agree with you on that point," Nukaya said. "But I don't think your mistaken decision was responsible for any change in his destiny. *No* senior manager at Nissei would have endorsed a continuation of the supermarket operation under the circumstances. So you, Inuzuka-san, have nothing to reproach yourself for. Aside from the question of blame, I agree: had Nakasato-san ventured into the supermarket business, he could have changed not only his own life but also the industry. The Nakasato of those days had tremendous energy and awesome conviction that showed me he was destined to make a lasting mark on the world—above and beyond the realm of Nissei's values."

"Easier said than done, you know." Even as Nakasato countered Nukaya, a sense of incongruity gripped him. How could he imagine any situation better than the one he had now?—a Nissei man secure in the strategic power base of the corporate hierarchy, with ambition to gain the highest post some day if chance favored him. Inuzuka and Nukaya's mental outlook seemed a bit out of focus. Both of them, curiously obsessed with values in some world outside Nissei. After all, nothing but the perspective of career dropouts—the sourgrape syndrome well known since Aesop's fox.

"That's right," Inuzuka said, breaking Nakasato's train of thought. "After the sight of the supermarket's meat room jolted me, I tried hard to recall everything you, Nakasato-san, said and did fifteen years ago. My memory was already vague, but I remembered how earnestly you asked for a transfer to Century Stores. 'You've got a lot to lose,' I pointed out to you. 'You gain nothing working yourself to the ground for a deficit-ridden subsidiary so far removed from Nissei's main operation. In the first place, I don't think your wife would like it. She married you believing she'd have an elaborate social life as the wife of an elite shoshaman with assignments abroad. She wouldn't be happy with her reduced status as the wife of a man who runs neighborhood supermarkets.' Do you remember how you answered that comment of mine?"

Nakasato hardly knew what to say. His answer to Inuzuka's unexpected question involved something of overwhelming importance to him in those days so long ago.

" 'If my wife fails to understand, I'll divorce her'—that's what you said straight out. You probably meant you had no use for a woman who couldn't understand what her husband considered his life's work. I don't think you remember it clearly: you weighed Century Stores and your wife on some kind of scale and unequivocally chose Century. Whether you could have carried out your plan is another matter entirely. But you did demonstrate your entrepreneurship. In my book, an entrepreneur is a leader without fear, who doesn't hesitate to sacrifice anything under the sun for the sake of saving his enterprise. At the time, however, I completely failed to understand you."

Maybe I made such a statement, Nakasato conceded to himself. But I meant something entirely different. All it proves is that I was seriously weighing the possibility of divorcing Rieko and marrying Masako.

"Inuzuka-san, I don't think you owe me any apologies for your past action," Nakasato said aloud. "But now I understand how you feel. Let's leave it at that. Tonight I'd like to enjoy your hospitality and eat this fabulous feast you arranged for us."

Nakasato tried to change the subject to keep his mind off the past, which threatened to open old wounds.

"No more serious talk, please," a soft voice suggested in response. A woman in a beautiful kimono entered the room and swept a radiant smile over the three men.

The instant he caught sight of her, Nakasato's heart skipped a beat. Here was a mirror image of Masako, the tall form and bobbed hair her exact double.

"The proprietor of this restaurant," Inuzuka informed his two guests.

"My name is Sakurako." The woman introduced herself.

On closer view, Nakasato perceived she was an elegant beauty, far more sophisticated than Masako.

What's the matter with me tonight, Nakasato chided himself behind a bitter smile as he felt a strange stirring in his heart.

4

The spring greens tossed in a Japanese dressing were refreshing to the taste. The soup base was incredibly thick and full-bodied. The shrimp and turbot sashimi arranged on a bed of crushed ice was an exquisite work of art. So Nukaya exclaimed his praise and joy at every dish of delicacies as it was set before them.

"Nakasato-san, I'll just have to write *Meals in Japanese Literature* next."

"You should," Nakasato chimed in but did not share Nukaya's enthusiasm. Here he goes again, was all he felt. Nakasato had heard Nukaya's story before but once and was not exactly bored with it. But it had released an undercurrent of antipathy in his heart.

Because of Nukaya's personal circumstances, Nakasato told himself, I ought to congratulate him for recovering enough to publish that book, *Meals in World Literature*. But if he lets it turn his head, if he thinks he accomplished something earthshaking, he's wrong. What can his book contribute to society anyway? One more trivial publication that's swallowed up before anyone notices. His writing got into print, that's all—no big deal by any standard. It means something only in a world of topsy-turvy values cherished by men no longer in the mainstream of society.

Nakasato was struggling to keep such thoughts from tumbling out of his mouth, when Inuzuka asked Nukaya, "What's that? Meals in literature?"

"Yes. Well, let me explain," Nukaya said, jumping at the opportunity to tell his story. The story of how he was on the brink of another nervous breakdown but his wife came to the rescue. . . Weary but duty-bound, Nakasato listened with half an ear. But Inuzuka took a lively interest, even interjecting suitable responses from time to time.

"How wonderful! That's great news!" Inuzuka exclaimed with particular emphasis when Nukaya announced the imminent publication of *Meals in World Literature*.

"Certainly!" Sakurako cried, beaming at Nuyaka, then glancing toward Nakasato as if expecting his assent. Nakasato forced a smile in return.

"Now then, let's celebrate your publication tonight."

"How marvelous!" Sakurako turned to Inuzuka. "But Sensei, isn't it customary to give a publication party after the book has come out?"

"Oh, well—in that case, we'll call this a precelebration. Make sure you let me know when the book is out, and I'll do you full honor with another dinner."

"We'll be at your service for that occasion, too," Sakurako put in.

Nakasato hid his mixed feelings behind a polite smile and sat silent as *Meals in World Literature* monopolized the conversation for some time.

"You did well to switch off your Nissei-only orientation. Now that's easy to say but very hard to do," Inuzuka said. Nukaya agreed wholeheartedly.

Just the sort of night to give me a nasty hangover, Nakasato thought as he went on drinking in silence. But the exchange between the other two showed no sign of slowing. Fearing he might not get another chance to broach a matter of greater importance, at last Nakasato made bold to cut in.

"By the way, Inuzuka-san, you went to New York City several months ago, didn't you?"

"What?" Inuzuka grunted, obviously perplexed. "Well, yes. I did."

"Did you go to see President Tobita of Nissei America?"

"I met Tobita all right. But that wasn't the purpose of my trip. My dance students in the New York area finally persuaded me to pay them a visit. It was good to see the city again after so long."

"New York City must be exciting," Nukaya sighed. In all his years with a trading company, he had never been to foreign countries. Somehow he had worked exclusively on domestic assignments, like many fellow employees of integrated trading companies, common belief to the contrary.

"Oh, you haven't seen America yet, Nukaya-san? When the royalties from *Meals in World Literature* start rolling in, you and your wife can tour the United States."

"No chance of such luck! My royalties will barely cover a weekend trip—to a nearby hot spring resort at most."

"Inuzuka-san," Nakasato interjected in a loud voice to steer the conversation back to his topic. "While you talked with President Tobita, did you by any chance mention my name? In connection with an American restaurant chain, perhaps?"

"Oh, that? Yes. I did. As a matter of fact, I told Tobita quite a lot about you."

"But how . . . ?"

"Tobita's seriously worried about the shosha's future prospects. Trading companies can't hope to survive much longer with the traditional policy of depending on commissions they earn as intermediaries in commercial transactions. As he sees it, now, while they still show profits, they should take measures to prepare for the future. So he proposed buying a restaurant chain—what was the name?—but he was frustrated. The shosha might be well-heeled, with funds to invest, but not with personnel to manage such a new venture. When he told me about it, you came immediately to my mind."

"Just what I thought."

"When I mentioned your name, Tobita didn't exactly get excited at first. He thought you were an *orthodox* Nissei man and wouldn't want to take on such a grubby job involving on-site work. I disagreed with him and insisted you were perfect for the project. 'He's a man with true entrepreneurship. In the past I failed to understand it and made a serious mistake,' I told him."

"What did President Tobita say to that?" Nakasato asked, his expression serious.

"He was surprised. 'I knew Nakasato was an elite shoshaman but never suspected he had so much gumption,' he said."

"What did he mean by gumption?"

"When I knew you, you were ready to give up glory in your own future for the sake of Century. You tried to renovate the meat-packing room with your own design—now fully vindicated. That is, you had everything an entrepreneur needed except the opportunity. That was snatched from you. I explained all that to Tobita."

"Thank you for a vote of confidence. But all that happened fifteen years ago. As for entrepreneurship . . . ," Nakasato began with deference but changed his tone in midsentence: "To be frank, Inuzuka-san, your presumption greatly inconveniences me. You're meddling not only in my life but also in the policy-making process of Nissei Corporation, when your talk influences the shaping of our downstream operation plan, for example. In fact, shoshamen have no idea what it means to start up an enterprise. Their idea of doing business is limited to support for enterprises that someone else built up: help in the procurement of raw materials and the sale of their products, financing when needed, and things like that. But these activities take up very little of all the business conducted in Japan—they amount to no more than 1 or 2 percent at most. What I'm referring to here is the shosha's margin of profit on sales. Yet the majority of shoshamen live under the misconception that they know all there is to know about business. Judging the elephant by its tail, I'd say. With all due respect, Inuzuka-san, I must say your perspective is not much better."

No doubt startled by the trenchant tone in which Nakasato began, Inuzuka and Nukaya had stopped drinking to pay him full attention. Her kimono-clad back upright and eyes downcast, Sakurako listened as well.

"The other 98 to 99 percent of business—the elephant's head, trunk, and body, say—is made up of critical activities like decisions on capital expenditures, ongoing intensive technological research, development of new products and distribution channels, and advanced marketing strategies. The production site is part of this larger picture. Unfortunately, shoshamen have no real understanding of such concepts as IE [industrial engineering], QC [quality control], and Toyota's famous *"Just-in-time"* Flow-card [supply of parts] System, because these have no direct bearing on the shosha's operation. How ironic, that precisely because the shosha deals in the widest possible range of products and commodities, shoshamen never come to grips with the inner workings of any specific industry. Yet most shoshamen are unaware of their own limitations."

Nakasato paused for a few moments but no one else made a sound.

"So they busy themselves with discussion of 'new businesses' and 'downstream' operations. They believe the tail is the elephant itself and plan to turn the shosha into one. Then someone like you comes along to fire them up. You probably mean well—but you stir up a lot of trouble," Nakasato said without mincing words.

Momentarily bewildered, Inuzuka blinked his eyes. He said mildly, "Forgive me if this sounds like quibbling. But you made yourself so knowledgeable in the area where most shoshamen are ignorant. You studied up on the issues you just explained to us. Don't you think all this proves my point, that you *are* uniquely qualified to lead a new business venture? I think it does."

"Knowing and doing are altogether different. Even if I'd been assigned to Century Stores fifteen years ago, for example, I couldn't have accomplished much. Worse yet, my brainstorm might have sent Century deeper into the red and done even more serious damage to Nissei. No telling what would have become of me then."

"I think things would have worked out absolutely fine."

"How can you use a term like 'absolutely'?"

"Well, that's . . . ," Inuzuka started an explanation but then smiled vaguely and fell silent.

"I beg your pardon, but isn't this exactly the same dogmatic and superior attitude that led you to make a number of mistakes you now feel compelled to apologize for? I have no reason to accept your gift and plan to return it. If you're really serious about making amends, I'd rather you changed your attitude. *That* would be the best restitution."

"Oh, no. I didn't mean to meddle in your life. But I beg you, keep the painting anyway. If it bothers you that much, please just consider it left in your keeping for the time being."

Matters between Nakasato and Inuzuka threatened to become more strained. Nukaya rushed in to arbitrate. "I'm afraid, Inuzuka-san, that you're causing Nakasato-san more trouble now than you ever did in the past. He's not the man you knew long ago. Today he's a gilt-edged stock, an acknowledged contender for Nissei's presidency. It's not fair to ask him to give up his career for an American restaurant chain."

Though Nakasato was well aware of his standing in the company, he was embarrassed to hear it put so explicitly.

For several moments Inuzuka looked as if he had trouble adjusting his mental focus. "I see. Nakasato-san has changed," he said after a while. His voice revealed deep emotion. "He's made Nissei Corporation his whole world."

Nakasato felt a bitter objection well up in his heart but held his tongue. Nothing to be gained by arguing with someone whose values were alien to his own.

"Oh, Nakasato-san, I had no idea. I shouldn't have intruded." Inuzuka shook his head in self-reproach. Then his expression cleared.

"Sakurako-san," he said, "will you dance for us? I seem to be a hopeless case—always bungling, stirring up trouble for other people. Now I'd like you to regale my guests with a beautiful dance to make them feel better."

"Great idea! Please do it for us." Nukaya pleaded with a note of relief in his voice.

"I haven't had a chance to dance for some time." Sakurako drew her alluring smile into a stage expression. "I can't seem to remember anything."

"How about 'Black Hair'?"

"Well, I might be able to manage that one. But I'm not good enough to perform for your important guests."

"I know that. So stop worrying and just do it."

"How mean! I may be a poor student, but you're a dreadful teacher, to say 'I know you're no good at it but dance anyway'!"

"I'd say so too," Nukaya said. "But please, dance for us, I beg you."

One of the waitresses sent for a samisen and plucked on its three strings as she sang:

My thoughts, tangled like black hair,
Came loose in the night
On a pillow I shared with no one.

As Sakurako began to dance, her body took on a resolute line and at the same time a more seductive charm. The fluid movement of her hand pulled an invisible comb through the long hair, charged with the sadness of a woman alone. The arabesque pattern of light and shadow that etched the line of her slender jaw against the straight black hair epitomized femininity in all its corporeality.

Masako. The sensation of a woman's physical presence came back to Nakasato from the past. Unaccountably, small tangible pleasures associated with Masako returned to his senses in random order. Masako's supple body, in his memory, overlapped with the body of Sakurako dancing before him now.

> Gone is night's dream this morning.
> How sweet, how dear! All this pining.
> Unnoticed, the snow deepens.

The music and the liquor allowed Nakasato's heart to drift in a realm of fantasy far beyond the real world. For some reason, he was back in a shabby hotel room where they held their study sessions twice a week over three years.

"Marvelous! Just great," Nukaya's voice cut in, bringing Nakasato back to reality. "What's this song?"

"It's a *nagauta,* a sort of feminine ballad," Inuzuka explained. "This one sings of the sadness of a woman who sleeps alone, her resentment, and her longing for the man she cannot stop loving. By the time she realizes, her blue-black hair has turned white."

"Ah, the deepening snow refers to gray hair, then. Amazing! I wish a woman loved me so much! To keep on loving until her hair goes gray. Stupendous! Don't you agree, Nakasato-san?"

"Yes. I envy her lover," Nakasato said aloud to Nukaya. But in his heart was the awareness, I was once loved like that. Why did Masako disappear so abruptly? Where is she now? Doing what? Barring an unlikely accident or illness, she has to be alive at this very moment, somewhere, somehow.

"Sensei is my savior," Sakurako was saying.

As Nakasato awoke from his reverie, Nukaya seemed eagerly attentive. His own mind totally occupied with memories of the distant past, Nakasato had not been following the conversation. Apparently Sakurako was into the story of her life now.

The only child born to the family that owned a venerable Japanese restaurant, Sakurako despised the hereditary business. She went to the United States in her junior year of college, determined never to return to Japan. Things happened to her in America, she said, with a tantalizingly suggestive smile, and she was going through a bad time when an American friend introduced her to Inuzuka. The friend happened to be taking lessons from Inuzuka, who was assigned to Nissei's San Francisco office and taught classical Japanese dance for relaxation. Before long Sakurako too became Inuzuka's student.

"I hated Japan. I revolted against Japanese cities, Japanese culture, and the Japanese people who created them—everything about my country. So I wanted to turn my back on Japan. But after I went to the United States I realized I could never turn into a true American, no matter how hard I tried. The way things were going, I was headed for disaster when I met Sensei. He brought me back to Japan. He saved me."

"What are you doing now? Rehashing a twenty-year-old story, no less," Inuzuka laughed.

A curious counterpoint, Nakasato thought: Sakurako failed in her attempt to leave Japan and was saved by Inuzuka. I tried to leave Nissei Corporation and was stopped by Inuzuka. He seems to have a strange knack of showing up at a turning point in other people's lives.

Sakurako still speaking.

Nukaya's and Inuzuka's voices interposed.

Nukaya and his *Meals in World Literature* again.

Inuzuka talking about his divorce.

"Remarried?" Nukaya asked.

"I have no intention of marrying again," Inuzuka said.

"Well now, you're really celebrating, aren't you! Make sure you don't catch cold." The waitress's voice seemed to come from far away.

"No problem," Nakasato said as he came to and staggered to his feet.

"Where are you going?" the waitress asked, again as if speaking from a distance.

"Washroom."

"Oh, it's in the other direction."

His legs felt wobbly. "No problem."

Nakasato remembered nothing after that.

.   .   .

When next he woke, he found himself in a car. He heard a door open and close, and the loud voices of Inuzuka and Nukaya.

"I'll see Nakasato-san home, so don't worry," Nukaya said. Inuzuka must have just climbed out of the car.

Should I sit up and say good-bye to him? Nakasato wondered but made no move. His befuddled head was reeling, and his body felt like a dead weight. Soon the car began to move. It rocked back and forth to negotiate a U-turn in the narrow alleyway. A wheel hit something, and the chauffeur grunted.

"All right, all right," yelled Nukaya, guiding the chauffeur. Now in the back seat next to Nakasato, he had his head out the window checking the rear of the car.

"What's all this commotion?" Nakasato sat up and looked out.

Through the window his upturned eyes caught sight of Inuzuka's back retreating into the night. Despite the narrowness of the alley, the two-storied house at its end had an imposing facade. The front door was open, and Nakasato could see into the entrance hall. A woman put her arms around Inuzuka to help him inside. She lifted her face and peered into the darkness toward the car.

"Masako."

No sooner did Nakasato whisper the name than the car pulled out. The alley passed from his field of vision within seconds.

"What's the matter, Nakasato-san? If you don't feel well, I'll stop the car."

"Are you all right?" the chauffeur asked, stepping on the brake pedal.

"Who was that?"

"Who do you mean?" Nukaya seemed perplexed.

"I wonder if it was Inuzuka's wife."

"Was anyone else back there?" Nukaya wasn't even aware a woman had come out to the front door.

"She was taking Inuzuka inside."

"Probably a relative. Maybe a maid."

"Masako can't be . . ."

"Someone you know?"

"No . . . just a resemblance."

"Nakasato-san, you must have been dreaming. You were bewitched by the 'Black Hair' dance or something," Nukaya laughed cheerfully.

Listening to his laughter, Nakasato began to dismiss the scene he had just witnessed as a dream. That was his last thought before he slipped back into insensibility.

FOUR

Lost Years

April

1

The day after the dinner with Inuzuka, Nakasato received a telex from New York City. Kano reported that Nissei America had opened formal negotiations with Griffin Securities to purchase American Gourmet Company. Nissei Corporation in Tokyo had twelve weeks to make the final decision. The offer would expire with the deadline.

"Griffin initially insisted on six weeks, but we won a major concession by explaining our need for intensive deliberations. Nissei America will submit a proposal within a week outlining our recommendation. Please expedite its processing at your end." Kano closed his telexed message with a request.

Drag it into early July, and the plan will die a natural death, Nakasato calculated in his mind. He could wait until the last minute to set up a situation in which some critical study would be found still pending. Of course, he must make certain not to be held personally responsible for the delay.—We tried our utmost to make the deadline, but in the course of our investigation we uncovered certain matters of grave concern. A new probe is under way but conclusive results cannot be expected in time. So would run an ideal scenario.

But it could backfire. Experienced hand that he was, Kano might very well manage to negotiate an extension of the deadline with Griffin Securities. Not only that, Nakasato would not put it past

Kano to play safe by misrepresenting the original terms. Suppose Kano had wrangled a much longer lead time and was keeping several weeks up his sleeve just to be on the safe side? If he'd been astute enough to draw a correct inference from his observation of Nakasato's reaction in New York, perhaps he anticipated Nakasato's covert scheme to kill the acquisition plan with procrastination tactics. It was entirely possible for Kano to have taken effective countermeasures to nullify Nakasato's effort. All the more reason why Nakasato must deploy multilevel safety devices regardless of the deadline Kano reported.

For the present, Nakasato telexed his reply to New York: "Studying the case with painstaking care. Twelve weeks you secured fall short of our need. To accommodate scheduled date of our managing directors' meeting, please make effort to extend till end of August at least."

This might get Kano to show his hand, thought Nakasato. Or it serves another purpose—it diverts responsibility from me when the time comes to drop the case by reason of insufficient investigation. This telex proves that at the outset I foresaw the lack of adequate study time.

Nakasato sent a young woman clerk to the telex room with the message. Relaxing in the departmental chief's chair he occupied by right, Nakasato leaned back and closed his eyes. His intent was to go over the strategic steps in his plan to scuttle the American Gourmet acquisition plan and check for potential weak spots. But his mind refused to obey his will.

It was Hozumi Masako's image that his mind conjured up instead. I thought I saw Masako in the entryway of Inuzuka's house last night, but was it a hallucination? I was drunk enough to hallucinate all right. But isn't it strange I remember it so clearly now? Her hair looked somewhat shorter, but still straight and bobbed just as in the old days. Night vision or not, I swear I saw Masako's face. The figure was hers, too. And yet . . . the fact that my visual memory is so vivid means just as likely the whole thing was an illusion. Come to think of it, it's not possible to get a clear sight of someone at such a distance so late at night. In less than one second of real time, to boot. The relief he derived from such rational explanation was mixed with a strange sense of disappointment.

Nakasato switched his mental focus back to American Gourmet. I ought to review Kano's proposal for starters. Acquisition of a company is a big enough project to contain any number of potential problems. In checking out each and every one, I'll need to go to America once or twice. Twelve weeks will fly by in no time at all. No, no doubt about it. It had to be Masako.

Again, Masako was crowding American Gourmet out of his head. Anyway, what *is* Masako doing in Inuzuka's house? If she's not a figment of my imagination, there has to be a good explanation. Maybe I was betrayed. Fifteen years ago, when she suddenly stopped writing to me, she might have been already involved with Inuzuka. Cold blue flames of jealousy flared up in Nakasato's heart over the love so long forgotten. No, absolutely impossible. Must have been my imagination, he told himself. At the end of his circuitous self-debate, Nakasato arrived at a sort of conclusion: no use puzzling over it; why not verify it?

Yet for two days Nakasato hesitated to act on his own recommendation. So what if it was Masako? No need for me to verify the fact. What's the good of meeting her again at this late date? A woman from my past reappears, involved with another man into the bargain. Things could get messy. If I poke my nose where it doesn't belong, I might end up hurting my social standing. I'd better keep my emotions under control and forget about checking whether or not it was Masako.

After all the vacillation, Nakasato succumbed to his impulse in the early afternoon of the third day. He closeted himself in the reception room at the office and picked up the telephone receiver.

2

The bell rang at the other end of the line. Holding his breath, Nakasato waited for someone to come to the phone.

If Inuzuka answers, I'll hang up without a word. Nakasato braced himself. Such an action would go against the grain. Nakasato had vigorously denounced rude and inconsiderate callers who hung up when someone other than the intended party answered the call. As a matter of fact, such behavior was typical of office lovers and all the more irritating for occurring at work. Be that as it may, fully prepared this day to commit the unpardonable breach of manners if necessary, Nakasato had dialed Inuzuka's number.

"Hello. This is the Inuzuka residence," said a slightly husky female voice.

Masako? Could be, but he was not certain.

"Hello, hello, Inuzuka . . ."

"Miss Hozumi?" Nakasato lowered his voice but spoke distinctly. If it was really Masako, he should be able to tell by her reaction. He refrained from calling out her first name, as he quickly reasoned that could cause Masako trouble, depending on her circumstances.

"Well . . ." The female voice paused on the line. Nakasato's heart skipped a beat as if in synchrony with the voice. He readied himself to hang up the minute it proved to be someone else.

"Miss Hozumi is at the office."

"What?" Nakasato cried out in surprise. "Office? You mean Nissei Corporation?"

It really was Masako the other night! His doubtful conjecture had been right on the mark. Nakasato was badly shaken. Even as his reason denied the connection as preposterous, his habitual mental association of Masako with Nissei made him blurt out the company's name.

"What's that?" The woman on the phone sounded perplexed.

"No . . . well . . . it's nothing. Can you give me the phone number of Miss Hozumi's office?"

"May I ask who is asking?"

"My name is Yamada. A friend from student days."

"Oh, you are?" After hesitating for a few seconds, she gave him a number. Its exchange indicated the Shinjuku district.

Only after he had put down the receiver did his heart feel the full impact of the unexpected discovery.

Masako is alive! It *was* Masako just as I thought. And at Inuzuka's house, of all places . . . What in the world does this mean?

What's the implication of Masako being in Inuzuka's house? Inuzuka said he had no intention of remarrying. Was he lying? Or are they merely living together without the formality of marriage? If so, she threw herself into the arms of the same man who'd torn her from her lover. Did Inuzuka by any chance scheme to send me off to an overseas post in order to take Masako for himself?

Nakasato tried hard to recall the sequence of events of the distant past. His speculation would hold up only if Inuzuka had been aware of the relationship between Nakasato and Masako at the time. Highly improbable.

What about the possibility that Masako had already been carrying on with Inuzuka? Absolutely none. There had been no lie in her frenzied cry, "I can't live without you!"

Inuzuka and Masako must have started their relationship after my transfer to Los Angeles. Then does Inuzuka know about my past affair with Masako? She could have told him about me. If so, when Inuzuka looked me up after all these years, was he apologizing in his mind about Masako as well as the Century Stores incident? But then—whatever made him pay a visit to Nukaya as well?

For some time Nakasato mulled over various possibilities. Hot anger surged through him at the thought that Inuzuka might have sent him out of the country to snatch Masako from him. The memories of their rendezvous carried a curiously bittersweet taste. At every turn of his mind, confusing emotions and sensations bombarded and unsettled him.

What frightened him was the unlikely but conceivable possibility that Inuzuka knew of his affair with Masako. Should Inuzuka happen to mention it to a former colleague, the secret might well reach the ear of President Ebisawa. Old as the story was, it could do him considerable harm on his way to senior management, which he expected to reach in the next several years. In the face of such danger, he doubted the wisdom of involving himself further. But in the end his desire to see Masako once more, if only to learn the truth, won over his prudence.

Picking up the reception-room telephone again, Nakasato dialed the number he had just obtained.

"Hello, this is M. Hozumi."

Nakasato failed to catch the company name, which sounded like a foreign word to him.

"Hello, I wonder if you have a Hozumi Masako there . . ."

"Oh, Hozumi, you mean our president?"

"No, no, I mean Miss Hozumi, Hozumi Masako."

"Yes, Hozumi Masako is our president. May I ask who is calling?"

"Well . . . my name is Nakasato."

"Please hold a moment."

Seconds ticked away as Nakasato waited.

Listening to the monotonous tune that took over the line, Nakasato felt his head would explode. President? What kind of company? Masako the president? Must be a small operation. However small this company may be, it's got at least two people working, counting the woman who answered the phone. Irrelevant thoughts flicked through his confused mind.

"Hozumi speaking."

"This is Nakasato. Can you tell?"

"Michio-san . . ." He heard the voice at the other end of the line break. "It's been a long time."

"I understand you are the president. What's the name of your company?"

"M. Hozumi, with my initial."

"Oh, is that it? Then it's your own company?"

"Just a tiny one."

"Even so, I'm impressed. Anyway, I can hardly believe I'm actually talking with you like this. If it wouldn't inconvenience you too much, I'd like to see you in person," Nakasato asked straight out, unable to contain his elation.

"Well . . . ," Masako faltered, thinking. "Yes. I've been prepared for this moment ever since Inuzuka decided to pay you a visit. But I didn't think you noticed me the other night from inside the car, at such a distance. Well, I'll be happy to meet you over dinner." Masako spoke as if choosing every word with care and suggested the lobby of an elegant hotel in Shinjuku. They agreed to meet there three days later, when both expected to be free.

"By the way, what's your company's line of business?"

"It's a chain of dress shops."

"Aha! That's it!" Nakasato exclaimed. "You've done it, haven't you? You made your dream come true after all!"

"I'm having a tough time trying to make it profitable, though."

"What's the name of your stores?"

"M. Hozumi, the same as the company name."

"I see, I see. That's how it is . . . ," Nakasato kept repeating himself. The next words stuck in his throat for a moment. "I'll be looking forward to seeing you."

For some time after Nakasato put down the receiver, his heart continued to pound and throb. He could scarcely believe he'd just heard Masako's voice. A shade deeper than he remembered, and the manner of speech crisp and businesslike as befit a woman executive, but the voice was unmistakably hers.

Not even in his wildest dreams had he imagined her president of a chain of dress shops. Hindsight told him it was a natural culmination of her staunch determination. But even after hearing it from Masako herself, he could hardly digest the fact that she had managed to realize such a fantastic ambition.

Nakasato investigated the status of M. Hozumi Inc.—this sort of research and investigation being the forte of sogo shoshas, Nakasato gathered the hard data in short order. M. Hozumi's figures made Nakasato gasp aloud in astonishment and admiration: capital—60 million yen; annual sales volume—8.5 billion yen; employees—284; number of stores—35.

Since its stock was unlisted, Nakasato had no way of ascertaining the profits, but the earnings reported on its tax return had been rising steadily to reach 300 million yen the previous year. Aside from Hozumi Masako, the president, there were several women on the board of directors. And on the list of their outside directors was the name of Inuzuka Keigoro.

Nakasato called the head of Nissei's textile goods department and quizzed him about M. Hozumi Inc.

"The company has no direct dealings with Nissei, but it has a respectable standing among the fashion apparel chains. M. Hozumi shops occupy strategic locations in department stores and rail station buildings. Apparently it's headed by someone who used to work for us."

"So I hear."

"Several years ago a staff member in my department noticed it and went over to negotiate business."

"And?"

"He was practically kicked out."

"What happened?"

" 'You have no capabilities for product development. In the first place we have no use for a department with a name like Textile Goods'—that's how our staffer was told off. 'What M. Hozumi Inc.

sells is apparel, not textile. Sogo shosha seems to have a particular fondness for the term textile. But that kind of material-oriented thinking gets you nowhere in retail marketing of consumer goods,' she lectured him. A formidable lady indeed.''

Nakasato tried to readjust the image of Masako in his memory to fit the woman entrepreneur capable of making such statements: my Masako, so hard and outspoken now? Not likely, he wanted to say. But at the same time he felt that such a transformation had of necessity come to his Masako.

Nakasato gave free rein to his imagination but soon realized the futility of indulging in conjecture. His dreams contained no other important values in life beside being a Nissei man on his way up the corporate ladder. Nakasato could imagine neither Masako's past nor her present as president of a chain of stores. Might as well stop wasting my time in useless conjecture, he told himself. Yet his heart rebelled. He compounded the folly many times over before the day came for him to meet with Masako, by wasting his energy in this oddly exhilarating mental exercise.

3

Bemused, Nakasato gazed at Masako across their table at the window of an exclusive restaurant with elegant pink and white decor. Outside the window of the hotel's top floor sprawled Tokyo's nighttime panorama.

Masako wore a simple outfit, a fawn-colored jacket with tan stripes and black slacks. It set off her fair complexion and the contours of her face. She wore her hair straight as before but much shorter now. Over a dark gray knit blouse beneath her jacket was a silver pendant shaped like a pair of boats.

At first its significance escaped Nakasato. Have I seen it somewhere before, he was vaguely wondering when recognition hit him— yes, I gave it to her, on the day of our parting! As a reflex he reached for his tie. The opal pin Masako had given him was no longer there. He had lost it so long ago that he could not recall when, where, or how. But Masako had not forgotten—she came wearing his gift this evening. The realization disconcerted Nakasato.

Masako looked no different. Or a bit more mature and self-confident? But she was too unchanged in appearance for his comfort.

After all his mental preparation, he found himself without a proper opening remark for the occasion. He need not have worried. When the time came, their greeting went as smoothly as between friends parted for a few days.

Saving him the necessity to ask her plan, Masako said, "You don't mind the restaurant here, do you?" She led him toward the elevator with the unthinking ease of habit.

"It's too much trouble looking for new places all the time, so I've taken out a club membership in this hotel. I do most of my entertaining here," she informed Nakasato with a smile. True to her words, she was so well known in the restaurant that the sommelier said, "May we serve you a Châteauneuf-du-Pape, which you enjoyed so much last time?"

"What wine would you prefer?" Masako asked Nakasato. He had no idea. Nukaya, the author of *Meals in World Literature,* would have risen to the occasion, but Nakasato's knowledge was limited to Beaujolais for red or Chablis for white. He was obliged to leave the selection up to Masako.

"Well, that's rather strong, but my guest tonight is a heroic drinker. It will suit him, I think," Masako said to the wine steward, smiling.

Neither Nakasato nor Masako was eager to touch on their past, and the conversation dwelt mostly on her business. In talking about herself she did not sound boastful, for her manner of speech was modest and her perspective detached. But it soon became clear to him that Masako had achieved a far greater success in her business than he had ever anticipated. Every casual reference she made in passing confirmed his observation.

"All day long I do nothing but meet people. Busy means your heart is dying, they say. It's true. It takes so much effort just to live without losing myself."

Masako's days seemed packed to the brim. Apparently she went abroad several times a year to buy merchandise or consult with designers affiliated with her firm.

"You're a spectacular success. I never doubted you'd succeed, but I'm really astonished to learn how well you've done. Congratulations! I could never praise you enough even with hundreds of toasts. After all these years, I'm still the same businessman working for a salary, a mere hired hand. I didn't have the gumption to take a chance and go on my own as you did. A man gets nowhere, probably because his job anchors him. By comparison, a woman travels light, you might say."

"Light? On the contrary, I was heavy."

"Oh? . . ." The significance of her comment eluded him, but he took it as sarcasm. "Oh, I'm sorry. I chose the wrong word. I don't doubt you mustered up tremendous courage to do it. I was just generalizing, on male-female differences."

"I mean I was actually heavy."

Perceiving the seriousness behind her tone, Nakasato studied her face.

"Heavy. No. Surely you can't mean . . . ?"

"Yes, exactly. I was heavy with child."

Nakasato put down a piece of French bread he was tearing off. He went rigid, his mouth open slightly in incredulity.

"Mine, you mean?"

"Yes, of course."

He could hardly believe his ears.

"Why didn't you let me know?"

"What good would it have done?"

There was nothing he could say to that. Masako was absolutely right. The best Nakasato could have done at that time was send her money from America to cover the cost of an abortion. Or perhaps not. Even so little might have been impossible to manage out of the fixed allowance disbursed by his wife.

"I see. Ignorance is no excuse, is it? I caused you great suffering. I burdened you with so much hardship, not only emotional but even physical hardship. Truly, I am sorry."

Nakasato repeated his apology many times, interspersed with sighs.

Suddenly a question surfaced in his mind. It had been nearly half a year after his transfer to Los Angeles that Masako cut off contact with him. She quit her job at about the same time. Then did she have the abortion while still working at Nissei Corporation?

"When did you have your abortion? By the time you left Nissei, it would have been too late to get one."

"I had no abortion," Masako said calmly. "I had the baby."

Nakasato heard her words distinctly, but they failed to convey any meaning. He fought an odd sensation of unreality. He remained silent for some time, trying to sort out his thoughts.

"Had the baby? Mine?"

"Yes," Masako said, perfectly composed.

"When?" Nakasato's heart began to beat violently.

"On the two-hundred-and-sixty-fifth day after our last meeting. I made a precise count."

"Wait a minute, is this real? You're not joking by any chance, are you?"

"I wouldn't joke about something like this."

His heart raced faster and faster. He found it hard to breathe. The dinner was forgotten.

"And what's become of the baby? Boy or girl?"

"A boy. He starts high school next year."

"Starts high school . . . then, in middle school now?"

In his astonishment, all he could manage was simple subtraction: before entering high school a child would go through middle school.

"Can't believe it," Nakasato mumbled and burst out laughing. Later, he puzzled over the psychological reason for such absurd behavior. But for the moment he just laughed and laughed. A long series of unrelated facts and ideas passed in front of his mind's eye. Images surfaced out of the past in random order. Some blazed, some gleamed modestly. The tour of Century stores together. Masako in the whiskey bar earnestly asking him questions. The twice-weekly sessions making love and studying. The discreet hotel entrance in the alleyway of a residential district. Masako speaks passionately of the fashion apparel business. Along with her dream, his own dream of running a supermarket chain grows and expands. So does the agony of being left suspended between hope and despair by an evasive superior.

A part of his mind remained lucid. He calculated. This child must have been conceived that night we made love for the last time. He was born and grew up—living right here in Tokyo at this very moment. Which of his parents does he take after? If he looks anything like me, does he also resemble my other children by Rieko? Or is he the image of Masako? Where do I stand now? Am I safe or am I in danger? I don't understand.

"Can't believe it." Aloud Nakasato repeated the phrase, which brought back the same sense of incongruity. The irony of it all! All the while he'd figured he was steering his own life on a neatly calculated course, but somehow he came out wide of the mark. Time had bypassed him. People who had crossed paths with him apparently kept right on living their own lives without him. Underlying Nakasato's laughter was a feeling of futility and impotence. It was bewildering to be so enmeshed in a situation over which he had no control whatsoever.

Waiting until Nakasato's agitation abated somewhat, Masako began to tell him about her life since they parted.

4

Masako discovered her pregnancy soon after Nakasato left for New York. She drafted a letter to report it to Nakasato, but no sooner did she finish pouring her heart out than a sober realization chilled her—this was one letter she could never mail: once she notified Nakasato, she must bear and raise the baby as his child. But how could she do that? Known as the father of an illegitimate child by a woman from the office, he would have no future left at Nissei Corporation. Masako's pride would never let her ask him to get a divorce. One taboo she had imposed on herself as she grew involved with Nakasato was against breaking up his home.

She tore up the letter he would never see and wept. Why consult anyone? There was no point. The only advice she could expect under the circumstances would be to get an abortion. So she did not even confide in her parents. She was determined to have the baby.

She hadn't the foggiest idea what becoming a single mother would entail. One thing was certain, however. It meant giving up her chance for a decent marriage with someone else. This prospect hardly bothered Masako, for Nakasato was the only man on earth in her eyes at that time. Weighing heavily on her mind was a financial problem far more real and urgent—how could she manage the expense of having the baby and bringing it up by herself? No doubt Nissei Corporation would do everything to get rid of an undesirable employee so reeking of immorality as a single mother. Masako had no intention of keeping her unchallenging job amid hostile stares merely to make a living. But where, then, could she find an alternate source of income?

The only key to the problem was her own ambition to run a dress shop. Masako worked out a desperate plan of action.

I'll stay on at Nissei until my condition becomes noticeable, several months more. In the meantime I'll use whatever connections I can find to raise funds and prepare myself. It won't be easy to get a dress shop of my own right off. After the baby is born, I'll go out to work at someone else's shop to pick up on-the-job training and professional knowledge that will stand me in good stead when I start my own business. But what to do with my baby? Well, unfilial or not, I have no choice but to impose on my mother to take care of the baby after weaning. One imperative, therefore, is to complete preparations for opening my own store before my mother gets too old to babysit.

What if all fails? In that case, I'll just kill myself. Life is no more than a dream, after all—from nothing to nothing. Even the love with Nakasato that had seemed so fierce and strong took no greater force than a transfer order to wipe out. Everything is meant to die anyway. When all hope is lost, best to give in with good grace and accept my end—a bit early. Alone in her room at night, Masako thought such thoughts and shivered in horror.

She wasted no time in securing introductions to a number of dress shops through clothing wholesalers doing business with her father. But it soon became clear they had no use for a woman in her midtwenties with no sales experience beyond helping occasionally in the family store. The most they would offer, if anything, was a part-time position as helper. Masako's plan stalled at the outset. At that rate, to raise a fatherless child on her own seemed hopeless.

Before long her colleagues at the office began to ask, "Haven't you put on some weight lately?" It was time for her to resign. She handed in her notice.

One afternoon, with less than a week left on the job, she fainted at the office. Earlier in the day she had hemorrhaged and planned to take a half-day off to see a doctor. As she rose from her chair to run some last-minute errand, she fell unconscious. She revived in Nissei's clinic in the same building. A threat of premature childbirth, she was told—she was under too much stress even for the most stable phase of pregnancy. Fortunately the attending physician's expeditious care prevented a mishap, but the incident betrayed her condition to her superiors and her parents. Her parents were aghast, but it was already too late for an abortion. At this juncture Inuzuka began to play an active part in Masako's private life.

The incident occurred during Inuzuka's brief stint as general manager of two departments, to one of which Masako belonged. Apparently he took it very hard when he learned that Masako, who had been in his charge once before in the Transportation Department, was about to become an unwed mother. She kept her silence, but he obviously believed the baby's father was a Nissei man, a subordinate of his from one of the three departments. It had to be a man with family, Inuzuka reasoned. If her lover were single, he, Inuzuka, could help get them married. Were the man childless, let him get a divorce and take his responsibility. So, involved with a family man, Masako had no choice but to bear an illegitimate baby. Driven by sympathy for Masako and anger at the faithless man, Inuzuka offered her help and moral support with such sincerity that for a while Masako's mother suspected he was the guilty party.

Masako quit Nissei Corporation and gave birth to a baby boy, whom she named Michio after Nakasato Michio. By the time she was ready to go back to work, it was Inuzuka who referred her to a prospective employer.

"One of my college classmates is senior managing director of a company that specializes in developing shopping centers. I asked him to find something for you, and he made contact with a fashion apparel store in the specialty-shops building in Shinjuku. Would you like to consider it?"

Gratefully accepting Inuzuka's reference given over the telephone, Masako decided to work in the store. Not that she took a job with them. Rather, she rented some 180 square feet of corner space to sell her own selection of merchandise. She was to pay 15 percent of her revenue to the store's owner, keeping the rest as her earnings.

Leaving the two-year-old Michio in her mother's care, Masako threw herself body and soul into her work. She ran from wholesaler to wholesaler to buy dresses and tended her counters to sell them. After closing time every day, she went over the sales slips to record the items sold and studied the files to determine what merchandise to stock next. One year later, her revenue from the modest corner amounted to fully half the total sales volume of the store, which had 1,080 square feet of floor space in all. In other words, she generated half the trade volume from her sixth of the space.

"Masa-chan has the best location in the store," complained the other saleswomen jealously. And the owner, apparently agreeing with them, reassigned her to a different corner. But in consequence her sales shot up instead of falling, the 108 extra square feet more than compensating for the less favorable new location.

Masako did make her share of mistakes, however. Once she was obliged to sell off her overstock at end-of-season bargain prices and took a loss roughly equivalent to her profits from two months of normal sales. Another time she went out of her way to stock dresses in a particular season's most popular colors only to end up apologizing to customers who complained of the poor quality of tailoring. But Masako's exceptional ability to memorize the names and faces of all her customers worked a miracle in public relations. In the crowded Shinjuku Station Building, she recognized a passerby and caught up with her to ask, "How did the dress you bought the other day work out?" The middle-aged woman was so moved that she not only became a steady customer but also brought many of her friends to Masako's place.

Two and a half years later she enjoyed an unanticipated turn of fortune. The fashion apparel store from which Masako was renting a corner collapsed through incompetent management. This incident propelled Masako toward her cherished goal. The owner of the specialty-shops building—who had heard of Masako's impressive sales record—invited her to open her own business in the space just vacated by the fashion apparel shop.

Masako did not hesitate to accept the offer. As a matter of fact, she practically jumped at it. But she needed more funds to cover the security deposit and the cost of remodeling, even though the landlord went out of his way to give her extremely generous terms. To borrow money, she made the rounds of acquaintances, among them Inuzuka. He had watched over her in the past, dropping in at her corner from time to time to make sure she was all right. Now in response to her appeal for help, he not only lent her a sizable amount of money but even put his name down as a guarantor for her bank loan.

"I have confidence in your business acumen, but nobody is immune to accidents. Please make sure you have sufficient life insurance coverage," Inuzuka said. She held back tears of gratitude: his dry and direct remark was meant to lighten the emotional burden on the indebted party.

Masako's company, M. Hozumi Inc., did not get off to a smooth start. At first she had trouble attracting customers—perhaps the negative image of her predecessor lingered to plague her. Fortunately, business picked up within several months. By the end of her first year she was breaking even. It had been a year of life-or-death struggle for her, but she made a fortunate start by any objective standard. M. Hozumi's subsequent evolution followed this pattern: Masako braved great vicissitudes but over the years her store rode the tide of fashions to grow ever larger and stronger.

When at last she took stock of her life, she found herself owner-manager of a solidly established enterprise well respected in the fashion apparel field. The trade sheets reported her activities in detail; whenever she attended dealers' meetings, a circle of people never failed to form around her.

When at last she was certain that M. Hozumi Inc. was managing well enough to stand on its own, Masako offered Inuzuka shares of her capital stock at their original value. Quite pleased, he accepted her shares by writing off a part of his original loan to her. At this point Masako pleaded with him to serve on the board of M. Hozumi Inc. as an outside director. He agreed. Self-confident in business matters as Masako was, she needed a personal advisor.

One day a young reporter from *Apparel Quarterly* came over to ask pointed questions about Inuzuka's appointment to her board. When she realized that nothing she said would change his preconceived scenario, she lost her temper and practically threw him out of her office. Perhaps sufficiently chastened by her genuine anger, the reporter never published gossip about her.

Ironically, when more serious trouble did flare up, it had an unexpected source—Inuzuka's wife. Mrs. Inuzuka became suspicious of the relationship between her husband and Masako and somehow convinced herself that Inuzuka had fathered Masako's son, Michio.

At first Inuzuka laughed off his wife's allegations. In time the truth would out and set her straight, he said, since her accusation was groundless. Masako agreed with his reasoning. But the issue proved far from simple. Obsessed with jealousy, Mrs. Inuzuka was past listening to her husband's explanations. When he stopped futile attempts to reason with her, she took this as a proof of his guilt.

Mrs. Inuzuka was a sensible and intelligent woman. Or so she had seemed to everyone. The wild and bizarre behavior she now displayed was so unlike her former self she seemed as if under the spell of some supernatural force. She went so far as to hire a private investigator to report on her husband's activities and tried to shadow him herself.

"It's most strange. My wife seems intent on destroying her happiness one way or another. Pop psychology or not, I wonder if she isn't starting to rebel against the traditional feminine way her parents raised her, now she's nearly fifty. Or at least that's about the only explanation I come up with." In his distress Inuzuka confided in Masako.

Maybe so, maybe not—because no one ever fully understands what's in the depths of another person's heart, Masako thought as she listened to Inuzuka, but she volunteered no comment.

Eventually Inuzuka made up his mind and divorced his wife with an unusually generous settlement. He and Masako became involved only after the divorce. Later, when they had begun to live together, he reflected.

"To be perfectly honest, I was as anxious to get out of the marriage as my wife was. No matter how you look at it, there's something dubious about marriage. I have an odd feeling, if my wife and I hadn't been married to each other but just living together, we'd have gotten along well enough and there'd have been no need for us to break up. As soon as two people get married, they tend to take legal protection for granted and stop trying to nurture love and affection for each other. An unlikely analogy, but it's no different with a salaried employee, who loses the driving need to serve the best interest of his company precisely because he's secure in his employment. But a morally scrupulous person can't tolerate such dishonesty for long. Security and protection, whether you earn them or not, might seem like a blessing, but they're not. In truth they're a kind of narcotic. Once addicted, you start to neglect your work, forget about public service, and lose your ability for love. Before long you turn into an arrogant incompetent and don't even know it. Worse even than the moral paralysis that the narcotic effect of dishonesty induces is this arrogance. And unawareness of your own disablement. In our marriage both my wife and I happened to wake up to the horror of it all. Yes, we must have."

Inuzuka discussed marriage and business life on the same dimension, Masako thought, probably because he was thinking seriously of resigning from Nissei Corporation at the time. Masako was in favor of his resignation. In her considered practical opinion as an entrepreneur, Inuzuka was not made to be a salaried employee. Unless he was lucky enough to come across an owner-manager enlightened enough to recognize and value the best qualities in him, Inuzuka would find little satisfaction working for someone else.

He quit the company, and opened his own school of Japanese theatrical dance.

·   ·   ·

Masako's story ended. Outside the restaurant window, night had fallen and an ocean of lights shimmered in the expanse of darkness.

"Was Mr. Inuzuka already qualified to teach Japanese dance?" Nakasato asked.

"They say it's auspicious to start taking lessons on the sixth day of the sixth month of one's sixth year. He, for one, did so. He was born in Kyoto to a family of hereditary grand masters of a dance school. In college, he agonized over the career choice between Japanese dance and business, he says."

"But it can't be easy for anyone pushing sixty to open a dance school and find enough students."

"His classes were filled. Can you guess why?" Masako asked, a mischievous gleam lighting her eyes. Her lips fluttered like butterfly wings and her face became a world all its own, innocent, charming. A long-buried sensuous memory sprang to life and coursed through Nakasato.

"Why?" he parroted, powerless to find words of his own.

"Americans."

"Americans? Oh, yes. I hear he has many American students." Nakasato remembered Sakurako's dance and her story of meeting Inuzuka in San Francisco.

"Apparently he's a marvelous teacher. And of course, he teaches in English. After he was transferred back to Tokyo, a number of his students followed him to Japan. Even before resigning from Nissei, he was already giving lessons to some Americans. They begged and pleaded with him—two-thirds of his students are Americans. He has fervent admirers who make me jealous. No wonder his classes filled up as soon as the school opened. It's doing extremely well. He wouldn't like me to put it in commercial terms, but I must say it's a profitable enterprise."

"Quite impressive," Nakasato muttered. "So he laid the first stone for his dance school while he was posted in San Francisco, so to speak."

"So it seems."

"Quite impressive," he muttered again. "He cleverly used whatever position he happened to be in at each stage of his life—to make provision for the future."

"Well, maybe so. But I can't agree with the way you put it. You make it sound as if he just coasted along on the job, half-heartedly, all the while scheming for his own interest."

"Certainly looks that way, doesn't it?" Nakasato insisted, with a perverse impulse to needle her.

"No. You are wrong," Masako said in an unequivocal tone. "All along he lived with a sense of mission to make himself useful to the world. He took his work seriously and gave his utmost to each assignment at Nissei. In fact, what he hated most about the shosha business was the sleeper commission. You know, the commission trading companies collect because of past ties but without any actual service or function at all for a client firm. 'Only if you have something to offer to the world can you get something in return. The basic principle of life is give and take.' That's what Inuzuka always says. Since he found it necessary to apologize to you, I assume he did make his share of mistakes on the job. But he was most certainly dead serious about his work. He made it a point of honor to act in the best interest of the company with sincere conviction. That's why he sometimes erred with conviction. He is a person who could not live with himself if he compromised his beliefs."

"In that case, can I take it that he meant what he said in apology to Nukaya and me?"

"Yes. He doesn't play psychological games, juggling the rhetoric of *tatemae* and *honne,* principle and ulterior motive—his word conveys his true feeling. What he says is what he means. He is utterly sincere, never double-dealing or double-crossing. He often spoke of the wrong he'd done you and Mr. Nukaya."

"True, Nukaya suffered real damage. But I've done all right in my fashion, no nervous breakdown or anything. He needn't lose any sleep over me."

"Well, come to think of it, you are a general manager of almighty Nissei Corporation. A fine position, you earned it with your own endeavor." Masako articulated slowly, choosing her words with care. "But to be honest, Nakasato-san, I think you passed up a precious chance. You should have taken the plunge at that time. I believe you could have worked wonders with Century Stores. The management approach you taught me turned out to be just what chain stores and retail outlets needed. It really works. Ah, yes, I brought something to show you."

She reached for a package on the chair next to her seat and pulled out a small pamphlet. The cover bore the notation "M. Hozumi Instructional Texts" and the title, *Theories on Chain-Store Management.*

"Why don't you take a look?"

Nakasato nodded and flipped through the pages.

His eyes chanced on a cluster in the phonetic *kana* script that spelled Henri Fayol.

"Ah, Fayol. A familiar name!"

"Yes. Please read on."

As his eyes skimmed the paragraphs, a sense of déjà vu came over him.

"These sentences . . ."

"You recognize them? They come from your letters. Look through the other pages. Most are filled with what you wrote, what you taught me. I put your theory into practice exactly as I understood it. It worked. That's why I'm teaching the same theory to my employees now."

I'm glad it helped, Nakasato tried to say, but for some reason the words eluded him. He felt he'd lost something.

"You could have made significant contributions to society even if you ventured out from the protective shade of Nissei Corporation.

You acquired so much knowledge and created your own management techniques. You could have gone your own way without rely-
ing on Nissei's name or credit. Now that I've become an entrepreneur myself, I'm all the more firmly convinced of this. With no
reservation whatever I say that the Nakasato Michio I knew then
was fully capable of accomplishing great things in whatever field he
chose."

Suddenly behind Nakasato's temples a whirling sensation erupt-
ed and spread through his head. A weird giddiness claimed him, as if
the contents of his skull had exploded.

"Watch it!" Masako cried, too late to stop the coffee cup from
falling out of Nakasato's hand to the table top. The cup broke with a
crash that reverberated throughout the quiet restaurant and spattered what remained of the coffee in all directions.

Nakasato scrambled out of the chair but caught a spray of coffee
over his jacket and pants. Masako's jacket was also splashed.

"Are you all right?" several waiters rushed up to ask.

The targets of curious eyes from every table in the restaurant,
Nakasato and Masako hurried to the restrooms.

"Sorry. I got caught up in my thoughts and forgot what I was doing," Nakasato apologized to Masako when they were back at their
table.

"Was I scared! I thought you'd had a stroke or something. You
got such a vacant look on your face. Are you really all right now?"

"I'm fine. See? Nothing's wrong with me." Nakasato spread his
hands on the table and moved all ten fingers to reassure her.

"Maybe my fault. I gave you a shock. I'm sorry."

Obviously Masako referred to their son. But Nakasato knew that
something else added to the impact on him: the weight of the lost
years.

The years in which Inuzuka taught dance to Americans in San
Francisco and offered a helping hand to Sakurako in distress.

The years in which Masako tended the sales racks of her 180
square feet of rented space, divined the needs and desires of each
customer, memorized faces and names, and sold one dress at a time
with utmost endeavor.

The years in which a fatherless child grew up to be a ninth
grader.

During those years Nukaya read through volumes of world literature, made notes of meal scenes, dined out with his wife to sample the foreign dishes, and wrote a book about his experience.

All of them had one thing in common—direct dealing with the world.

In the meantime, what had Nakasato accomplished? He worked at Nissei Corporation.

He mastered the skill to ensure smooth sailing of his projects through intrastructural channels. He took pains to acquaint himself with the names, personalities, and respective standing of other Nissei men and foster favorable working relations with them. He made a thorough study of the key men in power to learn their management styles and personal values until he could accurately forecast the chances of each project at Nissei Corporation. About the current president in particular, he came to know everything there was to know, from Ebisawa's mah-jongg strategies and his golf swing to the workings of his mind and the subtlest shades of his mood.

And what had Nakasato gained as a result?

Two things—promotion on schedule at the top of his class and reputation within the company. The promotion would guarantee him an income somewhat exceeding that of his year-mates, colleagues with the same seniority, and several extra years of employment beyond the general mandatory retirement age. And the reputation would make his job easier to carry out in the organization.

Now he noticed his loss, too. He'd lost nearly all ties with the world outside Nissei Corporation. No, that's not true, a part of his mind protested. I did cultivate social contacts with so many business associates in the United States as well as in Japan. Yes, another inner voice replied. Those people were a means to an end, a means to better my performance record and advance Nissei's causes. They were nothing, therefore, but gossamer shadows that paraded past.

Never love your work, never love anyone, if you want to succeed in business—Nakasato recalled the advice one of his senior colleagues gave him. He'd agreed with what seemed a poignant insight behind it.

Lose your heart to a particular job, and you are held back from moving on to other assignments of more vital importance to the company. Give your allegiance to a particular person, superior or subordinate, and you no longer function freely in the corporate human network—or so went the commonsense rationale.

Nakasato had little need to worry in this regard, though. Routine job rotation in the average cycle of several years would effectively prevent him from forming an emotional bond with any job or person. There was no way to cultivate love, in fact, even if he wanted to. And yet.

Even so, some men had dared to love under such circumstances. Take, for example, one contemporary who struck up fast friendships with Mexican people while stationed in Mexico. He requested extension after extension on his tour of duty until he became Nissei's leading authority on Mexico. But he earned low marks in the employee performance evaluation. He's practically turned into a Mexican himself, too besotted with Mexico to be of any possible use to Nissei Corporation, went the talk in the head office. Better than anyone else, this man knew exactly where he stood with the company. Eventually he resigned from Nissei, sent his wife back to Japan with divorce papers, and married a Mexican woman.

"Would you like to meet him?" Masako asked.

"What?" Nakasato gasped, startled from his racing thoughts. "Meet who?"

"Oh, no, Michio-san! Are you sure you feel all right?" Masako said, laughing. "I've been talking about my Michio."

"Ah, of course," Nakasato said to cover up his inattention. Instantly realizing the seriousness of her topic, he added in haste, "Yes, Michio. Mmm . . . well . . . I feel ambivalent about this. I mean, is it okay for me to see him? A bit scary, somehow."

"You can't tell him who you really are."

"But then, how do you expect me to behave?"

"Leave everything to me. I'll set the stage unobtrusively. Can you keep your morning free a week from next Sunday?"

"Yes, I can."

"I'll be playing tennis with Michio. If you don't mind coming to our tennis club in Setagaya Ward, you can join us for a game."

"What an excellent idea, perfectly natural. But I haven't even touched a racket for quite a while."

"Michio and I'll help you get back in shape," Masako promised, breaking into a smile. It was a radiant smile, glowing with healthy self-confidence. Slender fingers held her brandy glass poised for a toast.

Nakasato lifted his glass with a silent smile, but his heart was in chaos, a crowded battlefield where sensory images thrown up from fifteen-year-old memories warred with his will to suppress them.

5

At the appointed time on the third Sunday in April, Nakasato went to the tennis club in Setagaya. He found Masako already on the court, her pale legs provocative in tennis shorts. On the same court stood a tall boy topping Masako by eight inches or so. No doubt he was Michio.

Nakasato riveted his eyes on the boy as if trying to drink him up.

Big eyes. Thick eyebrows. Strong jaw. These features undoubtedly derived from Nakasato's genes. Oblong face. Straight hair. Shapely lips. These probably came from Masako.

As he gazed, his heart pumped faster and louder, making his breathing difficult. He felt oddly grateful. Perhaps I'd feel this way if I was assured of a bit longer life when the end had seemed imminent, Nakasato thought. He felt apologetic, too. He had the impression he'd shirked his responsibility, but in retrospect, he could not have taken responsibility for something he knew nothing about.

"Hi, Mr. Nakasato. Won't you join us?" Masako called out to him, as Nakasato walked onto the court after changing into his tennis outfit. In Michio's presence, they must maintain the appearance of old acquaintances running into each other at the court by pure chance that day.

"Thank you, I will. But be prepared for wild shots, because I haven't played for ages," Nakasato warned her. Taking a deep breath with mounting excitement, he swept his eyes toward Michio.

"How do you do? I take it this is your son?"

"His name is Michio. Will you play him?" Masako said, sending Nakasato what seemed to be a significant look.

"Hello. My name is also Michio, Nakasato Michio," he blurted out needlessly, in a panic.

"How do you do?" The boy returned his greeting with a bow.

Detecting the unstable masculine tonality of puberty in his rapid utterance, Nakasato was strangely moved. Subtly vulnerable, the plaintive note in it conjured up a vision of limitless future.

"Why don't you two practice together?"

At Masako's suggestion, the two males faced each other across the net.

"Here we go," Nakasato called, tossing up the ball he had in his hand. He swung the racket. The ball glanced off the frame to land in the net.

"Sorry."

Nakasato made another sequence of toss and stroke, only to send the ball on the same path straight into the net.

"Sorry about this. After such a long time, my racket just wouldn't meet the ball."

Noting that Nakasato had no ball left in his hand, Michio served. The underhand skimmed the net and came in a long vigorous streak.

In three unhurried paces Nakasato crossed the court to intercept the ball. Confident footwork of a veteran player—or at least that's what he meant it to be. But the ball bounced off the racket in tremendous flight high over the fence behind Michio and disappeared into the gutter on the far side of the wide city street.

"I beg your pardon." Nakasato found himself apologizing again.

Michio looked incredulously at Masako. Can this man play tennis at all?—the question was written on his open face.

"Even you get rusty, being away from the game so long, don't you?" Masako said in a fit of laughter, all but collapsing in merriment.

Is she reveling in the secret pleasure of noting resemblances between father and son? Well, let her—Nakasato said to himself, feeling reckless. Abandoning the wayward ball to the gutter, he gathered up what balls he could find around him.

"Let's go!" he yelled, gripping a ball in his hand.

Startled, Michio scrambled to receive the serve.

Nakasato made a high toss straight up above his head. A cannonball service—used to be his best stroke.

"Yei!" He shouted *kiai,* a battle cry.

In the wake of a resounding thud, the drive bounced deep in Michio's right service court.

Thwack! The boy executed a perfect return.

"Yoisho!" Nakasato whooshed aloud and scooped a forehand off the ground, all but praying. He managed a decent return. The rally continued. His heart swelled with a strange sense of happiness. He felt as if something genuine had been restored to him after many lost years.

For some time they were totally absorbed in the pursuit of criss-crossing balls.

"Let's play a game," Masako called to them fifteen minutes later. "We can ask Mrs. Kashiwabara in for doubles." She indicated the rather tall older woman who had come over to greet Masako a while ago.

Nakasato teamed up with Mrs. Kashiwabara, Masako with Michio. Nakasato's shots were erratic and cost his team a game.

"Hey, help! My heart is about to explode," Nakasato groaned.

"Not getting any younger, I see," Masako laughed.

Though Nakasato was eager to have a talk with Michio, the boy sped away toward the backboard and began to slam balls into it. A lump of pure energy, he probably needed more vigorous exercise than the one-sided game to work off steam.

Not that Michio was the only one with energy to spare. Mrs. Kashiwabara, who looked sixtyish, was still on the court trading shots with latecomers.

"Look at her. Young for her age, isn't she?"

"Can you believe she's sixty-two? Her husband used to be a managing director of Nissei Corporation. You knew him, didn't you?"

"Oh, that Kashiwabara . . . ," Nakasato said in surprise. He settled himself on the bench and took a more serious look at the older woman rallying with considerable skill.

"Mr. Kashiwabara passed on last year—or the year before, I think."

Masako sat down next to Nakasato.

"Yes, that's right. He was ten years older than his wife," Masako informed him. "He didn't know what to do with himself in retirement, she says. He just stayed at home and did nothing but complain and criticize. He'd been so long in a position of authority at work that he insisted on having his way at home no matter what. She invited him to play tennis with her, but he wouldn't condescend to start lessons at his age. He gave her a terrible time. It's really true that some people become totally useless after they leave their company, isn't it?"

"I can believe that of Director Kashiwabara at least. The talk at the office was that his only hobby was to read documents relating to company business."

"Maybe that's why he died suddenly before his time. But then what did his widow do but take a new lease on life! She keeps extremely active ever since, making the rounds of hot spring resorts and taking trips abroad. Whenever she stays in Tokyo, she comes here daily to play tennis unless it's raining. So full of vitality, in fact—playing for two or three hours at a stretch is nothing to her."

"Now you mention that, I see the deep tan she's got already, so early in the spring. By the way, the sunlight does seem to be getting stronger."

Looking up at the expanse of blue sky over the tennis court, he took deep breaths. Screening a third of his field of vision were branches of a cherry tree, its blossoms already yielding to the burgeoning young leaves.

"Michio-kun is a fine boy," Nakasato said, after a momentary hesitation to decide whether to tack the informal honorific *-kun* to his own son's name. "He takes after you."

"You think so?"

"I think he's like me in some ways, too."

"Very much like you. Now that he asserts himself, in the last phase of adolescent rebellion, I can see he's cast in the same mold. The very image of you, when he sulks."

"Of all the traits to inherit!"

"He has a will of his own. I don't mind a touch of nonconformist spirit in him. I'd like to see him grow into a resolute human being capable of standing firm by his own judgment instead of drifting along with the tide."

"Can he manage without a father?"

"I think so. I intend to have him come into my company. On an application for a job anywhere else, his family register with the father's name missing would be a serious drawback. But I can spare him that problem."

"Children don't necessarily fall in with their parents' plans."

"You may be right."

"Besides, he'll need certain abilities to run M. Hozumi, won't he?"

"Yes. More than abilities, he'll need personal qualities indispensable in a chief executive officer: passion, faith, fairness, love—in short, integrity of character in the true sense of the word."

"Cunning, insidiousness, duplicity, greed—aren't these what you mean?"

"Oh, no! Are you trying to make me angry?"

"No, just joking. Now I remember! Peter Drucker's *Practice of Management*. We read it together. His conclusion was: "One quality the manager of tomorrow must have is *integrity of character*.""

"That's right," Masako said, her voice breaking.

As Nakasato glanced at her, she turned her face casually away from him, but he saw her eyes brimming with precarious tears. Nearly brushing her pale face, several cherry petals floated down.

For the past few hours—more precisely, ever since the night of their dinner reunion—Nakasato had been fighting an impulse to consult with Masako. The impulse grew stronger or weaker but would not go away. What he had on his mind was American Gourmet Company. Masako succeeded in business. Why not me, too? Nakasato liked to think he was above simplistic logic, but that could well be the truth in a nutshell. Of course, there was no comparing. What Masako built up and what Nakasato accomplished in the same fifteen years were as different as the moon and a turtle, separate and unequal on any terms. This realization had been on Nakasato's mind since their reencounter. Fifteen years more at the most, and my career will end. Am I going to spend what's left of it as a turtle? The question lurked at the bottom of every thought.

He was of two minds about discussing the matter with Masako. She might think he was trying to compete, or she might come right out and say he wasn't up to the same task. Either way he'd find it hard to take.

"Hozumi-san," he tried a formal tone. "I'd like to learn more about chain-store management. Will you teach me?"

Masako looked momentarily puzzled but apparently decided to take it as a joke.

"Oh, no!" she smiled. "When I turned to you for advice, it took a monumental decision. But in retrospect I'm glad I had the courage to seek your counsel."

"That's why I'm seeking your counsel now." Nakasato briefed Masako on the American Gourmet Company acquisition plan—so at ease with her he somehow spoke more freely than he had expected. Considering the very real danger of losing the ladder from under him and getting stranded in America, he was right in trying to stay in his present position, wasn't he? Nakasato confided his intention to stall for time and eventually kill the plan.

"Well, I see you have something to lose now. That makes your situation different from the old days," Masako acknowledged. "But I don't think your move to American Gourmet is a big gamble in itself. After all, this project is like a field campaign—heading Nissei's expedition into new territory and diversifying the shosha's activities. And under the direct command of President Ebisawa, no less. Being picked to head such an ambitious operation counts as a big plus on your record, never a minus under any circumstances. Even if the project fails or President Ebisawa steps down while you're in charge of it, you stay in the sun as long as Nissei's top executives see you're doing your best."

"You really think so? Well, as long as I can return any time to the corporate path toward Nissei's boardroom, I might do well to take on this venture. Outside management experience will certainly give me leverage."

Masako said nothing for a few moments. A flurry of falling cherry blossoms danced in the soft breeze.

"If that's the way you feel about this project, better not accept the assignment. Whether you accept or not won't make much difference to your life in the long run, but I feel sorry for the employees of American Gourmet Company."

"What do you mean?"

"Any restaurant chain is doomed to fail under the management of executive officers whose only ambition is to race up the corporate ladder back at Nissei Corporation. As I said before, you have nothing to worry about, because if you are deemed loyal, even the failure of this project won't keep you from returning to Japan and climbing higher and higher in Nissei's hierarchy. But American Gourmet's employees won't be so lucky."

"The United States doesn't have a permanent employment system, and labor relations there are less *wet,* a lot more cut and dried than they are in Japan."

"Have you turned into a fool?" Masako lowered her voice but spoke decisively. "A chief executive officer has the same responsibility whether the company subscribes to permanent employment or not. He owes obligations to all concerned—customers, stockholders, business associates, creditors, employees, and subcontractors. Anyone who won't or can't discharge those duties and responsibilities ought to stick to a life of security doled out by the benevolent managers of a large corporation. What alternative would such a man have after all? He's destined to end up being utterly useless outside of Nissei. The only social service he can render after retiring is to die."

What a ruthless thing to say, Nakasato tried to interject. But the phrase stuck in his throat. Belying the merciless thrust of her words, Masako spoke in a quiet tone as if to persuade herself, and its impact on him was all the more powerful for the unemotional delivery.

"I haven't told Inuzuka about my relationship with you. Once I mentioned that at my request you instructed me in chain-store management. It was the day, in fact, when he came home from a visit to a certain supermarket and told me how shaken he was to find all your ideas from fifteen years before working like a dream. He was doubly surprised to learn that your theory had been responsible also for M. Hozumi's success. Inuzuka must have carried a double load of guilt ever since. When he happened to hear of the American Gourmet plan in New York, on the spot he recommended you to President Tobita, out of his unconscious desire to make it up to you. But I didn't agree with his opinion of you, because I expected you'd have changed. I wasn't wrong. You've turned into an ordinary businessman working for a salary. That can't be helped. But you can't run an enterprise on a salaryman's mentality." Masako looked up at Nakasato before continuing.

"How strange, to think that fifteen years ago it was you who said the exact same thing: the top management of Century Stores is strictly Nissei-oriented, a bunch of hired hands just killing time until transfer orders come. Neither at the supervising unit back in Nissei nor out at Century Stores do the managers take the supermarket project seriously as their own job. They can never make a success of it that way.—Remember how you used to deplore and rage in your frustration and exasperation?"

"You may be entirely right. But, Hozumi-san, it doesn't mean I've succumbed to the salaryman mentality. I'm just not as naive as I used to be."

Masako fell silent. For several minutes she seemed to vacillate, evidently trying to decide whether to say anything further, but at last gave voice to her thoughts.

"I wonder," she began as if elucidating to herself, "why anyone would take the trouble to contrive delaying tactics to kill a project beneficial to the company purely to protect his own interest, unless he is acting on the salaryman's mentality? I can't think of any other explanation."

Nakasato wanted to object. Any number of counterarguments passed through his mind. He could have furnished rationalizations powerful enough to sway his own beliefs. But he kept his mouth shut. No excuse seemed persuasive or weighty in Masako's presence.

Nakasato dropped his eyes. They fell on two legs, his own, emerging from a pair of white shorts. Covered by a thick mat of dark masculine hair, still firm and young on a body in its midforties. Nakasato touched the slightly sweaty skin and felt the vigorous resilience of the flesh against his palm. The question flared up: For whose sake have I used this body all these years?—For Nissei's sake. Until a little while ago, that would have been his answer. Now, however, his conviction was fading fast: Not in Nissei's service, but solely for the survival of flesh and blood, I've used this body. It has served the purpose of self-preservation in a literal, physical, sense. Nakasato felt a faint kick as something in his heart loosened and came free.

He glanced up toward the tennis court to find the match drawing to a close. From his vantage, the court appeared to be fringed by cherry trees just past their bloom. Further beyond the cherry trees, the fence edged a public street busy with streams of cars. Nakasato experienced a strange conviction that the world had turned a little brighter.

"I'm going over to Michio," he announced, getting to his feet. Masako said nothing but nodded in acknowledgment.

Nakasato strolled over to the backboard, where Michio was tirelessly driving balls. Michio saw him approaching and flashed a shy smile.

"Michio-kun, would you go another round with me?"

"Yes," the boy said, an earnest look coming to his face. In perfect likeness of Masako.

"You're going into your mother's business, aren't you?"

"No, I'm not certain. It's just my mother's plan."

"Is that it?" Nakasato laughed. "You haven't made up your mind yet. Just your mother, settling on the plan. I see. Well, then, if you won't carry on her business, what do you want to do?"

"I want to make movies. But if my mother catches me saying this, she'll give me a lecture."

Michio was picking up balls from around his feet. Nakasato helped him gather the yellow balls lying all about.

"Why would you want to make movies?"

"Why? I just like to. If it's my choice, I'd rather live my life doing things I like."

"I see. Doing what you like to do, hmm." Nakasato nodded his head several times. "That's why you want to make movies. I see."

Scattered under his feet were withering cherry blossoms. Nakasato's eyes traveled upward to a particularly large ancient tree, which continued to shed the remaining petals even as he watched.

"Shall we start?" Nakasato urged.

"Yes."

Leaving a crisp answer behind him, Michio ran full speed toward the other end of the court.

6

From that day on, Nakasato proceeded to reverse his plan of action. He made up his mind to stake the rest of his career on the task of managing American Gourmet Company. Can I really regard the restaurant chain as my life's work, he asked himself, and came up with what seemed an affirmative answer. But no sooner had he set his heart on the job than a new obstacle loomed up before him. It caught Nakasato by surprise.

Somehow he had taken it for granted that once he made his decision to accept the American Gourmet assignment, things would start rolling automatically. As he was about to take the plunge himself, however, he found it impossible to sit back and passively watch the proceedings. First, he reviewed the available data in their entirety. Past and present statistics on the American food-service industry, on the state of various companies in the field, on American Gourmet's financial and managerial performance record—all these indicated American Gourmet to be a safe investment. Nissei America's enthusiasm in proposing the acquisition seemed well justified. His own analysis of all the data, however, led him to conclude that the project was too hollow and insubstantial for him to stake his career on. The revelation surprised him.

The company may be operating in a good growth industry and showing satisfactory figures on its current balance sheet, but that's not enough to make me gamble my life away. There are far more crucial concerns. When I start work there, what will I be doing every day at the office? How do I greet people I meet in the morning? What business do I discuss in the conference room? What kinds of decisions am I to hand down? Who will carry out the orders I issue? Or, will they be carried out at all? For that matter, how much clout will I have? If their corporate culture is such that an Asian cannot find welcome as the chief executive officer, this project will be doomed from the start regardless of my own managerial skill or effort.

The more Nakasato thought along these lines, the more doubtful he became of the buyout procedure Nissei America promoted as the best format—a takeover in which the work force was to be inherited intact but the senior management replaced en masse. Nakasato considered an alternative of retaining the veteran managers whose experience and practical knowledge would be great assets to the new management, for he was certain that running a restaurant chain required critical know-how all its own.

Another important factor was American Gourmet's past policy in personnel management. Even in the United States, some companies looked after their employees with as much care as their Japanese counterparts under the permanent employment system, but others operated strictly on capitalist principles.

Not to be overlooked was the problem of labor unionism. In contrast to Japan's enterprise or company unions that formed the basis of the Japanese trade-union movement, the United States' dominant form of union organization seemed to be industrial and craft unions. How is American Gourmet's track record in labor relations?

"They have no adverse reputation as regards their dealings with labor unions," reported Nissei America, summarily dismissing the issue in one brief sentence. But *why* didn't they have problems in labor relations? That was the question. If the personal expertise and charisma of the present CEO were largely responsible for the absence of labor conflict, the planned change in the top management could very well put an end to the stable relations.

For that matter, none of the information available to Nakasato at the moment was of any use to him in reassessing American Gourmet Company from the vantage of a prospective CEO. His desk piled high with mounds of documents forwarded from Nissei America and study reports prepared by his subordinates, Nakasato was deep in thought.

What does this mean? Is this the way all our feasibility studies have been conducted in the past on potential objects of new capital investments?—Does the target industry show growth potential? Is the target company sound enough to be a low-risk investment? Is it possible to pull out without suffering a loss in case of failure?

As Nakasato recalled now, *these* had been the only questions addressed by what passed for feasibility studies in Nissei Corporation. On every level of the corporate channels, deliberation focused on nothing else. Nakasato himself used to consider it all proper and adequate. But now, viewing the prospects from the other side, he could not but note that Nissei's feasibility studies betrayed the moneylender mentality in their obsession with safe return on invested capital. In short, they were concerned with Nissei's interest and welfare as an investor, not with anybody else's. What a self-centered, arrogant attitude in conducting research! They operated on the premise that the world revolved around Nissei.

On recommendations derived from such feasibility studies, Nissei Corporation had made extensive capital investments in existing enterprises or in new companies that Nissei founded. Nakasato thought of a few from the past several years alone—Nissei Network System in new media, or information services; Nissei Electronics in electronic machines; Nissei Electrent in rental of electron-measuring apparatus; Nissei Finance in money markets; Nissei Sports Mail Order in direct sales of sporting goods. The media had hailed these ventures as the "new businesses" or spin-off operations launched by the integrated trading companies in their latest offensive. But all these new enterprises had fallen far short of expectations in their performance. Granted, these were still young companies. But none seemed even close to showing a glimpse of hope for the future.

Was there any connection between Nissei's approach to feasibility studies and the dismal prospects of their new ventures? Why didn't I notice it before? Nakasato was confounded by his own oversight. He was angry with himself for having overlooked something so obvious, and at the same time angry with Nissei's officers and managers who had been complacent enough not to question the adequacy of their feasibility studies.

Before long, however, Nakasato came to note a great change in himself. The self-revelation was triggered by Tamura's letter from New York marked "Confidential." When Tamura, a section chief of the Internal Control Division, had been transferred out of Tokyo headquarters to Nissei America, Nakasato had asked him to look into unmarketable stock Kano might have stashed away. The letter was Tamura's response to Nakasato's request. Tamura confirmed Nakasato's suspicion that some shipments of Taiwanese products were in storage with no sales prospect in sight.

"But no one knows the whole story except General Manager Kano," Tamura reported. "Kano denies the existence of any such stock, but what records of transactions and proceedings I was able to canvass all point to its existence. My guess is that Kano is frantically looking for buyers to take these products off his hands. If he fails to sell the entire stock, Nissei will be forced to absorb the loss because of its moral, if not legal, obligations to the manufacturers. But Kano is not one to let his own mistake of this magnitude come out in the open. He will probably maneuver to cover the loss with another business deal. So I shall carefully watch his moves for the next several months," Tamura closed with a promise.

Nakasato read Tamura's letter without emotion. Kano must be going to desperate lengths to hide the problem stock—all that seemed to be happening in a distant world absolutely unrelated to him. Poor man . . . No sooner did Nakasato hear himself mutter the words than he awoke to reality: What poor man? Why feel sorry for Kano, who conceals unsalable merchandise and contemplates ways to unload it on American Gourmet Company?

Or so Nakasato tried to reason. But he felt sorry just the same. Sorry for the man who is forced to conceal, maneuver, and grope for a way out in his natural desire to protect his interests and preserve his career. By the same token, then, each and every Nissei colleague was to be pitied. Every man who is under the delusion that he made the greatest accomplishment in the world by simply being ahead of his peers in the promotion race. Each one who buckles under to authority and dances to the tune of his superiors just to survive; who abuses his power and influence to dominate others; who whispers gossip and spreads rumors; who is mild-mannered but conceals his true self; who makes knowing remarks but never tackles anything head-on for fear of failure.

Working right alongside such men, Nakasato had never felt sorry for them until a few days ago. On the contrary, he had seen them as fortunate beings privileged to work for a top-rated trading company.

Apparently he'd been wrong. In their blind trust in the company as the only measure of worldly values, these men were no different from Ojima, who committed suicide because he had been passed over for promotion.

At last, Nakasato confirmed the radical change in himself. He was on his way back from Yurakucho, where he had his passport renewed for the second trip to America. He did not feel like returning directly to the office. He had no specific destination but strolled up to Sukiya Bridge. The famous bridge itself was gone, along with the newspaper building and the semicircular theater facade that marked a nationally known romantic rendezvous spot. Now there were two department stores crowded with young men and women even on this weekday afternoon. Soon the month of May would be upon them with the Golden Week packing in three national holidays.

The willows along the Ginza, immortalized in popular ballads, had fallen victim to exhaust fumes before the age of emission controls, but blue skies stretched beyond the zelkova trees lining Harumi Avenue. Nakasato let himself flow with the leisurely current of pedestrians and reached the police station at a wide intersection. For no reason in particular, his heart was light—airy and sunny to the core.

Crossing the avenue to the Hankyu Department Store, Nakasato stood at the curb for a few moments watching traffic. Then he sauntered to Sony Building and peered at motorized dolls moving about in the show window. As he turned into Namiki Street, the fresh green of plane trees replaced the zelkovas to fill his vision and invigorate his senses. Nakasato hummed a tune. He didn't know he was doing so until a young woman ahead of him turned round to look. He was embarrassed, but his heart grew all the more buoyant.

I'm free, liberated!

Nakasato at last grasped the true significance of the change in his heart. Old memories of the love shared with Masako came back to him in sweet nostalgic fragments. That love, painfully true, had measured his sincerity and courage in trying to live free, without fear or reservation. That love left a living testimony in the form of Michio.

I shall live free, too. Just like Masako. Like Inuzuka. Come to think of it, like Nukaya too. To Michio as well, I want to give freedom.

Nakasato all but pranced down the sidewalk from the busy Ginza to the side streets that would burst into life after dark.

I'm free!

Free from the invisible monster called the company. Free from the stiflingly small corporate world with its tethers and intricately webbed human relationships.

Lose your temper, lose your ground. Forbearance is to bear the unbearable. That's life. We're better off than most. I haven't sold my soul to the company; I can have my say whenever I want to. Hang in there—he can't be your boss forever. Your logic would not work with our company.

To hell with all the clichés!

I am FREE!

Off with the fetters!

Nakasato rubbed his throat as if he'd worn them around his neck until moments ago. The joy of freedom was so profound and intense that his heart regained a semblance of calm only after an hour of aimless roaming and two cups of coffee downed at a tearoom in the department store at Ginza's busiest intersection facing the Seiko building.

Between
Entrepreneur
and Salaryman

May

1

Prior to his planned second trip to New York, Nakasato asked for an appointment with President Ebisawa and made a progress report on the American Gourmet acquisition project. The report amounted to the declaration of his intention: I shall expedite processing of this project. But some matters still need to be cleared up before we can take definite steps forward. I intend to go to New York once more.

At this point Ebisawa gave him a quizzical look. In truth, weren't you opposed to this project?—Ebisawa's eyes asked. Now without doubt Nakasato knew that the president had seen right through his playacting.

"To tell you the truth," he hastened to explain himself, "our study has shown that the prospects for the family restaurant business aren't exactly as pessimistic as they first appeared. And American Gourmet itself looks better and better under our scrutiny."

The more earnestly he spoke, the more vacuous he felt. He thought he detected the trace of a smile flickering on Ebisawa's face.

"In other words, you changed your mind. Why?" Ebisawa asked.

"Well, as I explained to you just now . . ."

"Ostensible reasons, yes," Ebisawa cut him short. "But not your real reasons."

"No, I mean . . ." Nakasato stammered. For a minute he wondered if the president had somehow gained full knowledge of his old love affair with Masako. He felt warmth come over his face.

"Oh, never mind. I'm glad you're ready to get on with this project. Give it a thorough going-over."

Ebisawa folded his hands, rested his elbows on the arms of his easy chair, and stretched back in repose. This was his usual relaxed posture when he was in a good mood.

Nakasato respectfully sat upright on the couch.

"Yes, I will," he replied. "By the way, I have two requests to make concerning this project. May I tell you now?"

"What are they? Your conditions?"

"Well, first, when the acquisition plan goes into effect, I would like to be put in complete charge of it. Maybe this sounds terribly brash and conceited coming from me, but I believe I am the only person who can carry out this project."

"I see," Ebisawa smiled. "And the other?"

"Yes . . . I would like to request permission to resign from Nissei Corporation, if and when I am granted the appointment."

"Resign? What do you mean by that?"

"In my estimate, this is one job that will take at least ten years to complete. I cannot make a success of it unless I am prepared to turn myself into a real American."

Ebisawa's eyes blazed.

Daunted by the intensity of his gaze, Nakasato fell silent. To his surprise, it was anger in Ebisawa's dark eyes. A searing anger. His elbows had left their relaxed position on the chair arms.

At a loss to understand the abrupt change in the other man's mood, Nakasato was unable to utter another word.

"Are you testing me?" Ebisawa said at last, breaking a long silence.

"Not in the least! What do you mean?"

"Or perhaps you intend to kill the project in this roundabout way? If you oppose it, all right. Just come out and say so."

"Oh, no, far from it. I am all for going through with the project. Of course, pending the outcome of my on-site study. I mean to make sure there are no hidden hitches and snags."

Whether he heard Nakasato or not, the president sat immobile, a statue, with his eyes firmly closed and his arms now resolutely crossed over his chest. Ebisawa said nothing, and Nakasato had no choice but to follow suit. The two men were still for some time. Etched about Ebisawa's closed eyelids was a look of anguish. Or a shadow of deep sorrow. When at last the president's eyes opened slowly, Nakasato thought he caught a glint of tears.

The president rose from his chair.

Taken by surprise, Nakasato sprang to his feet a second later.

"Nakasato, you've become a salaryman through and through."

"Pardon me, sir, but there seems to be some misunderstanding . . ."

"For now, I accept your explanation. Go to New York and investigate some more. But if you are attempting to kill this project, don't waste any more expenses. Understood?"

"Sir."

"I know, I know. Get going. The end will justify everything."

Leaving the easy chair, Ebisawa returned to his desk and sat down.

Nakasato wanted to follow him, to exonerate himself somehow, but he dared not do so. There was unequivocal rejection in the president's attitude.

·   ·   ·

"Do you suppose I said something to hurt his feelings?" Nakasato asked Personnel Manager Yamabe.

After racking his brains to no avail, he turned to Yamabe for advice. Three years his senior at Nissei, Yamabe was a man he considered trustworthy. The general manager of personnel was also in the best position to intercede in a case involving a personal misunderstanding that needed to be straightened out.

They were seated opposite each other in a plain small room in one corner of the spacious personnel office.

"Sure you did. Don't you really know what you did?" Yamabe laughed with a look of incredulity. "You blackmailed the president."

"Blackmail?! All I said was, I'll commit myself enough to live permanently in America. How can you call that blackmail?"

"How? How can the worldly wise Nakasato Michio fail to get this? Don't you see? The president counts on you as his own man. One of the pillars holding up the Ebisawa regime, as it were. Even if he planned to send you off to American Gourmet, no doubt he figured on just two or three years. He assumed you were fully aware of your position and the scheme of things at headquarters. But then you suddenly hit him with the ultimatum: if it's an order, I'll accept the assignment, but then I won't be coming back to Nissei. Now, that's out-and-out blackmail, if you ask me."

"Did he take it that way, too?"

"Look, don't play the innocent with me. You meant to scare him. But it worked better than you expected—too well, in fact, and now you're worried. Isn't that it?"

"Nothing of the sort. I'm serious in my determination to live out my life in America if necessary. When a man sets out to run an enterprise, he shouldn't count the years before he comes back to Nissei Corporation—or to Japan, for that matter. I did a lot of thinking and came to a conclusion: if I want to accomplish this job to my own satisfaction, I must sever my ties with Nissei and be willing to live out my life in America."

"Are you serious, Nakasato?"

Yamabe peered searchingly into Nakasato's eyes as if examining a rare species of animal. Are you trying to fool me, too, with your joke?—Yamabe's skepticism was written on his face.

"I can't joke or lie about something like this. If ever I take on this job, I'll hand in my resignation before I report to New York."

"Impossible. Can't be done."

"What's impossible? I haven't quite given in to the salaryman mentality yet. I'm willing to stake my life against any odds."

"Nakasato, you're not yourself today, are you? Who's talking about mentality? According to Nissei's rule, you cannot become the CEO of American Gourmet if you no longer work for Nissei. Don't you see?"

Looking for a catch, Nakasato thought hard but found nothing wrong with his reasoning.

"I can't remember any such rule."

"Well, there's nothing in writing. But what we have is something even more binding than a written rule. A law—or a commandment, you could call it."

"How does it go?"

"It's unthinkable for the company to allow a valuable employee to resign and move out to a subsidiary. That's why Nissei's work regulations never stipulated any rule to cover such an unlikely contingency. No country or company ever makes laws and regulations about a situation that never arises in real life. Anyone who gets a compelling urge to become the first case for a harebrained hypothetical scheme should have his head examined."

"Wait a minute. If I express a desire to become a bona fide employee of a subsidiary, are you going to put me through a psychiatric test?"

"Well, we won't really go so far as to run a psychiatric diagnosis on you, but everybody will assume you've gone out of your mind."

"Why? Does moving to a subsidiary mean going to hell?"

"That's right. It may be just a fable, but Nissei's internal regulations are all built on it. If ever the fable is destroyed, Nissei Corporation loses the ultimate grounds for command over its employees. So the company can never change the fable, even if it's known to be wrong."

"That is to say, then, Nissei Corporation assumes the company is the sole source of all values in the world. It's taken for granted: Nissei's internal rating has precedence over the ranking in all other social units. Is that it?"

"Of course. That's why the company can never allow its own treasured employee to give up his right to return to the garden of happiness—that is, Nissei's headquarters—no matter how badly he wants to work for a subsidiary."

"What if he insisted regardless?"

"Your mind seems to be in low gear today. Of course you can quit Nissei, but then you disqualify yourself for the American Gourmet position. That's all."

"Makes sense all right," Nakasato agreed with feeling. Obvious as it was, this logic had never occurred to him before. He had seen numerous cases of assignees loaned out to subsidiaries. As general manager of development, he had been involved in his share of decisions on such job reshuffling. But never once had he come across a case like his own and had consequently had no occasion to wonder about how to handle it.

Why is there no precedent? After all, Yamabe may be right, thought Nakasato. Because it is "a situation that never arises in real life." It seems no Nissei man wants to sever his lifeline to the company, except perhaps under special circumstances—when he has reason to believe all hope of future promotion is gone. And leaving

Nissei for good to work for a subsidiary or an affiliate spells distinct unhappiness for the individual under Nissei's existing personnel management policy. Nakasato could think of no other explanation for the absence of precedents.

"But, Yamabe-san, Nissei can't foster the growth of its subsidiaries this way."

"Well, it does look that way, doesn't it," Yamabe conceded, unruffled.

"It isn't good for Nissei, is it? Especially now, when Nissei must fight its way out of the shosha winter by doing everything to create and expand new businesses in electronics and downstream industries."

"You're really out of it today. What's got into you? As I remember, your gripe was that too many Nissei men were spouting naive opinions like the one you've just handed me."

"Maybe it was, but . . . ," Nakasato tried to explain in another way, choosing his words with care. "In order to escape winterkill and make a new shosha image, Nissei needs to set up and build new groups of subsidiaries and affiliates. Wouldn't you agree?"

"I suppose such efforts are necessary in outgrowing the traditional shosha functions," Yamabe acknowledged with the resigned air of one answering a cross-examiner.

"The real purpose of investing in new enterprises is not to create more clients for raw materials or manufactured products. That's the shosha function of the past."

"No harm in continuing it, is there?"

"No, there isn't. But this type of service is no longer worth the commission it takes. That's why shosha business is depressed. It's time the trading companies went after dividends and capital growth— in short, capital gains should be the primary objective of investments from now on."

Nakasato had a strange feeling of déjà vu. As it hit him, he recalled he had said the same thing fifteen years before, when he was obsessed with Century Stores. No one had taken the slightest heed of his view at the time.

"In the past Nissei sought out low-risk, high-yield targets or used capital investments as leverage to increase the volume of trade with the invested company. But very soon the nature of investment will change. Nissei can send out a competent manager to help expand the operation of the invested enterprise and expedite capital growth—and use Nissei's own human resources. In other words, Nissei Corporation can turn itself into a training center for entrepreneurs. What's an entrepreneur? The antithesis of a salaryman. He's a man who doesn't compromise, who never stops until he finds the true and complete solution to a problem."

Nakasato paused. Yamabe's reaction was tepid. "In any event, Nissei needs mental restructuring."

"Nissei won't change," Yamabe said bluntly. "It's beyond even President Ebisawa's power and efforts to change. A big business of this scale can never change itself on its own energy. That's why Nissei tries its hand at new ventures without altering its traditional perspective or approach. There is no other choice—but this strategy is destined to fail sooner or later. The American Gourmet plan won't succeed, either. You'd better crush it if you can. I thought you were of the same mind."

Nakasato groaned inwardly. Personnel Manager Yamabe was the senior colleague he most trusted. Yamabe was of a different mold from most of his discreet predecessors, as his craggy face and massive frame indicated. He was generally believed to speak his mind. For all that, he displayed a surprising degree of sensitivity in what he said or did, as Nakasato often noted with admiration. Prevailing opinion also had it that Yamabe looked like a man of action but actually did very little. As a Yamabe fan, Nakasato had taken offense at such criticisms in the past, but now he understood what had given rise to them. Apparently Yamabe was a most dependable ally as long as Nakasato stayed within the boundaries of Nissei's common laws. But if he tried to step out of bounds—to change precedents and established practices—Yamabe would turn into a formidable adversary. It was entirely possible that Nakasato had fancied himself in tune with Yamabe only because he had not worked seriously enough to contribute to the remaking of his company.

"I'll explain everything to President Ebisawa on your behalf," Yamabe consoled Nakasato, whatever he might have read in the somber expression on the younger man's face. "Well, I don't quite understand your reasons—but let's not mention anything wild like quitting Nissei to take up permanent residence in America, shall we? You know our top management has high hopes for you."

"I understand what you say. It's just that I was afraid this project would get nowhere otherwise."

"Don't worry. Everybody talks a lot, but nobody's really serious about such a project. Even after we've gone into it, if things don't work out, we can always commission that American securities company—whatever its name is—to put American Gourmet up for sale again, on our behalf this time. Cut and dry is the way with the world-renowned sogo shosha."

They were talking at cross-purposes. Nakasato rose to his feet, taking care not to betray his acute sense of alienation.

"I have no idea what's come over you. You don't seem to be yourself today. There's nothing to get so excited about. Nissei won't change, but neither will it go under. If we put our accrued assets into term deposits at the bank, we can draw annual interest in excess of 10 billion yen. Our deferred assets amount to astronomical figures. Nissei will easily last until both of us retire at the mandatory age, I assure you. Just don't play with fire and burn anybody, company or individual."

Yamabe's consolatory parting lecture stayed in Nakasato's mind.

It opened his eyes to the glaring difference between salarymen and entrepreneurs. The same difference that separated the likes of Yamabe and the old Nakasato from Masako. One worked to get a share of established values, the other to create new values on her or his own.

At last, Nakasato faced the moment when he must choose one or the other way of life.

2

Nakasato wished to see Masako once more. It was easy for him to fulfill this wish, for he had a standing invitation. "I'd like you to see M. Hozumi stores," Masako said. "Let me know when you're free, and I'll rearrange my schedule to make time for you."

Next Sunday, she promised him on the telephone. After he put down the receiver, Nakasato noticed the coincidence: it had also been a Sunday when he took Masako out to show her around Century Stores. On the night of their second Sunday tour they had been united. The sequence of memories triggered a strange stirring in Nakasato's heart. But that history was unlikely to repeat itself. For a simple reason—he was scheduled to fly off to New York that very night.

"You'll be pressed for time then. Don't you have another day free?" Masako asked, but that was the only date he had open before his departure. Nakasato desperately needed to speak with Masako before going to America.

"All right. In that case I'll see you to Narita Airport. Please be sure to bring along your luggage."

"Thank you. I gratefully accept your kind offer."

In the morning of the appointed day, Nakasato loaded his large suitcase into a taxi and arrived at M. Hozumi's office in Shinjuku. Sitting outside was a Mercedes-Benz, Masako's car. Her chauffeur looked trustworthy and affable, an elderly man of few words and generous smiles.

"This Mercedes was virtually forced on me by the president of a wholesale house doing business with M. Hozumi," Masako began as they settled into the car, as if she needed to explain. "He says that in a modest operation like mine, receivables tend to become uncollectable if the president dies without a qualified successor ready to take over. This is the only car that can survive a head-on collision with a truck, he claims. In his view this car is collateral on my account with his firm. He had his own car dealer deliver this one with a price tag slashed down to a bargain rate."

"Sounds like quite a character."

"He is. What do you think I found in the car when it was delivered?"

"What? A big basket of flowers with a love letter tied on?"

"Nothing of the sort. Rope ladder, helmet, work gloves, heavy boots, and a pair of pants."

"Whatever for? Oh, emergency equipment?"

"Exactly. Just in case I get caught in an earthquake on the expressway through the center of Tokyo, he says."

"How thoughtful of him!"

Nakasato laughed out loud with a carefree air, but he was astounded by the discovery that Masako's world was so far beyond his own mundane perception. Most salarymen would make a conscious effort to avoid discussing physical safety as an impersonal matter of logistics: Earthquake on the expressway? Just have to cross that bridge when I come to it. Who's got the time to worry about it in advance? So an average salaryman would dismiss the issue with bravado—even as he kept a rope ladder handy in secret. He could not admit to taking such measures to protect his physical well-being, precisely because he must give top priority to his own survival above all else in everyday life.

In contrast to the salaryman isolated in his solitary struggle, how generous and gracious these entrepreneurs are in their mutual moral support and assistance! Nakasato marveled to himself. In their relation to employees and business associates, the entrepreneurs are fully aware that nobody else can substitute for their own physical existence. They never doubt that their management skills and decisions have direct bearing on their enterprises and society at large—they must consider it a social service to safeguard their physical well-being. Nakasato suppressed a rush of envy only with considerable effort.

Whether aware of his state of mind or not, Masako seemed to be in high spirits. Her choice of outfit for this day was a moss-green suit, quite conservative except for its fashionably padded shoulders. The flash of a collarless silk blouse beneath the jacket was the only bold touch. Nakasato's eyes discreetly traveled down to Masako's left little finger. He started in surprise. There was a platinum ring, with a pair of boats shaped much like bamboo leaves.

Masako kept up animated small talk in a sparkling voice, vibrant yet steady with the confidence of a person firmly in control of her own life.

"Here we are," she announced, and Nakasato found himself in front of the familiar facade of the specialty-shops building in Shinjuku. Masako led the way up to the fifth floor.

"This is Shop Number One, particularly dear to me."

Written on the glass door facing the arcade was a simple sign in the Western alphabet spelling "M. Hozumi" in plain white paint. The very lack of ornate embellishment in the lettering confirmed its sophistication.

"This store is small, only one thousand square feet. The sales volume has leveled off and it's no longer cost-effective, but I leave it as is, because not much more can be done with it."

"How neat it is," Nakasato said.

The floor was waxed to a mirrorlike gloss beneath the rows of racks from which hung dresses of all colors, serene and graceful as if they were works of art. A saleswoman in her midthirties approached and bowed to them, a smile flooding her face.

"This is the store manager," Masako said. "Three of our managers are women."

"Welcome to our store," the manager greeted Nakasato.

"My old sweetheart," Masako introduced Nakasato, startling him with her candor.

"Hello. Sorry to disturb you," he said lamely.

"Behind that pillar, over there, the recessed area to the left of the entrance—that's the space I rented to start my business."

"Tight, just as you said. Near the doorway but not exactly a prime location."

"But it made me happy to have it. My own place of business, all 180 square feet of it."

"Very impressive," Nakasato said.

His mind conjured up a vision of Masako at her 180-square-foot corner—she arranges her merchandise on the counters, forces a smile to her face, and waits for customers. Her man is in America having left her behind, and her baby is at home in his grandmother's care. If I fail to sell this dress, all hope for the future will be lost—such dire thoughts must fill her head crowned with the straight black hair as she waits on her first customer, her face tense and her lips quivering in an effort to overcome her innate shyness.

"Impressive indeed," he repeated aloud.

She built up her 180-square-foot stall into a chain of fashion apparel shops boasting thirty-five locations, all within a dozen years. Her life was a drama of spectacular leaps and bounds that defied his imagination.

"What's the ultimate secret of your success? In the beginning you were in no position to cut costs by volume purchases. Maybe it was your fashion sense? But until you established some influence and rapport with the wholesale houses, you must have had trouble getting specific items you wanted, I imagine."

"I just kept on doing whatever was necessary, as best I could, with stubborn persistence. There's no other secret," Masako explained and turned toward her manager as if she thought of something. "Minami-san, what do you think is the most important thing in managing this store?"

"It's communication," the manager replied without hesitation. "Communication among the staff, communication with the head office, and communication with the customers. I believe well-maintained communication never fails to solve any problem."

"Well, you have it right," Masako said, nodding in satisfaction. This was no longer the Masako Nakasato once knew or the Masako who carried on a casual friendly conversation with him in her Mercedes several minutes earlier. Standing before him at this instant was Masako the confident leader.

"It all comes down to human relationships. As long as you foster trust and communication among people and work out practical solutions to problems as they arise, you can make a go of your business, if it has any promise to start with."

This is what she used to tell me long ago, Nakasato thought. Do whatever you can to the best of your ability, and you can do well in your business. This credo proved the secret of her success after all.

They exchanged parting greetings with the manager and left the historic Shop Number One.

Within Shinjuku Ward, there was another M. Hozumi shop, larger, with eighteen hundred square feet of floor space.

"Can you tell our clientele by looking at this store? Mostly married women in their thirties. M. Hozumi supplies their complete wardrobe from formal dresses down to fashionable casual wear."

"It's necessary to define and narrow down your target group, I suppose."

"Yes. Dealing with a large number of random customers in our trade, we can't hope to satisfy everyone. So we start out clarifying our clientele and our role for the specific target group. I think it's no different with a restaurant chain."

Masako took the initiative to turn the conversation in the direction of his primary concern. Perceptive as she was, Masako had fathomed Nakasato's real motive in coming to see her on the day of his departure for America.

He gave her the gist of his conversations with President Ebisawa and Personnel Manager Yamabe respectively.

"What you told me the other day touched me to the quick. You're right. If I'm preoccupied with improving my standing back in Nissei's head offices, I can't do a proper job of running any enterprise. That's why I asked to resign upon my assignment to American Gourmet, but my intention was utterly misunderstood. According to the personnel manager, that move was an absolute impossibility—my request amounted to blackmail. In a sense, Nissei Corporation has all but institutionalized a system that stifles any growth or expansion of their subsidiaries and affiliates."

"It certainly seems that way. But you put Nissei in an awkward position. If they let you resign, how can they treat you afterwards? On one hand, Nissei owes you at least minimum protection against loss and failure. On the other, if the project proves a great success, what they do with you may raise the sensitive issue of equity with the other employees. A firm as old as Nissei Corporation is hardly likely to turn up forceful leaders who can overlook the apparent inequity vis-à-vis your peers and give you the reward you deserve."

Masako talked on in a low voice as if speaking to herself. On their way to the M. Hozumi shop in Kichijoji, she told Nakasato her conclusion on the issue.

"It doesn't matter whether you go through with the formality of resigning—some people leave their hearts in the company when they sever formal ties with it. The point is whether you're sincere in your decision to stake your life on American Gourmet Company."

"I am. I want to create something of value with my own hands. What I'm staking my life on is a chance to do exactly that."

"In that case, you should go to American Gourmet as an assignee from Nissei. Once you're there, you can make it your life's work and pour your body and soul into it."

"But I'll be recalled to Japan in two or three years."

"Then you *can* submit your resignation at last."

"That certainly is a way, isn't it?" Nakasato said vaguely, failing to grasp the significance of Masako's reasoning. Unless the company understands my logic, such a course of action will scar me for life, Nakasato thought. The reputation that took me over twenty years to build up will be wiped out in one stroke by an indelible brand—the rebel who defied the company order. And what if my resignation is accepted without question, instead of serving as a lever to get me an extension of overseas duty?

Nakasato pointed out such ramifications to Masako.

"If they brand you for insubordination or accept your resignation outright, it's time for you to quit anyway. That's all," she said simply. "You were quite ready to leave Nissei Corporation on your own, weren't you? Well, you have nothing to lose now."

"It's not quite so simple."

"Why?"

"Unlike you, I have to support a family. Once I quit Nissei, I'll never be able to get another job that pays as well, you see," Nakasato said, feeling sharp regret stabbing at his chest. What a shame, a terrible shame! he cried to himself. How I hate to admit it, but I can never be free. No use getting all fired up about a job, because I won't be allowed to do anything my way. The salaryman's lot—Masako can never understand.

"Don't worry. There's a perfect job for you that pays even better," she was saying. "By the time you get your recall order and hand in your resignation, you'll have served as the CEO of a restaurant chain in America for three years. Let's start from there. A failure could only crawl back to Nissei pleading for mercy under a white flag. But not you: with three years of hard work behind you, you'll have a track record as a successful entrepreneur. Even then, can't you give up Nissei Corporation?"

"Well . . . I don't know."

As Masako made clear, he had based all his projections on a faulty premise. He might arrive at a different conclusion, too, putting his new qualification as an experienced entrepreneur in the picture.

"After you leave Nissei, you can find another managerial position in the food-service industry right there in America. Experienced managers are handsomely rewarded over there, I believe. Not only that, your expertise will prove even more valuable back in Japan. The Japanese food-service industry has a long way yet to go in development and expansion. Their model is the American-style operation. Japanese businesses in the field will welcome you with high pay," Masako said with a warm laugh. "What's more, you'll have no need to work for someone else ever again. All you have to do is synthesize your experiences with American Gourmet, and you can make your living as a management consultant specializing in the food-service industry. If you're good at it, you can earn more in this way than any other."

Nakasato understood perfectly what she was saying. Her analysis seemed reasonable—at least, logically correct.

"Maybe you're right. I have no countertheory or alternative view to offer but . . ."

"But?"

"But there's no guarantee that what you say will come to pass."

Masako held her breath. Sitting next to her in the back seat of the Mercedes, Nakasato distinctly felt her reaction. I want to explain, he thought. I used the term guarantee, but I didn't mean to imply that I needed solid insurance. My point is that the way of life she is urging involves too much risk.

"You must have faith in the world. It's a mistake to put all your faith in Nissei Corporation. Even Nissei has people not worthy of trust. Remember that general manager, what was his name?"

"Natsukawa Tetsuji."

"That's it. General Manager Natsukawa of Food Department. Really a worthless type, wasn't he? Even rubbish like him swaggered around there—because Nissei men swallowed their company's formalistic value system without question. Going by more universal criteria of the outside world, he'd be judged utterly useless."

Masako stopped speaking. Nakasato kept his silence. A while later she somewhat reluctantly volunteered her conclusion on the matter.

"They say that for every man with insight, there's one without. Don't concern yourself with those who can't see. You must believe there's always someone with insight watching you. If you do an excellent job for American Gourmet, some people are bound to notice it. Good work earns due recognition—that's the law of this world, though of course it's not neatly codified, like Nissei's personnel management system that rates job qualifications by the number of years served in a specific field. As long as you're seriously committed to your work, it doesn't matter where you go or what job you take on. There should be no need for guarantees."

"Please, you need say no more. You're perfectly right. I can't refute you at all. I'm ready to take a big leap in the dark and accept the American Gourmet assignment. It's just that I find your reasoning hard to follow."

"I know what you mean. It must be difficult for you to see things in such clear and simple terms," Masako agreed. Her eyes closed, deep in thought, she sank against the back seat of the Mercedes. Some time later she said, "One thing is quite obvious, though. You don't trust President Ebisawa, do you?"

"What!" Nakasato stared at her in shock. "That's not true! I wouldn't breathe a word of this at the office, but I assure you that

President Ebisawa holds me in his favor, and I believe in him. You see, we have a relationship based on mutual trust."

"That's a lie," Masako stated unequivocally. "If you really believed in him, you wouldn't hesitate to take on any task that would benefit Nissei Corporation. Don't you see? First you planned to quit Nissei and devote yourself to management of American Gourmet. Alternately you decided to resign three years from now when you get the recall order. Aren't they both ways to help Nissei out of the shosha winter? Either way you'll be serving President Ebisawa's wish. Even if he doesn't understand you at this time, don't you think he'll eventually come around to see the truth?"

"There is that chance, I grant you," Nakasato said, punctuating each word with a pause. "A very good chance, in fact. But if he fails to understand me, I stand to lose everything. So I can't afford to take the risk. Why tempt fate when I'm content enough with what I have and where I am now?"

The chauffeur slammed on the brake to avoid something bolting across the street ahead of the car.

They broke off the conversation.

"Can't be helped, I suppose," Masako remarked a while later, as if talking to herself.

3

They lunched at a family restaurant, the suburban type with parking facilities, part of a chain—like American Gourmet's—that had recently burgeoned in Japan. As they gazed at each other across the table, both Nakasato and Masako felt nostalgia attack them. As if to break a tenuous yet dangerous sentiment that momentarily linked them, Masako opened a conversation.

"This morning I told you about the president of a wholesale house who made me buy the Mercedes. There's an epilogue to that story."

The waitress came over to take their order. As the uniformed figure hovered at their table, Nakasato found his mind drifting back to the American Gourmet project. I'm sure I know how to train Japanese waitresses properly, but what about American employees? Am I safe to assume they're no different from the secretaries I used to work with in our Los Angeles office?

Masako's quizzical eyes snapped Nakasato out of his musing.

"Soon after I bought the Mercedes," Masako continued, "I took the president out to dinner in the new car to show my gratitude for all his help and advice. The next day he telephoned. After duly thanking me for the dinner, he told me to fire my chauffeur."

"What nerve! Quite a tyrant, isn't he? He thinks he can run the world to his will. That's one reason why entrepreneurs of small businesses command little respect in society, no matter how successful or wealthy they become."

"That's not it at all. He called my chauffeur a rough driver. He said the man must have serious trouble at home or some illicit affair. He'd observed the brief exchange between me and my chauffeur and the way he handled the car, but that was all. So I ignored the advice."

"Then something did happen?"

"Yes, and on the following weekend at that. The chauffeur went for a drive with a woman who wasn't his wife. The car careened across the center line and was crushed by a truck. They both died. I had never been so shocked in my life. Apparently he was not getting along with his wife."

"You could have been in the accident."

"So true. That's why the wholesaler president hand-picked my next chauffeur, the one driving us today."

"Quiet but amicable enough. He seems like a natural driver. Dependable, isn't he?"

"Yes, he is . . ." Masako faltered briefly but continued in a moment. "He wasn't exactly born to be a chauffeur. He graduated from your alma mater, the national university."

"What?"

"A salaryman dropout, so to speak. Kawamura, that's his name, was manager of the Sendai branch of a top-rated textile manufacturer. He left this company, to start an apartment factory to make garments—a tiny business operating out of a rented apartment. Well, he had little business sense. When a dealer went bankrupt, he lost out too. So the apparel wholesaler who recommended a Mercedes to me took Kawamura under his wing and gave him a job selling dry goods, but it didn't work out. As the last resort, the wholesaler set up a small delivery service to handle the merchandise of his own company and let Kawamura manage it. Then what happened but a subordinate embezzled funds and put this fail-safe little company out of business. It seems Kawamura would have been better off as a salaryman after all. Of course this is only hindsight."

"I wonder what it was he lacked," Nakasato asked in earnest. He had stopped eating when the conversation took an unexpected turn to touch on a relevant topic. At last he understood why Masako began to rehash the story about her Mercedes.

"An ability to judge men, I think," Masako said.

"He lacked an ability to judge men, is that it?"

"If you're a salaryman, your company teaches you how to judge and whom. As long as you play by their rules, you won't be held responsible for a wrong judgment, provided it doesn't have dire consequences. Am I right? Decision-making power is precisely circumscribed for each level of management so that everyone knows what decisions a section chief, say, is allowed to make. But it's not so simple and easy for independent entrepreneurs. In deciding how much to trust each person we come in contact with in our own companies or outside, we have only our own judgment to rely on. That's why some of us get to be as perceptive as the wholesale-house president, who detected the disorder in my former chauffeur's private life just from casual observation of his manners and behavior."

Masako refrained from adding a didactic comment, but her intent was not lost on Nakasato. Don't exert yourself. If you have no self-confidence, you had better keep the status quo. I'm sorry if I seemed to goad you by making needless remarks—Nakasato sensed the same message behind her words once again. After the round of M. Hozumi shops, they were on their way to Narita Airport when Masako made a reference to Nakasato's family.

"It's anything but an optimum time for you to move to America, isn't it, when your children are facing the examination hell to get into higher schools. Furthermore, you must take into account Mrs. Nakasato's feelings about living out the rest of your career in the United States."

As he listened to Masako talking in this vein, Nakasato found himself oddly affected. Fifteen long years ago, he once thought of abandoning his family to marry Masako. Now she seemed to put herself in his position, expressing concern for the welfare of his family. Far from being self-contradictory, such an attitude was consistent with her personality. Through the mists of time that now thickened and now thinned about his heart, the embers of old sensations stirred to life. Nakasato was restive.

"Well, you're certainly right. But some shoshamen have overseas business trips so often, they practically live abroad. If and when the time comes for me to go with American Gourmet for good, I don't intend to say anything to my wife. The whole thing's too complicated for her to understand. I know she will put up no objection if it comes as a company order."

"Still, I don't think you should force the issue. It's a serious matter to go against the way of this world in your midforties."

"I'll be all right. It's a decision I must make for myself. Thank you," Nakasato said with more confidence than he felt. If anything, he was mired deeper in the maze now than he had been that morning before he came to see Masako.

They arrived at the airport with four hours to spare, too much time for him to wait alone even after the check-in procedures took up some of it.

"Thank you for seeing me all the way to Narita. If you can indulge me a little more, I'd like you to tell me about Michio-kun over tea."

"I'd love to."

They found a table in the airport cafeteria and settled down in opposite seats. Self-imposed inhibition had made Nakasato refrain from referring to Michio until this moment. But now his departure was imminent, a sense of urgency gave him a spurt of courage to introduce the subject.

"What would you like to know?" Masako asked with a mischievous look on her face. Her distinctive lips had a slight pout and her eyes were widened. The ring on her little finger tugged at a corner of Nakasato's mind.

"Now that you ask me, I don't exactly know."

"His blood type is B."

"Ah, same as mine."

"That's why he has your personality, I think."

"What are his best subjects?"

"English, math, Japanese literature—he does well in all the major subjects. He seems to have trouble with social studies, though."

"Exactly like me."

"He stays up all night recording rock shows on video cassettes. Oh, and he's made a video library of his own with the movies he copies off the television."

"He seems to have a fancy for cinema."

"A craze, I'd say."

No sooner did the last word leave her lips than she swept her eyes from Nakasato to fix them on the cafeteria entrance. Nakasato was turning around in his seat to follow her gaze, when Masako exclaimed, "Michio, what are you doing here?"

"Here you are, just as I thought," said a voice precarious with the subtle fluctuations of male puberty.

"What happened, Michio-kun?" Nakasato asked, springing to his feet.

He found the boy standing close at hand casually dressed in jeans and a checkered shirt, obviously feeling shy in the presence of two grown-ups.

"Hello," Michio greeted Nakasato in a faint voice.

"Is something wrong?" Masako asked, all mother now.

"Well, Mr. Inuzuka . . . he said, 'Run over to Narita, I have something I want you to deliver.' "

"Deliver to whom?" Masako pressed the boy.

"You *are* Mr. Nakasato, aren't you?" Michio said turning toward Nakasato, as if to confirm his name.

"Yes, I am. Remember, I played tennis with you the other day?"

"I remember. He wants you to take this to New York."

Michio pulled an envelope out of his satchel and handed it to Nakasato. It was addressed:

Mr. Tokihiko Tobita, President
Nissei America Ltd.

The envelope bulged a little at the lower end, probably containing a piece of jewelry or a watch by the look of it.

"All right. I'll deliver this. Don't just stand there. Take a seat."

"Yes, sir," Michio responded with commendable politeness but lapsed naturally into a boyish tone in speaking to his mother. "Mom, I'm famished. Mr. Inuzuka burst into my room and hurried me off to Narita. I practically flew over here on an empty stomach."

"Mmm, how good of you! But from your eagerness to run his errand in such a rush, I can tell you've come into quite a lot of extra spending money."

"Secret will out," Michio stuck the tip of his tongue out, looking like a little child for the moment. "Enough to buy three compact discs, to be precise."

"Mick Jagger again?"

"Whatever I choose. Anyway, get me something to eat, will you, Mom?"

"Oh, what a boy!"

Masako raised a hand to summon the waitress.

Her ring with two boats. Her son now in junior high. The short straight hair and the mobile full lips.

Nakasato hardly knew how to sort out his own feelings. There before his eyes breathed a reality provocative beyond his imagination.—Take this opportunity to have a good talk with Michio, he urged himself.—What's your hobby? . . . Do you belong to a club at school? . . . Are you popular with girls?

Nakasato posed questions at random as they occurred to him, but the conversation moved in fits and starts. The boy was doing his best to give an answer to each question, but Nakasato was unable to carry discourse any further. "Oh, is that so?" was the only response he could manage, and each topic just died there.

"Difficult to chat with young people, isn't it?" he remarked honestly.

"You haven't been doing too badly. No father and son could have conversed better than you two did just now."

Masako's words went right to his heart. Not that she referred to Nakasato and Michio as father and son, but her mention of a patrilineal pair in general was of great significance to Nakasato.

"About time you got going, don't you think?" she said glancing at her watch, after the desultory conversation had run its awkward course for a while. With the dinner time upon them, the cafeteria was becoming crowded.

"Yes, I'd better," Nakasato said, with half an eye on the watch. "Michio-kun, take care."

"Yes, sir," the boy said and stood up, his spirits picking up visibly now that an end to the constrained exchange was at hand.

On the way to the departure gate, Nakasato whispered to Masako.

"Thanks. I appreciate your thoughtfulness in arranging for this meeting. I enjoyed a good talk with Michio-kun."

"You are thanking the wrong person. I didn't arrange this meeting."

"Wrong person?"

"Strange. Maybe he does know, somehow."

They stopped dead in their tracks. Their eyes tangled in the air. Michio stood listlessly at a distance, waiting for them. The boy's tall slender form nearly seared Nakasato's eyes.

"You didn't tell him?"

"No, I didn't."

"About today . . . ?"

"I did tell him about today's schedule."

"I see," Nakasato mumbled, but it occurred to him that there was no use in discussing the matter at this juncture. He had something far more important to find out.

"That ring . . . did you have it made to order?"

"Ah, you noticed." Masako smiled. Starting from the butterfly lips, her face subtly changed into the remembered vision of many years ago. "Once upon a time, I had a wonderful sweetheart. This is a reminder of him. He was endowed with talent and ambition to live his life to the full and on his own."

Somewhere, that man is still alive and well, Nakasato wanted to say but restrained himself from uttering what seemed a smug platitude. Instead he turned to Michio.

"I'll deliver the envelope to President Tobita. Will you give my best regards to Mr. Inuzuka?"

"Yes, sir, I will."

Nakasato strode into the passengers-only area. Several paces later, he looked back at Masako and Michio, a tableau of mother and son seeing him off. Waving a large farewell to the rather incongruous twosome, sophisticated suit next to casual jeans, Nakasato descended the stairs leading to the departure gate.

SIX

Our People

Early June

1

By now Nakasato had lost count of the number of trips he had made between Japan and the United States. The exact figure would emerge from old notebooks and passports, but he did not feel like taking the trouble to count, any more than the average Japanese businessman would want to reconfirm the number of his trips between Tokyo and Osaka. For Nakasato, America was a familiar and routine workplace, no more distant than Osaka in his subjective perception. All the more familiar since the advent of jumbo jets.

But there was one thing that no amount of progress in aerodynamic engineering could eliminate—the formidable wall between time zones to be crossed in getting to America. His blood pressure being on the low side, Nakasato was not an easy sleeper. Consequently he suffered from jet lag every time. Practice never seemed to help. On a business trip of one week or less, he would be heading home just as he got over the effects of the first stage's jet lag. Direct flight to New York was the worst of all, day and night completely reversed to upset his biological clock. A senior colleague once gave him a useful tip— drive your body and mind to exhaustion and collapse into a good full night's sleep. For some time now, Nakasato had kept a membership in Andrews Club, a health club in New York City.

On checking in at the hotel, he would drop his luggage in his room and rush off to Andrews Club. There he would stay for the rest of the day, swimming and running. After he worked off the whiskey consumed during the flight and worked up a pleasant fatigue, he would return to the hotel and gorge himself on rich food. Then straight to bed and fall sound asleep.

This time again he followed the efficacious routine. He somehow awoke once in the middle of the night so that the cure fell short of complete, but in the morning he left the hotel in relatively good shape.

No sooner did he arrive at Nissei America's head office than Nakasato ran into Kano, who happened to be heading for the restroom.

"Hi, here I am, dragged out again," Nakasato greeted him by way of explaining his presence.

"Too bad about American Gourmet," Kano said without so much as a good morning.

Nakasato failed to get the significance of Kano's remark.

"What's that? What on earth are you talking about?"

"What! You haven't heard?" Kano cried, obviously surprised. "*Food poisoning.*"

"*Food poisoning,*" Nakasato parroted the English term. "You mean infection through ingested food?"

"Yes." Kano shrugged his shoulders, arms spread open in a gesture of helplessness. "Very serious. Some patients are on the critical list in Boston."

"What is it? The kind of poisoning that could lead to death?"

"An elderly woman and a young child are in intensive care. The worst is to be feared."

"Are you talking about American Gourmet restaurants?"

"Yes. Big trouble."

Nakasato hurried down to the Food Department. Hoshino was already at his desk reading newspapers with a fierce expression on his face.

A headline leaped at Nakasato's eyes: "Even Pasteurized Milk an Invitation to Food Poisoning?"

"Morning!"

"Oh, Mr. Nakasato. What a mess! Puts us in a fix."

Hoshino fairly sprang from his chair. He must have been waiting for Nakasato, but now that he was face to face with the general manager, Hoshino seemed too excited to express his thoughts in a coherent fashion.

"What's the matter?" Nakasato asked Hoshino, but the pile of newspapers on the desk made the situation clear enough.

The food poisoning occurred in three states—Massachusetts, Connecticut, and New Hampshire. The patients numbered well over three hundred, two individuals in Boston slipping into critical condition by Sunday evening. The symptoms indicated salmonella infection. Tracing its suspected course led health officials to the family restaurants in the American Gourmet chain. There they found salmonella in the milk. American Gourmet restaurants in the three states were ordered to suspend operations immediately.

"Several months ago, an outbreak of food poisoning was traced to salmonella in milk sold at supermarkets in Illinois," Hoshino informed him, as he calmed down enough to gather his wits. "But it involved raw milk. That's unpasteurized, meaning as it comes from the cow. Some faddists believe raw milk is good for heart disease or something, and there was a growing demand for it in certain areas. In the American Gourmet case, however, the culprit is pasteurized milk."

"That explains this headline, then."

"Right. Hard to believe pasteurized milk can cause food poisoning, isn't it?"

"It says here," Nakasato pointed to a side column in the newspaper, "that the possibility of deliberate contamination of the milk with a criminal intent cannot be ruled out."

"Certainly. American Gourmet's responsibility is by no means a foregone conclusion."

"Even if a criminal act caused all the damage, the company is liable to be held accountable for contributing factors such as loose security or sloppy operating procedures."

"In any event, American Gourmet faces a predicament. Tough luck indeed!"

Hoshino slumped down into his chair and let out a deep sigh, blinking his narrow eyes behind the glasses. "This couldn't have come at a worse time. I'm thoroughly disgusted."

"Well, don't take it so hard. The exact cause is yet to be determined."

Even as he comforted Hoshino, Nakasato felt drained himself, utterly deflated and heartsick.

I've come all the way across the Pacific cooped up in a tight seat, and for what? For absolutely nothing, maybe, Nakasato fumed inwardly, resenting the bad news more for hitting him right on arrival.

Too weary even to speak, he was reading the newspapers over a cup of coffee from the vending machine when Kano came looking for him.

"Nakasato-kun, President Tobita wants to see you. He's calling a meeting of all parties concerned."

"Concerned with what?"

"American Gourmet and food poisoning," Kano tossed off flippantly in English. Apparently the incident had prompted him to make up his mind. He seemed determined to have nothing more to do with the American Gourmet project. A shrewd salaryman—true to form, turning tail at the first sign of trouble.

Fierce condemnation momentarily rocked Nakasato's heart. What an opportunist, he raged internally.

When Nakasato walked into the president's office, Tobita greeted him with a quiet smile.

"Welcome. You must have been nervous flying over the Pacific, considering how hazardous air travel is nowadays," Tobita said, obliquely referring to the recent disaster involving a jumbo jet over the Atlantic. "But here in New York we've been hit by an accident, too. You didn't know about it until you arrived here, did you?"

"No. I had no idea, in fact, until I learned of it at the office this morning. It took me the better part of yesterday to get over jet lag, with no time to spare for TV news or papers."

"Hmmm, enjoyed a porn movie or something?"

"No, I swam in the pool. I make it a rule to work out at Andrews Club as soon as I come off the direct flight from Tokyo."

"Well, it's a sure way to get a good night's sleep."

Presently all parties associated with the project gathered in the room. Kano, Hoshino, and Emura, who had telephoned Nakasato at the hotel on his last trip to report Kano's problem stock. There were also Okawa, general manager of Internal Control, and his subordinates as well as several other men unfamiliar to Nakasato. All were soon seated in the luxurious couch and armchairs in the presidential lounge.

"What's the extent of the damage?" Tobita addressed the group, when all expected members seemed present. The meeting was now in session. Except on certain ceremonial occasions, most meetings at Nissei opened in this manner. Tobita, being his usual cautious self, started by seeking assessment of the actual damages. His men exchanged glances in silence, no one daring to hazard a guess.

"Well, then. Let me brief you on the outline of this case and the present condition of the casualties," Hoshino volunteered at last and with considerable finesse recapitulated the food poisoning incident as it could be gleaned from the papers. The men were apparently well informed, and some nodded in acknowledgment at the mention of certain significant points but contributed nothing new.

"What exactly is salmonella food poisoning?" Tobita asked.

"I can explain," Hoshino rose to the occasion. "Various kinds of food poisoning are classified largely by their causes. Aside from chemical elements such as methanol (wood alcohol) and mercury introduced artificially into food, the causes fall into two types—microorganisms growing in food products and natural toxins occurring in animals and plants. The second includes toxins of poisonous mushrooms and the blowfish we call *fugu* in Japanese. It goes without saying that salmonella poisoning is of the first type, caused by microbial infection."

Nakasato was impressed by Hoshino's concise but lucid exposition. Anticipating a request for such information at the meeting, he must have done his homework and prepared this abstract for presentation.

"The salmonella bacteria is transmitted mostly through meats and animal excrements. The symptoms are cramping abdominal pain, diarrhea, vomiting, and abrupt onset of fever. But milk, particularly pasteurized milk, is not counted among common causes of salmonella infections."

"But the unthinkable has happened," Tobita said. "Since this is America, there'll be hundreds of lawsuits. And their settlements will surely put American Gourmet Company out of business."

"Under the circumstances, what a lucky break for us that this incident happened before our acquisition talks went much further," Kano offered knowingly.

"I agree. What if it had come right after Nissei took over the management?"

"Oh, well," Nakasato cut in. "Could be a different story if it came two or three years after the takeover, when a Nissei assignee was settled in as CEO and able to take full control over operation and management. But who wants to shoulder corporate responsibilities to make amends for his predecessor's mistake?"

To Nakasato's surprise, what he meant as a casual remark provoked a wave of diverse reactions. Some men nodded in obvious agreement, but a few stopped nodding midway. Yet others seemed to contemplate the dire consequences of such an incident happening when a Nissei assignee was already in full command to assume all responsibilities. Apparently the likelihood of such a contingency had never occurred to anyone else present at the meeting. Their collective interest was focused on the fact that Nissei narrowly escaped involvement with the food poisoning case that American Gourmet Company brought on itself.

For a while no one spoke. Each man must have given careful thought to the issue raised by Nakasato's remark but, for lack of a simple persuasive answer, opted to keep his mouth shut. Reigning in the room was silence of that sort.

"Well, we're safe, at any rate," Tobita said, changing the subject. "We had Nakasato-kun travel all this way, but talks are at a dead end. We can't deal with a company that's so careless as to cause food poisoning."

"But the cause is still under investigation—and it's not certain American Gourmet has the legal responsibility to pay for the damage."

"Maybe so, but even assuming they're not held legally responsible, it won't be easy to repair their ruined reputation," Tobita said, his voice hardening. Naturally, Nakasato agreed with him on that point.

"Nakasato-kun, what are you going to do now?"

"I've been thinking about that. I'd like to go through with the investigation of American Gourmet Company as planned."

"You would?" Tobita looked at him quizzically. "Well, in any case, you do have to prepare a report for President Ebisawa, don't you?"

That was not what Nakasato had in mind but Tobita apparently convinced himself with his own logic.

"Nakasato-kun, an investigation isn't as easy to carry out as you seem to think," Kano put in again. "We're completely in the dark. And neither Griffin Securities nor even the owner, Zadick Corporation, is likely to know exactly where American Gourmet stands at this stage. Even if you want to see for yourself, all their restaurants are shut down."

"According to the papers, their shops in New Jersey and Maryland are still operating as usual."

"Oh, well. Whatever you do, don't drink milk—even for field research."

"Don't worry. Salmonella or typhoid, the germs will beat a hasty retreat when they come up against Nakasato-kun," Tobita quipped, taking up Kano's banter with a ready wit quite uncharacteristic of him. The meeting dissolved into laughter. The talk continued in a congenial mood for half an hour more, without generating any new information or ideas.

"Mr. Nakasato, am I to take it the American Gourmet acquisition plan's been called off?" Hoshino asked Nakasato with serious concern when they were back in their office.

"Looks that way, doesn't it?"

"But nobody—from President Tobita on down—came out and said so."

"That's right. But you felt the plan was to be dropped. Why?"

"What should I say . . . the atmosphere or something. Everybody just talked as if it were a foregone conclusion, and so I got the impression the plan was really dead."

"That's about it."

A sullen look clouded Hoshino's face, his lips tight over the protruding teeth and his brows drawn together over his angry eyes.

"I won't buy that."

"Buy what?"

"Two things. One is their conclusion, and the other's the way the meeting was conducted. Which should I explain first?"

"Doesn't matter which," Nakasato laughed in spite of himself. "Take your pick."

"Well. In that case, I'll start with the problem in procedure. Various types of meetings have different purposes. Exchange information, make decisions, plan projects, educate or train, generate ideas, build consensus, settle disputes . . ."

"And meet for meeting's sake—simply to go on record that it was actually held," Nakasato offered in a joking tone.

"Yes, certainly." Momentarily disconcerted, Hoshino lost little time in recovering. "Naturally each meeting has a style that fits its specific purpose. A meeting to exchange information, for example, ought to be set up to minimize the cost—in this case the time spent—of exchanging a given amount of specific information. The less time it takes to communicate the same information the better. At the other end of the scale is a planning session. Here the aim is to maximize the use of a given amount of time by producing plans of the best quality. Now, then, what in the world was the purpose of the meeting we just had?"

Nakasato kept his silence. Not that he failed to understand what Hoshino was getting at. Rather, he understood it so well that he felt no need to express his response. It was just as well, for Hoshino went right on talking as his wont.

"Answer: it had no definite purpose. In the first place, it didn't even have a moderator. All the staff associated with the project gathered around the boss, exchanged random impressions, and let the meeting drift to a close. For all that, a conclusion was reached somehow or other. What kind of meeting's that? Ridiculous! You wish you knew the purpose of the meeting ahead of the time, but it's too late to prepare pertinent data."

"What can we do about it?"

"I'd been with Nissei several years when this point began to bother me. At first what troubled me was the haphazard way our meetings were being conducted. So I asked around my college classmates working for other integrated trading companies. To my surprise, things were run more or less the same way in their offices, too."

"It's not surprising."

"At the time I reproached myself. A new-hire like me, fresh out of college, spouts all the presumptuous opinions on his mind but makes little impact on society. I have a lot to learn about the world first, I told myself. But then one day, I happened to mention it to a friend who was with a firm manufacturing home appliances. He opened my eyes to a whole new world."

Hoshino named a giant enterprise in the field, its revenues among the highest in Japan, who made it a point to do without a shosha's services in exporting its products. His friend was in marketing.

Hoshino recounted his story:

"That's substandard," the friend said when Hoshino described Nissei's practice. "Any manager who held a meeting like that in our company would be fired before the month was out."

"What do you mean?"

"In our company, every meeting has a moderator assigned to direct the proceedings. It's usually a manager from the unit responsible for the matter on the agenda. This moderator is commonly called the leader. His duty is to clarify the purpose of the meeting to be held. 'This is a meeting to define policies and directions in proceeding with the X project.' Or, 'This meeting is called to hear the reports of the project team so the information can be taken back and disseminated among all members of each section.' Most announcements run like that. Similarly, each man attending the meeting must speak up if he doesn't agree with the leader's explanation of the purpose. The one who voices no opinion on that occasion forfeits his right to raise any objection later about the purpose of the particular meeting."

"I see."

"The leader steers the course of the meeting at his own discretion. Even when a senior executive is present, the leader has the authority to preside. Working out the agenda and proceedings is an important task of planning and personnel management—any manager appointed as the leader naturally puts his best effort into it. The leader always writes out the agenda on the blackboard. After each item has been talked out, he reviews the results to confirm that for each item they achieved the purpose of the meeting."

"All this applies to special meetings of unusual importance, right?"

"No. Even an informal briefing session goes the same way. Or rather, all our personnel from the top down to the lowest follow this procedure. Our most important meetings include strategic planning sessions to launch new products, those to evaluate the outcome of some project, or even more crucial meetings to make investment decisions for overall research and development objectives. These meetings turn into a battleground where war is fought with words and ideas. Since our collective purpose is to ensure success of some new product that the corporate fortune may be riding on, all members of the project's team fight it out with no quarter or concession given. The leader regulates the debate's direction, analyzes all the arguments, and proposes a persuasive conclusion acceptable to everyone involved. The whole process can be quite awesome to watch."

"Ah, the cathedral of Cologne!"

When the inevitable cathedral of Cologne popped up in Hoshino's story, Nakasato said, smiling, "I see what you mean. Let's leave the rest for later and go to lunch now. This afternoon we can set out to visit American Gourmet restaurants."

"Yes, sir," Hoshino said, surging to his feet in his eagerness.

2

Making their way out of New York City, they drove across the Hudson River into New Jersey. The change in scenery was dramatic, replacing the sight of bleak Bronx streets with another slice of Americana, a beautifully lush expanse of green.

"Last time I was here, the dogwood was gorgeous, in bloom. Now it's gone." Nakasato noted the passage of time with regret.

"Charming flowers. They look familiar to me somehow. It surprises me to find something so imbued with Eastern flavor growing all over America."

"I wonder what Japanese flowers are comparable to the dogwood."

"Not the cherry. Cherry blossoms are clustered and shorter-lived than the dogwood. But doesn't it remind you of the *mokusei,* the Olea fragrans, that thrives in the residential areas of Tokyo? Of course the dogwood comes out at a different time of year and lacks the fragrance, but it has the red and white kinds—like what we call golden and silver *mokusei.*"

"Now you mention it, maybe so."

"I'm bitterly disappointed. I love the dogwood as much as the *mokusei.* I wouldn't mind living the rest of my life counting the seasons by the dogwood bloom."

"It's too early to give up hope."

"Really?" Hoshino's eyes lit up. "But no matter how much fight even you, Mr. Nakasato, put up, it'll do little good. Food poisoning—it's hard to beat after all."

Without responding to the younger man's comment, Nakasato kept his eyes on the scenery flowing past the car window.

Under the clear blue sky, houses with lawns and sprinklers going sailed into his vision one after another. As their car passed a church, newlyweds emerged into a shower of rice from well-wishers' hands. A familiar American sight in June. Only ten minutes earlier they had spotted a car marked "Just Married" and "Hot," rattling strings of empty cans in its wake.

"June bride, they say here, but nobody feels like getting married in June back in Tokyo."

"Right, seeing how it's not so much 'hot' as muggy there in the rainy season," Hoshino laughed.

"Differences . . . the same goes for meeting procedures," Nakasato said. "If meetings at the shosha appear less structured than those at the appliance manufacturing company, it doesn't mean shoshamen are less competent. Trading companies never needed planning or creative brainstorming to meet their primary shosha functions. The shosha setting doesn't lead to elaborate meeting procedures, any more than the June climate in Tokyo does to wedding ceremonies."

"But is that really the case? The shosha could use new ideas and careful planning in many traditional business transactions."

"But not necessarily ideas and plans coordinated into a system. Essentially, you see, the shosha carries out business on the individual basis. It assigns each man to a specific project. In contrast, to develop new household appliances involves companywide systems engineering. Each project needs input from many divisions—marketing, design engineering, technical supervision, product control, plant, and sales. Naturally, numerous meetings become necessary, to coordinate various units beyond the stage of data exchange. Consequently, at well-run manufacturing companies—especially makers of consumer products—management uses interface communication techniques. But the shosha has different needs. With all its units running independent of one another, it has no use for coordinating strategies. Shoshamen ask for meetings to obtain data and nothing more. The only trouble is, the new businesses the shosha explores—to escape from its winter freeze—are mostly enterprises like the appliance manufacturer. Including restaurant chains."

"In that case, the difference makes a cultural gap, doesn't it?"

"You can call it that. I learned my lesson fifteen years ago on a supermarket job. If the shosha doesn't work hard to close its cultural gap with such industries, it's destined to fail in most of its new businesses. We'll be stuck in the deep freeze unless we outgrow our impressionistic or simplistic perception. How far can we get, if we go cold on the American Gourmet acquisition plan at the mention of food poisoning? Just suppose, for a moment, that the appliance maker finds itself in a similar spot. No doubt it assigns a team to analyze the incident's causes and another to assess the impact on the company. The task force researches and evaluates all the data and then holds meetings on many levels. When it drafts a proposal of concrete measures to deal with the situation, it reaches the final decision through companywide deliberation. To my great regret, however, the average shoshaman has no idea that such procedures even exist."

"Look, there it is! An American Gourmet restaurant," Hoshino cried. "It's open all right. Shall we drop in?"

"Let's do that."

They suspended the conversation as the car crossed the curb into the spacious parking lot.

. . .

"Milk," Nakasato said to the black waitress with smiling eyes who took his order.

"Milk it is," said the woman. Surprise registered on her face as she pronounced the words with care.

"Yes, milk," Nakasato repeated solemnly.

The restaurant was deserted. Nakasato and Hoshino were seated at what they assumed was its best table by the window, boasting a view of the woods beyond the expanse of the parking lot.

Soon after the waitress disappeared, a brawny man came striding toward their table. White, midthirties, good-looking.

"I'm Robert Hancock, the store manager. I understand you ordered milk."

"Certainly, I did," Nakasato answered him.

"Thank you," the manager said. "You've read our notice posted at the entrance?"

"Of course. I read it carefully."

The notice to which the manager called his attention was a large piece of paper displayed on the wall facing the front door, so prominently that no customer could possibly miss it on entering the store. It outlined the food-poisoning incident and explained that a Massachusetts dairy farm had supplied the milk that caused it. The notice ended with a separate official report that meticulous tests found all other brands of milk served at the American Gourmet restaurants to be completely free of contamination.

"You mean you accept our statement in good faith?"

"Yes."

"Thank you. I'm glad you support American Gourmet."

"You aren't getting many orders for milk?"

"We've had some. But, I'm sorry to say, just a few."

"You have fewer customers now?"

"Yes. Today's figure runs about half our average for Monday."

"Every time someone orders milk, you come out to greet him?"

"Not necessarily just milk. But when a customer does order milk, I always thank him personally."

"By the way, Mr. Hancock," Hoshino interposed. "I suppose this incident is a serious blow to your company's reputation. When the exact cause is determined, the firm could end up with enormous damage settlements. Do you think American Gourmet can survive the trauma?"

Hoshino's question was so blunt that Nakasato instinctively glanced in sympathy at the manager's face. His smile remained intact, but he planted his long legs and set his shoulders to answer Hoshino's question.

"I believe American Gourmet will survive this setback. According to the latest report I just received from the head office, the contamination has been traced to an undetected faulty pipe connection at the dairy farm that allowed accidental seepage of raw milk into the pasteurized product. Whether this finding frees American Gourmet from all liabilities as the principal litigant in damage suits, I don't know. But it's been unequivocally established that the food poisoning was not caused by negligence on our part."

The store manager paused for a moment and looked at Nakasato and Hoshino as if gauging how much they understood. When they said nothing, he continued. "Even if the settlements are small, the damage to our reputation will still scar our image. But American Gourmet Company will restore its good name."

"I can understand why you as a store manager wish it to happen, but what specific measures can your company take to reach that objective?" Hoshino pressed him with unblinking persistence. Fully aware of Hoshino's motive in asking such a question, Nakasato felt so sorry for the manager that he averted his eyes.

"Gentlemen, this story may sound strange, coming from me." The tall man smiled and spoke with firm resolve. "But it's not the first time we had a brush with food poisoning. Nothing as massive as this case. Five years ago we had an outbreak of food poisoning from cream puffs—staphylococcus bacteria got in baked goods, because an employee at the bakery had a cut that festered. Danger to life isn't limited to food poisoning, either. Some ten years ago, hoodlums began to patronize several of our shops in a certain neighborhood in New York City, and regular customers gradually fell away. One day a shoot-out took place on the premises and two of our customers who'd come in unawares were seriously wounded."

"Frightening," Hoshino breathed. "Like machine-gun attacks on the *Untouchables*."

"Life's full of danger. Our job is to face each threat, figure out how to deal with it. Prevent a disaster from repeating itself—that's the most we can do. We've faced many problems and solved them in the past. I'm confident we can do the same this time."

"I'm glad you have confidence but . . . ," Hoshino temporized.

"What makes you believe it's possible?" Nakasato asked.

"Our people," the manager replied with a deep breath and pride lighting up his face.

"Our people?" Hoshino repeated the English words with a quizzical look.

"You mean you have faith in the people who work at American Gourmet restaurants?"

"That's right. That's exactly right," the manager said and took another deep breath. "I just knew you gentlemen had a vested interest in our business one way or another. A good guess, right? That's why I told you so much about my company. To be honest, I *am* terribly worried. Please pray that the seriously ill victims recover fast and all our customers come back to American Gourmet family restaurants soon."

"I understand. I'll pray, that's a promise," Nakasato said, and the manager gave him a warm smile and left their table with a nod.

"How did he guess we had a business interest in his trade?" Hoshino unloosed his pent-up question as soon as they were alone in the car.

"Two men in business suits show up in the middle of the day at a family restaurant implicated in a contaminated milk case and order a glass of milk. Anyone can tell they're more than casual customers."

"Come to think of it, that's true enough." Hoshino burst out laughing. "But what made him confide in us? Ah, I've got it! Maybe he figured us out and tried to make a pitch for himself. In short, he'd given up on American Gourmet. That could explain his behavior."

"I don't think that's the case. His speech was really impressive, wasn't it? He loves American Gourmet Company from the bottom of his heart. More than that, he loves the family restaurant or the food service business—that is, his current job. And he loves his co-workers."

" 'Our people,' you mean?"

"Right. I like the idea."

Nakasato leaned back in his seat, relaxing.

"Hoshino, now I know the reason why an integrated trading company has a hard time in global trade. It's because the shosha has little love or concern for the industry to which the 'new businesses' belong and the people who work in them. The shosha assesses any enterprise only as a likely investment target with potentials to increase earnings. Small wonder . . ."

"Small wonder," Hoshino took the words out of Nakasato's mouth, "that Nissei men immediately came up with a collective wish to drop American Gourmet as soon as it was touched by food poisoning—that's what you were going to say, isn't it?"

"Exactly."

Hoshino hit upon the truth, but Nakasato was far from being in the mood for a laugh.

Occupying his mind at the moment was the thought of Masako. "Have you turned into a fool?" her incisive words echoed in his memory. It was her response when he said he would not mind going over to American Gourmet, if he could come back to Nissei a great success. At the time Masako pointed out that the responsibility of an entrepreneur was no different whether he worked in Japan or in America. With his newly gained insight, Nakasato wondered if in fact she'd been referring to love for the enterprise and the workers.

During the next four hours, Nakasato and Hoshino combed the area for American Gourmet restaurants. Less and less inclined to speak, the two men rushed from shop to shop as if propelled by some unseen force.

Every time one of them ordered milk, the store's manager never failed to make a personal appearance. White, black, Asian, jaunty, quiet—they were as different as they could be in type and background, but the pattern of their action did not vary. Each manager would thank the two men courteously, answer their questions, and walk away in dignity.

"This can't be coincidence. The head office must have issued a directive," Nakasato remarked in the car heading back to New York City.

"Most likely. You order milk and the manager shows up to call attention to the notice on the wall and explains the officially identified cause of the contamination. That much was the routine all of them went through. But beyond that point, each man had his own style," Hoshino observed with considerable insight.

"I agree. Very interesting. The head office regulates the companywide operation to a certain extent, leaving the rest to the independent judgment of the on-site management. This may be the key to the chain-store system."

"Quite sophisticated as a technique of systems management, isn't it?"

"The role of the head office and that of the individual shop are perfectly in gear," Nakasato muttered as if reshuffling his thoughts.

They had covered a considerable distance in silence when the church in front of which they had seen a June bride on their way out reappeared into view. Hoshino broke the silence at last, obviously at the end of his endurance.

"Mr. Nakasato, do you think the American Gourmet plan is really finished now?"

"I don't think so." Nakasato's voice was strong with a confidence that surprised even himself. "If anything, the food poisoning helped firm up my commitment. Now I see the project's real significance."

"I was right after all, then," Hoshino cried, louder than necessary in the confined space. "To tell you the truth, I had a feeling you were all fired up—but it seemed too good to believe."

"Hey, watch it! Keep your eyes on the road, will you?"

"I'm all right. To be frank, Mr. Nakasato, you may be set to go, but you can't expect a green light when everybody else is spooked by the food poisoning."

"Not necessarily. I'm going to give it a try."

In his mind Nakasato was already drawing up a plan to expedite the acquisition procedure. First, he must take as accurate a reading as possible of the impact of the latest incident. Food poisoning was a problem inherent in the food-service industry, couldn't be avoided. But once the company was found responsible for an actual outbreak and saddled with huge damage settlements, he'd be ill-advised to recommend its acquisition.

I'll confer with President Ebisawa as soon as I get back to Japan, Nakasato thought. I must convince him that the key to making success of "new business" is love for the enterprise. "Why buy a company cursed with food poisoning?" the president may ask me. "Love? Well, love may be a necessary thing, but how can you run business on love alone?" he is likely to say. I'd better be prepared to answer both questions. Probably to expand on the differences between the shosha trade and the restaurant operation.

Presently Nakasato snapped out of his musing and turned to Hoshino.

"By the way, you mentioned after this morning's meeting that you couldn't buy two aspects of it. One was the procedure. But what was the other?"

"Couldn't buy . . . ? Oh, that! It's all settled," Hoshino announced breezily. "I wanted to say, food poisoning is something the food-service industry fights to prevent, not something that keeps any company from the field. But now I feel you already understand all that."

"I suppose, Hoshino, the construction of the Cologne cathedral cost many lives in numerous accidents. Its builders invented ingenious measures to hold the sacrifice to the minimum over the centuries and completed it. Guided by love all the way."

"In this case, love for God was involved, too, don't you think?" Hoshino turned his head sideways to look at Nakasato, taking his eyes off the road in flagrant violation of safety rules. The Japanese eyes behind the glasses glinted, and his lips moved as if to say something more, but no audible word came out.

"Watch where you're going!"

"Yes," Hoshino responded meekly, turning to face forward, and pressed down on the accelerator. The old Ford surged ahead in a burst of speed, hurtling toward the great bridge spanning the Hudson. As Nakasato reclined against the back seat, his wife drifted unbidden into his thoughts. He had borne nothing but negative feelings over the years for Rieko, who seemed to be smug, at her ease in the marital sanctum. But now it occurred to him that her complacency might have mirrored his own attitude as he coasted along in the salaryman's sanctum during the same long years. Announce a decision now to stake his business life on a new career path, and it might put their relationship on a new plane and create rapport between them. And yet Rieko might object, saying, "This is no joking matter. Why should you choose to take such a risk?" Entirely possible she'd prove impervious to persuasion no matter how he presented his case.

Let come what may, Nakasato told himself. Instead of accepting a life of endless compromise at home and at work, in a cage marked Safety consigned to a terminal called Regret, I ought to talk with Rieko, discuss how we want to spend what's left of our lives. For her as well as for me, the coming years are too precious to waste. Whatever the outcome, at least I won't regret having the talk, Nakasato thought as the car's motion gently rocked his jet-lag-weary body into a comforting fog of sleep.

Just before his consciousness faded out, he felt the tangible presence of an absolute force, time, whose constant and relentless speed carried him in its wake.

3

The thought flashed into his mind as soon as he opened his eyes. When his vision cleared, Nakasato glanced at the clock—2:30 A.M.

How can I get Ebisawa to understand?

In daylight with Hoshino chauffeuring him around, it had seemed natural that his appeal would touch a responsive chord in the president. But late at night in his hotel room after an evening of social drinking with associates from Nissei America, Nakasato began to doubt it was as easy as all that.

There was nothing wrong with Ebisawa's power of comprehension. If anything, the president and Nakasato had an ideal relationship as the top executive and a middle-management planner. For all that, there was one sensitive issue that Nakasato found hard to explain to Ebisawa. Namely, his wish to devote 100 percent of his remaining career years to management of American Gourmet Company.

Why was it hard to explain to Ebisawa? Before going to bed earlier that night, he had figured out why: it would constitute a mutiny against the president in the primal sense. Up to this point, Ebisawa had backed up Nakasato's status within the company. Of course Nakasato had amply demonstrated his own competence in corporate planning, project coordination, and negotiation skill under other superiors. Besides, he served directly under Ebisawa only on his American tour of duty. So he had not depended on Ebisawa's patronage to survive at Nissei all these years. But he had to admit that ever since their Los Angeles days, he'd been conscious of Ebisawa's warm regard. Ebisawa was never out of Nakasato's thoughts, and he never failed to consult with Ebisawa to secure his approval on matters of importance. For Nakasato, Nissei Corporation was personified in the mortal man called Ebisawa Shiro.

Ebisawa himself knew what he meant to Nissei men. In their corporate cosmology, Ebisawa was a great presence watching over the employees from above; in turn their dedication and concerted effort put him in the president's chair and supported the Ebisawa regime. Such human configuration was a salient feature of Japanese corporate power structure. Any action incompatible with this structure was doomed from the start, and a man who unwittingly threatened to undermine it would be digging his own grave.

Evidently Ebisawa found it imperative for Nissei Corporation to launch its own brand of operation downstream—say, to break into the food-service industry. He took an active interest in the American Gourmet acquisition plan proposed by Nissei America. By all indications, he had Nakasato in mind as his trump card from the outset, with the idea of committing him to this daring new project for a few years. But Ebisawa had no intention of relinquishing him for good, now or ever. For the president, keeping Nakasato in Nissei Corporation, that is, close at hand right in his own clique, was a fixed assumption. But here was Nakasato's very problem: he was convinced that his project would fail unless this assumption was modified.

Nakasato had a task cut out for him, clear and simple in one sense: press Ebisawa into making a choice between two alternatives—change his assumption and venture into the downstream, or give up the planned expansion into new territories to preserve the assumption intact.

He expected Ebisawa to be reluctant to overturn what must be his bottom-line condition. Destruction of this assumption could very well start a chain reaction leading to the fall of the Ebisawa regime and, ultimately, even to the total collapse of Nissei's corporate structure. For it would mean intrusion of a structural principle utterly alien to the existing one.

Nakasato got out of bed. He went to the bathroom, had a drink of water, and stood at the foot of the twin bed to stretch his back. Moving one area of his body at a time, he tested his muscles. Perhaps from fatigue, they seemed to creak in protest.

"My mind is made up," he said aloud as he went through his calisthenic exercise. "I'll get the president to modify the premise. There's no other way to solve the problem."

For some time he paced the room, distracted in thought. At last he sat down at the desk and spread a sheet of stationery before him.

"Hozumi Masako-sama." He addressed her with the formal honorific, beginning at the top of the sheet as customary in the Western-style horizontal writing. After dating it, he paused briefly. Transcribing her name had brought back the memory of his countless letters to the same addressee fifteen years ago. He felt a faint ache deep in his chest.

"Dear Madam," he wrote and grinned to himself. Never had he dreamed that one day he'd find himself starting off a letter to Masako with a "Dear Madam."

"The night deepens into the small hours. Here I am, wrapped in my memory of you as is my wont," he would have said for a starter in the old days. But this letter was to be a study in contrast.

Dear Madam,

I thank you most sincerely for your kindness in seeing me as far as Narita Airport. Still earlier on that day of my departure, I learned a great deal from your guided tour of M. Hozumi shops.

Your success is stupendous. I bow down before the extraordinary endeavor that certainly went into it.

Arrived in New York safely and am proceeding with my work as scheduled—that is what I would have liked to report, but reality had an unpredictable trouble in store for me. American Gourmet Company, which we had been studying with a view to acquiring it, became entangled in a serious outbreak of food poisoning.

Nakasato outlined the incident, summarized his prognosis, and went on to describe the impressive manner in which the American Gourmet's store managers had dealt with this crisis.

I felt greatly encouraged to note the diversity in their ethnic origin and skin color. Many management-labor disputes in America are said to be rooted in ethnic prejudice and discrimination. The U.S. government has created the Equal Employment Opportunity Committee, Human Rights Commission, and other new regulatory offices to deal with problems of this nature. The fact that the American Gourmet employees of various ethnic backgrounds work in concert toward a common objective indicates that the company has maintained excellent labor relations over the years. I am well aware, of course, that the true state of employee relations isn't clear to casual observation, and I intend to engage a reputable firm of consultants specializing in this particular field to run a full-scale study for us any day now.

No doubt the food-poisoning incident couldn't have come at a worse time. But on the plus side, it opened my eyes to many things. I think that the calamity gave us an X-ray of American Gourmet's corporate anatomy. In this sense, we could say that the timing was perfect.

The problem is actually the attitude of the staff at Nissei America. Most of those who had promoted the acquisition plan switched sides in reaction to the incident and began to voice opposition to the plan. This makes no sense. Food poisoning is a problem for the food-service industry to overcome, not something to render an enterprise unfit for investment.

Nakasato wrote on steadily, giving Masako his critical comments on the Nissei staff to conclude this section of the letter. "Now, to get down to the real business," he said aloud and stopped writing for a few moments. The next section must be charged with sincerity and prayer. A missile in the form of a letter addressed to Masako, it was to be launched on a precisely calculated trajectory toward Ebisawa in Nissei's presidential suite.

Strange as it may seem, the food-poisoning incident has driven me in the opposite direction from most of the staff at Nissei America. Now I want to join the people who work at American Gourmet Company and help build it into the best restaurant chain in America, or even in the world. To me it somehow seems possible.

Come to think of it, my heart has undergone a great change within the last two or three months. Meeting Mr. Inuzuka again, hearing Nukaya's story, and learning of the trail you blazed in your life—these recent experiences affected me tremendously. I was forced to confront myself, a man deluded into believing that Nissei Corporation was the whole world, a man who had coasted along all these years compromising his fundamental values and principles at work and at home.

Of course, I am not belittling a salaryman who loves his company, takes pride in it, and dedicates his entire business career to one particular firm. If anything, I have admiration for such a sensible and sound way of life.

The problem arises when a salaryman becomes caught up in his relationship with his company to the exclusion of all other relationships that exist—say, between his company and the world or between the world and himself.

Business enterprise is primarily a means to link individuals with the world. Students take jobs to get out into the world. But as soon as they realize that this means nothing more than getting into a company, they lose interest in the world—in other words, they come down with *corporatism* (as I recall, a popular Japanese term coined from *autism* a while back), characterized by disregard of external reality and withdrawal into the corporate self.

I was totally unaware of my symptoms. You can hardly imagine how shocked I was to discover that my eyes, which had been wide open fifteen years ago, were totally closed to the world.

How did I contract corporatism?

To my shame, it was because I had been blessed with Mr. Ebisawa Shiro's patronage. The instant I realized I was in his grace, my sight became fixed exclusively on Mr. Ebisawa Shiro until I could see nothing but him.

Now I must see the world once again. I must undertake the job that I owe the world to accomplish. I hope it will be Nissei's significant contribution to the world as well.

My final decision is of course contingent on completion of our feasibility study. The findings we have on hand at this moment indicate that American Gourmet Company has the making of a worthy project on which I can test my mettle and stake my business life. Provided no further problems arise, I intend to process the acquisition plan with dispatch on the understanding that I will be granted a permanent assignment.

In the event that this project is summarily turned down, I am determined to leave Ebisawa Shiro and Nissei Corporation. What shall I do afterwards? Or what can I do? I shall think about it if and when the time comes. The world is full of people who do not understand me, but there must be some who do, as you pointed out to me. I would like to live my life trusting in those who understand me.

I want you to know how I feel, since it was you who opened my eyes to new possibilities.

I wish you good health and ever greater success.

Please give my best regards to Mr. Inuzuka.

Sincerely,

Nakasato signed his name and put down his ballpoint pen. As he read over the letter, he felt that the ending might be a little abrupt, but it seemed to accentuate the message he wanted to convey—that he was ready to leave Nissei if necessary. Nakasato folded the letter and touched it lightly with his lips. The heat of the passion he had known fifteen years ago flared in his heart.

"Masako, I'm counting on you!"

In his scenario, Masako does not fail to read between the lines. She wastes no time but shows the letter to Inuzuka to ask his opinion. He immediately sends word (and possibly encloses a copy of Nakasato's letter) to President Tobita in New York. Shortly, via a confidential fax or a telephone call, Nakasato's wish reaches his ultimate target, President Ebisawa.

Nakasato estimated the whole process would take two or three weeks. One more time he went over the entire route in his mind to make certain there was no break in the circuit. From Masako to Inuzuka, the passage was inevitable. From Inuzuka to Tobita, it seemed certain also, judging from what Nakasato knew of Inuzuka's character; no doubt Inuzuka would do everything to forestall a situation in which his own action might cause Nakasato's resignation from Nissei Corporation. The unknown area lay between Tobita and Ebisawa . . . Communication along this line was difficult to predict, but Nakasato believed the odds were in his favor. In the first place, Inuzuka would most certainly ask Tobita to pass the message on to Ebisawa.

As Tobita's name popped into his head, it reminded him of something that had slipped his mind. He unfolded the letter and picked up his pen once again.

"P.S.," Nakasato wrote. "As for the package that Michio-kun delivered to the airport, I handed it to President Tobita upon my arrival. My best to Michio-kun."

As he spelled out the boy's name in ink, he registered deep in his chest a warmth distinct from the emotion that had returned to him moments earlier.

"Masako, I'm counting on you," he murmured with profound feeling. Once more he kissed the letter and sat for a while, his eyes closed.

The Insubordinate Loyalist

Late June

One evening in June when the trees surrounding the hotel across the street showed vivid green, Ebisawa's secretary called Nakasato on the phone.

"The president wishes to see you," she said.

Nakasato was poring over a thick report in English on the prospects for new investment in Hong Kong. He dropped everything and hastened to the president's office. But could the missile of a letter I launched from New York have reached him so soon? Nakasato deliberated on his way over.

The door of the president's office was always kept open to the corridor of the executive row, but just the same Nakasato knocked on it to announce his arrival. Unhurriedly Ebisawa lifted his eyes from the papers and rose to his feet. Offering the couch to Nakasato, he sat down in the armchair.

"How's the food-poisoning case going?"

"The telex that's just come in reports that American Gourmet is likely to escape indictment."

"That's good to know," Ebisawa said and fell silent. His expression was unreadable, but he was apparently absorbed in thought. Nakasato refrained from interrupting.

"Have we got anything on their labor relations?"

"Not yet. The report from Cottrell and Lowell Associates won't be due for another month. We may have a better prognosis on the food-poisoning case by then."

"I see," Ebisawa observed but said nothing more. Nakasato was transfixed by a silent gaze so intense that he could not but avert his eyes.

"Do you have confidence?"

"Pardon?"

"In your ability to run an American food-service business."

My missile hit the target! Nakasato exclaimed in his heart.

As if he could see right through Nakasato's mind, Ebisawa had a gentle smile hovering about his mouth.

"I wouldn't presume to say I have confidence, but I feel that if I do a proper job of whatever I'm supposed to do, I can produce proper results."

"It'll take time."

"I am prepared."

"Did your wife consent?"

"I intend to talk it over with her when I have the official notice in hand. If it's a company order, she'll follow me without question."

"You have a good wife."

"Yes, sir."

"Yesterday Inuzuka dropped in to see me."

No wonder, Nakasato thought to himself. My missile bypassed intermediate stops and took a more direct path to the target.

"Inuzuka once worked under me. I knew him to be a man of unswerving conviction who never compromised his principles. He hasn't changed a bit. He spoke highly of you."

There was nothing Nakasato could say in response.

"Run a thorough check on American Gourmet Company to make certain it's worth betting your life on," the president said.

"Yes, I will."

"If you find it trouble free, go ahead with the acquisition plan."

"Yes. Thank you, sir," Nakasato said, getting to his feet. He bowed his head deeply.

"I have something for you." Ebisawa walked over to his desk. He wrote a few words on a memo slip and came back to hand it to Nakasato.

"Defy the order to benefit the lord, for that is loyalty," read a sentence written in Chinese.

"Does this mean that going against an order is an act of true loyalty if it's in the best interest of the company?"

"Yes, more or less," Ebisawa agreed. "Shigetou Yoshikuni, one of Nissei's former presidents renowned for his management expertise in the prewar times, often inscribed this adage in calligraphy. Dedication to work takes this much resolve. I believe you're now at a point where you can appreciate the full meaning of the words."

"Yes. I think I can understand."

"I have been waiting for this day. Drive everything else out of your mind. From now on, concentrate on the best interests of American Gourmet Company."

Nakasato had taken his leave with a reverent bow and was already at the doorway when Ebisawa stopped him with a question.

"Weren't you a contemporary of the late Ojima?"

"Ojima? Yes, I was."

"Did you know him well?"

"Yes. We shared a room in the new-hire training camp. He was a sincere and serious man."

"Why do you think he chose to end his life?"

"I heard he had a nervous breakdown."

"Of course he must have suffered some kind of breakdown to kill himself, but can we leave it at that?"

Nakasato remained silent, waiting.

"It might surprise you to hear me, your president, put it this way—but I suspect Ojima was too preoccupied with the company."

"You're right. I noticed that tendency in him, too."

"Promotion is an important measure of values within the company, but it's not everything. A cosmology that sets Nissei Corporation apart as a paradise of happiness for the insiders and labels the rest of the world a hell is pure nonsense. First of all, Nissei itself is no transcendental absolute power but merely one of the multitude of enterprises in Japan's twentieth-century capitalistic system. As such, it's destined to perish sooner or later."

How refreshing it sounded to Nakasato when the president admitted that his own company would perish sooner or later.

"For over two months after Ojima's death, I sought out the opinions of people who knew him. It was a shock to me that an employee with such loyalty and devotion to the company should kill himself. Eventually I found out he'd been a fanatic believer in companyism. He mistook Nissei Corporation for a god. That's why he couldn't stand the fact that, for all his unparalleled faith, the god had seen fit to relegate him to a lower rank. That's how I interpreted his motive. Just when my mind was occupied with such thoughts, Inuzuka happened by and talked of you.''

In unhurried strides Ebisawa reached the spot where Nakasato was standing. There was a smile on his face.

"I never viewed the company as my god. But maybe I led my men to believe it represented some kind of absolute value. If so, I was wrong. If the company were a god, you couldn't defy an order and still serve its best interest. Well. Go now and blaze the trail to your frontier. The company, which is no god, can live on if only we work together to demolish its outmoded form from within and build a more viable framework.''

"I understand. Thank you, sir.''

Nakasato stepped into the hallway. As he closed the door quietly behind him, his eyes fastened on the thick wooden door of the executive conference room. Had it really been almost three months? Inside this very door on that fateful morning in April, Nakasato made Management Grade One and Ojima crashed the ceremony. At the time Nakasato viewed Ojima's death as a fall of a loser in the race for glory. But now he had a different perspective of his own, aside from Ebisawa's interpretation.

Nakasato was in no position to speak ill of the dead man. Until recently he himself had placed blind faith in the same religion without realizing it. Since he had made his way straight up the corporate ladder ahead of competition, he had never tasted defeat. Consequently he'd had no occasion to question the doctrine by which he lived.

In truth, he thought, companyism is a religion without salvation, promising nothing but defeat for all except a handful who attain the presidency. The defeated, however, do not turn apostates. They gain self-satisfaction quickly, remembering how much better off they are than those whose defeats were bitterer or came earlier than theirs. Companyism is a sinister religion of ultimate social discrimination.

Nakasato joined his palms to bow before the sturdy door of the executive conference room. Whoever happened by to catch sight of him at that moment would have gathered an impression exactly opposed to Nakasato's intent. But for Nakasato, the gesture was a requiem to a friend killed by his inability to break the spell of companyism. And, at the same time, it was a ritual to pledge his own apostasy.

As he raised his face, Nakasato felt a heady sense of liberation. He began to move slowly down the carpeted hallway. Reaching unthinkingly into a jacket pocket, he found the slip of paper on which the president had written, "Defy the order to benefit the lord." Ebisawa's aristocratic face and his words came into Nakasato's head.

What a surprise to learn that Ebisawa had taken the trouble to probe into Ojima's motive for suicide and had even analyzed his philosophy of life. Nobody would have objected if Ebisawa had blamed everything on Ojima's lack of judgment or on a nervous breakdown. But to have arrived at such a conclusion as he had revealed to Nakasato, the president must have put himself in the employee's place and objectively reexamined himself and Nissei Corporation.

As he recognized Ebisawa's greatness anew, Nakasato had to admit he might never be able to outgrow the great man's influence. But he felt no sense of defeat. On the contrary, Nakasato was elated to think that Ebisawa, the chief executive, had confided in him his true feelings for the first time in their association. It was as if the president had acknowledged him as a fellow manager.

The point, nevertheless, was not what Ebisawa thought of him. Can Nakasato Michio grow into a truly competent manager and entrepreneur? That was the question.

Nakasato shook his head as if to clear it, opened the thick glass door at the end of the hallway in the executive row, and stepped outside. Beyond the horizon lay America and the great expanse of a world altogether different from sogo shosha.

AFTERWORD

The theme of this novel—the nurturing of the entrepreneur spirit—may be the most urgent problem that contemporary Japanese businesses need to tackle if they want to progress. In fact, I considered calling the novel *The Road to Entrepreneurship*. Ultimately, I discarded the title as too straight-laced for fiction. But what I have tried to delineate is the difficult road that a middle-echelon salaryman must follow as he matures into an entrepreneur.

I have been a "shoshaman" for thirty years. For the first ten years, I worked in the offices of Sumitomo Corporation, a sogo shosha (integrated trading company). Then I had myself assigned out to an ailing supermarket chain within the Sumitomo Corporation Group. I have had the opportunity to observe the workings of the trading industry for a total of three decades, and those of the large-scale retail field for two, always from the inside and at close range.

Throughout my long career, I have gained much firsthand knowledge and derived many insights that have proved invaluable in writing business novels. My odyssey spanned many phases and facets of the business world, from rookie shoshaman to veteran to manager, then from retail-chain manager to senior executive officer. I moved from a high-yield corporation to a failing operation that, revitalized, burgeoned into a spectacular growth industry.

My work has also brought me into contact with many people whose interests lie outside large corporations. Although I never belonged to a union, I was led to think seriously about labor management because of an assignment to the Personnel Department during my sogo shosha days. I have also done liaison work for the parent company and its subsidiaries.

In the course of these experiences I have met many people who fall into either of two categories: salarymen and entrepreneurs. The ones I met because of my sogo shosha connections are all salarymen; the ones I met in the supermarket industry are either owner-executives or other, similar entrepreneurs.

I have found myself in the rather contradictory position of being a salaryman in status but an entrepreneur in practice. Looking back on the past thirty years, I realize that I have switched back and forth between the two positions depending on the occasion and the environment, that is, the type of people I happened to be dealing with. I am a veritable social chameleon or—to put it in a more positive light—a bimental creature capable of thinking with two minds. Just as a bilingual person can manipulate two languages simultaneously without conscious effort, I seem to have learned to cross the mental bridge between salaryman and entrepreneur with spontaneous ease. I have developed a sort of sixth sense for spotting the thought processes and mental attitudes that distinguish the one from the other.

The story line of *Shoshaman: A Tale of Corporate Japan* evolved out of this sixth sense. There are no particular models for the organizations or individual characters featured in the story.

Some time ago, the term "the winter freeze of the sogo shosha" came into the popular vocabulary. It implies that the integrated trading companies can no longer rest easy solely on their traditional shosha functions and must transform themselves to adapt to a new age. But a cold season has not descended merely on sogo shosha. At best, more than half of Japan's industries are weathering a late autumn chill, even if they have not yet reached midwinter. One way for a company in a business field threatened with chilly prospects to branch out into a new field with better market opportunities is to start a new venture. The indispensable key to the success of such an undertaking is the entrepreneur spirit of its executive officers.

Not all salarymen are driven by the salaryman mentality, nor are all business leaders brimming with the entrepreneur spirit. Yet the correlation is staggering; it demonstrates the impact that environment has on the human psyche. The problem of a business field entering a winter phase lies in bridging the wide, deep, and very real chasm that separates the salaryman mentality from the entrepreneur spirit. Although most companies do expect their employees to nurture the entrepreneur spirit, in actual practice they provide nothing but infertile environments.

As a salaried employee, I find it regrettable that salarymen are denigrated for their "salaryman mentality" *(sararīman konjō)* rather than praised for their "salaryman spirit" *(sararīman seishin)*. Whenever I meet someone endowed with a superb entrepreneur spirit, I am forced to admit anew the difference between "spirit" and "mentality," as measured in the quality of mental attitude and outlook on life. It may be that salarymen know the difference better than anyone else.

Rare is the salaryman who has never agonized over his own impulse to quit the company. Many must have contemplated the possibility of earning professional qualifications as, say, a CPA or a tax consultant, or of starting a small business of their own. They roam through the bookstores in search of how-to guides and helpful references. But in the end they beat their usual path to the drinking holes, where they mourn the death of their short-lived dreams and pour out their hearts in criticism of their immediate superiors. This kind of behavior indicates nothing so much as their loathing of the salaryman mentality with which they are saddled. The anguish of their quest for a meaning in life makes me hope that salarymen can and will develop the entrepreneur spirit if only they are accorded a different environment.

Arai Shinya
Tokyo: May 27, 1986

ABOUT THE AUTHOR

Born in 1937, Arai Shinya graduated from Tokyo University's prestigious Department of Law in 1960 and immediately entered Sumitomo Corporation. He served four years in the General Affairs Department in Tokyo, five years in Personnel in Osaka, and then one year in Tokyo in the Foodstuff and Fertilizer Department.

In 1970 he requested a transfer to Summit Stores, Inc. (renamed Summit Inc. in 1988), a supermarket chain that Sumitomo Corporation had founded in cooperation with Safeway Stores, Inc. After opening two stores in the Tokyo suburbs, Safeway withdrew in 1964. Over the next several years Sumitomo tried to build up the chain by adding more stores, but performance declined steadily until 1970, when the corporation sent in an entirely new senior staff, including Mr. Arai as assistant manager of operations and of planning.

In 1973 Mr. Arai was made a director of Summit Inc. and placed in charge of management planning and sales planning. He became managing director in 1978 and senior managing director in 1983. In 1988 he was appointed executive vice president of Summit Inc. and a director of its parent company, Sumitomo Corporation. As of 1990, Summit Inc. has fifty-three stores, including its two most recent additions in Taipei.

Using the pen name of Azuchi Satoshi, Mr. Arai published his first novel in 1981—*Shōsetsu ryūtsū sangyō* (Downstream industry; Nihon Keizai Shimbunsha). A paperback edition, retitled *Shōsetsu sūpāmāketto* (Supermarket), came out from Kodansha in 1983. *Shoshaman: A Tale of Corporate Japan* is his second novel, originally published by Kodansha in 1986 as *Kigyōka sararīman* (Entrepreneur salaryman). He is hard at work on his third, set in the business world of the near future.

Mr. Arai's other writings include *Nihon sūpāmāketto genron* (Principles of Japanese supermarket management; Parusu Shuppan, 1987) and a survey of the field entitled *Supermarket Chain* (Nihon Keizai Shimbunsha, 1990). Since September 1988 he has also had his own column in the *Nikkei Business* biweekly magazine.

Shoshaman was made into a television miniseries featuring the well-known film stars Baishō Mitsuko and Watase Tsunehiko. Broadcast in prime time over three Sundays in November 1988 by the Terebi Asahi network, it won the ATP (Association of Television Productions) Prize. Perhaps because the story was part of an ongoing drama series entitled "Man's Decision" *(Otoko no ketsudan)*, the network chose to make several changes in the ending. The social standing of Nakasato and Masako was reversed: in the television version, a bankrupt Masako is seen drowning her sorrows as she concedes defeat. Nukaya's book comes out with the dedication, "For my wife, with gratitude." Nakasato himself moves to New York to become president of American Gourmet, and his wife prepares happily to join him, leaving their children behind in school dormitories.

—C.M.

Designer: Barbara Jellow
Compositor: Miller Freeman Publications
Text: 10/13½ Baskerville
Display: Baskerville
Printer: Haddon Craftsmen
Binder: Haddon Craftsmen